Sleek Bodies

Also by Mark Daniel

MARK DANIEL
Sleek Bodies

MICHAEL JOSEPH
LONDON

MICHAEL JOSEPH LTD

Published by the Penguin Group
27 Wrights Lane, London W8 5TZ
Viking Penguin Inc., 375 Hudson Street, New York, New York 10014, USA
Penguin Books Australia Ltd, Ringwood, Victoria, Australia
Penguin Books Canada Ltd, 10 Alcorn Avenue, Toronto, Ontario, Canada M4V 3B2
Penguin Books (NZ) Ltd, 182–190 Wairau Road, Auckland 10, New Zealand

Penguin Books Ltd, Registered Offices: Harmondsworth, Middlesex, England

First published in Great Britain 1994

Copyright © Mark Daniel 1994

Filmset by Datix International Limited, Bungay, Suffolk
Printed in England by Clays Ltd, St Ives plc
Set in 11.5/13.5 pt. Monophoto Photina

ISBN 0 7181 3552 0

This one's for David Grenfell,
above all, but also for Eddy and Tessa
Fitzgerald, Tony and Beatrice Ensor,
Peter Richardson, Johnny and Valerie
Jobling-Purser – the gang, in short –
and, of course, the *capo*, Andy Redmond,
and all his clan.

PART I

F REDDY GLAISTER had no thought of dying that night.

Oh, his mind was filled with the squelching and sucking sounds of feet wrenched from mud and steel from flesh. He could hear, beneath the Sibelius and the spluttering of the log fire, the howling of shells, the answering screams of men and of horses, the teeth-jolting thuds as missiles hit earth. Death was much on his mind, but he had no thought of dying.

Not personally, as he might have said.

Freddy had left his problems behind him. He was reading about Passchendaele. The First World War was Freddy's idea of good stuff. Light reading.

He liked the First World War.

In his dressing-room, he had bayonets and helmets, soldiers' notebooks and steel-wrapped Bibles, puttees, cap badges and the Lord and Freddy knew what else. He also had a nigh complete set of *Wisden* and six cricket bats signed by West Indies' teams.

Freeze-frame, then.

Just look at him, in his velvet slippers and beige cords and his check open-necked Viyella shirt, frayed at the collars and the cuffs.

He looks young. Even the shadows cast by the courtly, sprightly flames cannot give him an ounce of gauntness or gravitas. The cheeks are round, the skin smooth and shiny as billiard balls. The short dark hair is swept back in a quiff. He looks contented. He looks to be that strange,

3

fortunate sort of man who can open his mail without a tremor.

Yes, you can see him enjoying the First World War. For five minutes. *Come along, chaps, salt of the earth, play up and play the game. England expects . . .*

Pow.

And quietus.

You didn't think they made his sort any more.

He turned the page, a heavy page which flapped like a sail. He uncrossed his legs and crossed them again, this time the other way round. Both his hands held the book. There was no drink beside him, no cigarette, nor did his fingers fidget or flutter. He was very still.

Until the rolling thunder came from the knee-hole of the desk.

Then he was up and out of the armchair fast. He shoved the book aside as he pushed himself forward. He strode to the doorway and out into the hall. 'I'm off to the yard!' he called. His voice bounced around the stairwell. 'There's someone out there!'

A woman's voice called, 'What?' from up there, behind one of the doors on the gallery. Freddy had strode through into the back hall and pulled on his Barbour and boots by the time that his wife, Alison, appeared on the landing. She wore a thick blue towelling dressing-gown. She flourished a cloak of steam. Her dark hair was up, but its ends were wet and squirmed like leeches on her neck and shoulders. 'Sorry, what?' She frowned as if at a painful sound. 'What's the problem?'

Freddy had the front door open. Sibelius was faint now. You could hear the sigh of the wind and, beneath it, the slow, deep breathing of the sea. 'Someone's out there,' Freddy called up. 'It may be nothing. May be bloody Jim blundering around. Don't worry. I'll just check it out.'

'For God's sake, leave it,' she called peevishly down to him. 'It's only a bloody horse . . .' But he was gone out, into the darkness.

She was left mumbling to herself, 'Jesus, all this drama . . .' As she turned back to the bathroom, she raised

4

her head and lowered her hands at her sides as though catching twin cannon-balls.

'Christ!' she sang, and the steam reached out wraith-like tentacles, and dragged her in.

Freddy jogged once he was on the gravel. There was a half moon, but charred fragments of cloud scudded across it. There was more wind up there than down here, where the hydrangeas barely bobbed their flowerheads like courtiers their hats as he passed, then returned to their whispered gossip.

He took a shortcut. He scrabbled up the steep bank of turf, through an archway in the holly and so into the walled garden. He jinked to his left, leaping over flowerbeds until he reached the wrought-iron gate, the shape of a tombstone, in the wall. He hissed as his warm hand touched the cold metal. The latch clicked, and he was through.

There were dim lights scattered about the boxes, but they only served to make the darkness in the corners and at the centre of the stableyard seem deeper. Freddy knew his way. His eyes were fixed on one box, down at the far left-hand corner. He was panting slightly, but he swallowed his breath and, with a little nod to himself, sought the cover of the water-butt at his left, the shadows in the lee of the moonlight.

He ducked down. Crouched and on tiptoe, he scurried down the line of boxes beneath the noses of incurious horses.

And he was right. The double-door of the box on which his eyes were fixed was a mere black oblong, a grave the night before the corpse arrived. Freddy could hear someone moving in there. The footfalls on the straw were lighter and more frequent, the breathing shorter than that of the horses in the boxes all around.

Freddy set his back against the wall. For a second or two, he paused. He had not considered the need for a weapon. This was England, where the police went unarmed, and villains, for fear of doing needless accidental murder, packed nothing more dangerous than a cosh.

Now came the problem as to exactly what you say in such a context. Briefly Freddy searched his memory for an example of etiquette. Something from Dornford Yates, perhaps, or Raffles . . . ?

A television addict would no doubt have called, 'I know you're in there. Freeze!' or, 'Up against the wall, mother-fucker!' but Freddy watched only wildlife programmes and cricket on television, in neither of which were motherfuckers explicitly discussed and, anyhow, he had the Englishman's innate fear of looking foolish. When he swung round the doorframe, therefore, he uttered nothing more menacing or worthy of *ODQ* than a very loud 'Ha!'

It was his last deliberate utterance.

Other sounds were to come from him – the punctured airbed 'Whoof!' as a fist drove deep into his gut from the darkness, the sound of an ill-oiled hinge as he doubled up and sank to his knees, then the ghastly donkey tritones as asthma took hold.

His eyes were already brimming with liquid as he looked. Light from a torch smashed at his sight. The man in the box was moving towards him. Freddy's right hand arose to fend off the light as much as any further blows. His left hand scrabbled at the flap on the pocket of his Barbour. He needed his inhaler, fast.

The man with the torch squatted before him. His hand reached forward and grasped Freddy's just as it closed about the inhaler. 'Easy, now,' the man's voice said. It was a familiar voice, but it bubbled into Freddy's consciousness, all blurred beneath the roaring in his ears, the desperate honking of his lungs. Air was oil, heavy to inhale, heavier still to be rid of, but the soft touch of the breeze told him what air could be – cool and fluffy as a virgin's spine.

But it was all right. The man had his own inhaler. He was levering the spike to puncture a blister. Blessed, familiar relief was moments away. The nozzle was to Freddy's lips.

He managed to exhale. He sucked in deep. He felt the

powder grains lightly spattering at the back of his throat. Already a grateful smile formed on his face.

But the expected lightness did not come.

Freddy's heart drummed faster. The weight would not shift from his chest. Each breath seemed no more than a mouthful.

The fingers of his one hand gripped tight to the other man's wrist. Those of the other scrabbled at the beloved plastic of the inhaler. His chest was palpitating now, three breaths a second. The darkness span.

'All right,' the man before him was saying. His arm was round Freddy's shoulders, forcing his mouth down on the inhaler again.

Again Freddy did his damnedest to inhale. But this time he understood. His hands and his legs shook violently. His wheezing gave way to a clattering rattle deep in his throat.

His heart exploded, showering his chest with acid. He could actually feel his oxygen-starved limbs jerking like those of a palsied conductor; he could actually feel his tear-filled eyes rolling upward.

He had had no thought of dying that night but, when it came to the point, to stop breathing at all was a pleasure.

The pink silk A-line mini-dress was just a puddle on the flags, and Audrey Hepburn was – God, forget the sweet little innocent bit – she was going it, doing beautiful, wild things to Philip up there on the Whispering Gallery of St Paul's when the telephone shrilled.

He said sadly, 'Oh . . . ?' and rolled over on the mattress. He clutched the sheets to him, but Audrey was gone, unlaid but exorcized by the noise at his ear.

He rolled back, sprawled, just getting his bearings. He opened his eyes. Atlas did a couple of pirouettes. He closed his eyes again. He licked his lips, tried 'Oh,' again, then cleared his throat. He propped himself up on one elbow. He reached for the receiver.

'Hmm?' he said. 'Yes?'

'May I speak to Mr Philip Glaister, please?'

'Speaking, just.'

'Philip, good morning to you.' The Irish voice was high and good-humoured. 'Did I wake you, by any chance?'

'Hmm?' Philip blinked twice. He could smell his breath in the mouthpiece. 'Yes. What's the time?'

'Over here it's just on nine-thirty. Must be later with you. Rough night, was it?'

'You could say.' Philip hammed it up.

'I will not say that you have only yourself to blame. People who say that should be ritually disembowelled.'

'I agree, Ivan.' Philip reached for the Disque Bleu packet on the floor beside him. 'You just didn't say it. I heard you just not saying it. I am deeply grateful. What's the news, then?'

'Visitors. This evening. Arriving around five. They'll be staying three days.'

'Thanks for the notice, Ivan.' Philip flicked the lighter. He inhaled. He fumbled on the table above him for paper and a pen. The paper which came to hand was a Turnbull & Asser catalogue, much ringed with coffee stains. The pen stood in a Winnie the Pooh tin which toppled and crashed to the floor. Philip wedged the receiver between his jaw and his naked shoulder. 'Right,' he said at last, 'so who are they?'

'Sorry. Another strictly incognito number, I'm afraid, Philip. They'll be bringing their own security and their own staff. A nice easy one for you. Nobody's to know. If they want the *Fionnuala*, they'll send their own man to pick it up and they'll take the tender out from Cap des Gyrs. Just like last October. All right?'

'Sure,' Philip nodded wearily. 'So, likes and dislikes?'

'None. No, listen, just get up there, if you would; see that everything is clean and warm, fires laid, flowers, all that, then clear the staff out, ensure that the house is completely empty by, say, four o'clock. That's it. Just don't mention that anyone's up there, OK?'

Philip shrugged. 'Sure. As you know, it won't do much good. The whole town'll know someone's there within minutes. Still, leave it with me.'

'Right. Thanks, Philip. I'll try to get down next month – oh, and if they need anything while they're there, your contact will be one Angela Duncan, OK?'

'Got it.' Philip scribbled down the name as, back in London or Dublin, Ivan Duggan briskly said, 'Bye,' and replaced the receiver.

Ivan Duggan owned L'Hermitage, the converted monastery overlooking the town. He also owned the *Fionnuala*, the biggest, glitziest yacht in the bay, but then, Ivan Duggan owned loads of things. Once he had been a fairly successful amateur jockey. Now he was a brewer, and owned a television company.

According to the *Sunday Times*, he also owned thirty-four million pounds.

Of these, he paid one hundred Irish punts a month to Philip Glaister.

Philip's duties were, generally, none too taxing. Duggan kept a skeleton staff of housekeeper and gardener at L'Hermitage. A boat-boy, Luc, and his girlfriend, Jo-Jo, lived on the *Fionnuala*. Whenever Duggan invited a friend or business associate to avail himself of the boat or the house, it was up to Philip, as a bilingual French speaker and *'un gentleman'*, to draw up menus, ensure that flowers and sheets were fresh and drink and bath-oil bottles full, and that Jo-Jo's damp knickers were not left lying around the state rooms. In exchange, Philip had the run of the *Fionnuala* whenever he needed a bolthole or a chance to put on the style.

Only once before had Philip not known the identity of a guest. That was the previous October. He had subsequently learned from the newspapers that the mystery man had been a junkie rock-star attempting to accustom himself to sobriety. Philip was incurious about such things. He was not a reader of *Hello* magazine.

He showered, dressed, rang this morning's pupil to postpone the lesson, and set off up the hill to do his duties.

Everything was spotless. Perfect.

L'Hermitage was grand without grandiosity. The ground-floor bedrooms had vaulted ceilings and white walls bare of all save a few small paintings and old-master

9

drawings. All had marble baths. All had views over the sea but gave, at the rear, on to cloisters which now surrounded a swimming-pool. A nimble Lothario, therefore, could visit all eight bedrooms in torrential rain without getting wet. Equally, guests could step directly from their beds into the arcades and out on to the grass to plunge into the wriggling blue water.

The chapel of Saint Fiacre had been converted into a spacious games-room, done out like a *West Side Story* milk bar, with orange formica tables, pinball machines, an original Wurlitzer jukebox, one-armed bandits, pool and ping-pong tables and the whole front end of a turquoise Oldsmobile emerging from one wall.

The *hospitium*, formerly separate, was now attached to the chapel by a long, broad passageway which doubled as a conservatory and a sculpture gallery. The monastery's old guest-house was the only part of L'Hermitage on two levels. Upstairs were the staff quarters and the offices. Philip did not bother to inspect up there. Downstairs, in the drawing-room and dining-room, things suddenly became richer, sedater, more English – more Irish, no doubt Duggan would say. The drawing-room walls were of green watered silk. There was a great Irish Chippendale library table and two console tables, rich with intertwined acanthus leaves. There was a giant Lavery, a stunning Leach, a dark little O'Connor and two Cézanne landscapes. The dining-room too was traditional. The table was a flame-lit reservoir, the sideboard heavily charged with silver. The paintings here were of the Duggans' horses, by John Skeaping, Pauline Fitzgeorge-Parker and Peter Curling.

Philip led Berenice, the housekeeper, into the kitchen – a custom-built extension. He glanced quickly around, strode over to the fridge and peered in. He straightened with a smile. 'Berenice,' he announced, 'you are a treasure, a marvel. Will you marry me?'

Berenice was the shape of a successful soufflé, but none the less managed to curvet and to squirm. Philip averted his eyes until the process was complete. 'I must say,' she said at last, 'I don't like leaving everything to strangers.

Who knows what damage they might do? And I'll never find anything in here once some silly chit has been so-called cooking. Still . . .'

'Don't worry,' Philip reassured her. 'Mr Duggan wouldn't allow just anyone to stay here.'

'Huh.' Berenice's whole torso shifted into upper-case then back again. 'I've seen some of them. Cleaned up after them. Princes, musicians, artists – pah!' She gathered the entire Lilliputian nobility and corps of Parnassian mountaineers into her scaly and capacious hand, squeezed the juice from them and ejected them on to the terracotta tiles.

'Yes, yes, strange people, often very strange,' Philip mused, all innocence. 'Stressful lives. That's the problem. But not vicious. Troubled, spoiled, perhaps. They don't have your advantages.'

He could not have spoken more diplomatically. Berenice had raised three sons. One had died; two had emigrated. She now gave to this house all the fussy, fractious care which she would otherwise have devoted to her grandchildren. 'Well, yes.' She made a cradle of her hands before her crotch. 'They often have nice manners. I'll grant you that. And not everyone is as lucky as us. Secure homes, that's what counts. You and I, we don't have those problems, do we?'

'Absolutely not,' Philip nodded sagely. 'We must be charitable. No, I'm sure everything'll be looked after. Everything'll be fine.'

'Of course it will.' The voice was a soft contralto, but somehow it rang in the walls more than Philip's more strident tones. The copper pans buzzed above the marble worktops.

Philip started. He swung round. Berenice turned slowly, solidly, but none the less raised a hand to her left breast and squeaked, 'In the name of God!'

A woman leaned on the doorframe. She wore a clinging black body and tiger-print leggings. She was all soft curves, but trim and tight as a sausage in its skin. Philip's eyes did what eyes do in such circumstances, following the curves of calves and thighs, the lovely long, concave line from her flanks to her lowest rib. Her eyebrows were thick cutlass-blades, raised in sardonic amusement. Her hair was dark and sleek as dolphin skin. It was twisted up on her head, trim again. Philip put her somewhere between thirty-two and older-than-the-rocks-in-which-she-sat. When she moved, it was with arrogant laziness.

'Who on earth are you?' Philip demanded.

Her eyes flickered over him, toe to top. 'Well, I know who you are,' she drawled in English. 'I was warned to expect directness. Philip Glaister, I assume?' She held out a languid hand.

'You assume right,' Philip scowled. 'So how about answering *my* question?'

'Me?' The smile, when it came, was devastating, two hundred-candle stuff. 'My name is Angela. Angela Duncan. I think you're expecting me?'

Philip nodded. He took the hand. It curled softly about his. The nails were long and narrow and painted maroon. She stood so close to him that he could feel her breath on his lips, his cheeks. It was very sweet.

'Right.' Philip cleared his throat. 'I'll show you round. Berenice,' he switched to French, 'this is Miss Duncan, the representative of the people who will be staying here. Miss Duncan, Berenice, the housekeeper.'

Her eyes swivelled sideways for a bare second to acknow-ledge Berenice's presence. 'Hello,' she said, then, looking back at Philip, 'Yes, if you would. Thank you. And Angela, please.'

'Hm.' Philip grunted. 'Right. Come with me. Berenice, you OK?'

But Berenice was mumbling to herself and wringing her apron as if it were Angela Duncan's neck.

Philip had led Angela Duncan through the reception rooms and back down the corridor to the games-room. She had languidly trailed her fingers over furniture and sculp-tures. Here, however, she became all girlish. She whooped. She laughed. She sat in the Oldsmobile and sounded the horn.

She danced across to one of the pinball tables, said, 'Take you on,' and Philip watched, admiring, as, buttocks tight, back arched, she flipped the flippers and shoved at the table with her pubis. She was good. Philip had played this table a hundred times. He only barely won.

'This,' she said, 'is fun.' She skipped over to the Wurlitzer and stabbed at a few numbers. Brian Hyland, 'Ginny Come Lately', puddled from the speakers. She turned and leaned back on the jukebox, her mind apparently unaware, her body all too aware of all that straining, fingering fabric up front. 'I like this. It's the only place in the world where a misspent youth makes you the boss. You had a misspent youth, didn't you, Philip?'

'I thought I spent it very nicely, thanks,' Philip growled. Their voices echoed in the chapel's vaults.

'Yeah. So did I.' She giggled. 'I like you. You don't fawn and paw.' She hummed along with the music. 'Talking about "Ginny Come Lately", you had Camilla Seaforth, didn't you?'

Philip winced and frowned. 'That's a curiously phrased and rather impertinent sort of question,' he said.

'Well, I did, and I'm not ashamed to admit it.'

'You did what?'

'Had Camilla, of course. I wonder how often our paths, so to speak, have crossed. It's an exciting thought, isn't it?'

'A peculiarly unattractive one, actually.' Philip's lips were a thin straight line. 'I have to say, Miss Duncan, that I enjoy sex in all its forms and, so far from having anything against those of your persuasion, have frequently been the dandelion in a daisy-chain. Your sexual predilections are no concern of mine. And that is precisely the point. They are no concern of mine, and I'd rather keep it that way. You can do what pleases you, but I'd sooner you didn't come bragging to me about it afterwards. Good sex doesn't travel. It withers in the light.'

'Pompous, hypocritical load of crap.' Angela Duncan raised her chin. She sneered. 'You disappoint me, Philip Glaister. I know your reputation. I'd hoped for something better. You're prepared to do it, in other words, but not admit to it. Typical English middle class.'

'I will admit madam, to more sins than you have had

13

time, energy or imagination enough to dream of,' Philip retorted. 'What I will not do is broadcast them. There is a crucial difference. Now, let's leave this subject, shall we?'

'Pity . . .' Angela shook her head slowly and smiled her condescension. 'Such a pity . . .' She sauntered across to the window through pools of green, red, blue and gold cast by the stained glass. 'I'd hoped we could party. Still – ' She gazed out at the white sandy track which trickled down to L'Hermitage's private beach. 'We'll need two girls tonight, if you'd be so kind.'

'What?' Philip's voice was husky, but a whisper would travel from one end of this room to the other.

'Girls, dear, remember? Two of them. Pretty, slender, no more than, say, thirty-five, and broad-minded – more broad-minded than you, anyhow. To arrive here at nine o'clock this evening. Thank you.'

Philip eyed the girl's silhouette against the leaded windows. He eyed it with displeasure. He had developed such a dislike of her over the past few minutes that his earlier appreciative interest in her body had hardened into an intense and urgent desire.

A deep growl like something heavy being pushed over gravel thrust up from inside his stomach. 'I'm not a pimp,' he said.

'Oh, yes you are,' she sang lightly. 'We know all about you, Mr Philip Glaister. You have introduced girls to others of Mr Duggan's guests in exchange for a small fee. Does no one any harm, does it? The girls get money and a good time. The guests get lucky. Don't get all priggish with me, for God's sake.'

It was true. There were girls along the coast who enjoyed a party, a trip on a yacht, good food and wine, flash company and folding money. There had been guests willing to afford these to girls along the coast. Philip saw no harm in introducing the one group to the other, nor in taking a small sum from both in recognition of his labours.

'I'll see what I can do,' he said at last, 'but I'll need to know something about your employers. I'm not sending my friends up here without knowing more.'

14

'How touchingly chivalrous.' She turned and folded her arms. 'The floozies of the coast weren't so fastidious in my day. What do you want to know?'

'Well,' Philip shrugged, 'who are they?'

She shook her head. 'That's not part of the deal, I'm afraid. They're a middle-aged businessman – wholly respectable – his wife, me and some young man or other. That's the lot. Clean, safe, no violence, just a lot of lovely, naughty fun. Your girlfriends will be looked after.' Her lips wriggled in a little smile. 'Very well looked after indeed. They may not walk straight for a week, of course, but I never heard anyone complain about that, did you?'

There it was again, that full, halogen smile. Philip wanted very much to rip those leggings, perch her up there on the pinball table, ram it into her, make her whimper and sweat. She disgusted him, so she was of his kind. 'So,' he said angrily, 'all right. What's in it for me?'

'Well, now.' She cocked her head. She walked towards him. Each leg swung round its pair. 'I'd hoped we could invite you to join in the fun,' she cooed, 'but I don't think such a prude would enjoy it.' Her fingers slowly arose to stroke his cheek. 'So, what shall we say? Three hundred? Pounds? If they're nice.'

Her wide brown eyes smiled into his, daring him. She wanted action, so Philip, who wanted it too, steeled himself and simply said, 'You do their dirty work. I'll do yours. The only difference is, I'm not such a whore as to enjoy it. I'll be off now.' He pushed past her. His shoulder hit hers so hard that she span. 'Enjoy your evening.'

'Oh, I will,' she called after him, 'and you'll be wishing you were here come nine o'clock. I guarantee it. Bad luck. You blew it.'

Philip's stomach was churning as he stepped out into the bright sunlight. He cursed her, then himself.

He suspected that she was right.

'Oh, charm, I may grant you.' Douglas Snaith nodded vigorously. His rectangular bifocals flashed. 'Not that I've ever been aware . . . not that I've seen any evidence. Still, yes, each to his own, I say.' He looked about his office, gauging the effect of his dictum on the other man who sat at the table. Such effect was not visible. 'What I'm saying is that charm is scarcely what is needed here, in these unfortunate – these tragic circumstances. Charm – anyone can be charming, and it doesn't last.' He smiled his most charming and, at the same time, his most dismissive smile. 'Come on, let's face it. Young Mr Glaister has had his chance. He failed. He's . . . well, not to be mealy-mouthed about it, and I know that you have a softness for him, Mr Kilbride, but . . . No, to be absolutely frank he's . . . well, not a suitable sort of person. If you ask me.'

'Oh, dear!' Gerard Kilbride folded plump pink fingers. His pale violet eyes were amused. 'Suitable for what, pray? First of all, I must take exception to what you say about charm. Charm is precisely the one thing which does endure. The voice may go, the dugs may sag, the eyes may droop, but the birds will not stay on their perches nor the stones remain lifeless merely because Orpheus is getting on a bit. Anyhow, howsoever that may be, it is true that Philip made a cock-up of running Swynsmere, but there were many mitigating circumstances, many of which no longer prevail.'

'Mitigating circumstances?' Snaith snorted. 'What? Young man, newly married, inherits a lovely place like that? Every advantage, Eton education? I should be so lucky, is all I can say.'

'Yes,' Kilbride intoned softly, 'Philip could be said to have been fortunate in that he inherited Swynsmere. I for one do not envy him. There are many advantages, you know, to being the younger son. I was one. I know. You can be amateur, irresponsible. You have all the advantages of privilege and none of the burdens of trusteeship. Philip was such a child – sensitive, intelligent, easily hurt, sensualist . . .'

'Sensualist!' Snaith seized on the word. 'Well, there you have it.'

'. . . and grossly abused by his father,' Kilbride finished precisely.

'Oh, come, come. That is going too far. Colonel Glaister was a charming gentleman . . .'

'No,' Kilbride sighed, 'that, I'm afraid, he was not. You were his solicitor, I know. I was his friend. Tom was amusing, pompous, grouchy, and an opinionated bully through and through. Harmless to me. I just laughed at him. He liked that. He liked people who stood up to him. But to a child who saw him as a just god? No. Philip couldn't stand up to him, and Tom made him feel inadequate from the beginning. Alexander – oh, Alexander could do no wrong. He didn't muck up his mind with books and art and things. He was too damned stupid to be afraid, and little Freddy was Catherine's son, so he was different, he was the little one, he was special. But poor Philip was his mother's son. Tom treated him like dirt. Strange irony, really. Philip, trying to prove himself, ends up in the army, while little hero Alexander ends up on drugs at university. It was Tom's fault, all of it. No, he had no charm, Tom. The gauche ingenuousness of a spoiled child, perhaps, but that, my dear Snaith, is not at all the same thing.'

'Oh, well, of course I bow to your superior knowledge. Charm, as I say, is not my thing; but none of this, none of this stuff, alters the fact that Philip Glaister ruined a working enterprise. There must be someone better to sort things out.'

'Philip Glaister,' Gerard Kilbride explained in a voice like a bowed cello, 'will have the yard's best interests at heart. He knows most of the staff, he knows many of the horses, he knows the business. He may have lost money while he was training, but he had more placed horses *per capita* than any other trainer in his first two seasons. Look, Snaith, I know it's difficult for you, but just try putting yourself in his position. His older brother dies when doped up to his eyes. Philip inherits. When his father died, Philip was young, unprepared, newly married to a beautiful but spoiled girl. They invite their friends down. Of course they do. They play poker, back horses, have weekends in Paris, all that. Of course they do. They're nice, civilized young people – '

'I don't see what that has to do with it. It is quite possible to be *civilized* without having orgies.'

'Not, however, without *having* had at least one,' Kilbride said smoothly. 'No, but what poor Philip and Linda didn't realize was that the whole shooting-match was appallingly under-capitalized. All right for old Tom. Let's face it. For him, it was just a snobbish hobby. If it hadn't been for the one horse . . .'

'Erebus,' supplied Snaith.

'If it hadn't been for him, Swynsmere would have been pretty much a nonentity. Philip could have been an infinitely better trainer than his father, given time. OK, so he reacted badly under the strain, drank too much, tried that ridiculous scam – '

'*Ridiculous scam?*' Snaith pushed back his chair and stood. He walked over to the fireplace and directed his words up at the dark portrait which hung above. 'Mr Kilbride, we are talking about large-scale fraud. He was – and I do not think I am defaming him – he was exceedingly fortunate not to be imprisoned for a considerable period.'

'I know that, Snaith,' Kilbride said patiently, 'but I cannot see that that is germane to our discussion. All that concerns us is that Freddy is as good as dead and Swynsmere and its horses are at present untended, or, at least, inexpertly tended. It is the tail-end of the season. I think we are agreed that the interests of the trust will be best served by selling the entire property in the spring. Even if Philip wished to come back and train, he has lost credibility in the racing world. But in the meantime, there are horses – valuable assets – that need expert feeding and training.' Kilbride's smooth voice took on more resolve. 'Now, listen, Snaith. An idea. My goddaughter has been on holiday in those parts, and I've got her to do a little research for me on her way back. The D'Estes, you know. She could call in and conscript Philip tomorrow. Now I maintain that Philip is the only man with the knowledge and experience to do the job. You maintain that he was lucky to stay out of chokey. Can I now have your views on the short-term stewardship of Swynsmere?'

Snaith shooed dust disapprovingly from his jacket lapel. 'There must be someone else,' he snapped.

Kilbride shrugged. 'Name him, my dear chap.'

Snaith swung round. His shoulders were hunched. His fingers clasped and unclasped. He stared down at them as though they were doing it against his will. 'I don't know,' he mumbled. He slumped down in his chair again. 'I just don't want that man back. He's – what do you horsey types call it? A rogue?'

'A wrong 'un.'

'Yes, well, if you ask me, Philip Glaister's a wrong 'un, through and through. I'm sure of it. However, you are a trustee, so ask him, but it makes me nervous. I tell you, Mr Kilbride, wherever Philip Glaister goes, disaster follows.'

The moment he saw the girl, worry whispered.

She appeared in a frame the shape of an upended coffin between two peeling ochre houses. The bright sea was behind her head and shoulders. A jet-ski unzipped the water from her eye to Charlot's rickety veranda. She walked briskly across this frame and was lost to view.

The sea's sound swelled and healed, high-speed. The water trembled and glittered. Philip frowned.

He frowned because she was incongruous in her nicely-tailored clay-grey jacket and her tapering skirt, her dark blue Lavallière and her clattering courts, incongruous here, where the sunlight lay heavy on one's shoulders as a sleeping pet and the more usual quayside uniform consisted in a single pouting sliver of fabric.

He frowned too because she carried with her like a scent the memory of that world which he had fled, of business, property, propriety. He told himself that he was being absurd.

He feared that she was here because of him.

The hell with it. He shrugged. He returned to the more pressing concerns of Sylvie and sole.

Sylvie and he were the only customers for lunch at La Vieille Auberge. They sat in the tiny *place* at the top of the steep and narrow street. At Philip's right, a dark jigger wound upward between balconies which almost touched. Beneath the fiesta of frocks and tea towels, a dark boy in tiny blue shorts sat on a doorstep, gravely flicking marbles as though reading the auguries. On the other side, a broad flight of steps climbed to the Rue de l'Horloge. A marmalade cat lengthened and shortened like a caterpillar as he stopped at each step to undulate, stretch and flex his claws.

This sole, like all Tante Agnes's soles, appeared to have lived virtuous and died content. In its honour, Agnes had eschewed all flowery obsequies. She had let its fragrant character speak for itself. She had anointed it with a chrism of olive oil, stale breadcrumbs, parsley and lemon juice before consigning it, otherwise naked, to the flames.

Philip ate one of this philanthropic fish's relations every Thursday lunchtime. He had won *la patronne's* grudging approval by insisting that it should be served with no more distracting accompaniment than fried potatoes and washed down with nothing more assertive than icy *bière blonde*.

He had, in short, found fish, chips and ale on the Mediterranean.

It did not make him wistful for home.

Sylvie sat opposite him in a tight white tank-top and tight white pedal-pushers. She ate with the delicate coarseness of the south. She tore bread as though it were jointed, but popped each piece into her mouth from between long red fingernails as though it might burst should it touch her teeth. She sighed and thumped down her glass with piratical relish, but she dabbed her lips almost daintily and left her plate looking always ready to sit for the local painters.

She was an Indo-Chinese half-breed in her early forties. Her black hair, fine as spun sugar, was coiled loosely on top of her head. Her cheekbones were high and fine, her eyes sole-shaped and dark as coffee. The left one was lazy, which gave her a *malin* look. Her skin was dark by nature, darker by virtue of her beach-bum life.

'So I told her . . .' She gulped and coaxed a flake of crust

20

from the corner of her mouth. She spoke a clipped, *boule-vardien* French. 'I said, "You must meet my friend Philippe. He is an English gentleman and a writer so pure that he cannot bring himself to write so much as one unworthy word. You should see some of the books that he has not written. He will teach you English," I said, "and, if you are very lucky, he will take you to bed with him . . ."'

'Ah, Sylvie,' Philip sighed, 'you are to my PR what Herod was to Montessori.'

'Well, why not?' she shrugged. 'You can talk to her of horses and maybe marry her and have lots of disgusting fat Italian babies. I shall visit you in your Torinese palazzo as a very dear old friend and steal the family *bibelots*. Perfect.'

'Sorry, darling.' Philip pushed his plate away. He tipped and tapped a bent Disque Bleu from its packet. 'Oh, I'll teach the bint, but I'll not marry her. Or anyone else. Been there. Done it. Not for me.'

Sylvie leaned over to steal a neglected potato from his plate. She chewed as she spoke. 'She is quite *mignonne*,' she nodded, 'if you like them pear-shaped.'

'Yeah, well, I don't.' He exhaled twin columns of smoke.

Sylvie pouted. She leaned backward and stretched high. Those long nipples jumped beneath the tank-top. Philip allowed a licensed eye to roam. They would probably spend the afternoon in bed together. The thought was agreeable.

Agreeable was about the best that he could conceive just then.

She read his mind. It needed no Enigma. 'I think this afternoon,' she cocked her head, 'I shall go down to the beach and torment that big *boche* with the gruesome red bits dangling beneath his big belly. Why these *roux* think that they can lie in the sun all nude . . . So anyhow, now he is all swollen, and peeling like Pinocchio stuck his nose in paint-stripper. I shall go there and lie close beside him and rub oil in my body and he will writhe in agony. This should be diverting.'

'You will do no such thing,' Philip growled. 'You will

21

come and smooth almost everything in me which is furrowed, and cool whatever in me is heated. I'm only just waking up. It's an unpleasant experience.'

'Ah, poor Philippe.' She reached across and ran a hand somehow cool as apple skin down his unshaven cheek. 'Did you have a hard night? I shall send you a pear-shaped Italian.'

'No.' He grasped the hand and pulled it to his lips. He breathed salt and Mitsouko. 'You. Pear-shaped Italians for dessert. And I shall beat you.'

'We shall see.' Sylvie sat back, replete now with good food and his desire.

The proprietress's giant, idiot son emerged from the auberge. He showed Philip his teeth. All four of them. Philip nodded. The boy shambled over to clear the table. *'Deux marcs,'* Philip told him.

Over the waiter's arm and Sylvie's shoulder, Philip saw the mystery girl again at the foot of the street. She walked more aimlessly now in the direction from which she had come. She held a flat black briefcase before her loins. Her dark blonde or light brown hair gave off a phosphorescent flash like salt beef. Even up here, you could hear the rattle of her heels.

Philip made it casual. 'Who's that?'

Sylvie's head swivelled. 'Who?'

'Down there, in the grey.'

For a moment, Sylvie's chin rested on a shoulder freckled and glossy as a pippin. She turned back with a shrug. 'Bah? She has the English air. Maybe an agent of police sent to find you.'

'Could be something to do with Major Waghorn, I suppose,' Philip suggested. 'Solicitor or something. Stockbroker.'

Sylvie released the obligatory giggle which always bubbled up in her when that good yeoman was mentioned. 'Or his daughter.'

'There is no daughter. Just the two sons – John who lost his toes in the Arctic and Tom, also known as Tanya, who works out of a *boîte* in Cannes.'

'There is your answer. This, then, is Tom/Tanya Waggle-horn.'

'Uh uh. That,' Philip informed her with solemn certitude, 'is no transvestite.'

Sylvie scowled. Again she turned her head. The girl was gone. 'Oh, no. She is some little English girl that you met at a party, perhaps, and now she has twins and has come looking for you.'

'No.'

'You are sure?'

'Sure as I can be.'

'Which is to say not sure at all.'

'OK, OK, it's possible. I can't be expected to know everyone, but most of my associates would know better than to dress for Holborn at the seaside. Naked on Holborn, maybe . . .'

'So. I tell you,' Sylvie leaned forward, elbows on the tablecloth, hands raised for expressive finger-painting, 'she is the personal private secretary for the EC in Brussels, which means that she spends all day lying on her desk with her legs in the air being force-fed potato-chips. She has a story with her boss, and they have planned a few days of making love in the sun, so she, because she has to look as though she is on business, wears business clothes. Well, but he, his wife – who is very *petite bourgeoise* and comes from Toulouse – she has found the letters and the tickets and has tied him to the bed with his ties from Hermès with no thought of pleasure. So now the poor mistress, she wanders back and forth. She dare not telephone his home. She does not know if she should wait a few hours more or return to Brussels or simply suicide herself in the harbour and it is all very tragic and I think I am going to cry. There.'

Philip vaguely smiled, but worry was nagging now. The liqueurs had been delivered as she spoke. He picked up his glass. He swirled the liquid once, just to mark time, and drained it in one. He flicked away the cigarette. 'Come on. Drink up. Let's be on our way.'

'Hold on,' Sylvie frowned. 'What's the rush? Let me finish my drink, will you?'

'All right, all right.' He pulled out another cigarette. He bummed it on the pink damask. He lit it, exhaled noisily and rested his forearms on his thighs. Rope-soled espadrilles don't tap too well, so he contented himself with a lot of eloquent jiggling.

Up there on the hill was the sanctuary of home: Big Mama Thornton on the tape-deck, an open bottle of Lirac rosé in the fridge and a mattress on the bare boards in the zebra light from the blinds.

Hell, he wanted to be there. Now.

Sylvie, Philip noted with approval, was not one to linger simply because he wanted to hurry. In Philip's book, such people would linger long in hell. She drank quickly, stroked her hair just once and shouldered the string bag.

Even as she did so, Philip was up and leaning through the bead curtain to call farewells and thanks. He had no need to pay. He settled all bills on the first of each month, never bothered to carry more than a hundred francs in cash.

Sylvie was standing when he returned to her. She cast a resentful little pout and a smile up at him. 'OK,' she said, *'bourru.'*

He walked round the table and took her elbow. He made to steer her up the dark alley – the quickest and safest route homeward – but she raised her arm and pulled it free. 'No, Philippe!'

He was all innocence. 'What's up now?'

'What do you mean, what's up? What's wrong with you? I've got something to do in town. I told you.' She set off down the hill towards the sea.

Philip caught up with her in three strides. 'OK, OK,' he said, 'so what is this something?'

'I told you this morning. I have to see the Crow. She has been mending a pair of jeans and making a sweet little dress for Antoinette for this *fête* of your friends, the Duggans. You want me to go back home and tell 'Toinette that I have not brought her dress and she must go to the party in an old one because her friend Philip was too impatient to wait, huh? She would weep very poignantly for a night and a day, then she would sharpen a good knife and disembowel you.'

24

'Fine, fine. Did I say I wanted to stop you? Let's get on with it, that's all.'

'There is a sack of time, Philip. All afternoon. This will take only a few minutes, and it is a lovely dress. Little pink flowers and a *gilet* of cerise velvet. You will like it. Now, be nice, or I shall go and entertain myself with fat Germans.'

'You do what you like,' he mumbled. 'I don't mind. Go home on my own, wait for you. I don't care . . .'

'Bah,' she giggled. She slipped an arm through his as they emerged into the bright light and the swooping soft breeze on the quayside. He looked quickly to left and right. No grey girl. He was almost disappointed. Sylvie was saying, 'The big English bear *bourru*.'

Bourru was a term often used about Philip. It means grumpy, testy, crusty. *Bourré* means drunk. They'd said that about him too, on occasion.

He resented this grumpy tag. 'I am *jolly*,' he would protest. 'Everyone says so. I have several medals for jollity and for the spreading of sweetness and light. "Aha," cry the bereaved and the melancholy as they see me approach, "here comes Glaister, as ever with a spring in his step and a sparkle in his eye and a jolly jest to cheer our mournful hearts and enliven our humdrum lives!"'

He positively exuded cordiality now as he and Sylvie walked along the quay. He nodded to Madame Regis where she sat gape-legged in dusty black before her front door. She licked her beard in response. He waved to Christian, the bovine blonde who owned the jet-skis. Christian showed Philip neon teeth and raised a golden-roasted arm. Philip hailed Felix and Charlot, the local villains, where they sat on a plank hanging from the side of a rusty old schooner. A bottle of wine, a couple of baguettes, paint pots and brushes stood between them. Only the pots and brushes seemed untouched. And now, at the end of the promenade, a jerk at Philip's arm tugged him sideways through a chattering bead curtain and down a step into darkness.

It was always deep dusk in here. A large mottled pot-plant occupied the only window. The floor was the colour of dried blood, the walls that of wet sand. There was a large dark press against the far wall on the right and a large dark table on the left. A sewing machine stood like a stuffed pug amidst scattered patterns and swatches. A madonna made excuses in a corner niche. Holy cards and pages from old fashion magazines hung askew on the walls. There was a dark armchair spurting horsehair from its many wounds. There was an old woman in the armchair.

Of these, somewhat to Philip's and Sylvie's surprise, it was the old woman who spoke.

A litter of hamsters seemed to reside in each of her cheeks. They jostled blindly beneath the walnut wrinkles. She rasped, 'I don't know. No point in asking me. I'm just a poor old woman. Oh, no. No gratitude. Never there when she's needed. Typical. What do you expect? *Salope*.' The hamsters tussled a bit more, then gradually sank into sleep as the old woman's jaw dropped into her collar. Signora Rastrelli's Italian accent had been transmuted into a broad Provençal twang – '. . . kong dong a berswang . . .' Now she contented herself with snuffling and crooning.

Sylvie paid no attention to the old woman. She swept past her to the door at the back of the room. 'Anna?' she called up the stairs. 'Anna! *Ciao*! It's Sylvie. Have you a moment?'

There was some shuffling and thumping upstairs, then a flurry of footfalls. La Corneille swept in, smiling. She told Philip she was delighted to see him, then opened the cupboard and pulled out hangers covered in rustling tissue-paper. She cleared a space on the table. She and Sylvie got down to some heavy-duty oohing and ahing.

The Crow's nickname had nothing to do with her appearance. Anna Rastrelli was tall, strong and slender. Her grey-blonde hair was pulled very sleek and tight back off her face. Her nose was straight and strong, her skin of that soft, powder-pink variety which never seems to wrinkle. She wore bright gypsy colours.

26

She had won the name in the war. A sixteen-year-old in Piemonte, she had caught the eye of a lieutenant in the occupying army. He had not proved displeasing to hers. For this crime, her gallant fellow-townsfolk had one night stripped, shaved, tarred and feathered her and rolled her, trussed, from the back of a cattle-truck into the town's principal square. Her mother – the crone who sat steaming and festering in the corner – had not spoken to her from that day to this.

Philip understood barely a word of the cooing at the table. He concentrated instead on the pictures on the walls. He was studying a particularly ghoulish representation of the Sacred Heart when the beads in the doorway stuttered, and light slid in.

Light from the sea squirmed on the ceiling. A fine hand with a knuckleduster of light punched through the beads. Then a head appeared. From what little Philip saw before returning to his devotions, it was a good sort of head.

'Excuse me,' it said, and the vowels were more open, the tone more confident than the schoolgirl French warranted, 'I have a reservation at the Hotel Athenée, but there is no one there. Is it that you know where is M. Pierrefeu?'

Sylvie and the Crow had picked up on the accent. Both had turned to Philip. He did not turn to the girl but answered quickly in French. 'Emile? Yes, he will be with his mistress above the *tabac* at the top of the Rue des Martyres. Unless they've had a row, in which case he will be out in his boat getting drunk. Either way, he will be back prompt at five.'

'Just let yourself in and find a room,' Sylvie advised with a quick frown in Philip's direction. 'Don't go above the second floor. The wallpaper gets seriously noisy.'

Philip could not see the girl, but he fancied that she was studying him as she said, 'Oh, I see. Extraordinary. Thank you. Oh, and do you know where I find Villa Locarno, please? An Englishman? Philip Glaister?'

Again the two women's heads swivelled. Sylvie managed to get out, 'Ma . . .' before Philip overrode her.

'Straight along the road,' he rattled in brusque French,

27

'up the hill towards the Duggans' place, monastery up
there. About a mile-and-a-half out of town. Locarno's up
on your right. Pink place, wild garden, beehives, top of a
steep little drive. No point in going up there, though.
Glaister's away. Italy, I think. Business. Won't be back for
a fortnight.'

'Oh,' the girl said. She muttered. Little soft plosives, like
pine-needles on the fire. 'Typical.'

'If you want a message to him,' Sylvie spoke coldly and
in halting English, 'I can assure that he will receive it as
soon as he returns. Or you could leave it at the Post. He
may be back more early.'

'Nope,' Philip told a lamb with a banner. 'Two weeks,
maybe three, he said.'

'Surly bloody peasant,' the girl said softly in English,
then, to Sylvie, with lots of gender solidarity, 'Thank you
so much. I'll see about a message.'

There was a long silence. A bluebottle buzzed inside, a
Vespa outside. The girl was considering Philip. He was
sure of that. Still he did not turn. At last, the beaded
strings crackled. The heels chimed.

'Right,' Philip said loucly before anyone else could speak,
'all sorted? Good. Let's be on our way.'

Sylvie contained her exasperation for just three minutes.
As soon as they were out in the sunshine and trudging
homeward, it burst from her. 'I just don't understand you!'
She put in two steps to his every one. 'What harm can she
do, in the name of God?'

'Dunno. Probably none,' Philip shrugged. 'I just don't
want whatever it is – England, business, all that – to break
in on me here. I like things the way they are, thanks.'

'But, Philippe, it could be important!'

'Not a chance. If it was urgent – something to do with
Sam or Linda or something – they'd have telephoned,
right? If it's not urgent, they could write. I've got no debts
back there, no obligations. I cleaned up thoroughly before
I left. And that's the way I like it. So no. Most likely thing

is, she met someone who wanted to impress her. She says, "I'm going down south." The someone goes, "Oh, Philip Glaister's living down there. You should drop in," and she just happens to be one of those extraordinary social liabilities who take people at their words. Oh, I forgot. You wouldn't know. In England, the truth is quite properly considered improper and is restricted to medical notes and drunken, late-night discussions. Whatever is said in mixed company is untrue, which is why, for example, we speak marriage vows with straight faces. We're used to that sort of thing. But there is a group of naive and vulgar aspirants who actually believe what we say. We say, "Do pop down for a weekend," and the buggers actually do so! We say, "forsaking all others", and they call their lawyers as soon as we go back to our mistresses after the honeymoon. This girl's one of those. I'd lay odds on it.'

'But aren't you curious?'

'Not a lot,' he lied.

'Well, I am.'

'Of course you are, my darling.' He shifted her daughter's new outfit from his left arm to his right. He threw back an insistent bang of hair. 'And doubtless by judicious enquiries at the hotel or wherever, you will soon know all. I imagine that it will all prove very mundane and boring.'

'She is pretty,' Sylvie objected.

'Yeah, yeah,' he admitted. 'She's pretty. Lots of people are. I can live without one of them just this once.' He stopped suddenly, and leaned against a low wall. Beneath, silver scrub bounced steeply down through olive trees to the grey rocks and the sea. To his left, the coast hooked back like a scythe. 'Look,' he sighed, 'I am happy here. Everything's organized. Everything's fine. The cash comes in, the sun shines, there's you, a bit of work here or there – I just don't want England and money and family and all that crap seeping back in. I've had all that stuff, and I made a balls-up of it. I want to be left alone to get on with my own business. Someone like that turns up, all business and do-you-know-so-and-so, it messes things up like a note from the pox-doctor on your wedding night. I don't need it.'

'You mean you don't want to feel nostalgia.' Sylvie, leaning against the wall beside him, looked up at him over her shoulder like a cyclist. 'You love your England. You know you do.'

'And you love 'Toinette's dad. Doesn't mean you want to live with him or have him turn up here. Anyhow, the England I love has gone. Used to be a gay old girl, pretty, buxom, maternal, all dressed in a plush frogged get-up of green and gold. Not now. Stripped bare and raped by gangs of opportunist little gnomes. Hunters, herdsmen, northerners, midlanders, west countrymen, cockneys – all gone. Only greedy south-eastern troglodyte wankers now. Don't speak their mealy-mouthed language. Better off here.'

'Which is why you religiously read your London *Times* every day.'

Philip tried another 'hrmph'. It didn't come out quite right. 'Just the cricket,' he said.

Down at their left, the town was awaking after the lunchtime break. It was built on a slope, an old Remington keyboard with cottages for keys and the quay for its spacebar. Human figures in varied states of undress were visible down there, heading back to work or to the beaches. Christian's powerboat coughed then miaowed as it bounced out into the bay, stitching a dart of lace into the silky blue. His orange paraglider pursued like a predator. Philip and Sylvie were too high to see more than the bare legs beneath the awning.

'. . . no need to make friends with her,' Sylvie was saying. She had turned and now leaned back against the wall, her face turned up to the sun. 'Just find out who she is and what she wants. No harm in that, surely?'

'I don't know; probably not,' Philip admitted. 'Could be. Say she's a journalist. Nice little story. Pay for her holiday. Quick run through past history, get an update, a picture, publish it in some weekly gusset-moistener as an object lesson as to the wages of sin. Thanks, my love, but no. No,' he straightened, 'I'm alone and I intend to stay that way. Come on.' He extended a hand. 'Let's get home.'

*

Jenny Laing flung her jacket then herself down on the bed. Heat had made the once crisp jacket flaccid as cooked pasta. Her shirt clung to her sides and was clammy on her back. She lay on her back and stared up at the plain white ceiling while her right hand worked the shirt buttons free. She flicked the shirt open at her either side. She wore a white bra, though her breasts were not large. The skin over her well-defined ribcage and her stomach was tanned to the colour of a year-old dime. She parted her legs a little, just to let the air in. She puffed.

OK, so she had been dumb, dressing up in Costelloe for the hired-car run up from San Remo. What was wrong with a T-shirt and cut-offs, Christ's sakes, like she'd been wearing for most of the past couple of weeks?

But she'd told herself it was because hers was a grave and sensitive charge, that she should dress respectfully to bear bad tidings.

Balls. Bad news is made no better by the messenger's sombre dress. Worse, if anything. No, the reason had been simple and stupid. The reason had been Philip Glaister.

She did not know him, but she knew his reputation, knew what he had done to her step-sister, Theresa. She reckoned that she knew his type, and she did not like it. He was a philanderer. Treated women like objects. He was a crook. She had heard all the stories.

Sure, but why had that made her dress as if to play at a lunchtime concert at Queen Elizabeth Hall? She could look after herself. Even in the unlikely event that he should wish to, he was hardly going to get into her knickers just because she was more skimpily and practically dressed. Shit, his type couldn't get in her knickers if that was all she was wearing. Jenny Laing liked to be respected and treated respectfully. The brutish love 'em and leave 'em type were for schoolgirl posters only. In real life, you wanted them kind and supportive.

No. In the end, the sole, fatuous reason that she had donned this sober uniform was that she felt that it, together with a suitably polite and frosty manner, would somehow serve as a reproof to the good Mr Glaister and all that he

31

stood for. She was damned if his arrogant Ovid's flea of an eye would wander over her limbs as it had over Theresa's – this despite the fact, which she ruefully acknowledged, that she had been content for hundreds of strangers' eyes to do just that for the past two weeks.

Oh hell, she grinned at her own foolishness as she pulled herself to her feet, unfastened her skirt and unzipped her suitcase on the bed. She disliked what she knew of Philip Glaister and had suffered a fit of the priggish school-prefect in consequence. That was all there was to it.

To punish herself, she very deliberately pulled out a little cream go-silk number which would almost pass for a tennis dress. It was as inapposite in its own way as her original outfit but, shit, it would be comfortable. Give the lout an eyeful, why not. He was no threat.

For Jenny's original suspicions had hardened into near certainty. Glaister was in town. She had checked that young man's story with two locals on her way back to the hotel. Neither knew anything of a trip to Italy. Both confirmed that they had seen Glaister within the past twenty-four hours.

And a further suspicion made her blush with anger as much as embarrassment. She had not seen Glaister since she was fourteen and he twenty-five. In those days, he had occasionally, always briefly, called at the house to pick up Theresa. She remembered him only vaguely. He had been fairish. He had been slender. He had had bright blue eyes and a long, gaunt sort of face.

Eleven years had passed. By now, given what she took to be his lifestyle, Glaister might be stooped, grizzled and haggard. If, on the other hand, he was one of those rare people who mocked the concepts of natural or poetic justice by appearing young and fit despite vice and excess, he might, just *might*, look like that surly young man in the dark little dressmaker's.

And if that were the case, Jenny vowed as she unfastened her bra, pulled down her white knickers and stepped up into the shower, if that were the case, Mr Philip Glaister would have cause to rue her coming.

*

32

Philip was restless and irritated. He could not work out why.

He eased his right arm out from under Sylvie. It stuck and juddered on her skin. He rolled from the mattress on to the boards. Sylvie creaked contentedly. The curtains billowed and subsided in a sudden, brief breeze. He stood. He plucked a damp towel up from the floor and slung it around his shoulders. Otherwise naked, he strolled into the warmer air outside. The paving stones were hot to his feet, the dangling bougainvillaea cool to his shoulders.

The white sun was turning yellow. The pool was just a flashing field of fire. He dropped the towel and dived in. He was glad of the rush of cool, cloudy water which seemed to peel layers from his skin.

He crawled two lengths fast, then rolled over and allowed himself to float, eyes closed, on the bobbing water until the sunlight began to thud at his eyelids. He swam to the side and pulled himself out. He picked up another towel. He rubbed his face and hair. His footprints evaporated almost as soon as they were left. He walked over to a wicker chair and slumped down. He tapped out a cigarette. He lit it, exhaled noisily, spread the towel over his lap and sprawled. He picked up *The Times*.

He went at it in the usual order: Court and Social, Levin, letters, cricket, then a crack at the crossword. He never looked at the racing now.

Ten minutes later, he laid down the newspaper and his pen. He picked up the blues harp which lay on the white iron table. He started on a low, sucked B natural, bent a semitone down. He triple-tongued it, worried it, spurted in a series of squibs up the scale and back until he had his motif, but what started out as a chirpy blues stomp quickly and without his permission turned into a chocked, Sonny Boy style Chicago wail, so he stopped that too.

Then he heard the car. It grumbled up the hill. It slowed with a whine. It was her, the grey girl. He was sure of it.

Clasping the towel to his groin, he scuttled round the pool and back into the house. He shut and locked the kitchen door behind him. Sylvie lay reading *Vogue*. She

looked up with a puppy's frown. He winced, pointed. He
scurried to the window above her.

'What is it?'

'Our friend in the grey,' he hummed.

'Oh, go on, Philippe, find out what she wants.'

'No. There's the post, there's the telephone.'

'Mad,' Sylvie sang contentedly, 'quite mad.'

He looked down at where she lay curved like a strung
bow on the twisted sheets. Something Way Down There
growled like a double-bass string in his stomach.

He turned back to the Cinerama field of vision between
the blinds. A taxi waited on the road below. The driver
leaned on the car roof. The girl was already halfway up
the moss-splodged steps. He noted the little cream dress,
noted how it showed off her long legs to best advantage.
Jenny would have been pleased to hear the little hiss
which seeped from his lips. The V at her throat framed
shady hollows and the wink of a gold cross which bobbed
between freckled quarter-moons. Her glossy bay hair had
rebelled. A peaty tributary had broken free of the main-
stream and now tumbled and splashed over her left eye
and cheek. Otherwise, she looked cool and pristine.

She *was* pretty, if that was the right word, but, more
than that, Philip liked the purposeful, almost angry way
she walked, the way she held her shoulders back and her
head high and unprotected. She had what strippers and
drag queens absurdly ape. He liked, as his father would
have put it, 'the cut of her jib'. He did not, however, think
that he liked her.

She reached the final flight of six steps. There were grey
strands already about her brow. Philip put her at twenty-
six, twenty-seven. Her eyes were very pale and wide. She
cast a glance which may have been wistful in the direction
of the pool. She pressed on.

Philip ducked down. His hand touched warm flesh, its
back still warmer fur.

Sylvie at once flicked shut the magazine. She stretched.
The fur nuzzled harder at him. 'Where is she?' Sylvie
asked.

'Sh!'

The girl's form cast a scudding shadow about the room. Inside, they could hear the panting of her dress as she walked. They were expecting the sound of the doorbell, but still they both started when it came, a rusty robot's death-rattle.

The girl outside was humming. Some adolescent bolshiness as much as lust made him move his left hand rhythmically against Sylvie. His right hand grasped her left calf and raised it to his lips.

The visitor's heels clicked four times. She was humming *Satin Doll*. The bell clanked again.

Philip slowly worked his way up Sylvie's leg. She made a noise like Dracula's door. *'Ta gueule,'* Philip whispered.

The girl's shadow fell across them again. She was above them, barely a yard away, but the angle was too steep for her to see them. Philip stopped what he was doing and waited. That crisp pelt arose and fell just inches from his nose.

The girl outside muttered, 'Damn it!' Her footfalls clicked around the house. Philip raised his head. The door through to the sitting-room was ajar. He pulled back a foot which might just be visible. The footfalls scraped and stopped. The sitting-room window-panes rattled under three hard knuckle-knocks. Either this girl was just naturally bloody intrusive, Philip thought, or she had reason – the drinks by the pool, he supposed, the strewn damp towels – to believe that someone was here.

Sylvie wriggled further down so that her pubis now scratched at his cheekbone. He frowned. He raised a halting hand. 'I shall scream,' Sylvie whispered.

'Don't you bloody dare.'

'Continue, then.'

'Wait.'

'No,' she said out loud. She giggled. Her knees arose. She grabbed his ears with both hands. She pulled. 'Now.'

The hell with it.

For the next few minutes, as the girl outside growled, muttered, returned to the front door and with some

35

difficulty forced a sheet of paper beneath it, the house, for her, was silent. From where Philip was, it sounded like a tidal wave just hit.

'But that was the whole idea!' Richard Heron squeaked in frustrated protest. 'That's why we're here, woman. For Christ's sake, why didn't you invite him? He's a randy little shit. He'd have come.'

Angela Duncan sat with her back to him at the dressing-table. She was naked but for the briefest of black and white bikini briefs. She leaned forward, tweezers poised, and plucked at a wild hair which had presumed to grow apart from her carefully arched eyebrows. 'Oh, he'd have come all right. God, I could have had him this morning. No problem. But you've misread your man this time, Richard. He's not the sort to give away state secrets in exchange for a little pussy. He's close, and rather disgustingly principled in an old-fashioned sort of way, *and* . . .'

'It would have given us an entrée, persuaded him we were friendly, reduced his precious dignity –'

'*And*, I was about to say . . .' She stood and, moving past him, picked up a skimpy flowered kimono from the bed. 'He happens to have been your dear wife's closest friend at Cambridge and before, way back into their childhood. Think about it. He's hardly going to love you because you offer him someone he played hopscotch with. Double standards, maybe, but commonplace ones.'

'Christ.' Heron sank on to the bed. 'I didn't know. I knew he was buddies with Vane . . .'

'He goes far, far further back with Eledi.'

'Why didn't you tell me before?' he grumbled.

She tied the belt of the kimono and sauntered to the french windows. She pushed them open. 'Because, my dear Richard, I didn't know till a day or two back, and you were incommunicado in Buenos Aires. I'm always cautious about this sort of thing. Your wife may have an exemplary past, but that doesn't mean she hasn't got a past.'

'Bitch,' Heron brooded. 'So how do we get to him?'

'I don't think we do, is the answer. I think our American friend is the answer. We'll be extra nice to him, and get a few nice pictures just so we know we can trust him, then he can make the overtures. He doesn't strike me as particularly bright, and he's got the hots for Eledi.'

'She'll object.'

'Of course she'll object, but that's never stopped her. It's a drug. Once the action gets going, she has no more will power than a junkie. You know that.'

'So we leave Glaister alone for now.'

'For now, yes. But don't worry.' She strolled out on to the baking paving stones. She clasped a strand of bougainvillaea to her nose, sniffed deep and gasped. 'Philip Glaister will have his uses. He will, most definitely, have his uses.'

This, now, was a good part of the Glaister day – so good that Philip always put it off until he could wait no longer. Sylvie had returned home. Philip had slept and read by the pool as the sun had turned yolk-yellow; he had swum some more, read some more, showered and pulled on a fresh shirt – Sea Island, but it felt rough as sandpaper on his stiff baked skin. Fumble with cufflinks, then, and give up, bang sand out of the espadrilles, pour a glass of Sancerre, stroll about, locking up and conducting Rossini. Great. Think about another glass; think about calling a mate or two – hi, you up to anything? – but hell, who needs a commitment to be attentive and amusing? Take a good book instead, just see how the yarrow-sticks fall.

Right, and off, that fertilized yolk of a sun now pierced and dribbled or streaked across a rumpled sky. There was a wriggling breeze from across the bay, strong enough at moments to raise the hair off his forehead, but not chill enough to still the creaking of the cicadas. The sea looked like coffee-sugar.

Dear Mr Glaister, the girl had written in a surprisingly loose and loopy hand, *Gerry Kilbride asked me to call in on you on my way home. I have some rather bad news and had hoped to see you before I left so that I could give it to you in person. Someone has told me that you are away, but I know you are here. Anyhow, I'm at the Athenée and look froward to hearing from you. If not, I'll leave a letter at the Bureau du Poste. Yours aye . . .*

Then there was a big, bubbly spume of pen swoops, translated beneath as JENNY LAING.

Some rapid Holmesian deduction gave Philip so much: Jenny Laing, of Scottish descent (Yours aye), was a friend or associate (Gerry) of Gerard Kilbride, Philip's father's friend and pet gadfly, former barrister-at-law, now an amateur art historian and a trustee of the Glaister estates. Said J. Laing, whose writing was less confident than her manner and her speech, probably due to early dyslexia (froward), was returning from holiday down the coast.

Now. The bad news. As he had told Sylvie, it could not be that bad. The only truly ill tidings that he could imagine would relate to Linda or Sam, and of such he would have been notified direct rather than by such roundabout means. No. Ms Laing's, he was sure, must be a dove's, not a raven's mission. Gerry Kilbride wanted something of him. Dearly as Philip loved him, he was not disposed to grant him whatever it was.

Worst imaginable, then, given the circumstances?

His younger brother, Freddy, had invested the paltry family fortunes in one of the many sure-fire, copper-bottomed Titanic-type flotations around these days. The Glaisters were bust. Philip's remittance was gone.

Four years ago, such a concept would have terrified him. Now it constituted little more than an irritation. A few less soles at Tante Agnès's, a few more Stocks and fewer Glenlivets, a degree of caution, perhaps, where formerly there had been blithe recklessness, but that was all. He would survive.

His English lessons brought in a healthy subsistence. Michael, the younger son of a German banker, paid Philip 150 francs every Monday for discussing the contents of *The Times* with him and his boyfriend over lunch. Then there was the Sicilian princess who lived in a tumbledown twenties palace five miles inland. Tiny and fluffy, with a voice like chalk on a blackboard, she closely resembled the bantams which flapped and squawked about her veranda and, frequently, her drawing-room. She used Philip as a sounding-board for her memories of the quality. 'Now I think I have understand him. The earl is married himself to the countess. I have right?' Philip would nod. 'Ah, yes, I remember I am meeting the Earl of Launceston once in Trieste . . .' She would then shift into low Italian and high gear for the remainder of the lesson. Philip charged her 300 francs an hour. That way, she felt she had a real status symbol of a tutor.

Then there was Thibault, a podgy nine-year-old cherub who looked as though he had fed upon the Bread of Heaven till he could want no more. He wore Juicy Fruit T-shirts and baseball caps. He already had a substantial English vocabulary of the 'bitch', 'bastard' and 'bottom' variety. Philip tried in vain to teach him English. He preferred the lingua franca of bad movies and worse pop songs – 'Hey, baby, you good guy. I lerv you. Give me five and get down, yeah, holy shit . . .'

In winter, too, Philip bought and sold antique knick-knacks. When he found an old Provençal bread-drier, he packed it off to associates in Penzance and pocketed the profits. When he didn't find an old Provençal bread-drier, he had a mate up in Saint Remy who would knock up a particularly ancient specimen for a few thousand francs. Occasionally too a villa on the coast came privily on the market and he as privily steered it in the direction of a friend of a friend.

As for the Villa Locarno, Philip had bought it many years ago in partnership with his schoolfriend Bobby Herbert. Bobby had last been seen some six years ago, in pursuit of the Ultimate in the mountains of Nepal. He was sorely missed by his many friends and by many casino-owners throughout Europe.

When first Philip had slunk in here, dressed in a blazer which he had rarely worn since and cream flannels which had long ago been shrunk by seawater and cut short as bum-bags, when first he had come, chock-full of resentments and self-pity, that annual remittance of eleven grand from home had seemed a pauper's portion, a pittance which barely preserved him from the annoyance and his family from the embarrassment of a life – or a death – on the dole. Now, astonishingly, a fully qualified pimp, a lay-about, a bum, he could look calmly upon the prospect of its loss.

Eledi Heron sat up in the steep-sided bath of rose marble. She caught sight of herself in the mirror at her left. She started, frowned and rested her chin on her upper arm. She stared solemnly into her own green eyes.

Behind her, she heard Richard, her husband, on the telephone. 'I don't care what . . . Things can't be that bad . . . All right, tell him seven mil two fifty for the half share. So, Monastique – what happened, for Christ's sake? You told me she had that race in the bag . . .'

Horses, horses . . . Stallions, broodmares, foals, thousands of horses in training. Eledi travelled with him to Melbourne, to Kentucky, to the Curragh, to Epsom, to Chantilly, to see horses winning, horses beaten, horses covered, horses foaling. They all belonged, entirely or in part, to Richard.

Funny, really. Eledi had hunted in her youth. She had even been a proficient junior eventer. Richard – she had insisted that he accept their host's offer of a ride in Maryland last year. Christ, it was funny. She and Johnny Goodman, whooping and heading off at a gallop, flying posts and rails, and Richard behind them, bouncing, slipping, yelping. He didn't know horses. He didn't even like them. He just owned them.

Sometimes Eledi could remember what it was like back in those hunting days, before her skin became open-pored as pigskin and those lines appeared about her eyes. She remembered her Catholic schooldays, her days at Cambridge, her aspirations, her juvenile successes as an actress. She remembered poor, devoted Charlie Vane, now Charlie Kilcannon, who had carried a torch for her for years until

40

at last she had relented, said, yes, go on, I'll marry you, just because he was nice through and through, because she made him so deliriously happy by just being with him. And she remembered those days, the childish Charlie days, when her fellows backstage had resented her engagement to a member of the nobility while she had never felt at home in that cheery, hunting and racing Anglo-Irish crowd.

She was in no doubt as to Richard's motives for seducing her. Richard resented the nobility and the Jockey Club. He resented Charlie Vane who, through snobbery and some imagined slight, had consistently blackballed him from all his clubs, and he had recognized traits in her of which she had not been aware herself, traits which made her vulnerable. Charlie had said it, back then. 'Stuffs bigger men than he by stuffing their wives.' God, she smiled affectionately, poor Charlie never knew the half of it.

Sometimes, these memories made her angry, as though they stood before her as accusers. Then she declared herself glad that Richard had seen through the conventional mask that she had worn through those years, swore that one day the truth must out – the truth that she was out of the ordinary, that she was, if you must, bad by nature. One day, perhaps many years into a loveless, unhappy marriage, there would have been emotional meltdown and its consequent terrible fallout. On such days, and at such thoughts, she would pour herself a stiff drink, snort a line, feel better, ask, when was the next party, then?

But sometimes, like today, those memories seemed precious. They reassured her, not only that she had been loved, but also that there was – there might be – some routes other than that to which Richard was irrevocably committed. Then she watched children's television, rang childhood friends or Micky and Jenny Brennan, Charlie's oldest friends. Occasionally, she even rang Charlie's number, only to lower the receiver when she heard his voice.

Sometimes, then, she watched videos.

Richard had a lot of videos. Most of them were of horses

41

– foreign horses racing, past triumphs, stallions covering Richard's mares (a peculiar foible, this. He claimed that he liked to have a record of his foals from the moment of their genesis). Then there were the other tapes, of parties, threesomes, crazy times.

Sexuality was a bitch. Sometimes these tapes worked like fire in her blood. Sometimes they made her sick. But on those wistful, hopeful evenings, Eledi averted her eyes from the flesh films (she was inclined, then, to see glossy racehorses and glossy humans as indistinguishable – sleek bodies, all fit, all engaged in hot-blooded strivings, all short-lived), and, with thumb hovering over the 'STOP' button against Richard's or Angela's intrusion, watched a beautiful little girl in plaid or cords or floral prints, dancing, playing canasta with her family, sitting on her father's lap, or a beautiful young woman, playing in Wilde or Coward.

On those nights, she was incredulous of her Dionysian alter ego. On the other nights, she could not believe that ever she looked towards sobriety and propriety with nostalgia.

Yet she looked at her face now, saw the open, flirtatious child in this gaunt yet slightly sagging frame, and said softly, 'Stuff it,' for no better reason than that others, somehow knowing her, had granted liberty to one aspect of her nature but had denied it to the rest of her.

Richard had understood the playful exhibitionism which had made her seek privacy and solace on a stage. He had understood why she was listlessly marrying Charlie as 'the best of the rest', because no man had ever commanded her passions. In the early days, he had ensured her continued compliant participation in group sex, bisexual antics, drugs, all that, by more or less explicit threats that the films and the photographs might find their way to the newspapers or to her parents. Gradually, though, she had come to accept that she could not live without the werewolf nights. Her rebellions became less frequent. She had even – and still remorse had power to move her to a blush, a sick sneer – she had even organized scenes for herself when Richard had been away for a month at a time.

42

She stood, and the water and foam were peeled from her like layers of winter skin. Her head was gone now. All that she saw was a body, with twin hooks of toffee-coloured hair on the shoulders. The body was slim and well-conditioned. It bore no stretch marks, no signs of use.

She had slept with women whose bodies bore such vestiges.

She wished that hers did.

Not because stretch marks meant children – well, partly, perhaps, that. Eledi's body had been caressed by lovers, manipulated and pummelled by beauticians and masseurs, but it was a lightweight thing, a buffed, streamlined arte-fact. It wanted gravity. It was a girl's body on a grown woman. Richard liked his women slender as boys.

'God!' The door swung inward. Richard emerged from behind it. He was six foot, but somehow he always gave the impression of being a small man. It was the baby plumpness, the soft contours, the sleek, flattened down seal-grey hair. She hated him very much, but it was the hatred of a faithful dog for a cruel master – no, the hatred of an ace fighter pilot for his enemy, for they were initiates both and, though he disgusted her, she disgusted herself, and there was some strange, consoling bond in shared sin. He had taken everything from her, yet somehow she was in his debt, and grateful. He had blackmailed and slyly bullied her, yet they were united in predation. She could never be as bad as he, yet a strange, vengeful passion made her aspire to such equality.

'God,' he said again. He did not look at her as he walked to the window. 'Bloody awful day. I've told them to sell San Ignazio. At least property prices are holding up there. Monastique doesn't get the mile, Christ knows why not. Blew up at the seven-furlong marker. Jesus, what's wrong with the bloody animals?'

'Can I have a towel, please?'

'What?' He turned his head towards her but still did not look at her. 'Oh, yes.' He turned back to the towel rail. He tossed the deep maroon towel to her and resumed his gazing out of the window. 'Aren't you ready, then?'

'Relatively asinine question,' she said. She wrapped the towel about her and stepped from the bath. 'No, I am not ready. Don't worry. You go and play your little games without me. I'm sick of the whole thing.'

'Don't start,' Heron sighed. 'We've been through this a hundred times. The same bloody pure-as-the-driven-snow routine. How can you use a poor maiden so. Jesus. Half an hour, you'll be down there scoffing anything comes your way. I know you. No use coming the Home Counties virgin with me, dear.'

'God, you are a filthy little man,' she sneered.

'Yes, well, that's as may be, but what would you do without me, hmmm? You might find it a little difficult to indulge your tastes on quite this scale . . .'

'Your tastes, actually, Richard. I can live without your squalid little scenes, thanks.' She saw his sardonic smile. 'Oh, sure, so I'm human. You can get anyone all worked up – I mean, OK, things can be erotic. Doesn't mean . . . Christ! Why can't I just have a normal life?'

'Because you're not a normal woman, darling,' Heron answered smoothly. He sidestepped past her into their bedroom. 'Now, come along and stop being silly. Young Glaister is sending up some choice little numbers for our entertainment.'

Behind him in the doorframe, Eledi's head arose. Her hand, which was towelling her crotch, froze where it was. She swallowed. 'Who's Glaister?'

'Oh, yes, of course. Sorry. Your childhood friend. Well, he's pimping down here now and working as Ivan's gofer. You grand county types aren't doing too well really, are you? Should know the sort of thing we like, though. So, have we done with our protestations, or do I call Angela down?'

She was thinking. It was a second or two before she answered. 'No,' she said wearily. She threw the towel on the bed. She plucked up black cami-knickers. She took a deep breath. 'No, I'll be there. But don't you even think of touching me.'

'Oh, don't worry, darling,' Heron grinned, 'I wouldn't dream of it.'

'And leave me alone to get dressed.'

Heron made a deep bow. 'My sweeting,' he said.

She said, 'Christ, puke.'

Dusk swarmed in corners as Philip came back into town and strolled along the quayside. Boats groaned and jostled one another like bloated cattle. Beyond them, the *Fionnuala* lay serenely at anchor. Two or three lesser gin-palaces were also in harbour, but the worst of the Plutocat invasion had ended with the jazz festival two weeks ago. Philip was not displeased to see the Von Kauzes' schooner bobbing by the far harbour wall.

There was already a crowd at Les Oliviers. Philip stepped up on to the trellised terrace beneath a green awning and twining, trailing vines. Below table-level, the whole place was a jungle of bronzed limbs beneath floral shorts and skirts and shirts.

Philip was greeted by the usual rumbling mumble, a sound like someone moving a baby grand over bare boards. He sat at his usual table in the corner which Theo had kept free for him by chasing tourists away from it. Theo liked Philip. Philip drank his most expensive whisky and told him that his food tasted of badger droppings.

He nodded just once to the dainty young waiter, who flicked the table with his napkin as though it had goosed him and bustled off.

Philip sat back and surveyed the scene. Over at his left, burly Charlot and spry Felix played briscola. Charlot was impatient with the cards; Felix was impatient, as ever, with Charlot. Charlot's thick, muscular limbs, for all their strength and all the sunshine, seemed always white and plush as suet dough. His black hair looked as though someone had steam-rolled a Mohican. He lumbered through life in a permanent state of mild puzzlement, quick to anger or to laughter on the rare occasions that an idea found a foothold.

Felix, on the other hand, skittered about the place like a squirting filly subjected to an unending Kruper solo. His cobwebbed eyes shifted to and fro. A tic pulsed between his ear and his jawbone. His fingers drummed on tabletops or twiddled the grotesque jadeite signet which, together with gold identity bracelet, gold cross between non-existent pectorals and slithery satin shirt, constituted his full-dress uniform.

Then there was Luc, the Duggans' boat-boy, and his 'wife', blonde, buck-toothed Jo-Jo. Jo-Jo caught Philip's eye, simpered and wriggled. Luc looked over quickly. He scowled.

A fair proportion of the usual crowd was already gathered here amidst the vines and the gabbling tourists. The waiter placed the chuckling glass of pastis and the Ricard water bottle in front of Philip. Philip nodded. He broke the spine of *In The South Seas*, and was soon wandering the hills and the lagoons of the Marquesas in his mind.

Two drinks later, darkness had closed in all around. The fairy lights along the quay made bouncing springs in the water. Theo was very red and shiny. The noise all about had swelled. Major Waghorn showed up. He raised his eyebrows. Philip nodded. They called for the chess board and the Major's whisky-and-soda. Philip set aside his book. Once during the next hour, Waghorn said, ''Nother of those ghastly potions, Glaister?' and Philip nodded. Once Waghorn said, 'Still a lot of fuckpigs around, eh?' and Philip nodded. Once Waghorn said, 'See the Von Kauzes are back,' and Philip nodded. Otherwise they played in silence.

Philip was not a good chess player. He would set up some carefully researched, classic defence, only to cock it all up by being seduced into a death-or-glory charge. Death was commoner than glory.

He lost the first game ignominiously. The second proved one of those reckless games of sacrifice and counter-sacrifice. The bloodshed attracted an audience. Theo stopped by, mopping his brow, to give Philip advice. Philip told him he'd as soon consult a Frenchman about strategy as a Belgian about colonialism – or, he added for diplomacy's sake as he saw Hanni Kauz blowing in like tumbleweed –

a Hun about humour. So Hanni engulfed him in diamonds and liver-spots and spoke a lot of German all at once, and Philip told her to take her filthy throat complaint away from him and not to wear that revolting Lily of the Valley mixture and what age did she think she was anyway? She made a noise like an airlock and hugged him again. She sat down beside him.

Then Anne-Marie, an ex-pupil of Philip's, glided in in slacks slick and sinuous and shimmery as a brace of fresh mackerel, and Philip remembered just how much difficulty he had had in teaching her until they had overcome certain fundamental problems; how readily she had learned thereafter. She too embraced him, then sat on his other side and leaned her damned head, the colour of winter dawn, on his shoulder. She wanted Waghorn to win, she said.

Charlot and Felix had tired of cards – or, more probably, Felix had tired of cards when he saw what Anne-Marie had so strenuously cling-filmed – and they too sauntered over to lean on the table and murmur encouragement with every move. Philip and Waghorn had become momentary celebrities. It grew hotter. There were people all about them. Philip won that game. They set up a decider.

Suddenly an English voice sliced through the Gallic burble. 'Ah, Mr Glaister,' it said in that matter-of-fact tone which Britons adopt to announce the breaking of world records, 'why is it that you consider it so bloody amusing to waste my time?'

Philip turned round, mouth agape, for a bare second, before returning to the game. The good Ms Laing was directly behind him. One of her eyebrows was raised in a quizzical, arrogant, mildly pitying expression calculated to evoke memories of parents, calculated to annoy.

'Forgive me, Laing,' Philip told his pawns, 'but I did not invite you to come here. Your time is yours, and mine, I think, mine. I certainly have nothing to say to you, and whatever you have to say is of no interest to me.'

'Oh, come now, Glaister ...' Waghorn vaguely protested.

She breathed a bit, in a considered, projected sort of way. 'Mr Glaister – ' she started, but Philip was ready for her.

'Laing,' he said sternly, and sternly plonked his king's bishop where no self-respecting angel could have trodden without shitting himself, 'I am playing chess. There are conventions, you know, even here.'

She breathed a bit more. 'May I sit?'

'Of course, of course,' John Waghorn shifted along. 'Sorry about our friend. Touch of the sun. Churlish bugger, isn't he? Come along now. Serious game. Needle match. Decider. Concentration, all that. Drink? Theo will see to it. Theo?' he bellowed.

Jenny Laing introduced herself to Waghorn with a thin smile. He presented her to the rest of the party. But when he came to Philip, he said, 'And of course, but you know Glaister.'

And Jenny simpered lethally. 'Oh, yes,' she said, 'I know Mr Glaister all too well . . .'

Through the darkness of the arcade, Eledi Heron watched the taxi as it drew up by the front door and the two girls climbed out, smiling aimlessly and nervously. One was dark and fine-boned and elegant – probably Eledi's age. She wore a soft blue jersey and black stockings. Eledi liked black stockings.

The other girl – oh, she was much more Richard's style: blonde, pretty, slightly pudgy, wide-eyed, full curves barely wrapped in pink satin. The overgrown, overblown child-star, all pouts and mock reproofs. Eledi's residual snobbery instantly branded her as 'common as muck', but then, she had had fun on the muck heap in her time.

She sighed and wondered, not for the first time, where she had acquired this infinite capacity for surrender. She would go to that room cold, even scornful, but the sights and the sounds and the smells would get to her and she'd let anyone save Richard touch her and soon all dignity would be gone. It was the only freedom which she knew,

48

yet, when the heat had passed, she knew that it enslaved her totally.

She padded in stockinged feet to the bedside cabinet. Her hand shook slightly as she drew out the little blue and gold Sèvres box. With the razor, she scooped out the cocaine and chopped and scraped, chopped and scraped. God. She had seen her mother doing the same thing a hundred times with herbs from their garden. She rolled a banknote from the pile on the table, held a nostril closed and, with the other, chased the line from one end to the other. She transferred the rolled banknote to her other nostril and snorted the other line. She blinked up at the ceiling as the ice trickled down her throat. She shuddered. Her tits tautened.

'Are you set, then?' Angela's voice was deep with excitement. Eledi turned. She blinked at the apparition in the doorway. It was pure burlesque – brash, tacky and sexy. Angela was dressed in fringed white buckskins – a stetson, a little bolero, chaps, high-heeled boots, and nothing else. Her eyes splashed light. 'Like it?' She raised her arms. The little jacket arose above her nipples. She pirouetted. Her bare buttocks flashed.

'Well, there's nothing to prevent access,' Eledi said drily.

'That's right. It feels very sexy, all this leather on your legs and the air on your pussy.'

'Why do you do it, Angela?' Eledi sniffed. 'What's in it for you? I mean, I know Richard pays you well, but . . .'

'I like it,' Angela shrugged, 'just like you do.'

'I don't.'

'Oh, come *on*, darling,' Angela laughed.

'No. I mean, OK, I'm susceptible. So? It's like an alcoholic. He doesn't like drink, but when he's had a couple, he's got to have more. OK, but he still doesn't like the hangover, he still doesn't like it when he's sober. I don't like it. It's squalid. It's . . . debasing.'

'I know,' Angela purred, 'that's what's so nice about it.' She looked at Eledi then, a deep, naughty, seductive look. She licked her lips. Eledi looked away. A moment later, she felt Angela's naked arms encircling her. 'Come on,' the

49

words were soft and warm on her ear, the lips dry on her neck, the breasts plush against her back. She found herself leaning backward into the warmth. 'I'll tell you something,' Angela sighed between small kisses, 'which will cheer you up. Don't tell Richard I told you, but a very old friend of yours sent the girls up tonight.'

'I – I know. Philip.'

'So you could get one of them to pass him a message, couldn't you? Arrange a meeting. That would be nice, wouldn't it? Hmm?'

'Yes,' Eledi gasped as Angela's right hand swept smoothly and surely up her stockinged thigh and two fingers dipped and gently rubbed. Her head rocked back until her crown rested on Angela's collarbone, and suddenly Angela's lips were on hers and her tongue slithering about her gums. Eledi closed her eyes. Her whole body shook.

'Come on, darling,' Angela croaked. 'Let's go and have fun.'

One last kiss, one last soft rub, and Eledi suffered herself to be led from the room, docile as a broken yearling.

Bonaparte merely had piles, and he couldn't cope. He didn't have Jenny Laing's chalk-stream eyes upon his every move, nor Anne-Marie's hand upon his upper thigh. Philip didn't stand a chance. He stumbled into a trap as subtle as a choirboy in an Intourist hotel bed. His queen looked reproving as Waghorn twitched her from the board. Three moves later, Philip said, 'There we go, Major. Thanks.' He turned over his king.

He excused himself and stood. Anne-Marie remained attached to him. He pushed her gently back. He sidestepped out into the aisle between the tables, stretched and plunged into the café.

The light was brighter in here. A few voices and hands at the bar were raised to greet him. The pinball-table rushed forward to bite him in the groin. He made his way with hellos and apologies through the crowd to the loo out at the back of the restaurant.

He was being petulant and childish. He knew that, but somehow, what had started as a spontaneous reaction to the invasion of his privacy had escalated into a battle royal between himself and the accursed Laing. Instead of apologizing and retreating, suing for his attention or throwing a scene and storming off, she had remained cool and persistent. She had given not an inch. It was like serving aces at a stone wall.

As Philip left the loo, he saw her standing in the café doorway. She looked good there on a backdrop of vine leaves and darkness, framed by a swoop of fairy lights. He strode over to the bar. He ordered drinks for the whole unbidden party round the chess board. There was no point in holding out further. She had him cornered. Best get it over with.

But she was approaching now, that handsome face still cooly disdainful. Beside Philip, a genuine antique fisherman was arguing with his son about cycling, a subject which held about as much interest for Philip as, say, paddling-pool manufacture or the sex life of the common accountant. He none the less sought refuge in ardent discussion as to the relative merits of two pedalasts of whom he had never heard.

'Come on, Mr Glaister,' Jenny Laing spoke briskly at his shoulder, 'I have wasted quite enough time and effort on you. Now . . .' Philip turned and opened his mouth to speak, but she swept on. 'Now. That's enough, thank you. Just listen, you have got to listen to me.' Her speech became more emphatic. 'Your brother is on life-support and is not expected to regain consciousness. Your assistance would be appreciated. That is the message from Gerry Kilbride. I have now done as he asked. If you want to speak to me, I shall be at the hotel until midday tomorrow. Thank you. Good night.'

Philip found himself making noises like a sheep with a stammer. By the time he had a basic 'baa' ready for production, Jenny Laing was halfway across the room. By the time he had it produced and was getting something more cogent together, her red rump had swivelled, she had

51

passed through the crowd and was lost in the darkness outside.

What at last came from Philip's throat was a croak. 'Hold it . . .' He set off after her. He drained his whisky as he went. He banged it down on the table nearest to the door. Theo appeared in the doorway with his tray. They danced for a second or two, then Theo pressed his back against the doorframe and Philip squeezed past. 'Hold it!' he called into the darkness. Hanni or Anne-Marie shouted out to him. He swept past them.

An amorous couple walked laughing towards him. He jumped across their path and off the pavement. Jenny Laing was already thirty yards down the quay. She walked purposefully. Her hand arose to her crown. Her cream shirt was all cubist contours as she passed beneath the different coloured lights – now pink, now green, now yellow. 'Hey!' Philip shouted. He broke into a run. Jenny Laing did not so much as check her stride.

He caught up with her outside La Corneille's. 'Look, Miss Laing – ' he said, but she didn't stop. 'Look – ' He overtook her and walked backwards in front of her. 'OK, I'm sorry, all right?'

'First,' she addressed an invisible giant at his left shoulder, 'first, I do not believe you. Second, no, it's not bloody all right just like that. I don't see why I should spend a whole day chasing around after you like a blue-arsed fly just to do you a favour. I appreciate your desire for privacy, but I do not appreciate your downright discourtesy.'

'All right, all right,' Philip nodded. He was still walking backwards. 'Thank you, nanny. So we're not going to be best best friends. OK. I'm sorry about that, but it'll have to pass. I can't undo today. I can only say sorry and please just stop for a moment before I crick my bloody neck, and tell me what's happened. Please?'

She stopped very suddenly. A woman appeared from behind him with a bottle-brush on a lead. Both woman and bottle-brush turned to look at Philip and Jenny.

'Very well,' Jenny Laing drawled. 'We'll just stop and

talk here. I don't know very much, anyhow. Just what Gerry told me on the telephone. By the way, I'm sorry about your brother.'

'Thanks. Half-brother. A lot younger. But, please please tell me what has happened,' Philip rambled.

She walked across the road to the harbour wall, and sat on one of those iron nail-heads that you tie ropes to. She smoothed the red cotton at her thighs. She sighed. 'Right,' she said. 'Come on, sit down. Not going to talk with you hovering above me.'

Philip sat with his legs hanging over the quay's edge. Beneath him, the water nibbled at the narrow strip of sloping shale. The boats rocked and moaned like old men. 'So . . .' he prompted, 'you work with Gerry?'

'No. He's a godfather, that's all. I teach.'

'Oh.'

The water lapped.

'Right,' Jenny then said, 'apparently your brother – Freddy?'

'Yup.'

'Right. Freddy was found in the yard late the night before last. His heart had stopped. Acute asthma attack seems the general consensus. Your sister-in-law got it going again, but there was brain damage. He'd hit his head hard, I know, when he fell, but I don't know if it was that or oxygen starvation that did the damage. Anyhow, he's – er, comatose. I gather there's no chance of a recovery and it wouldn't be desirable even if there were. Brain's gone. Sorry.'

'Poor bloody Freddy . . .' Philip murmured. The water seemed to murmur it back. He looked down at his feet then up at the string of lights. 'Poor bloody Freddy.'

He looked for grief's solace. He spun the dial through a hundred half-remembered combinations in hope that one might cause the tumblers to click and the door to fall open. It remained shut. There were only glimmerings, none of them sufficient or sufficiently clear to constitute an identity for the man or a cause to mourn. There was the brash, wriggly, eager child, all teeth and spaghetti limbs, a noisy, play-with-me puppy who could be reduced to blushes and tears with a single sharp word. Then the gauche, increasingly incomprehensible adolescent with healthy enthusiasms, like *Wisden* and First World War history, whereas Philip had been obsessed with morbid things, such as tits. Then the keen, well-meaning, glossy-cheeked young man, disapproving even as he apologized for doing so, eager to please, eager to do the right thing – a nice, unimaginative, middle-class, over-aged schoolboy. Bit of a prat, really.

But now he was all but dead, and you can't get much more grown up than all but dead. Philip's baby brother was somehow suddenly exalted by his propinquity to the Great Tinker. He had acquired status where formerly he had been negligible. You could laugh in death's face, but you could not pat it on the head and tell it to cut along.

So, as he gazed at the worms of light in the water, Philip's image of Freddy strangely changed. He must now assess the man as a whole, for all prospects of his changing were now gone. The pattern, however dull and random, was complete.

Affectionate – yes, Philip could cling to that. Freddy was always affectionate, absurdly and vulnerably so. He had wanted to please Philip even as he had recited his endless mantra, 'It can't go on like this, Philip, it really can't.' It got to the point where Philip would greet him with those words. 'It can't go on, Philip, it really can't,' he would mimic as Freddy scurried into the library, bearing brown envelopes in his hand, and Freddy's hurt was as palpable as his sense of duty. Trouble was, he was one of those whose hurt served only to make you want to hurt him more. He was gauche, transparent, petulant, apologetic, intolerant of all that he did not understand. As far as Philip was concerned, he understood precious little.

Philip's occasional sexual peccadilloes, his more raffish friends, his predilection for the odd drink, the odd bet, all were to Freddy somehow admirable in the abstract and despicable in reality. The younger man would squirm in embarrassed delight as some erstwhile mate of Philip's told tales of his sins, but would tut and sigh as though nanny were watching when he brought in the wadge of bills in the morning. He would have fitted in perfectly had he been born the son of a West Byfleet sort of bugger, but instead he had been brought up in a training stables and sent to private schools where they made him read corrupting literature such as Stevenson, Henty and Meade Falkner.

Poor, mystified Freddy, a mother's boy who wanted to be like his father, but didn't know how, or, for that matter, why. Freddy with his pre-Raphaelite view of women, his pre-pubescent view of Empire, his jolly, crimson, unmasked face – he had done his best to find his level. He had even become an accountant, surely the ultimate resignation barring suicide. But their father's will (and Philip's lack of it) had dragged poor Freddy back to the amoral world of racing, in which he was lost. His last conscious thoughts must have been of those great, stupid animals which he had always feared and never understood, the last scent in his nostrils that of horse piss and straw.

'You were close?' Jenny prompted softly.

Philip slowly focused on the girl beside him.

'No. No, not really. He was ten years younger. No. Just like – I don't know – like a dog, you know? You share so much. Don't have to speak the same language. Just . . .' He shrugged. 'Ah, well. Always had asthma. Thought he had it under control. Bugger. Poor little sod.'

'The thing is . . .' Jenny interrupted Philip's dronings. She stood and talked down at him. 'Apparently the business is just creeping back into the black, and there's no one left to look after it. Gerry thought – '

'No,' Philip said, quietly at first. He went on saying it as she continued.

'Gerry thought you might be able to help. The thing is, he says, you know the place, the staff know you, you know the routine and all that. You used to run the place. You're the obvious person.'

'*No.*' Philip was definite. 'Forget it. Thanks for coming. Sorry to have wasted your time. Send my love to Gerry, but absolutely no.'

'Gerry says it could be just for the rest of the season.

There are horses in training for specific races. If you could just take charge of that, supervise the winding-down of the business . . .'

'No. Send the horses to other trainers. I made a bollocks of the whole business before. I have no intention of making a bollocks of it again. Sorry. *J'y suis et j'y* bloody *reste.*'

Jenny very suddenly turned on her heel and walked back towards the promenade. Philip jumped up and followed her. 'Look . . .'

'It's no skin off my nose. I don't know anything about this, but you have done nothing to endear yourself to me, so I might as well shove in my pennysworth. As far as I can gather, your son is the heir to Swynsmere,' Jenny hummed. 'I don't think that at five years old he's quite ready to supervise his own patrimony.' She turned to her left and headed back towards the hotel.

'Just sell the bloody thing,' Philip snapped.

'And the horses owned by your family? Who's going to train them?'

'I don't bloody know. Not me, that's all I can tell you.'

She looked straight ahead. 'Gerry says to tell you that there's an animal called Plutonium . . .'

'I know there is.'

'Apparently, and I quote Gerry, "He's the hottest thing on four legs in the kingdom."' Her head turned to right and to left as she scanned the road for traffic. She swung to her right and clicked across the road. 'Gerry says your son could be heir to a great stallion.'

'Sure, sure. And Plutonium's effing grandsire was the hottest thing in the kingdom too, and what happened to him? There's always a champion in the making in that game. It's what racing people feed on, for Christ's sakes. No, sorry. This is my home. I've had all that. Why can't Ali take on the licence?'

'Because, and again I quote Gerry,' she reached the pavement and executed a military left-wheel, '"Ali – Alison Glaister – doesn't know which end bites or kicks."'

'Dermot, then. He knows a sight more than me. Jesus, he was headman when I was in short trousers.'

'Which is why he's now far too old. He retired in the spring and has moved down to somewhere in Devon. New boy's generally deemed to be unreliable.'

'Got all the bloody answers, haven't you?'

'Obviously Gerry anticipated your objections. Apparently he needed all the bloody answers to persuade the other trustees, too.' She stopped on the second step to the hotel's front door and at last she turned to Philip. 'Even they had to admit that there's no one better qualified. They don't love you, in case you didn't realize, but they need you back.' She turned away again to climb the last two steps.

'Look, Jenny!' Philip almost howled at her retreating form. 'I can't and I won't go back, all right? I hate bloody horses and I hate bloody England. They've both dragged me down in the past and I'm buggered if they're going to get their claws into me again. I'm happy here. Lotus eating, OK, but I'm happy. I don't want – ' But a slice of light fell on him and the door said 'Shhh' as it swung slowly shut. He was left in darkness looking down at a hand raised and half-clenched like a claw. He was shaking.

He abused the door a bit, but he did as it bade him.

Back at home, Philip prowled.

He hit things which had done nothing to provoke him.

He poured himself a large straight malt. He switched on the television. A French Barbie-doll jabbered at him about the Right-wing revival. He hit the remote. Clint Eastwood sauntered down the main street of the frontier town. When he spoke, it was in French and in a silly deep voice. Philip tried again. This time he got two Americans grunting in Italian and in silly deep voices. He switched the machine off.

He prowled a bit more.

At the last, unable to read or relax, he went to bed.

He couldn't sleep either.

He lay on the mattress and stared up at the wriggling shadows on the ceiling. He cursed Freddy for his sudden, last-minute run into importance. He cursed Jenny Laing for her self-possession and for bearing bad tidings. He rolled on to his side and worked his cheek into the pillows. He closed his eyes.

Five minutes later, he was on his back again. He felt as though someone had dropped a fag end in his brain's firework store.

The sanctimonious would tell you that you cannot escape from yourself. If they were seriously unbalanced, they would then sing 'Climb Every Mountain' at you, which advice were best ignored. They are right about the first bit, though, Philip thought. You can fling the albatross back over your shoulder so you don't have to see it, but in time, it will stink.

Here it was, the cold blast from the past which smashes down doors and scoffs at provident layers of insulation.

Swynsmere had summoned him.

He hated Swynsmere with all his heart.

It was not the house in which he had been brought up. The word 'home' for him yet conjured visions of the much extended, white New Forest cottage in which he had spent the first twelve years of his life. There had been orchards, a rose garden, and lawns which sloped down to the Avon. There had been ponies and dogs and ducks. It had been a Blytonesque idyll – an idyll interrupted.

For the first six years, the interruptions had been few. Philip's father had been away on service and had returned but rarely. Philip and his older brother, Alexander, had been brought up by their mother and their nanny. Otherwise, their closest companions had been the gardener's boys. They had come each day of the school holidays to mow, to scuffle and to battle with briars. Alexander and Philip would follow them like imprinted ducks, teasing them, competing for their favours and generally getting in their way. The Jenkins boys were always ready to set down their hoes for a game of football or a rough-and-tumble.

Philip tried to recapture the earliest moments. Glimmer-backs remained, scents and sounds of a quieter England, emptier of humans, fuller of life. Had he idealized that lost England, where you could ride on your neighbours' land and the stars were many, where the common were referred to as common and the poor as the poor? Undoubtedly he had, yet the stars had been many for all that, and life free of fear. Of the unknown, at least.

His mind drifted there now, to that prelapsarian time, sank into it gratefully as into a familiar bed. The spell was simple as the clicking of the ruby slippers. 'Home,' was all you had to say.

The rain had stopped now, not that you'd have noticed it starting. It had drifted, rather, in fine white waves like a veil dragged across the lawns. It had bobbed the montbretia and the lilies, it had darkened the grey wall on the eastern side of the garden, but it had not touched the windows at the front of the cottage nor that other orchard wall. It had pearled the netting on the thatch and the horns of the grazing cattle. It had left a slippery sheen on the turf. Wormcasts gleamed.

As soon as it had passed, everything woke up. Birds emerged from the hedges and hopped across the lawns. They stabbed at the softened turf and leaned back to pull. A small breeze pursued the mizzle like a dog at heel.

The french windows opened outward. A woman's voice called, 'It's over. Yes, come on, Philip. You won't be needing that. Come on.'

The woman stepped out into the garden. She wore a red blouse over a full white cotton skirt. She was slim and handsome. Her hair was dark. Over her arm she carried a trug in which gloves and secateurs lay. When she set her high-heeled foot on the turf, it set up a crackling for yards around, like a swarm of ants on cellophane.

Behind her, a small child bent to lever a plastic tractor over the window's frame. He wore blue shorts and a shirt adorned with pictures of aeroplanes. He straightened and followed his mother. He was no more than three years old.

His hand waved loosely behind him and held tight to

the string as he ran gapelegged after her. Halfway down the lawn, the tractor jinked and toppled over on its side. The boy stopped, stamped and, still looking ahead, said loudly 'Oh!' in a vexed tone borrowed from someone else. The woman only turned, laughed and disappeared into the yew tunnel which led to the rose garden.

He turned and tottered back to the plastic thing. He tugged at it and struck it as though it were a naughty child and he a frightened mother. When it was once more set on its wheels, he picked up the string and headed purposefully for the arch in the hedge.

The garden was empty again. Only now did you notice, though it had been there always, very faint from the other side of the house, the clinking and rasping of hoes in flinty soil.

Philip Glaister emerged in the rose garden. For a moment, he panicked. His mother had vanished. The garden was walled in on all sides. Pergolas looped a cruciform path of cracked grey flags which split it into four beds, all full of red and white roses. A granite sundial stood at its centre. Philip stood tiptoe to see over the towering roses. She was not there.

Then he saw the white of her skirt in the corner away to his left. She sat on the path with her legs tucked up beneath her. The skirt had ridden almost up to her knees. Philip sighed and gave a tolerant shrug. He trudged over to where she sat. She greeted him with a vague smile.

He let go the string and stood still to watch her. She would lean forward and precisely select the point at which to cut. Then her left hand would rise to grasp the stem between the third finger and thumb – and click – the rose would topple sideways. Each time she stretched forward, the underside of her bare forearm flashed and her hair caught the sunlight.

When he had fixed that movement and that rhythm, he walked around her. He reached out to touch a flower of his own.

'Careful, darling,' said his mother, 'better leave them alone. No, Philip. Stop that, Philip. You're ruining them. Don't! It's not the flowers' fault! I – said – stop! There.'

For the boy had struck at the flowerheads with his open hand like a kitten cuffing again and again as the petals tumbled on to the soil. Now he stopped and examined his hand. He was affronted. A high keening sound seeped from his throat.

'There. I told you. Serves you right.'

He saw blood, screwed up his face and screamed at his mother as though she had conspired with the thorns.

She laid down the secateurs and held out her hand. 'Oh, darling, does it hurt? Come on, come here, then. Now, it's not that bad, is it? Come on. There.'

Claire Glaister took her child on to her thigh and cuddled him close to her in the old walled garden. He sniffed and leaned his head on her breast. He accepted it all as only normal.

An idyll. Interrupted.

'Three foot six?' Tom Glaister's laugh was strangely sheeplike after the gruff roughness of his voice. 'You? Jump three foot six? Bollocks.'

'I did. I think,' said Philip, now a lean, long-faced six-year-old.

'Three foot six?' Tom Glaister shrilled. 'Alexander couldn't jump three foot six. Bragging nonsense. Makes me sick.'

'Oh, leave it, Tom.' Claire's voice was weary.

'No. No. He said it. He can darned well show us, then. Right. Right.' He removed his blue blazer from the back of the deckchair on which he had been sitting. He laid it carefully across his wife's lap. He folded up the deckchair.

He was not a tall man, and affected brisk moustaches which sprang upward like a splash. The hair was grizzled. He propped the deckchair on its side. 'All right, then, Philip,' he sighed. He spoke with a softness which made the boy's skin seethe. 'There you are. That's probably – what? Three foot? Off you go, then.'

Philip stood, sulky. His head hung downward but his eyes were on the striped canvas obstacle. It was chest high. His eyes flickered briskly about his audience. Four other people sat about the detritus of tea on the mosaic conservatory table. Eledi, the little girl with pale orange hair, looked solemn and abstracted on the swing chair. Beside her, her daddy, Mr Donovan, smoked a funny flat cigarette. He leaned back because his right leg was plastered rigid to the hip. Then there was Alexander, beaming, enjoying this, with his thick brown curls and his spank-pink face, then his mother, in a flared frock printed with big black flowers.

'Go on, then,' Alexander urged.

'I'm sure he just got the figures wrong, that's all,' Ivo Donovan appeased. He sipped iced coffee. He gave Philip a quick supportive smile, which hurt.

'Yes. For God's sake, what does it matter?' Claire Glaister was impatient, scornful. She had let the blazer slip from her lap on to the floor. 'Let's just have a nice, peaceful tea, can we?'

'No. Come on, old boy. You said you could do it. Off you go, then, Philip. Got a long enough run up? Jolly good. Come along, then.'

Philip did not understand. He knew that he had jumped something at his primary school. He believed that it involved a '3' and a '6', but it had never been anything like this – this barrier. For a second, to the watchers, it seemed that he could only resort to collapse and tears, for his lower lip trembled and the rims of his upturned eyes were filled with thick liquid, but he gritted his teeth, lowered his head further and took three loping, slow-motion strides. He flung himself at the deckchair.

The top rail hit him low in the stomach. The chair keeled over and smacked on the stone flags. Philip sprawled. Stone struck his knee, his elbow. His upper lip was flipped back by his mother's outstretched hand as she sprang up from her chair. Then the clattering stopped. He lay still. The sobs jerked his ribcage. He wailed, he gasped for breath.

'Come on, come on.' His father was pulling him up. 'You're all right, old boy. No bones broken.' Philip filled his lungs with a deep, prolonged honk. He hurled his yell at the ceiling. The glass of the conservatory buzzed. Then he succumbed to a coughing fit.

'There was absolutely no point in that,' Claire Glaister snapped. 'Completely pointless.' For a moment her eyes flashed white at her husband, then she knelt to enfold the shaking Philip in her arms.

Philip raised his head from under his mother's shoulder and, this time, flung his scream full in his father's face.

'Well, all I can say, you're in fair danger of creating a poor bloody milksop, you go on like that.' Tom Glaister rolled his eyes heavenward. 'God. Well, come on, Alex. Time to get the gee-gees in. Three foot six. I don't know.'

'Tom's so bloody unfair sometimes,' Claire told Ivo. Philip lay at her side, his thumb thrust deep in his mouth. Beneath them all, on the lawn, Eledi was picking flowers to take home to her mother. 'I'm not an over-indulgent mother, am I? I mean, I don't think a few cuddles or a bit of a fuss when a child hurts himself can do any harm, that's all.'

'No, no. Course not,' Ivo said sleepily.

'I mean, children are different. Alexander – God, he's never been frightened of anything. He's got no particular gifts, but then, it's sometimes not so easy to have special talents. He's just good at everything. First in his year at running, jumping, I don't know. Philip's different. He thinks about things. Things hurt him. He's got imagination. Life's just not so easy for someone like that. But Tom – I mean, away all those years, he comes home and finds Alex all ready-made. When he was home before, nanny was at great pains to make sure that Alex never bothered him. He didn't have to see the mewling and puking and tantrums and wet beds and all that. So it's all, "why can't he be like Alex?" but, I mean, Alex is ten, for heaven's sake!'

'Mmm. Same with puppies, you know. You can tell their general predispositions pretty damn young.' Donovan

63

sipped at his Turkish cigarette. Its scent mingled with that of the lavender beyond the conservatory doors. 'You can see. Young Alexander, now. Life's going to be a stroll for him. Philip, God knows – could be a genius, poor sod. He's certainly got the application, but, as you say, it'll go hard with him. Eledi, now – dreamy sort of chit, pensive, likes to study something before she makes up her mind. World of her own. Life and soul of the party, then just cuts off. Strange.'

'She's so pretty,' Claire smiled. 'Trouble there.'

'No, problem is – I don't want to talk out of turn, but – Tom's used to getting his own way and he's used to getting the best out of his men. Expects a lot, you know? Understandable, only poor young Philip there hasn't done his basic training yet, have you?'

Philip shook his head and turned away from that friendly smile.

'No, he takes after his grandfather – my father. You can see it.'

'Well, he might end up an Arabist too, that sort of thing. Don, explorer . . . Nothing wrong with that. Wouldn't suit me, but . . . Ah, don't worry. Tom'll adapt to domestic life. We all do in the end.'

'Pru's lucky. At least you're out of the forces.'

'I dunno.' He kicked his stiff leg as he flung the cigarette through the window. 'Captain of industry isn't a lot better. At least I get to see Eledi growing up. That's a plus.'

'It must be. No, I just hope you're right. Tom's not a natural with children.'

'You can say that again,' Ivo laughed.

'You can say that again,' muttered Philip now in the darkness, and for a moment his air-cushioned mind drifted over to L'Hermitage to nose like a wind at the windows and doors. Then he was back in the past. The idyll had fled.

The first casualties had been Glenn and Cary. With Alexander now at his father's side, and increasingly well-versed in the social distinctions between him and his erstwhile playmates, Philip alone 'helped with the gardening'. Tom Glaister came home early one evening to find them all playing football. He bawled the boys out. Why should he pay good money for them to amuse themselves? He expected a good day's disciplined work for a good day's pay ... The boys took exception. The age had newly dawned when the likes of Glenn and Cary could announce that they weren't going to be spoken to like that.

Increasingly, then, Philip spent time with books, with horses and with dogs. His father took him and his elder brother to the races on his Saturdays off. Alexander professed to love it. Philip as frankly hated it. It meant long hours in a car filled with his father's cigar smoke, then long hours being dragged from smoky bar to smoky bar, where the only discussions were of odds, distances and weights in races which he was too small to see and too young to understand.

Philip's estrangement from his former tranquillity and security was made the greater by his mother's repeated and prolonged absences. He was vaguely aware, as one is vaguely aware that a familiar child is growing, that her nature was changing, her customary vigour waning. She tired quickly. Sudden noise appeared to pain her. She spent mornings and sometimes whole days in bed. She received guests from the sofa, in negligée and slippers. She grew thin and pale. Philip would turn to find her staring at him with an eery fixity in those eyes made wide by weight-loss. It would annoy him.

The friends that called were few now. Occasionally, Tom Glaister's colonel, Major-General Tiffin, called, stuffed with bonhomie and, it appeared, an inexhaustible supply of half-crowns. Occasionally some middle-aged women from the village came with sympathetic clucks and coos and unwelcome caresses from their thick-fingered hands. Otherwise, there were just a few old friends – Gerry Kilbride, Ivo and Pru Donovan ...

Dermot Redmond, formerly Tom Glaister's batman, now in charge of his stables, started to take an avuncular interest in Philip. He taught him about horses, with particular regard to their legs. Dermot was a great leg man. He took him back to his bungalow for high tea, and his wife, Margaret, spent a deal of time tut-tutting and shaking her head.

That was the way they did these things, back then. It was better that children should not know. There were some things, however, of which they could not be kept in ignorance. Death was one of these. Claire Glaister died of cancer of the breast two days after Philip's ninth birthday.

'Well, it's jolly bad luck. A bugger, but everyone did everything they could, and at least mummy had the happiness of knowing that she had two splendid, brave boys, and that was what really mattered,' Tom Glaister told his sons that evening. Alexander, released from public school, looked splendid and brave. Philip, who felt neither, snivelled. There would be time enough to cry.

'Now,' his father went on briskly, 'thing is, I've had to take a lot of compassionate leave over the last few months, and, well, much as I'd like to be with you chaps all the time, someone's got to bring in the readies, and I've a regiment out there that needs me, so ... What I've arranged ... Well, you know Uncle Bernard and Auntie Di? Well, and you get on well with Oliver and Caroline, don't you? Course you do. Well, they've got lots of space, so they jolly kindly said, of course, they'd love to have you, so, it's all arranged. Of course, soon as I'm settled in, you can come out to Hong Kong in the school holidays, that sort of thing. And I can't go on soldiering for ever, so, you know, one day soon, I'll come back, start up the stables and we'll all be together again.'

And that was that. The idyll was done. The light did not slowly fade, it was snuffed.

Alexander was all right, or, at least, so he said. He had the extended family of Eton, where he proved competent, bright and popular as ever. For Philip, however, the betrayal was total. Every constant in his life had proved ephemeral. Within a week, his mother abandoned him, his father abandoned him and he lost his home. He moved –

or rather, was moved – to a dark, echoing Victorian mansion not dissimilar to his prep school, where he was ignored by the adults, pinched by his cousin Oliver and mendaciously 'told on' by his cousin Caroline.

He was bullied at school.

It was a very solitary eighteen months.

Books again came to his rescue. By dint of adopting the voices of the great literary wits, he developed a formidable vocabulary and a gift for the one-liner. A black eye might hurt, but, with the aid of matron's gentian violet, soon healed. A Glaister put-down would remain with a boy throughout his school career and even into adult life. Half-a-mind Mander and Fluffy Fitzpatrick, one now a stock-broker, the other an earl, were both still so known to their contemporaries. Both names sprang from some conceit of Philip's in his first years at Eton.

At the end of eighteen months, Auntie Di made a moment-ous announcement at the breakfast table. She did so, as was her wont, with many a sucked breath and with a variety of pitch and emphasis that made her sound like a diva sitting astride a washing-machine. She triple-underlined and spiked her speech with exclamation marks.

'Daddy's written, and guess what, boys? No, you'll *never* guess. It's just *too* exciting! No, well, the *first* thing is, he's giving up the *army* and he's coming *home*, and he's bought a *lovely* house *and* a stables and it's in beautiful, beautiful *Sussex*, on the *downs*, so you'll be able to live with him as a proper family! Isn't that splendid? And – it's even *better*! I just can't *believe* it, but if anyone *deserves* a little happiness ... *Anyhow*, he's met this *lovely* girl called *Catherine* and they're going to be *married*, so you'll have a new *mummy*! Isn't that *wonderful*?'

'Enthralling,' said Alexander. '*Step*mother, actually. I bet she looks like the back end of a bus.'

In fact, the boys were later to decide, Catherine re-sembled a more ancient and animate form of transport. She had a long, pasty face and she wore her dark hair in a pudding-basin fringe. Her calves and ankles were broad of girth and in shape recalled balustrading. She was a true colonial product. She knew Kipling's *If* by heart and had taken part in many amateur productions of Gilbert and Sullivan. She thought the Beatles disgusting and noisy and complained, though she was herself no more than twenty-nine, that you couldn't tell boys from girls these days. She was moved by *Dr Kildare* because Richard Chamberlain was swoony and Raymond Massey's brother had been Governor-General of Canada. She was hygienic to the point of sterility, arranged flowers in spare, 'Japanese' style, made abundant pastry, after eating which it was unwise to swim for some days, and retired to bed for three days every month with what she referred to as her 'visitor'.

Three months after her arrival in England, manifesting similarly improbable delicacy, Catherine retired to bed full-time until Freddy's squawking rent the stillness.

The new house was Swynsmere.

It had long been Tom Glaister's fantasy, his promised reward, that one day he would train racehorses. He had inherited money and lands in Rhodesia. Now he ploughed the lot into his new establishment. He did not seek an assistantship in order to learn his new trade. He relied on his experience as a cavalry officer and former amateur rider and upon his reading. A few friends brought horses to train, but owners were never going to be plentiful for an unknown, untried ex-soldier, not in Sussex. Tom Glaister did not mind. He had money enough to indulge his fantasy. A winner at Brighton or a touch at Windsor was celebrated like a Derby.

The same old comparison between the older boys was made. Philip had carefully schooled and brought on a young potential hunter-chaser named Chanticleer. Urged on by his father, Alexander put the animal at a five-bar-gate. Philip pursued them, screaming at them to stop. Alexander purled over the horse's head and no harm was done, but the older boy was congratulated for his gameness whilst Philip was chid for his fears. 'Damned pig's breakfast of a boy, ask me,' said Brigadier Glaister, and relapsed into gusty silence.

Alexander's life was mapped out for him. He left school

and moved to the Curragh, where he was groomed to be his father's assistant and ultimate successor. Philip's future was less certain. He was a proficient scholar and had facility with language. It was vaguely thought that he might join the Foreign Office – 'shirtlifters and Wyke-hamists; should suit you,' – or try his arm as 'some sort of scribbler'. No one – save, perhaps, Philip – was more surprised than Brigadier Glaister when his second son enrolled in his father's regiment, but then, maybe that was the whole point.

He went to Cambridge at the army's expense. Eledi Donovan had gone up the previous year, and was already established as a beauty and as an actress at the ADC and with the Marlowe. She introduced him into her circle, and something very remarkable occurred.

He found himself popular.

His quick and acerbic wit, formerly a defence, now earned him friends, admirers and, most remarkable of all to a young man who had always thought himself ill-favoured, women. It was the early seventies. Only nuns were not on the pill. Antibiotics had done for syphilis, gonorrhoea and NSU. Aids had never been heard of. Pussy was à la carte, and Philip, incredulous and delighted, gorged himself. Three years of drinking, disputation and fornication led to a moderate 2:2 in history. Then came Sandhurst and five years' service in Northern Ireland and in Germany.

He was in for another surprise. He liked the army. His men admired and liked him and his superiors were more amused than exasperated by his eccentricities and rebel-liousness. He discovered in himself a talent for confronta-tion. Courage was a bloody silly word. Other men, men with deep, genuine fears, were doubtless braver than he. He merely discovered that he could switch off his imagina-tion in crisis. When something unpleasant needed to be done, he could do it coldly and efficiently. Neither his body nor his mind let him down.

He had also learned that such coolness worked. Oppon-ents backed down in its face ninety-nine times out of a hundred. So when a drug-crazed, fully armed squaddy ran amok at Castlereagh, it was Philip who strode past the makeshift barricades, told him brusquely to behave himself, slapped him hard on both cheeks and doubled him up with a deep right to the gut. When Corporal Davies hesitated, gibbering, on seeing that the sniper in the Glenalina flat was a pretty girl, it was Philip who knocked him out of the way and shot her between the eyes.

It was the same with fences. Throughout those army years, Philip rode as an amateur, both chasing and eventing. He was second in the Foxhunters' two years running. He even made the trip to Czechoslovakia, confronted the awesome Taxis with its seventeen-foot drop. Same thing applied. There was no point in falling in your mind before even taking the fence. Sit into your animal. Go for it.

He was at Sandown, unsaddling a winner in the last year of his army career, when they brought him the news. Alexander, apparently high as a kite, had sought to take flight from a fourth floor window of the Shelburne Hotel. Gravity had behaved more predictably than, at that moment, he had expected. Gravity had been stone cold sober. All those aspirations, all those simple, happy impulses and abilities had spattered the spitting wet asphalt and trickled down the gutter.

The Brigadier's version of grief was blind, bitter, snarling anger. He was angry with God, angry with Ireland, angry, above all, with Philip, for surviving.

What then, in the name of all that was unholy, had made Philip return to Swynsmere, to a father who despised him and a business for which he did not care?

As well ask why one human being marries another. Philip shook his head now, still bemused. Too many ingredients had gone into the broth for it to be given the name of any one. Pity, of course, played its part. The old man's desolation was palpable. Like an itinerant from Shangri-la, he seemed to have aged twenty years in a night.

At the time, too, Philip had no excuse to dodge the supplications of everyone save his unbending father. Catherine begged him for the old man's sake. Freddy, now nine-

70

teen, felt that really it would be the decent thing, you know. Dermot, now Swynsmere's head lad, probably carried the day by insisting that Philip was the only horseman in the family and by introducing him to a beautiful and brilliant dark brown filly named Acheron.

Philip agreed to stay on. At least until the end of the season, he said.

There is a form of coercion so evident as almost to be subtle. The mistress who wishes to be a wife can be so blatant that you cease to suspect her. Her flatmates pester her and snore. Her furniture needs a temporary home. Of course she can store it in the stables. But then there are twenty for dinner, so the fish-kettle and the armchair move in, and the vases because all you have is old pickle-jars. Then the rats are getting at her books, but not to worry. She'll initial each one before putting them on the shelves. In pencil.

And it's such a waste not to be collecting benefit because she has no fixed address, and is it all right to tell Uncle Sebastian that he can come and stay next September . . . ?

It is the greatest of grand illusions. The conjuror informs you that he is working a trick, and so preoccupied are you with catching him out in subtle sleight of hand that you fail to notice the removal truck.

Such was the trick wrought by the grumpy old Brigadier. That first year, Philip was subjected to many groans and much despairing rolling of eyes towards the heavens as he displayed his supposed ignorance of racing history or practice. At night, however, he would be consulted about the placing of runners. Often, his suggestions were mocked, but the Brigadier would shake his head and make a punctured noise with his nose and snap, 'All right. Have it your own way. I'll lay you a hundred he's not good enough.' As often as not, Philip won those bets. Damn it, he had always had flair, always had sympathy with the accursed beasts.

And then he had enjoyed the scrubby little meetings to which he was sent when his father was playing *grand seigneur* at Epsom or Ascot. And he had liked the little cottage which had been built for Alex just before his death. And there was always another animal, another bet that promised well . . .

And there was always Acheron, the beautiful and brilliant dark brown filly.

Little darling. Dream machine.

Tom Glaister's passion for racing was inherited from his mother and sustained by a provocative myth which she had also bequeathed him. That myth was the Vespertine gene.

Vespertine was a sport, a deviation. Officially, he was by Gladstone, a washy bay who had won the Wokingham and had come second in the European Free and in the Stewards' Cup, and out of Sophonisba, a pale chesnut, unraced full sister to the brilliant Monbretia, who had won the Middle Park, the Royal Lodge and the Guineas. Both horses had had placid temperaments. Vespertine, however, was black as coal and his mind appeared to have been wired up by Jackson Pollock. Legend supposed that, before she was covered, Sophonisba had been allowed to run with an extraordinary looking animal which had been brought over by Mrs Glaister's friend – some said lover – showjumping White Russian Prince Menshikoff, and that it was the Russian animal (who, for all Menshikoff's efforts, was never subdued into service) who planted the seed which wrought such strange magic. For Vespertine was a genius. And a killer.

He, like his putative sire, won the Middle Park, spread-eagling the field with a staggering time of 1 minute, 10.56 seconds. He finished last in the Guineas. Returning to six furlongs, he returned too to brilliance and won the July Cup by the sprinter's equivalent of a distance. That night, he went berserk, trampled and severely damaged his – admittedly drunk – handler, then, apparently trying to jump out of his box, shattered his off-fore.

Vespertine's sperm count proved low. He got two progeny only before dying at eight of a twisted gut. The first, Vestal Fire, a bay filly bred by Ivo Donovan, proved useless. The second, Sanaro, a replica of his sire, proved a tempera-

72

mental, competent sprinter who never competed at Group level. He won four times, in unexceptional style and in unexceptional company save once when, at Windsor one evening, he smashed the course's six-furlong record by more than half a second with his nearest rival eight lengths back.

One day, Philip thought grimly, the people who tinker with such things will discover the gene responsible for, say, alcoholism. One day, they will be able to excise and thus destroy that gene and, being idiots, will probably do so. The world will be free of drunks. It will also be devoid of poets, for no one gene, it seems, plays just one part. The Vespertine gene meant brilliance, instability and infertility, for Sanaro too, having got only one foal in eight seasons, was destroyed.

That one foal was Acheron.

She won everything in her two-year-old term. She was second in the Free Handicap as winter came. The leader of the Free was Pendennis, whose family was notorious for dodgy legs. The Glaisters owned Acheron, nose to tail.

After one major row with his father, Philip had made a last bid to break out. He took a job as researcher for a Swiss market-research company. A big American soft-drinks manufacturer wanted to offload a vast surfeit of inferior orange juice on to the European market. Philip had travelled to Paris, to Geneva, to Milan . . .

It was there that he had met Linda Tovey.

As a somewhat lackadaisical model, Linda had no short-age of panting hoorays at her heels, but Philip had made her laugh. Back in England, the old man too, canny to the last, gruffly wooed her. They stood together on the owners' and trainers' stand as Acheron kicked, and spurted up the Newmarket straight like a sliver chipped from the rest of the field.

Philip and Linda hugged and cried then, and held hands as the stewards' enquiry was announced. They hugged and cried when the verdict was announced. Acheron was officially placed third for bumping and hampering the favourite, Foxy Lady. That night, one of them asked the other about this marriage thing.

Oh, and God, they had been happy, those first two years.

Others talked of happiness as a state negatively defined, a sort of featureless terrain, distinguished only by ease of passage, by absence of obstacles. Philip and Linda discovered a fertile, varied landscape full of obstacles which they surmounted with reckless joy and astounding ease. Everything worked for them. Each morning seemed a rich child's birth, full of prodigious promise, each night a childish heaven of giggles and cuddles and games. Philip had not known physical warmth and responsiveness like that. It had scared him at first, but he had taken to it like a performing dolphin to the open sea.

When Sam was born, it seemed still more evident that they had been elected by the gods for particular blessings. Sam was entire and perfect. He looked like Linda. He slept through the night from the first. The two-year-olds looked good.

Brigadier Tom Glaister and his wife, Catherine, took their first holiday in years, a safari in Zimbabwe. They died when the gas water-boiler in their cabin blew.

So Philip and Linda became master and mistress of Swynsmere.

Brigadier Glaister's mistrust, however, endured even after his death. He had bequeathed the house, the yard and the estate in trust for Sam and any other of his grandchildren. Philip and Freddy were appointed just two out of five trustees. Freddy, now a quietly successful accountant up in town, was to look after the finances. Philip would tend the horses and could live off such income as they might generate. There was a total of £37,000 in the bank – the total working capital.

Oh, maybe they could have made it, had they drawn in their horns from the outset, but they had been young and convinced of their immortality. They had entertained – not lavishly, perhaps, but their friends were expensive, and they liked to do things right. And there was always tomorrow, always the big win just round the corner . . .

It never came.

Seconds – oh, there were seconds aplenty, but second

74

place makes no money for trainers. The 'loyal old owners' proved dilatory payers. When pressed, they took offence. 'Sharp little sod, behaves like a bloody tradesman. Never should have had control of the old place. Not like this with poor old Tom . . .' They neglected to recall, however, that poor old Tom had had a sizeable military pension with which to finance his playing at trainers.

The only way out was to borrow, but the trust was not empowered to do so. Philip spent long hours in the office with the bills and the whisky bottle for company. He tried to get out with a few big bets. For every good thing that proved good, there were three that failed.

One memorable day, Freddy had come round to urge caution and restraint. Philip had flung a Newmarket boot at him and told him to bugger off. He had made his way to the drawing-room then, to find Linda surrounded by young men with faces like gobstoppers and their doxies, all grinning and yapping and yodelling, all drinking his booze and chomping on his food.

He had told them to bugger off too.

Linda, offended by his now constant belligerence and by the financial clipping of her wings, left soon after that, taking Sam with her. Philip found a perverse satisfaction in his solitary gloom. He brooded. He drank. He let the bills pile high.

There was one last chance. Erebus, Acheron's only son, possessed the Vespertine gene. He had shown a startling turn of foot at home, but hated the stalls. Twice the field had set off without him. Philip had worked on him, and had him entered for the Coventry. Had he succeeded . . .

Well, to Philip's mind, there never was a chance. Not because Erebus did not have the ability, but because Philip was by now firmly convinced that his and Vespertine's family were somehow linked in some dreadful, inexorable curse. It afforded him something like pleasure when Erebus swallowed his tongue in running.

The end, whatever that might be, was that much closer.

The trustees were on the doorstep every day now. Freddy was solicitous, Gerry Kilbride sympathetic and avuncular,

75

Snaith and Festing, the Brigadier's solicitor and bank manager, snidely disapproving.

Philip had tried his pretty scam, but there had been this bloody little insurance investigator who came sniffing around. Freddy and Gerry Kilbride had saved Philip from prosecution, but when they stood on the doorstep that last frosty morning, it had been obvious what they had to say.

Freddy was to take over at Swynsmere. Philip was to live on the dividends from his mother's legacy. 'What about Linda?' he had asked. 'What about Sam?'

Freddy and Gerry had exchanged glances. 'Don't worry about them, old chap,' Freddy had told him.

'No,' Gerry had soothed, 'they're fine.'

And, very gently, they had delivered the final kick to the poleaxed fighter. As soon as the divorce was through, Linda was to marry David Nugent, a glossy, plump, millionaire owner who kept llamas in his fields and for whom Philip had trained.

Not only had a chapter ended. There would be no turning back of the pages . . .

The three light knocks at the back door did not surprise Philip. It was not abnormal for the braver of his acquaintance to drop in after dinner. They risked an ill-aimed missile and a volley of abuse, but they also stood a chance of welcome and a drink. Tonight, he was ready to embrace anyone who offered the prospect of company. If that someone should prove to be that bitch Angela Duncan, wanting to play further games, he would embrace her more violently than she might expect.

He pulled on boxer shorts and a shirt. He felt his way through the kitchen to the door. He blinked a bit as he fumbled with the latch.

The security light showed a friendly and familiar face. He said, 'Hi. Come on in.' He stood back. He switched on the inside light.

Corinne Poirier sidestepped past him. She affected weariness in her slouch and her bent, beast-of-burden gait, but she looked good.

The little blue dress was perhaps a little crumpled; a few strands of dark hair were out of place, but her skin was bright, and her eyes surrounded by nothing more than the usual laughter-lines.

He shut the door and leaned back against it whilst she slumped into a chair at the kitchen table. 'Good party?' he asked.

'*Suis crevée!*' she squealed. She laid her forehead on her forearms, then looked impishly up at him. 'Oh, it wasn't bad. There was a nice English girl, very nice. I liked her. And a sweet American man. The others . . .' she held out a hand and rocked it, 'bah, not my type, but yes. Fun.'

'Pay well?' Philip pulled out another chair and straddled it.

'Not bad. I don't think I did as well as Anick. She put on the show of her life. She likes them big, Anick, and she likes them rich. God, fake orgasms by the million. I was more – discreet. My friend – oh. I could fall for her – she is a friend of yours too, she says. Can I have a drink?'

'Sure.' Philip suppressed his curiosity. 'What would you like?'

'Have you cocoa?'

'Yup. Hold hard.'

'I can't pinch your bed tonight, can I? Or your sofa?'

'Sure.' He slammed the fridge door shut. 'Bed has me in it. Sofa's vacant but cold.'

'I'll take the warm bed,' she stretched and yawned.

Philip nodded. He lit the gas flame and stood warily over the milk pan. He would be glad of the warmth and the company. He and Corinne would never be lovers. They were too much equals for that. 'So,' he said casually, 'this "friend" of mine.'

'E-lady,' Corinne announced. 'She is, oh, so beautiful. Very sensuous.'

'A lady?' Philip frowned.

'That is her name. E-lady. She says you were friends in childhood.'

'A lady . . .' Philip tried it again, then, quietly, 'Eledi?' He was suddenly pale. 'You're saying that Eledi was . . . ? A . . . what colour was her hair?'

'Autumn leaves,' Corinne said dreamily.

'Oh, Christ, no.' Philip perched on the chair opposite hers. He leaned forward. A muscle in his cheek was pulsing fast. 'Her husband? Tell me. What was he like?'

'I didn't like him.' Corinne shuddered. 'White and sleek like a slug. Charming but obvious. Cold eyes in a little boy's face.'

'Hair?'

'Dark brown going grey. Smoothed back, like he had an iron cap, you know?'

'Oh, Jesus, Jesus, Jesus,' Philip was up again, and gnawing at a knuckle. 'I don't believe this. Eledi? What . . . ? What did she say?'

'Philip, calm down.' Corinne's smile was concerned. 'She's OK. I think she is very unhappy, but she is fit and she is well-dressed and she had fun tonight . . .'

'What did she say?' he demanded.

But Corinne had yelped and flung herself towards the stove, where the saucepan was erupting. There was a lot of sizzling then, and sniffing of the air. Corinne insisted that she should manage the cocoa, thank you, and where were the cinnamon sticks, please . . . ?

Philip was shifting from foot to foot and looking dangerous when at last she turned back to the table, nursing her drink.

'Corinne, please. Just sit down and tell me. What did she say? Eledi. About me. Did she send a message?'

'Yes, I was going to say. She said she would like to see you but she doesn't know how. It is all very fairy-tale princess in tower. She is watched, she is followed. I said, but Philippe knows this place so well, he can get in or out with no problem. She says, yes, but there are security guards. You saw them. I said, pah, Philippe will not be worried. He will come, I am sure. She is all frightened. Tell him to be careful, she said. She is in the room third from the left, the one with the pink bath and the Dufy. Her husband does not sleep with her, so it is best you go now.'

'Now?' Philip considered. 'These security guards, did they have dogs?'

'Not that I saw,' she shrugged, 'but guns, yes, and batons, yes. But you will slip past them, yes?'

Philip did not share her faith in his burglarious skills, but he nodded grimly. 'I will slip past them,' he said. 'Yes.'

The night was still, and deep blue, not black, though Philip could see neither moon nor stars as he stepped from the house and jumped down the steps. White things – the yachts moored out in the bay, the sand of the beach ahead of him and to his left – showed very clearly.

The cicadas had given up their chirping. The sea was discursive rather than disputatious. It mooted and muttered rather than roared. Its hushing was just a soothing suggestion.

The road to L'Hermitage led up to the principal, electronically-operated gate, which would certainly be guarded. The perimeter wall, too, was high and topped with the usual outward-sloping ramp of sharp wire and assorted spikes.

Philip had been obliged by Her Gracious Majesty to jump from high walls into deep mud. He had even, on occasion, been requested to jump out of aeroplanes, but he had not found this sort of thing to be his forte. His soldiery had been of the meditative, not the Milk Tray variety. Heights did not agree with him. But then, he did not agree with heights.

No. He must play his ace – his solitary ace.

Philip's knowledge of the coastline and of means of access to L'Hermitage was derived from various nocturnal excursions he had made with Felix and Charlot to the North African coast and back. The boat was invariably heavier laden on its return journey than on its way out. L'Hermitage's beach was private, its draught more than adequate and its slope gentle. L'Hermitage, furthermore, had the advantages of being frequently empty and of capacious cellars, formerly the crypts.

The only part of L'Hermitage's grounds which was not walled was the clifftop stretch, and the guards, Philip reasoned, would hardly expect journalists or burglars to approach by sea – or, at least, not in silence.

Philip intended to approach in absolute silence.

At this sort of thing, he had had a lot of practice, and if the British army was not a match for a bevy of Mediterranean muscle-queens in fancy uniform, he would be more than a little surprised.

He jumped and slithered down the little straight track towards the rocky shore. When at last his trainers hit pebbles, he swung to his right and, keeping low, scrambled over the rocks towards the scimitar-blade of white sand.

And, as he went, he thought of Eledi Donovan, now Eledi Heron. He could not reconcile the Eledi of the night's reported orgy with the Eledi whom he had known, but then, he had never been able to reconcile the Eledi of his childhood, of Newnham, of the ADC, of endless Pitt Club dinners and assignations at the University Library, with the concept of Eledi, Mrs Richard Heron, glossy, haute coutured consort of one of the flashiest little sods ever to set his millions against the Nemesis of the turf.

Ivo and Pru Donovan had been friends and neighbours of the Glaisters from the first. Ivo Donovan and Tom Glaister had been brother officers during the war. Philip had not seen Eledi between his mother's death and that party in Jesus Lane, just two weeks after he went up to Trinity.

She had become, quite simply, the loveliest thing, let alone creature, that he had ever seen. Aside from the evident physical attributes – that flashing, toffee-coloured hair, those tourmaline-green eyes, those broad, smiling lips, that body – she possessed a rare and joyful luminescence.

Philip's first reaction had been obvious. He had wanted to be near her and then he wanted to have her, but somehow, for all the incandescence of her skin and hair, her eyes, though bright and friendly, never sent back precisely what he was transmitting through his. He would be sending, 'I'd love to have your breasts in my hands,' and she would unscramble it as, 'Yes, let's have a bottle of champagne on the backs.' He would be sending, 'Let's be alone. Let's rip off our clothes. Let me worship your body,' and she tossed the message back as, 'It's so nice to have you here. Let's find loads of friends and go for a ride.'

And he found himself liking her version as well as – though never better than – his. Once she confided that, although fans had written panegyrics and poets poems and painters begged to paint her, no one had ever made a pass at her.

He could see why. One way or another, he never got round to it himself.

They were friends. That was all. He used to surprise himself by spending hours in testing her on her lines for the various roles that she played at the ADC and the Marlowe.

When Charlie Vane had appointed himself Eledi's No 1 dog-at-heel, the quality of diversion had improved. Now there were trips to London in Charlie's Rolls, trips to Ireland for the Dublin Horse Show, for the coursing at Clonmel, for the hunting, the spring fishing, but again, Eledi insisted on keeping herself from the intimate, the challenging *tête-à-tête*. She travelled with a family of friends, in which Philip played an elder brother. Charlie, good-natured as ever, welcomed Philip. They got on well.

It was some years before Charlie and Eledi at last announced their engagement. The gossip-columnists cooed. Philip congratulated them.

Mere weeks later, the gossip columns were shrieking. Eledi Donovan, aspiring actress, was to marry Richard Heron, bloodstock and leisure tycoon, sixteen years her senior, as soon as he had obtained a divorce from his third wife.

Philip barely knew Heron, but Heron hated him.

It was mutual.

Heron had started his career running illegal poker games. When gaming was legalized in the early sixties, he had been well placed to move into the new, luxurious club market. His clubs were glamorous, but much of that glamour was derived from the rumours of young women and men luring prospective punters in, from the rumours, too, which said that various big winners had received visits from large persons in Heron's employ who encouraged them to settle for less.

Victoria Vane, Charlie's older sister, was married to a widowed farmer named Guy Allingham. They had two children. She was lured into Heron's club in Mount Street. Heron let her run up debts of over seventy-five thousand pounds.

She could not pay without ruining her family and her marriage. She could not bring herself to seek help from Charlie or their father, Benet, the old Lord Kilcannon. Heron told her not to worry. There were plenty of other ways for her to pay.

She paid in a hundred different, degrading ways before at last she swallowed a whole lot of whisky and a whole lot of pills. Benet Kilcannon had been in Ireland, so Charlie, then at Cambridge, was called by the hospital. Philip and Micky Brennan had been in Charlie's room at the time. They had travelled down to London with him. They had sworn never to reveal what she told them. Charlie had smoothed things over with Guy Allingham. Victoria was now a respectable, middle-aged, gentleman farmer's wife.

Heron had moved into racing. He had found his social progress occasionally obstructed by Charlie Vane, who blackballed him from every club to which he applied. He had also heard himself viciously lampooned by Philip. His financial progress, of course, met with no obstructions. His revenge on Charlie was to steal his wife-to-be. Charlie had never told Eledi the truth. By then, anyhow, she would not have believed him.

Charlie had been shattered by the announcement. Philip had been furious. Both had telephoned. Both had encountered a palisade of secretaries. Both had written. Neither had received a reply. Philip had sent an offensive telegram to the wedding.

And that had been that.

Philip had been twenty-eight when she vanished, but she vanished almost as effectively as a white-slaver's victim. Of course, a noted beauty and the wife of a multimillionaire could not, in these days, completely evanesce. There was the odd picture of her in the papers, always identified as an appendage of her husband – 'Mr Richard Heron and Mrs Heron' – but there had been no stories on the circuit, no 'I sat next to Eledi the other night,' no 'D'ye know what Eledi told me?' In social terms – the terms, that is, of the society of her childhood and her youth – Eledi Donovan had died.

And had returned to life, it seemed, in the south of France, metamorphosed into a swinger, a party girl.

Above, at the top of the cliff, the moon broke suddenly into smoky cloud. Philip froze. The moon, all but full, slid back into darkness. Philip veered to his right, hugged the shadows of the cliff. Black was the colour for night, but not on a strand of imported silver sand. He had to assume that a guard was standing up there, looking down.

Ahead of him, Philip could see the noticeboard that identified this as a strictly private beach, and, above it, the sandy path that ran steeply halfway up the cliff to three flights of zigzagging steps.

When L'Hermitage was empty, Philip climbed that path and those steps, but they would not do tonight. He would keep them hard at his left, as markers.

Before he started, he reached into his pocket for his inhaler, shook it, then, having exhaled, squirted in two puffs. He needed clear lungs for the climb. He clambered up on to a sloping slab of rock and scurried across it. He reached up and grasped marram grass. Slowly, hand over hand, feeling for handholds and footholds, he started to climb. It was not sheer. Had it been so, not fifty damsels in distress would have induced him to climb. At certain points, he could have stood, but he needed to keep low, so continued to crawl. Halfway up, he became aware of music drifting down from the clifftop.

The moon broke from the clouds just twice as he made his ascent. He was in no hurry. He just lay there, recovering breath, until darkness returned.

Once he raised his head and peered upward through gloved fingers. There were no silhouetted figures on the cliff's edge.

He was just six foot from the top when he heard the voices. At first they seemed just a distant rat-a-tat, then a man laughed. The voices were coming nearer. Philip pulled himself up another few feet so that he could curl up on his side in a slight indentation just below the lip of the cliff.

There were two male voices. The deep one was broad Provençal. The higher was Parisian. They were discussing horse racing, for God's sake. Philip briefly wondered whether they knew they were working for one of the biggest owners of horseflesh on God's earth, then he stopped wondering because they seemed to be heading straight for him.

'No trouble,' the deep one sighed, immediately above Philip's head.

'Sheesh. Do these people never sleep?'

'Would you?' the Parisian giggled.

'Seen the women they've got in there?'

'Yeah. Greedy bastards, and still they import it from the town. God, that little blonde one. I'm going to look her up.'

'Find out her name, did you?'

'No, but . . . Can't be too difficult, this area . . .' The man sighed. 'Ah . . .'

Something moved behind Philip. Something tapped at his ankle. He started, shifted his leg. He winced at the tell-tale rustle, but for the men up there it was lost beneath another sound, a hissing, pattering sound coming from just below Philip's left boot. Above his head, twin arcs of silver wavered in the half light.

Philip wanted to curl up small. He wanted to let go, to slide fast down the cliffside. He could do neither. He had to lie still as the initially great arcs of piss shrank, pattering on the legs of his ski-pants, on his black T-shirt, on his hair. He shuddered. He resisted the temptation to yell abuse or to take evasive action.

It seemed to go on for ever.

When at last it ended and the zips screeched, the warmth

was already seeping through the fabric of his clothes. His hair was warmly glued to the left-hand side of his head. The giant shudder shaking his frame had become a constant thing.

He very sincerely and very irrationally wanted to kill those two Frenchmen.

But they were strolling away now, their voices growing fainter. Philip spat and kept spitting. He reached for his inhaler, worked it fast, took two hard draughts of Ventolin, then spat some more. He wrenched up clumps of grass and mopped ineffectually at his neck and his hair.

He slithered swiftly downward. Thorns plucked at his sleeve and scratched his skin. Shale slid after him. A sharp, bouncing stone hit his temple hard. A twisted rock near the bottom jarred his knee, blasting discords of pain up his thigh to the small of his back. He did not care. He wanted only to be away from his assailants up there.

They had taught him much in the army – about moving silently, about camouflage, about climbing, about avoiding enemy fire . . .

They had never warned him of the dangers of being used as the enemy's pissoir.

He lay on his back on the pebbles and stared up at the moon. This was unpleasant. It did not happen to the heroes of penny-dreadfuls nor of chivalric romances, nor did he have their justification that he was engaged in a bid to save a maiden from a fate worse than death. From Corinne's account, Eledi – whom, after all, he had not so much as seen in years – embraced her fate with considerable enthusiasm. Philip was probably no more than an object of amused curiosity to her, or perhaps, in common with many women that he had encountered, she merely wanted to deny tonight's excesses by expressing her shame and embarrassment and by blaming someone else to a disinterested party.

Philip looked down at his left arm. In raising his head, he tasted blood at the corner of his mouth. There were a hundred little cold scratches on his arm and on his stomach where the sweater had been pulled up to tit level. His sleeve was in tatters.

Corinne was keeping the bed warm at home.

It was four or five minutes before curiosity and bloody-mindedness got the better of him, another five before he had splashed his face with sea-water and calmed himself sufficiently to consider action.

He scaled the cliff again, this time slowly, stiffly, almost carelessly. He pulled himself up to the cliff's lip and peered across the lawn. The house was just twenty open yards away. There were still lights blazing back there in the games room – Heron continuing his jollies, no doubt – but only a dim pink light glowed through the curtains in Eledi's window. He hoped that she was prompt in opening it – hoped, still more, that she was alone.

He had two choices. He could run for it across open ground and pray that no one was watching and that the moon stayed modest.

The alternative was more laborious. He could make his way along the cliff's edge without breaking cover until he reached the row of poplars at his left. He could then make use of their sporadic cover almost all the way to the steps down to the door of the crypt. He had a key, could creep in there, but that would mean waiting until the whole house was asleep, because the crypt stairs led only to the chapel – the games-room.

This, he acknowledged grimly, was the wise course, but he was damned if he would sit in a cellar for hours in his present state.

So. He must make a run for it.

He ran.

He resisted the conditioned reflex to run zigzag. He sprinted straight.

He had run just three strides when the moon came out.

There was a big black shape right on his heel.

He leaped and nearly fell. He would have yelped had he not sucked up so much cold air in that first moment of terror.

Then he realized, and ran on. The black dog was only his shadow.

He was halfway across the lawn when another, darker

86

shadow joined his. It was moving a whole lot faster. And it made a deep, guttural noise like a burp before the shadow stretched. And vanished.

The weight which hit the small of his back bent him, staggered him. It forced the breath from his lungs in one huge gout. He stumbled forward on to his hands and knees.

He rolled against the weight on his back.

Philip's face was so close to the dog's that its heaving breath made him nauseous. The heat of it wrapped itself like smoke about his nose and mouth. Its panting rasped.

He raised his arms and legs to fight. He struggled to remember what he knew about fighting dogs. He should feed it his left arm in order to keep the teeth occupied. He should attempt to gain purchase, then force the forelegs apart until the spine snapped. It was all in the books. As with pornography and seed catalogues, he had never found that books and real life tallied too closely.

He had already forced his forearm between the animal's jaws when he realized that the creature was showing no fight. He raised his head. The swinging shadows were projected by a wagging tail. 'Dog?' Philip gasped. He lowered his arm. The black Labrador-cross took the opportunity to slurp at his face with its tongue. Something like a giggle sawed at Philip's throat.

Moonlight was a hallucinogenic drug, Philip decided as he pulled himself to his feet. It made passions of cheap lusts and monsters of mutts. 'Dog' had been hanging around the coast for years now, scrounging treats from holiday-makers and scraps from the likes of Philip, scavenging gulls and bad mussels on the shoreline. Hence, no doubt, the beast's enthusiasm; hence too that filthy breath.

Philip was gulping for air. He needed to get his breath back – more, he needed a drink. He needed to be one hell of a long way away from here.

He bent to pat the dog. He raised a finger to his lips to hush it. Then, with a quick glance over his shoulder, he ducked down and scampered to beneath Eledi's window. He tapped twice. The music from the games-room was slow and soupy now. The breeze broke it up into sudden bursts, sudden silences. Philip stood shivering for a minute, glancing back and forth, then he tapped again, this time in the six-and-two rhythm familiar to every child.

The curtain was scooped upward. There was long reddish hair in there, and white smocked cotton, a smiling face, but aftershock had set in. Philip saw it all as if through wind-swung net. He was shaking. His breath was fast and shallow.

'Philip? Philip!' The squeak of delight above the whisper. The dog whimpered at his side.

'For God's sake,' he croaked. 'Help me in . . .'

'God, come here,' she beckoned. 'God, that is you, isn't it? God, what's the matter with you? Jesus . . .'

Her hand reached his shoulder. He mumbled, 'Can we keep the religious observance? Get me fucking in, will you?' He fell over the window-sill and let her pull him in. Then he sat on the floor and groaned his own invocations to a maleficent God.

'What happened?' Eledi asked softly as she led him through to the bathroom. 'God, you're bleeding, Philip. Are you OK? Come on, it's all right. I'll take these things off. Gaw, did you know you stink?'

She poured a bath of steaming hot water, stripped off his shirt very gently and dabbed at the wound on his shoulder. 'Ow,' she said repeatedly on his behalf.

'Is there a drink in this place?' Philip almost burped.

'Sh! Yes. Hold on. Are you sure you should?' She half rose and stood bent, gazing almost wondering into his face.

'Stuff the ethics,' Philip growled. 'Get me a drink. Now.'

She smiled in recognition. She said, 'Stay here,' as if he might be considering evaporating, and went back into the bedroom. She returned with a tumbler of champagne. Philip dimly noticed the high colour in her cheeks, the heaviness of her eyelids, the slight list with which she walked.

'So . . .' She sat beside him. 'God, it is so good to see you!' She leaned across and planted a clumsy kiss on his cheek. Philip found himself toppling. His left hand flailed. His right pulled him back upright. 'So, what happened?'

'What happened,' Philip said grimly, 'is that your husband's nannies out there used me for a pisspot and that I was subsequently tested as a new variety of Pedigree Chum.'

'I'm sorry!' she said simply.

'You're sorry. Great. How about getting to a telephone? I'm in the book. Or jumping in a car?'

'I can't, Philip. You don't understand!' She took his hand. 'Come on. Let's sit down. There's a hell of a lot to tell you.'

'From what I hear, I reckon there just might be,' Philip said sarcastically. 'So, let's catch up with the news. . . .'

'Oh, for Christ's sake.' She rolled over on the bed half an hour later. Her head hit the pillow hard. 'You're just like all of them. Piss off, will you, Philip.'

'Sure,' he shrugged, 'but it looks like I'm your only hope.'

'Hope for what?' She looked back at him over her shoulder. Her eyes were wet and bleary. Her cheeks were flushed. 'Hope for what? Go back to Puffas and Sloane Street and idiots who sound like they're related to frogs?'

'They're people, Eledi. They're getting by as best they can. Not for me, not for you, but they're doing better than you.'

'Oh, sure. So how come . . . ? You. Look at you. You're such a jolly decent chap, are you? Balls. You're corrupt, aren't you? You've done the same sort of things as I have, haven't you?'

'Yes . . .'

'But you're OK, socially acceptable, morally . . . Me, I'm destroyed. I'm despicable. Is that right?' She took a deep breath. 'Do you know . . . Do you know how many housewives are sitting out there longing to do what I do?'

'Yes, darling,' Philip was stern, 'but they keep longing, that's the point. Watch a dirty movie, sit on the washing-machine . . .'

'Or the gardener, or their husband's best friend, or they

89

hit the bottle or the Valium, or plunge into good works, God save us, but they all have their ways out, don't they? So what right have you to look down your nose at me?'

'Eledi.' Philip wearily stood. 'I know the werewolf in me, in all of us. I accept the need for the Lord of Misrule to take charge from time to time. God knows, I should. But the Lord of Misrule moves on. He doesn't rule our day-to-day lives. I see sado-masochists all around me. They make the same mistake. If they got into bed, played games, beat one another, whatever, they'd be healthy. Instead, they play out their domination and submission games in their God forsaken sitting-rooms, tear one another apart. Sure, you get raunchy, you should get laid. No harm in that. But organize your misrule. Not the gardener, not the secretary, not your best friend's wife. Be honest enough just to get laid and that's that.'

'Well,' she mumbled into the pillow, 'that's what I do.'

'Yes, darling.' Philip leaned against the wall and looked down on her. 'But you remember whatsisname? Greek Philosopher. Going into the whorehouse. And his disciples all going tut-tut, disgraceful. And he turns to them, says, "The sin lies not in the going in but in the never coming out."'

That did it. She curled up, clutching her belly. Sobs seemed to pick her up and punch her again and again. She jerked with each blow, and the whimpers and wails forced from her were smothered by the pillow.

Philip sat beside her. 'Eledi . . .' he said after a while, but that only seemed to make things worse. He reached out a hand and grasped her heaving shoulder. He said, 'It's all right. I'll get you out of this. Shh, now. Easy. You'll be all right . . .'

These were not a model's tears. When at last she looked up, she looked ravaged. Her eyes were red. Her mascara had run down her cheeks in speckled rivulets. Her hand shook as it flicked back sodden hair.

'Oh, forget it,' she said with a little smile. 'I'm no good, Philip. Leave me. I'm bad, through and through. OK, so it's Richard who drew it out in me . . .'

'We're all bad through and through,' Philip soothed. 'All it takes is a Mephistopheles. God, give me Helen of Troy and I'll go down. No one offered is all.'

'It's too late now. I can't come back.'

'Oh, yes, you can.' He leaned forward to kiss her moist cheek. He plucked hair from before her eyes. 'Some Orpheus, me, but you can come back.'

'No,' she gulped. She shook her head. 'I don't even know if I want to. Anyhow – anyhow . . .' She sat cross-legged. She brought her joined hands down with a thump into her lap. She looked down at them. 'Richard's got pictures, films. Not the ones of him. He'd produce them in court. I couldn't deny any of this . . .' She waved, 'This stuff. And . . .' Her voice was suddenly small. 'I don't know if I could live without it.'

'There are other excitements,' Philip soothed. 'Just wait. Babies, the stage – God, just a garden somewhere.'

Her shoulders arose in a little laugh. 'Hmph,' she said. 'You, Orpheus. Do you still play that silly mouth-organ?'

'Beautifully. Stones walk.'

She held out her arms. She hugged him to her. For a moment, to his surprise, he found his own eyes smarting. He kissed her. He pulled back.

'Stay with me,' she said, and she was acting now. He knew those wide doe's eyes, those working lips.

'Fuck off, darling,' he said softly.

He leaned forward and kissed her gently and quickly on the lips. He drew back before she could cling to him again. 'I don't sleep with virgins,' he said, 'and, though you don't yet realize it, doll, that's exactly what you are. Lots of orgasms. Never the real thing. See you.'

He turned and, still bare-chested, walked to the window. He peered out. 'I'll be in touch,' he murmured.

He clambered up on to the window-frame, jumped down, and ran.

Philip entered the hotel like a storm wind the following morning because storm winds have an easier time of it than apologetic breezes. He banged the brass bell on the reception desk. 'Emile?' he called. He banged the bell again.

He hopped over the desk and peered into the office behind. The bed in there was crumpled. So was the Carlos-Clarke calendar which Philip had given Emile for company. 'Emile, damn you!' he bellowed, and this time he found the bolted and hinged section of the counter. He let himself out and strode through into the dining-room.

Everyone is a stranger at breakfast, he noticed. There is a peculiar silence, marked only by the snicker of newspapers, the clink of steel on china, the occasional experimental mumble, as men and women attempt to reconstruct themselves from the debris of the night. Ten or twelve breakfasters still sat at their tables, crumbling croissants and gazing dolefully out at the hot blue sky, the cool blue bay. Philip greeted them with a cheery 'Morning!' It seemed to do little to alleviate their gloom. Only a little brown-haired English girl shouted 'Morning!' back at him. Her parents hushed her. Philip rewarded her with a salute and a bright smile.

He barged through the swing door into the kitchen. Emile was coaxing eggs from a copper frying-pan.

Poor, emaciated, doleful Emile had been widowed only last winter when some drunk punk in a Fiat had side-swiped his wife, Eugenie, as she waddled back from her shopping. Eugenie had been good-humoured, obliging and gentle. Now, Emile complained, he had no escape from the sympathetic ministrations of his mistress, who looked like – and shared the vivacity of – a kipper.

'Monsieur Philippe!' Welts appeared in the long blue face. It could not quite be called a smile.

'Morning, Emile.' Philip clapped him on the back. 'How's it going, then?'

Emile shrugged and slid the eggs on to a plate. 'They come,' he said. 'They go. Next year they come again.'

'Thanks, Emile,' Philip nodded. 'Feel better for that. Nothing like a cheery aphorism to start the day, brighten up the morning.'

'Bah,' he shrugged again, but one corner of his lips actually twitched. Probably a nervous tic.

'English girl,' Philip said, 'arrived yesterday. Laing, J. Pretty girl. Where is she?'

Emile put the plate and a coffee pot on a tray, the napkin over his arm. He picked up the tray and shuffled past Philip. 'Dunno,' he said. 'Paid her bill at seven-thirty. Left her luggage in reception. No breakfast.'

Philip reached over his shoulder to push open the door. 'Wearing what?' he asked.

'Very nice,' Emile carried the tray over to the English family in the corner. 'Shorts. Pink, with flowers. And the same on top, like an old-fashioned bra, you know? Nice legs.'

'Beach-bag?'

'Mmm . . . ?' Emile placed the eggs before the young paterfamilias in his Aertex shirt. 'Yes, I think so. Yes.'

'Thanks, old mate.' Philip turned away. 'She comes back, tell her I'm looking for her, OK?' He caught the eye of the little girl, 'Morning!' he called over and winked at her as he left.

He sloped along the promenade, keeping an eye on the café *terrasses*. At the very end, he left the road and followed the sandy path through the hillocks of scrub towards the beach. 'Beach' was a euphemism. In fact, he looked down on a few yards of shingle enclosed by conveniently flat grey rocks. Yet this was the town's principal, or, at least, most exclusive beach. Already towels were spread on the rocks nearest the sea. The bodies spread on them ranged in colour from aspirin-white to mahogany, with various uncomfortable tones of pink between.

La Laing was not amongst them. Philip saw her from a hundred yards off, swimming a sedate but fluent breast-stroke on the far side of the little cove. Her hair was not yet wet, save at the ends which fanned out about her like weed. As he neared her, she dived. He watched her through the blue-grey water, her hair now blossoming and billowing, her slender legs pumping her in and out of the rocks on the sea bed. Her shadow dulled pebbles which shone bright as jewels when she had passed. She surfaced a good ten yards from the point at which she had dived. She flipped on to her back and kicked herself seaward. She was the only woman here wearing a bikini-top which, Philip thought, was a pity. She was one of only two or three here who, if France were properly governed, would have been granted a licence to go topless.

He strolled around to the towels which were quite clearly hers. There were two of them, one ginger, the other pale blue. They bore Horrocks's labels. A paperback copy of *Of Human Bondage* lay open, jacket upward, on the blue one. Philip unbuttoned and pulled off his shirt. He sat. He picked up the book with the vague idea that he might appear cool and disinterested. Soon, however, he had leaned back against the rock, seduced, engrossed.

'*Excuse moi,*' said an appeasing American voice. 'No, no. Don't move. Sorry. Just let me get my towel.'

Philip looked up. He looked like a corpse when the shroud is unwound. The woman above him was drying her face. Her arms were thin, but so was the skin on them. It wobbled like a chicken's crop. The arms dropped to reveal iron spikes of hair, a hooked noise, eyes like beaten nailheads and a broad, perfect smile. The breasts were small and sagging, twin carrier-bags with only an orange in each, the nipples inverted and an alarming pale pink. The stomach bulged. Little else did.

It was unfair, of course. The woman, whoever she was, was well preserved for her years. It was just – when you look up expecting a Laing, anything else comes as a shock. Philip said, 'Er . . .'

'You like?' The woman pointed at the book. She dabbed her breasts and folded herself on to the towel beside him. 'You like more ham?'

Philip smiled sort of solicitously. He thought, sure, it happens. The sun gets to them. 'M – more ham?'

'*Oui,*' she nodded. 'More ham. You like?'

'*Non. Merci.* Oh. Ah.' He nodded frantically as at last he got her drift. '*Oui. C'est à dire, non. Je ne le comprends point. Pas un mot. Pardon, madame.*' He struggled to his feet.

'*Non!*' she reached up to lay a bejewelled hand on his forearm. '*Assieds-toi. C'est OK.*'

'*Non, non.*' He pointed vaguely out over the water. '*Je croyais . . . je cherchais . . . il y a une amie . . .*'

'*Oui, oui. Une amie,*' the woman smiled and cooed. 'Come on, honey. Sit down. We talk. *Parle,* huh?'

'*Non. Mille pardons, madame.*' Philip bowed and gently loosened her fingers from his arm. '*Je me suis trompé. Pardonnez-moi. Je ne comprends rien. Excusez-moi . . .*'

Suddenly from behind him there came a giggle – a deep wriggling sort of giggle which rose in pitch and suddenly stopped. He swung round. Jenny Laing was not to be seen – just a few rings of wrinkles on the water, a wraith beneath.

He jumped down on to the beach. The pebbles shifted beneath his weight. He picked himself up, quietly growling obscenities. He slapped gravel from his bum. Radiating aloof dignity, he took up a position at the water's edge. He stood as if for his portrait.

Jenny Laing surfaced, sparkling. She saw him. She did the nose-trick. She submerged again.

Until yesterday lunchtime, life had been orderly. Life had been Laingless. Now, it seemed, the bloody woman must disrupt his every waking moment.

She was under the water for a long time. Philip allowed himself the luxury of imagining that she had drowned. He would go to the funeral, of course, and no doubt the odd tremor of the lips, the occasional bark of triumphant laughter would be put down to a proper and affecting grief . . .

She pulled herself from the water just five yards from him. When she stood, the water was knee-deep.

She did not look at all like a teacher just now.

As Emile had faithfully recorded, her bikini was pink, with a pattern of large pink roses and green leaves. It was not a slight bikini. The top was strapless and the waistline high. It was, perversely, quite seriously sexy.

'I do believe,' she laughed as she made her way tentatively towards him, 'I do believe that I saw the famous Mr

Glaister running scared. Ow!' She bent forward. 'Damn these stones.'

She extended a long arm towards him. He took her hand and, with just disdain, drew her up the bank of shingle.

'Thanks,' she panted. Water dripped from her hair on to his forearm. He looked down at it. His skin was pale gold. Hers was darker.

And he remembered. 'Oh, bloody hell,' he winced, 'I left my shirt up there.'

Laing spluttered. She wheezed. She convulsed. It was not nice to witness. 'And – and you don't dare go back and get it?' She laid a cold wet hand on his shoulder. 'You think she'll eat you? I think you might be right. Don't worry. Auntie Jenny is here. I'll explain about my idiot brother.'

She kept her hand on his shoulder as she hopped and danced up the beach to her rock. She plucked up a towel. 'Oh, that was good,' she sighed. She dried herself quickly, spread out the towel again and sank down. She searched in her bag for sun oil. She rubbed it briskly all over where she could reach and slowly lay back. She closed her eyes. 'What's with the plasters?' she murmured.

'Hmm?'

'Your arm.'

'Oh. Accident.' He sat beside her. He looked down on her. 'Place not your bust in chintzes,' he said because he'd often thought he'd like to, and this seemed a good opportunity.

'Tee,' she said slowly, 'hee. So. You changed your mind?'

'No. I don't know. Bugger it. Why can't the world leave me alone?'

'Doesn't work that way, Greta,' she droned. 'The world gave to you, didn't it? Perhaps sometimes it wants a quid pro quo. You have to be very, very poor or very, very rich to have total freedom.'

'Yeah, yeah, thanks.' Philip raised his knees to his chin. He looked down at the slow swelling and sinking of her glistening ribs, her long, flat stomach, the gentle slope of her pubis beneath the floral print. He looked away. He picked up a pebble and flung it hard towards the sea. 'All I bloody need,' he grumbled. 'Sunday-school teacher. Maxims for a Good Life. Muscular Christianity. Jesus.'

'So,' her left eye opened again, 'are you coming back?'

'OK, so, what if I did?' He found another flat pebble to skim on the water. 'It'd really be just for the rest of the season?'

'If that,' she shrugged. 'Gerry said the main things were to supervise Plutonium's last race, dispose of the other animals as best you can and wind the whole business down. He reckons you could be back here munching lotuses in no time.'

'What time are you leaving, then?'

'Two o'clock flight out of Nice. You coming?'

'I told you. I'll think about it, OK?'

'You do that,' she sighed, and she rolled over.

Angela watched as he trudged up the path towards L'Hermitage. Dust puffed from his heels and swirled up to shoulder-height. He walked fast, head bowed, frowning as though studying his crumpled linen trousers or his tan leather sandals. He drew deep on his cigarette and threw it hard away from him. It was an aggressive gesture.

She liked his aggression. She liked his fine, long hands. She liked his reputation. It was a shame, really, that he could not have been there last night, but he had other uses, and, whilst Angela had no objection to mixing business with pleasure – her life, it might be said, was devoted to attaining that amalgam – it would have caused needless complications here.

She strolled unhurriedly to her bedroom door and out into the vaulted cloister. She would be the first to meet him. Richard could not bear the sight of him, the sound of his name, but that would not stop him from laying on the charm if Philip had something he wanted, and Philip had. It would do him no good. She had sussed that within seconds of meeting Philip, just as she had realized that sex would never bend him to their ends. Oh, he would fuck her all right, given half a chance, but he was not such a mug as to pump out his sense with his spunk. He would thank her brusquely and walk away. She knew it. He would feel that he had won.

At her right, Eledi swam breaststroke away from her, hair spread out behind her like jellyfish tendrils in the clear blue water. Angela ignored her.

Last night . . .

As a Very Personal Assistant, as she liked to dub herself, she felt that she had excelled. It had all worked so beautifully – the movies up on the screen, the low lights, the lines of coke already cut and laid out on the marble commode. As usual, Eledi's holier-than-thou pose had worn off once the vodka and coke, the sights and smells and sounds had got to her. Predictably, she had got all soppy and silly about the chic, bony dark girl that Philip had sent up. Richard had promised the tall, dumb Yank, Ernest Cormick, first crack at Eledi, so Cormick had had her while the dark girl had soothed and caressed her, and then the two girls had retired into a corner to kiss and croon and slaver over one another for the rest of the evening. 'A gooey twoey,' Angela called it, always with the postscript, 'Yuk.'

Angela, though, had been the star. In her cowboy gear, she and that little blonde with the arse had taken it in turns with Richard, Cormick and that damned dumb bronzed stud she had found last year in Antibes. When the men flagged, the two girls got it together. Anick had been complaining of soreness by midnight. She must have been a whole lot sorer by the time she staggered home at four in the morning.

And in the meantime, Philip Glaister had been crawling around for secret assignations. She had known that he would come, had even drawn the dark bit aside as she prepared to leave: 'Now, you will be sure to pass on Eledi's message to Philip, won't you?' and the dark bit had nodded keenly.

Angela now opened the front door even as Philip raised his fist to strike it. 'Good morning, Philip, *mon ami*,' she smiled slowly. 'You're not meant to visit, you know, but I suppose you just couldn't keep away from me.'

'No, I'm like a fly that way,' Philip told her curtly. 'No, actually, I just came up to apologize to your employers. I'm going to have to go back to England today.'

'Oh, dear. Problems?'

'Yes. So I won't be on call should you need me.'

'I can't imagine how such a need could possibly arise, but thank you for the thought.' Again she laid a long hand on his patched forearm. 'Poor you. What have you been up to?'

'Right, well, I'll be going.' Philip's eyes scanned the building behind her.

'No, no. Now you're here, you must come in and give your message to my employer's wife. I hadn't realized that you were such old friends.'

'We are?' Philip frowned.

'Yes, indeed. Childhood sweethearts, I imagine. Eledi. Eledi Heron.'

'Eledi?' Philip raised his eyebrows. 'Good Lord. Well, I won't be welcome. Mr Heron is no friend of mine.'

'Oh, rubbish, rubbish. Richard's not one to bear a grudge. Anyhow, he's at work in his office. Come in, come in.'

Philip followed her into the hall. He was surprised and bemused. According to Eledi's account last night, she was not allowed to mix with her own friends, and Angela was chiefest among her warders. Why, then, was he being granted such ready access to her? It was like finding a lift in Rapunzel's tower.

He followed the swaying buttocks beneath their black wrapping down the gallery into the cloisters. Eledi was just clambering from the pool. She wore a skimpy gold bikini. Her eyes were wide and bloodshot. Without make-up, she looked older than her years. She stared suspiciously at him.

'Eledi, darling,' Angela grasped her left shoulder, 'look

99

who's come to see us! Poor Philip has to go back to England, but I thought you just must get together before he goes.'

Eledi shrugged off the hand. For an actress, she wasn't doing too well. Her dull eyes focused on Philip, then on Angela. They returned to Philip. She laboriously painted a weak smile on her face. 'Philip! How lovely!' She shuffled forward and proffered her cheek. He leaned forward to kiss it. 'I wish I'd known you were here before. And now you've got to go. Oh, drat it. It's been for ever. It's so good to see you. Gosh, you're looking fit.'

'Can I get you a drink, Philip?' asked Angela.

'Er, yes. Thank you. *Citron pressé*, please.'

'Back in a second.' Her hand trailed along his arm as she moved off.

'What's *happening?*' Eledi squealed under her breath. She looked quickly from side to side. Angela's flip-flops slapped on the flags beneath the cloisters' arcades.

'That's what I want to know.' Philip was grim. 'I could have got killed last night because of your fairy stories.'

'They're not fairy stories, Philip. I promise. This is un-heard of. That woman is planning something. Think. Why would she ask you to supply girls then introduce you into the house? Jesus, it's suicidal. OK, you're you, but how does she know you're not going to run off to the *News of the World* and sell the story for thousands?'

Philip considered this whilst he unwrapped a new packet of Gauloises. 'True,' he growled. 'I don't like this. Heron doesn't like me. I wonder if he's setting me up some way ... God, I'm becoming paranoid. Look, we've only got a minute. I was hoping to be able to leave a message somehow. I'm going back to England. If you were serious about getting out of all this, I'll do my best to help. You're going to have to trust me. Do you think you can get hold of some of these famous pictures he uses to blackmail you?'

'Oh, God, yes, I should think so. He taunts me with them. He's got the negatives, after all. I can tear the prints up to my heart's content.'

'Get them to me, somehow.'

'We'll be in London in ten days' time.'

'Right. We'll have to meet up there. But we need to think of a plausible rendezvous, fast. Have you any definite plans, going out somewhere, so I could accidentally bump into you?'

Eledi screwed up her face in concentration, her eyes now mere red slits. Then, 'Yes, yes. Fraser's. They'll believe that. The twenty-first. It's my birthday. I can insist we go there for lunch, it's my favourite. It makes sense.'

'OK. One o'clock, Fraser's on the twenty-first. Leave them in the Ladies. Securely wrapped. Jam them behind the bog, or the bin or whatever. If there's more than one bog, use the one nearest the door in.'

'You can't go into the Ladies!'

'Why not? Damn few ladies do, I can tell you. No, don't worry. I'll worry about my end.'

'I'm serious about this, Philip,' she murmured gravely, 'I want to get out. Goddamn it. It started as dirty fun. Now I'm being given away as a business perk. It's killing me. Please. I do trust you. You won't let me down, will you?'

'My dear girl.' Philip at last contrived to pull a cigarette from the packet. He glanced over his shoulder to see Angela returning down the cloister with a tray in her hands. 'Leaving aside familial ties and the love I bear you, I have plenty of reason for wanting to do Richard Heron. I'll do it for Charlie, if not for you.'

Eledi winced. 'Oh, God, poor poor Charlie.'

PART II

'WELL, WELL,' said Vincent Lovelady. He inhaled coffee noisily. When Barbara did not respond, his moustache twitched, he sniffed, he said, 'Well, well' again.

'What's that, then?' Barbara asked.

'Oh, nothing.' Vincent gave a little smile. 'Just an old friend of ours. Mr Glaister. Oh, the troublesome Glaisters. See this? Now it's the younger brother. Had a massive asthma attack. Coma, they say. Pity. Nice fellow. And people creeping about the yard, they say. Well, well. Well, well. It never rains, as they say.'

This pronouncement appeared to satisfy them both. Vincent and Barbara Lovelady ate toast. Barbara read *Hello*. Vincent leaned a long way forward to study the *Telegraph*.

He had his little way with newspapers, did Vincent. He first folded them double, left to right, then again, top to bottom. He then read the paper in quarters, three columns at a time. This, he would have told you, was kinder to neighbours on the train. It also allowed Vincent to watch his immediate world whilst gleaning the news of more distant human doings.

Vincent eyed all human doings with interest and benign suspicion, as an old terrier, heavy in years, battles and pups, might watch youthful antics and the approach of prey. The world, for him, was full of naughty people, all desperately attempting, within the ever fuzzier bounds of their morality, to fulfil their own ideas of themselves. Sometimes this desperation caused them to steal money,

105

because these people wanted to become or to remain grandees or great lovers. Vincent, although he had no such desires himself, sympathized. But it had been his business to stop them.

He was lucky, and acknowledged the fact. His idea of himself was neither expensive nor tiring nor too far removed from the physical reality which others perceived. He did not wish to own a power-boat, nor to sleep with Michelle Pfeiffer. He did not wish to plunge from the skies to pluck up derailed trains nor, particularly, to change the world. The world, like Vincent Lovelady, was as it was. Take it for all in all, it wasn't at all bad.

When he looked in the mirror, Vincent did not for the barest millisecond see Clark Gable. He saw a smallish, baldish man in his early sixties with largish ears and a weakish chin. His only vanity was the moustache. Barbara liked it, and it made up for the chin.

Even Vincent, however, if pressed, would not claim to be free of vanity. His vanity lay in the camel-vulva hat, the pipe, the cardigans and car-coats, the Terylene trousers and galoshes. Vincent's father had been a costermonger, a spendthrift, a Methodist and a drunk. Vincent's mother had been a dreamer, an ooher and aher for whom reality began when darkness fell on the one-and-nines. She had named him after Vincent Price.

Vincent, reacting, had embraced the security and predictability of middle-class order and Mr Pooter respectability. He was that rarity – a man whose dream of himself was smaller and cheaper than the real thing.

The house in which they sat was a bungalow near Guildford which differed from its neighbours only in the wealth of security installations on the walls and in the absence of a satellite dish. Vincent Lovelady believed in security, and got the equipment cheap. As to television, he and Barbara watched it for two hours every night, and the BBC was good enough for them.

'I wonder . . .' he said as he laid down the paper.

'Mmm?' Barbara, a thin woman with salt-and-pepper hair, raised her eyebrows.

Vincent dabbed at his moustache. 'Glaister,' he said. 'You know me and my nose, Barbara. I just wonder if we've had a claim from the Glaisters. I'd be interested . . .'

'Well, of course,' Barbara said proudly. In all the years that she had known him, her Vincent's nose had never let him down, bless him. 'You'll be looking into it, then?'

'I rather think I might,' Vincent mused. 'Yes, if I have time . . . My nose, you know. And those Glaisters.' He shook his head sadly. 'A troublesome lot. Too much imagination by half.'

His wife nodded, understanding. In Vincent Lovelady's book, imagination was the root of all evil.

Philip had a headache within minutes of arriving at Heathrow.

Each time the tube train's doors opened, it was to gulp in more people. You could hear it chomping on them between stations. Just occasionally it spat one or two of them out, but in general the pickings got richer and the laidly worm's belly more congested as it wound and growled its way towards the centre of town.

There was the usual bristling drunk which London Transport seems to import specially from Scotland. He said 'foh – foh – blee – foh' and then, rather surprisingly, 'Knickers'. Somewhere about Hounslow Central a man with a guitar got in. He told everyone to be happy. Perversely, he then played Dylan worse than Dylan while his mate plied the cap. Philip threw in a franc.

Swedes and Dutch and Spaniards were there with knapsacks. Men who had plainly passed their childhoods being other children's imaginary friends hid behind their *Standards*. A plump, putty-faced girl in a mini-skirt stood gazing at her reflection in the windows. A Marks and Spencer bag sagged sadly from her hand. Tears dripped from her jawbone. Then loud young men in striped shirts swaggered in, and negroes who wore menace because they had no striped shirts . . .

Philip got out at Hyde Park Corner. London hit him.

107

If the people had been bad, the stones were far, far worse.

Up there, up flashing Park Lane, he had danced and drunk and talked – made plans for races over breakfast in the Dorchester, attended charity balls and stable-lads' boxing at Grosvenor House, hotsheeted at the Hilton. Just back there, in South Audley Street, he had been married. Five o'clock in the evening – by some strange theatrical conceit of Linda's – and all the guests in white tie or ball gowns, coaches waiting outside to bear them to a ball at her daddy's gaff at Kew.

He could not face Piccadilly.

He hailed a taxi. As it bore him past Piccadilly's palaces and down Whitehall, the driver recited the usual jeremiad. No tourists. All scared of bombs. Gawd. Insult. Had London been scared of bombs fifty years back? Shit. The bloody jungle bunnies, Christ. And bloody minicabs. And bloody child molesters. And nobody safe, not nobody in this town after dark. Recession. Silly bastard, where's he fucking think he is? Brand's Hatch? No, guv, what I say . . .

Philip tried a few 'Hrmphs'.

He tried to forget that every stone here, every staring window held a memory and an accusation for him. No. Not him. A child who had had tea here beneath a Fragonard swing; a student who had fucked here, sought adventure here, fallen in love, eaten beyond his means here, even, when those means had run out, had dossed here in all-night cinemas. He had partied and not even understood why he did so. Because he was good at it, he supposed. Certainly not because he enjoyed it. It had left him with – what? A few friends, a trance of hazy memories, a lot of notches on a philanderer's gun – only he had never been a philanderer – just a lost child seeking refuge in the one sure thing that he understood once the BL reading room was closed.

Not him. Just the accusing ghost of another incarnation, a ghost who no doubt still wandered these streets, still smiled at girls in hope of a returning smile, still wrote cheques at antique shops and sale rooms and restaurants, still occasionally found dark and lonely bars in which to brood and to complain that this could not really be IT – the realization of a thousand dreams of glamour, of social success.

A dog twitches and whimpers as he dreams of hunting. He wakes up in a town flat, gets a rush of adrenalin as he pursues the only available quarry. Just occasionally, he too must get the feeling that there is something missing, something wrong, that there is a hunt finer, a chase more exultant, and a purpose higher than the pursuit of his own tail.

Even in the four years of Philip's absence, pus from the Great Wen had spread. There was the odd cosmetic patch of grey-green spattered with cow, but the train was forty minutes out of London before he saw a proper hedgerow.

The dusty scarlet of the bryony berries twining through the hawthorn told him that summer was all but done. So did the slightly anaemic colour of the beechwoods which studded the hills, the yellowing rushes by the canal. Ragwort on the sidings was shrunken and venomous. Rosebay willowherb showed silver seedheads amongst its withered flowers. When at last the downs barged into the picture, many of their fields had been ploughed into bedspreads of purplish candlewick. If there be a just God, Philip thought, there is surely a grand slurry-pit in hell for downland farmers.

He arrived at Wykeham just as dusk closed in. Last night at this hour he had been strolling in sunshine down to Les Oliviers. It seemed years ago.

He walked to the only taxi on the rank. He peered in. There were NO SMOKING signs everywhere. Philip opened the back door. 'St Dympna's, please,' he said, 'wait a while, then out to Swynsmere. And I intend to smoke. Thank you.' He flung in his grip, then slid in after it. 'And if you object, I shall break your head,' he added, just to make everything quite clear.

'Fair enough,' the driver told the rear-view mirror. 'It's

only the drunks I'm worried about. Swynsmere, eh?' The car bounced out on to the road. 'Police, is it?'

Philip frowned. 'What? No.'

Philip considered. Suntan, tweed jacket and trainers might, he supposed, suggest police to a television watcher. Talk of breaking heads inevitably turned thoughts in that direction. But it had been the mention of Swynsmere which had prompted the assumption. 'Why d'you think that?'

'Oh, nothing. Dunno. Just a thought.'

'Come on. Must be a reason.'

'Nah. Shouldn't have said anything. Just, chap out there keeled over sudden, didn't he? Suspicious like. You know. Probably just talk. You know what they're like. Dead chicken, they say devil worship or something.'

'Yes, but what do you mean, suspicious?'

'Ah, nothing, really. Just sudden, like I say. Papers say there was burglars or something. Poor chap gets a shock, asthma attack. That's what they say. Shouldn't have said anything. Probably just these bloody travellers – hippies, so called. Hippies my arse. Me, I was a hippy, believe it or not. Peace and love, huh? These sods, nothing like it. Probably after tack. Big market these days, bridles, saddles, bits. I mean, OK, not murder or anything. Just bad luck, creeping about, just happen to run into a guy turns out to be an asthmatic. Still, I was out that way next morning. Police was out there – ooh, three cars at least.'

'Were there, indeed?' Jenny Laing had not mentioned interlopers in her account of Freddy's accident. Perhaps Gerry had not told her. Perhaps Gerry had not known. But there was no particular reason why finding burglars should trigger a fatal asthma attack. Freddy, like Philip, would go nowhere without his inhaler. If burglars there had been, and if their presence and the asthma attack had been, as Philip assumed, unrelated, it constituted a coincidence, and a curious one at that. Obviously the police had thought so too.

Philip leaned his head on the window and watched Wykeham's steep high street. The Victorian red brick was hot against the dark grey sky, and smeared by the rain on the window.

This, for some reason, was not as bad as London, perhaps because he had never been so desperate or so lost here. There was the Black Swan, now homogenized by Trusthouse, where he had dined and drunk in the school holidays, and there Pearson's the stationers, Tooley's the feed merchants, and Craven's the wine merchants, all of which he had been forced to skirt in that last year when money had been too short to meet their bills.

But it had been home, this staid, slightly shabby market-town. The shopkeepers and the publicans might not greet him with embraces. They might not even acknowledge his return with smiles but, in the event of a brawl, they would judge the Other Chap to blame. He was a local.

'Cook's has gone, I see,' Philip murmured.

'Yup. What? Two years back? Safeway's have made a difference. Lovely.'

'Supermarket? Lovely?'

'What? Well. Yeah, this one is.' The driver's eyes arose to watch him in the mirror. 'You from these parts, then?'

'Yes.'

He kept looking at Philip, waiting for a potted autobiog. At length, he shrugged and looked back at the road in time to miss the left-hand pier of the railway bridge.

St Dympna's hospital stood on the hill above the town, an ugly orange Gothic building now boxed in by uglier grey blocks and bunkers. The light from its hundreds of windows turned evening into night. The car rustled to a halt on the wet forecourt. The driver said, 'There we are,' like a midwife.

Philip stepped out under the concrete awning. He pushed through big glass doors, and again, and he was in the hospital's brightly lit but somehow dingy foyer. He side-stepped a speeding trolley, bowed to a matching pair of nurses, kicked a plastic ball back to its child and made his way to the horseshoe-shaped desk. There were two women behind it. One, a large, square creature with pudding-basin black hair, stood tiptoe to peer into the top drawer of a

111

filing cabinet. He walked up to the other, a slight, greyish cadaver with pale primrose curls.

She ignored him very carefully. She sighed a bit. She looked at a blinking VDU. She picked up papers and banged them on her desk. She said to the woman behind her, 'Why he should think he can get away with it. I mean . . .'

There was no bell on the counter – only a wooden prism on which ENQUIRIES was printed. Philip picked it up, then he slammed it down on the surface of the counter so hard that it split. It made a good sort of sound, a sharp rap like that of snapping bone, much enhanced by the ringing echoes in the vast hall.

The burble about Philip subsided. The yellow-haired woman stopped talking and at last looked up at him. She forgot to shut her mouth. Her teeth were tanned. Her lower lip and her empty crop wobbled. Her eyes stared, alarmed at first. Their expression was hardening to disapproving disdain, but Philip was not going to give her time to put her apology for an identity together again.

Philip spoke fast and loud. 'Right, let's start with, "Good evening, sir, can I help you, sir?" Even "Excuse me, sir, I'll only be a moment" will, at a push, do. Now, let's give one of those simple little sentences a try, shall we? "Good – evening – sir . . ."'

Her goitre bounced, her whole torso curved as she regained breath. The words when they came had plainly been robust when bottled but had lost bite with age. 'How . . .' she gulped and tried again, 'How dare you? Are you aware that that is hospital prop . . . ?'

'No, no,' Philip smiled patiently. 'Try again. Smile – remember? And – "Good – evening – sir – how – can – I – help – you?" Not very difficult, hmmm? Come along. Give it a go.'

A shiny black beetle in a white coat breezed through the door behind her. He vaguely smiled and vaguely blinked through ice-cube glasses. 'Hello, Dora,' he said cheerily, 'any trouble?'

'Yes,' Philip informed him. 'I am doing nothing more

112

than demand common courtesy from this constipated harridan, and she has refused to acknowledge my existence.'

'He called me a . . .' the woman interrupted shrilly. A small crowd had gathered.

'Now, now,' the beetle raised his hands. 'Let's have some hush. What was it you wanted?'

'I want, sir, to see my brother, at present lying comatose and close to death within these walls. My name, since no one has seen fit to ask it, is Glaister.'

'He broke hospital property!' The woman had decided that tears might help her cause. 'He called me . . .'

'Yes, yes, yes,' the beetle soothed. 'That's enough from everyone, I think. I'll take care of this. No need for excitement. If you'll come with me, Mr Glaister . . .' He strode quickly to his right and let himself out through a small door. He joined Philip out in the foyer. 'This way,' he said.

Philip accompanied him down blue-green passages, through dirty cream wards and up grey stairs. He moved fast, sweeping down more blue-green passages, past noticeboards and NO SMOKING signs and rusty conical fire-extinguishers, until at last the beetle swung to his right so suddenly that Philip was three strides past the door before he realized that his guide was no longer with him.

Philip followed him into a little cream anteroom, then into the room where Freddy lay.

The curtains were drawn. The room was dully lit. Green and red lights on silent steel machines cast eerie little flushes on the walls. There were flowers – apricot and white gladioli and red roses. Otherwise, there was just a bed. And Freddy.

Poor little Freddy. There were tubes in his nostrils, but Philip could still make out that characteristic, puzzled-puppy cock of the eyebrows, which made women want to pick him up and men to kick him. The drip-feed was taped to a pale, thin forearm. He still looked like a boy.

The doctor had picked up the check-board. 'Poor chap,' he said softly. 'I was here when they brought him in. His wife had done her best but – well, frankly, in his position, I'd sooner she hadn't.'

113

'He's not in any discomfort, is he?'

'Oh, no, no. Brain dead, I'm afraid. I was here when he came in. Nothing anyone could do.'

'Asthma did this?' Philip stepped nearer to the bed.

'Yup. God knows why they do it.'

'What's that?'

'Asthmatics. So many of them. Steroid preventatives can improve the quality of life one hundred per cent, but they stick to their inhalers, damn them, and every wheeze could be their last.'

'Oh, God,' Philip murmured, 'don't start on that.'

'You too?'

' 'Fraid so.'

'Well, sorry to be pi, but here's an object lesson if ever you wanted one. What happened here – I gather he surprised someone down in the stableyard, got a bit of a shock, I suppose. Acute attack. Only this time he puffs away on his inhaler and it doesn't work. The tubes just get tighter – well, you know how it feels. Each breath in weighs pounds, each breath out . . . Air becomes treacle. Anyhow, apparently his wife heard something, came out, got him in the car. Heart stopped somewhere along the way. She made a hell of an effort. Good woman. Did the business. Kiss of life. But too late. You know how long it takes for brain death? Just one hundred and twenty seconds is all. Not much is it? Two minutes. Anyhow, she gets him here, but the ECG shows no electrical impulses and there's no respiratory effort . . .'

'Sorry?'

'He's not breathing for himself. First thing we do, we shove the ventilator down him, poor fellow, but that's what's doing the breathing for him, and the heart's just ticking over under its own steam. Forty beats a minute. Man's gone.'

Philip was standing over the body now. It was hard to believe that air was still pointlessly pumped through that still, flat chest, that that dark hair still grew, that under that smock a heart still slowly pumped. His face was as he remembered it, but it was empty. It sagged where it should have moved, drooped where it should have bulged.

114

And Philip remembered: Freddy, enthusiastic and eager as ever to please, had resolved at twelve, thirteen, that he would be a conjuror. One Christmas, he had put on a show. The high point involved one of his pet rabbits. He popped the poor beast into a white satin bag, and even as he made passes over it and delivered his stammering patter, you could make out its contours as it twitched and kicked inside. Then he flourished his cloak. For a moment, the bag was out of sight. He held up the bag, released the drawstring and turned it inside out with words which were to become a family catchphrase – 'See! *Oryctolagus cuniculus* has evanesced! The rabbit is no more!'

That was all that Freddy's body had to tell Philip now. '*Oryctolagus cuniculus* has evanesced,' he crooned. He touched the back of the still hand. 'The rabbit is no more.'

'Mmm?' said the doctor behind Philip.

'Nothing.' Philip turned to him. 'So – what happens? You can't keep him here like this for the next forty years or whatever.'

'Tell that to Mrs Glaister. Jesus, but I wouldn't mind having a woman like that on my side, I can tell you. Not that I'd like to be left like him, but all the same. Be good to have a woman that frantic to keep you in the land of the living. Pocahontas stuff, you know? "He is not dead! His heart is still beating! You remove that ventilator and I'll have you up before the highest court in the land – for murder if necessary." Ah, great stuff. Gibberish, of course, but straight out of *Dallas* or *Stella Dallas* or something. Hair all everywhere, eyes spraying tears as she jerks her head, hands shaking, but fierce, you know? Wow! So I took her aside, tried to explain. There is no hope. None. Best thing's let nature take its course, right? But she's not having any of it. Sister has a go. Still no change. I mean, all we've got here – heart's not receiving instructions from its captain, right?' He pointed at the back of his neck. 'The captain's dead. Heart's just the engine on the *Marie Celeste*, right? That great old pump thumping slowly away ... Normal thing, you don't catheterize him. He's not passing water; urinary tract infection finishes the job. But she's wise to

115

that. Amazing. And the other usual thing. Pneumonia. She tells us, "And if he contracts pneumonia in the next three weeks, I'll have your guts for garters" or words to that effect. Weird. I mean, the attitude's that of an ignorant woman, but she seems to know it all. So. There we are. We're just pumping air through like a punctured tyre.'

Philip nodded slowly. He too was puzzled. Alison might conceivably have become passionately amorous towards her husband over the past few years. She could not, however, have developed medical ignorance – she was a qualified nurse. She knew well enough what brain death meant, how purposeless was this charade. 'Right,' Philip took a deep breath and cast a quick glance back at what remained of his half-brother. 'Thank you, Doctor. I'll have a word with her.'

He walked quickly and in silence back to the hospital's front door. He blinked away the smudging of the rain before he realized that he was still indoors.

Philip might have been a conquering hero, the number of joyous cries of, 'Philip!' and 'Good to see you, mate!' and, 'How's it going, mate?' that greeted him as he lugged his grip into the public bar. His shoulder was clapped, his hand shaken, his back patted. He waved. He nodded. He said, 'Evening, Joe,' and 'Evening, Tony,' and tried to look gruff. It felt good to be welcomed by the tribe, and he didn't want a display of emotion.

'I said you'd be back!' Dick, the landlord, thumped the bar with a hand like a cigar case. 'Didn't I say it? Our Philip'll be back, I said. No one believed me. There you go. Pint of best, is it?'

'Yup, thanks. Look, I need a telephone before I go any further, then we can settle down and have a session.'

Dick bustled along the bar to fetch him the telephone. Philip slipped a coin into the slot and tapped out the old, familiar number – his number. The telephone at Swynsmere rang just once, then there was some rustling and sighing and a breathy 'Lo?'

'Hello, Alison?'

116

'Oh . . .' a groan, a bit more rustling, 'Philip. Er, hi. And what can I do for you?' Her tone was suddenly brisk, businesslike, insulting by its politeness.

'Nothing,' he reciprocated in kind. 'Just rung to say I've arrived down here and I'll be coming round tomorrow morning, if that suits.'

'Can't stop you, can I, Philip? I may be in. I may not. Still, treat the place like your own, please.' A bitter dig, this. Goddamn it, when would the woman realize that he would willingly have given the place to her had it been in his power, that it was his father's bloody-mindedness that had left them in this ridiculous situation, that the house and the yard were neither hers nor Philip's nor Freddy's, but the property of a trust? It wasn't his fault that hers had proved a pealess pod, so that there were no little Glaisters to inherit but his son.

'Thanks, Alison,' he said above the scratchy laughter in the bar. 'I dropped in on the hospital. Sorry about old Floozo. Bloody bad luck all round.'

'You noticed he wasn't well, then?' she snapped; then, 'Oh, stuff it. I'm glad to hear you're concerned, anyway.'

'Of course I'm . . .' A pint was pushed beneath his nose. He took a deep breath, nodded and murmured thanks. 'No. Poor old fellow. Have to talk to you. Make plans. I'll not disturb you first thing. Have a look round the yard. Be up at the house round – what? Ten thirty?'

'Any time you like. As I say, I'll either be here or not.'

'Right,' he said. Her coolness was meant to depress him. It was working. 'See you. Good night.'

'Sounds as if your good night's already started. Do please have fun.'

'Thank you,' he said over a clatter at the other end of the line, 'I will.'

He laid down the receiver. He picked up the pint. He nuzzled into the pubic bush of foam. 'Ah,' he gasped, 'almost worth coming back for. Now, who's going to bring me up to date?'

The talk burst over him.

*

117

St George's flag was flying on top of the dovecote, which was crazy. The flag had only been bought as a grandiose joke on the day Linda brought Sam back from hospital. Philip had hoist it just twice more – once when a boring Welsh owner had been staying during the rugby world cup and once on the day that he returned to find Sam and Linda gone.

Irony had been the general idea.

The sloping lawns were drenched, the gossamer spangled. Blackbirds hopped and rocked amongst the wormcasts. It was a fine cold morning. Philip had walked down from the village, and now crunched up the washed gravel drive to the house.

Swynsmere was a plain, grey stone oblong halfway up the valley's side. Its plainness was relieved by the castellations along its eaves, the Gothic niches set between the ground-floor windows and the vast domed and crenellated conservatory which curved around this nearest corner. It was a bold provincial stab at Strawberry Hill.

Philip walked round to the 'front' door – there was no door in its ornate façade. He rapped rapidly. He shouted up, 'Alison? Hello?' He proceeded over the threshold into the black and red tiled porch. He rapped again. 'Alison? Alison! Hello?' He pushed open the door and went into the hall.

His voice tripped up the oak staircase and along the gallery, trying the stained-glass windows as it went. There was a strong smell of solvent.

'Oh, so you're here, are you?' Alison emerged from somewhere beneath the stairs. She held her hands palms outward at her sides. They appeared to be covered with glistening blood.

'Bad penny,' she said out of the corner of her mouth. 'Hello.' She looked at the study door behind him.

If she had been looking to shock, she wasn't doing badly. She was smaller and thinner than Philip remembered her. She was painfully thin. Her cheesecloth shirt hung loose. Hamlet-style. Her faded jeans bunched at the knees. Her dark hair was cropped short. It made her large grey eyes seem larger. They shifted from left to right but never once fixed on him.

He would not give her the satisfaction of seeing him recoil. He put together a smile. 'Hello.'

'So. The vultures gather, right?' she sneered.

'No, no, no, Ali. Nothing of the sort. No, just back to lend a hand if I can. Damn bad luck, Freddy.'

She cocked a leg and slouched. 'Oh, you must be desolate.'

'No. Just sad, and if I can help . . .'

'I suppose you don't mind if I stay on while you're doing all this helping?' Her raised chin jutted up at him. 'I'll try not to get in the way, of course . . .'

'Come on.' He laid a tentative hand on her left shoulder. 'Don't be silly. It's your home, for God's sake.'

'No, it's not.' She sidestepped from his touch. 'Or rather, it is because I've got no other, but it's not my house. It's yours, isn't it? Yours or Sam's or . . . I just work here. I just scrimp and save. No, you can't have that new dress, no holiday this year, Ali, love. Get the place on its feet . . . Fine, fine. We get the place on its stinking feet, Freddy has an accident, and oh, look, guess who's back on the doorstep with his tongue hanging out. What a surprise. Thank you very much, Alison. Bye bye. Good little skivvy. Done your job. Whole lot goes to another bloody Glaister, doesn't it?'

'There's no question . . .' he began, then it burst from him, 'Anyhow, if you'd had children, you'd have been in the same position as me. It's just . . .'

'Don't start,' she jabbed a finger at him. Her voice was ripping fabric. 'Just – don't – start. We couldn't *afford* children, could we? Maybe next year, Ali, dear . . .' She rocked her head in gross, childlike mimicry. 'Jesus.'

'OK, OK, I'm sorry, but it's not my fault. If it's anyone's, it's Dad's. Let's just make the best of a bad job, shall we? The trust isn't going to leave you high and dry, for God's sake.'

'Yes, sir. The voice of reason. Just keep your mouth shut, Alison. Take what we give you. Oh, I suppose you'll be wanting my services. *Droit de seigneur*, all that?'

'Leave it out, Alison.' Philip shook his head, bemused by

119

the barrage of foul thoughts which spewed from her. 'I'm not here to make trouble. Don't even bloody want to be here, if truth be told. So let's just tiptoe around one another, shall we, not just charge one another head on? Is that possible? Just for a matter of weeks, OK? Let's make it easy on both of us.'

She stood stiffly to attention. Her red hands now squeezed the juice from the air by her thighs. It was cold in here.

She trembled. Tears trickled down her gaunt cheeks, but she did not blink, just stared like a doped puppy at the skirting-board. When she spoke, it was in a deep, airlock moan. 'Oh, you were ready enough to charge into your brother's place before, weren't you? Didn't worry you then.'

Irritation again welled up in Philip. 'Oh, for Christ's sakes, woman.' He strode towards the kitchen, then swung on his heels. At his right, he saw the source of all the gore. A little green rug lay crumpled beneath the stairs. Two large tins of car spray-paint stood drooling beside it.

Alison had been painting a red carpet against his arrival. As with St George's Flag, irony, he assumed, must have been the intention.

'Look, how come you're always the bloody victim, hey?' Philip narrowed his eyes at her. 'Nice Edwardian little maiden – "the nathty man made uth do it" – sure, except when it suits you, then it's "I'm as good as you. I'm independent. Don't patronize me." Can't you face up to your own responsibilities! I didn't go to your fucking hen-party with the intention of tangling saliva and pubic hair with you, and I don't remember being the subject of a major international dragnet for rape. We both behaved like drunken, lustful little shits, you as much as I. Don't rewrite history with me as the villain and you as the poor little victim. We fucked, right? Good fun, bloody stupid, whatever. Shitty. Just don't burden me with your guilt, that's all.'

She had run out of original lines. 'You – you bastard!' she shrieked. She charged towards him. 'How dare you?'

Her eyes flashed. Her hair splashed. Her cheeks shook. This was what the doctor had described to Philip. The woman was frightening.

She swung at him, but he had seen it coming yards off. He grasped the flailing wrist, caught the other hand and bent both backwards until she was on her knees. Then he let go of her as though she were something sticky.

He walked to the study door and peered in. He turned to his right and looked into the drawing-room. Behind him, the squeaks of protest turned into little clucking sobs.

'It's always all right for you,' she groaned at last, building herself up again. 'Big, tough Philip. Just stop for once, just, just stop and take a look at what you've done to poor Freddy, and me and . . . Big heroic brother. Yes, I fell for it. Silly little girl, and Freddy was just boring, nice, wasn't he? And you. Blow the family fortunes, so we have to give up everything, everything. Nice home, good future, everything, just to mop up after you. Do you know what Freddy's boss in the City told me? He said Freddy was the brightest young accountant he'd ever had on the firm. He'd have been a partner in a matter of a year or so . . .'

Philip watched her as she pulled herself to her feet. Her shoulders sloped now. For the moment, she was defeated. He did not blame her. He would have liked to have liked her enough to have given her the hug that she so plainly needed. Instead, he said, 'Alison, I've travelled my road, made my cock-ups. They should have affected no one but me. I'm sorry that your wagon was hitched to my star. But it's like parents, country of birth, whatever. You have to make the most of what you've got. I'm here to wind up this bloody enterprise for once and for all, and I guarantee you'll be OK. You just carry on as best you can. I'll make the best deals I can, run the horses that have to run. Don't worry. I'll not move in on you here. I'll stay up in the village, with old Ma Bradley. We'll have to talk a bit, but we'll keep it to business, OK? Otherwise, I'll stay in the yard.' He paused as his words sank into the fabric of the house.

'Just one thing,' he said into the silence. 'Did Freddy have any life insurance?'

121

'Fifty grand.' She spoke sullenly. 'Term. It was all we could afford.' She stiffened again. For a second, there was light in her eyes once more. 'But he's not dead. He's *not dead.*'

'No,' Philip nodded. 'OK. We'll talk about that another day. I'll go out to the yard now.' He walked across the hall to the swing door which gave on to the kitchen and the back hall. 'Sorry about everything, Ali. I'll do my best.'

She said, 'God help us.'

He wished people would stop saying things like that.

In the back hall he moved as fast as he could. He needed protective clothing and footwear. He did not want Alison to come upon him there, to continue wrangling. He pulled down a full-length Barbour which might just be big enough. He flapped quickly through the rank of wellingtons. He found a pair of tens. He added a suede jerkin to the bundle in his arms and quietly let himself out of the side door.

He was halfway up the back drive and sheltered from the house by brownish rhododendrons before he stopped and changed into the boots and the coat. The weight and the rustle of the waxed cotton were unfamiliar now. He sank his hands into the pockets. In the left-hand one there was a length of string and a crumpled-up ball of loo paper. In the right, there was something cold, flat and hard.

He pulled it out. Freddy's inhaler. One of the newfangled, revolving variety.

He frowned. This little plastic container could have saved his brother's life.

He shoved it back into the pocket.

To work.

Philip stopped in the archway beneath the clock-tower. He took a deep breath, just taking it all in.

Every morning for years he had swaggered, staggered or shuffled through here, every morning seen the sand-coloured walls, the doors painted in the Glaisters' primrose and blue colours, the cobbles about the central square of grass and the municipal-style flowerbeds.

There, in the office down on the right, he had plotted the careers of his animals and dreamed his dreams.

Just one win could save the day. That was the intoxicating horror of this game. One win could wipe out all the misjudgements, all the ill fortune of the years, so, by nature an optimist, he had planned and dreamed where he should have cultivated resignation, and, time after time, had raised his head at the juddering growl of the returning horsebox to see glum faces and shaking heads.

There, too, he had sat and drank whilst the yard clattered about its business without him. There he had read bills for light relief as his jowls and his eyelids grew heavier and darkness closed in, knowing that all that awaited him was a cold and empty house and Mrs Berry's dinner waiting with a note on the kitchen table.

And there he had concocted his last-ditch, half-baked plan.

Erebus's brilliance was by now a mere memory. After his failures at Ascot and Newmarket, he had still been expected to do great things in his three-year-old term, but he had overwintered badly, put on no weight. Philip had known that he had little chance in Group company, so had wangled him a second place in a four-horse 'preparatory' race at Newmarket and had then let slip rumours about coughing to justify his failure to reappear.

Erebus was still insured for £1,250,000. He had to remain so.

With the highly-paid connivance of Diarmid O'Donellan, his alcoholic vet, Philip had also established that Erebus was all but infertile. His sperm count was minimal. Whilst newspapers speculated as to whether Erebus might reappear and carry all before him, he was cavorting in a field ten miles from Swynsmere. Every time that a Glaister mare came on, Philip sent her out to join him for a holiday.

Just one of the mares had tested in foal.

Now all that Philip needed was a dead or dying horse.

123

Diarmid had turned up with the corpse late one August evening. A dark brown horse of the blood had broken his neck at a bullfinch during a team-chase.

Philip had called an old friend of his father's who had repeatedly asked him for a retired racehorse. 'His name's Hades. If you'll pick him up right now,' he had told her, 'and let Diarmid castrate him first thing tomorrow, he's yours.'

That night, there was a fire in the isolation boxes at Swynsmere. Diarmid signed the necessary documents.

Philip had recognized an anomaly in bloodstock insurance. In the event of accidental death, such as death by fire, no check was made of the casualty's DNA print-out, nor would anyone assume that there was advantage to be gained by the death of so gifted and valuable an animal.

Nor was there, Philip thought ruefully, save to one so accursedly sentimental and soft-hearted, so accursedly *stupid* as to shudder from burning to death a healthy horse.

Still, Erebus was officially dead.

And would have remained so, had it not been for an unwarrantably intrusive, moustachioed little bugger named Vincent Lovelady . . .

Philip now braced himself. He set his shoulders in a short of swagger. He stepped into the yard.

And a ghost hobbled towards him.

The ghost was a gapelegged old black and white collie with a grizzled mask. His banner of a tail waved. He could not trot, but did his best, dropping on the off-fore, the one leg which yet bent, with each stride.

Philip frowned. He said. 'Myshkin?' Then he fell to one knee and called, 'Myshkin!' and the dog came up to him, climbed on to his knee, raised his stiff forelegs on to Philip's shoulders, and rested the soft side of his nose against Philip's cheek. He snuffled softly. Philip found himself responding in kind.

'Come on, my old darling,' he growled at last. He scratched the dog's ears and stood. Myshkin put in a little, rocking bound of joy and fell in at Philip's heel.

124

At his left, horses' heads hung over the box doors. It was Sunday. Most of the animals were barely awake. At a quick scan of the yard, he counted nineteen heads.

And another surprise, though this one, he supposed, he should have expected. Halfway up the yard, Myshkin swung to his left and disappeared into one of the boxes. Again Philip stopped. Again he stared. He had cut the hole in the door so that Myshkin could walk in and out of Ludo's box at will. Ludo, his hack, was one of those horses which were only happy when they had pets. Sometimes you would find Myshkin curled on Ludo's sleeping body, sometimes in the manger.

Why had Philip not expected to see that slightly common bay head at the box's door? Ludo had been only sixteen when Philip had gone into exile. Yet it was somehow touching that Freddy, who would have supervised the string from the Range Rover rather than from a hack, had kept the old boy on, even when the yard was short of cash.

Philip reached up, stroked Ludo's snip, tugged at his ears, said softly, repressing a gulp, 'Hey up, boy. Good to see you. How're you keeping?'

He unbolted and opened the door. The hot, familiar sweet smell hit him. He did not bother to shut the door again. In his day, Ludo had had the freedom of the yard. He had known his way to the field where he grazed and had let himself back into his box at night.

Philip crooned softly as he went through the horseman's reflex inspection, running his hands down the neck, the shoulders and the legs, feeling for tell-tale heat, but not really. It was just a way of saying, 'hello' to this animal who had plodded to something like glory over seven years of service. Twenty starts, six victories, placed five more times . . . Tough and genuine and honest as the day is long.

It was Ludo who had carried Philip in the best of his amateur races, Ludo who had been buried at the Taxis in Czechoslovakia, Ludo who had scraped third in the Swedish Grand National. Philip had ridden him – disastrously – at Badminton. They had hunted together. The horse had taught Philip as much as Philip could ever have taught him. He had earned his pampered retirement.

'All right!' The twanging, drawn out vowels slithered about the concrete walls long after the consonants' rap had faded. 'What the 'ell do you think you're doin', then? Stand up slowly.'

Philip turned his head to the silhouetted figure in the doorway. 'Hello,' he said.

The man stood sideways on, pitchfork advanced, like a foot-soldier with bayonet fixed. 'I'll hello you, mate,' he said. 'Come on. Up with you. Who the fuck are you?'

'Mr Glaister.' Philip straightened. 'Philip Glaister. You?'

'Oh.' The man lowered his pitchfork. He wiped his right hand on his jodhpurs. 'Oh. Um. Sorry. Jim Dobbs. Sorry.' He wriggled. 'Yeah, well, you know. I was – you know. Sorry. I wasn't to know. I'm sort of, well, head man here, you know?'

'I know.' Philip nodded. He stepped forward and offered his hand. The man who took it was five-five, five-six. His face was pale and prematurely graven with deep lines. He had a shock of auburn hair which looked as though someone had just dropped a boulder on to his head.

Philip said, 'Good to see you so alert. Sorry to give you a shock. Still, glad you're here. If you've got a moment, perhaps you can give me a quick rundown on the animals here. Ludo, I know.'

They left Ludo's box and went into the next box along. 'Well, we got this bitch, Royal Straight. She's Mr and Mrs Nugent's. Sire's Straight Flush, and she's one-paced over the six. We was hoping she'd get the seven last season, but she blew up last time out, still, she's got some growing to do, Mr Glaister says . . . Whoops. Mrs Nugent – that's –'

'My ex-wife. Not to worry. No, Mr Glaister's right,' Philip mused. 'She's got scope. It'll be someone else gets to enjoy it, though. Nice.'

Jim Dobbs led the way out of the box and held the door open for Philip and Myshkin. He bolted it after them. Philip was already at the next box when he caught up. 'Now, this . . .' Dobbs began.

126

'You don't need to tell me.' Philip glared grimly at the lean, black, flashing form which, though darker, somehow seemed to shine brighter than the shade about it. He glared at the eye which, though full, was twitching and leery. He glared at the smooth, undulant contours, every muscle exaggerated by the contrast between black shadow and phosphorescent light. He glared at the lean, long limbs and the short back of an animal which promised everything. A speed machine.

A bastard.

'Plutonium,' he muttered. 'God almighty, it's a fucking reincarnation. Tell me.'

'Well, 'e was a pig to get into the stalls . . .'

'I know,' said Philip.

'But he ran green first time out, left and wandering, but, Jeez, you should've seen 'im hit overdrive . . .'

'I know,' said Philip.

'So we goes for the Dartington. Walks it, 'e does, turning 'andsprings. Magic.'

'Magic horses.' Philip shook his head. 'They all bloody are.'

'Oh, well.' Jim Dobbs shrugged. 'You know it all, I reckon.'

'No, no. Sorry. I knew the bugger's sire and granddam. I hate the sight of the haematite bastards. Nappy, is he?'

'Ah,' Jim smiled. ' 'E'll take a chunk out of you, you give 'im a chance, and I'd not advise you to stand behind 'im.'

'Rearing?'

'Well . . . 'E 'as, yeah, but not often. 'E's got a screw loose, I reckon, but, Jeez, he shifts, it's like watching a – a bullet. I tell you, nothing's gonna touch him in the Dewhurst. Licentious can't 'old a candle to 'im. Don't think much of the French thing neither. French form's shit, you ask me. You saw that Plus Tranquilly at Epsom? Meant to be the superhorse, but stuffed all ends up.'

'That was three-year-old form.'

'Yeah, but. Nothing to match this boy.'

'You reckon?' Philip sighed as the bolts were shot. Straw hissed beneath his feet. 'Yeah, well. Maybe you're right. I'd not lay much on it, though. If I know this family, he'll stop and read a book two furlongs out, or have a heart attack or – oh, God, the bugger's beautiful, isn't he?'

And he was, as, doubtless, the Hound of the Baskervilles would have been beautiful to a Kennel Club judge. Plutonium stamped. Plutonium glared. But Plutonium looked, like certain very fit men whom Philip had encountered, ready to win or, if he could not concentrate his energies to that end, ready to kill.

'Take the blanket off 'im, sir?' Jim Dobbs asked.

'No,' Philip almost growled. He knew what was there. 'No. Let's see the rest of them, shall we?'

Half an hour later, the horses all checked, Philip went into his old office with Jim Dobbs.

'No, but, funny thing was, see, guv'nor,' Jim had warmed to his theme, 'I 'eard this sort of banging, right? Like, you know – well, like I don't know what. Sort of metal, you know? I don't know. I mean, back of my mind, I know that sound, but I just can't think what it was. Sort of clanging, rumbling sort of. So I wakes up, says, you know, Gawd, like, what's that, then, you know, like one does. And I'm thinking I dreamed it, you know, or maybe it's a cat or old Mysh 'ere. But then there's fuckin' footsteps, and I'm up out of my pit like, you know, getting dressed. And there's this – Gawd save us, now I know what it was, but it sounds like someone's sanding something, you know?'

'Mr Glaister's asthma,' Philip nodded. He sat back with his feet crossed on his old desk.

''Sright. Makes you shudder, dun'it?' Jim perched on the windowsill. He sipped at the mug wrapped in his hands. 'Then there's more footsteps, but running, like, just as I gets to the door.'

More likely, thought Philip, the good Mr Dobbs had been waiting inside his door until he heard just that sound. He did not blame him.

'So I came out, and there you are. There's poor Mr Glaister laid out on 'is side on the cobbles, stone cold still

128

and staring, like, and just the occasional twitch of 'is legs and Myshkin standing over 'im sort of nuzzling 'im, only 'e 'adn't barked. Jeez. So I tries, you know, artificial respiration, like. You know, turn 'im over, push down, like, on 'is back . . .'

Dear God, Philip sighed. This would-be rescuer was an inch away from manslaughter . . .

'Then out comes madam – Christ, I mean, I was scared. Gawd knew 'ow she knew what was goin' on. She must 'ave 'eard something too. She's just got this, you know, shirt on and some jeans, and she's shrieking and running. Never forget it, I won't. Like something out of a horror movie. So she shouts – well, I'll not tell you what she shouts, but it's not nice, but then, you know, even a lady, I suppose, you know, sees 'er 'usband, like . . .'

'Yes, yes,' Philip reassured him.'Quite natural.'

'Well, she tells me "phone for an ambulance," and she's down there on the wet cobbles, really professional, like, puffing into 'im. And I sees 'is chest going up and down, and I think, "thank Christ," you know, "'es going to be OK." Any'ow, I rings the ambulance, say, "Get a bleedin' move on," and they're 'ere in – what? five minutes? 'Mazing. And madam is supervising everything, screaming orders, like do this with the oxygen, do this with glucose. God, fierce she was. I dunno,' Jim shook his head sadly. 'Still shakes me up just to think of it.'

'So where was this?' Philip lowered his feet. His chair rocked forward. He rested his forearms on the desk. He picked up a pen.

'Ah, now,' Jim was triumphant. 'That's the thing, in'it? Slap bang outside Plutonium's box, it was, and the box door wide open. I didn't think about it at first, but then, I begins to put two and two together, like. I mean, you open Plutonium's door, 'e'll be in Timbuktu before you can blink, right? So I come to close the door, I think, well, there'll be no 'orse in there. 'E'll be well gone. Nope. Look in. There's old Ludovicus, Ludovicus, mind, calm as calm. So you tell me, what's 'e doing in Plutonium's box, eh? And what's Plutonium doing on the other side of the yard?

You tell me that, guv'nor? Weird, the 'ole thing. Fuckin' weird.'

'Very odd,' Philip agreed. He looked as though he were taking notes. In fact, as ever, he was doodling horses. 'And when Mr Freddy was found, did he have his inhaler on him?'

'Nope.' Jim Dobbs was certain. 'Nope, 'cos I looked and madam looked. Near frantic she was, and I know, like. I mean, I'd seen 'im often enough before – you know, in stress, like, or in a smoky atmosphere, first thing 'e always done, reach for that disc thing, lift up the whatsit and "hoooff!"' He mimed inhalation.

Philip looked down. He sketched the galloping animal's mane. 'He'd never go anywhere without it. I wouldn't, I know.'

'Well,' Jim shrugged again, 'not that time.'

Philip reached into the coat pocket. He pulled out the Ventodisk. 'This is the thing, right?'

'Gawd. Yeah. That's it.'

'So – ' Philip pulled off the semi-circular cap. 'I still use the old puffers. Let's see if I've got this right . . .'

He looked down. There was a disc of foil blisters. 'Let's see . . .' Philip raised the plastic flap. 'So,' he said, 'the spike punctures the blister in which the Ventolin is contained. I put the tube to my lips and suck . . . Yup. The powder comes out . . .' He swallowed. 'And the disc moves on one, like a revolver, to the next blister. Simple enough.'

''Sright.' Jim stood dolefully looking down from the other side of the desk. 'Seen 'im do that a hundred times, I 'ave.'

'And he didn't have it with him, and the dog didn't bark . . .' Philip shoved the little machine back into his pocket. He put an eye into the doodled horse's head, then pushed back his chair. He paced the length of the room. 'Quite simply,' he said, 'it doesn't make sense.'

'No sense at all,' Vincent Lovelady sipped his beer and licked his lips. He leaned smugly back against the curtains

130

in the Snooty Fox, the public bar attached, as it were apologetically, to the Swan Hotel. 'The man goes out there, perhaps uniquely, without his ventilator, or whatever the thing's called. On this one, extraordinary occasion, he meets interlopers, suffers a serious shock and has an acute attack. It's possible, of course, but unlikely. And then we add the other extraordinary facts: that something – some sound – drew him out there in the first place, and that something – perhaps the same thing – caused his wife to run out there too.'

'On the other hand,' Detective Constable Andrew Markham said, 'she did everything she could to save him. Without her, he'd be dead today. You can't suspect her.'

'Oh, I can suspect anyone.' Vincent gave a brief grin. His moustaches jerked into a shallow V. 'It's a talent of mine. I start with the premiss that no one's motives are pure and philanthropic. That way, I sometimes get some really pleasant surprises.'

Markham giggled, a shrill zigzag of sound. It was a strange sound to come from so big and outwardly manly a man. His paisley tie matched his handkerchief. Both accorded with his pink shirt. His hair was blond and quiffed. His skin was tanned. His hands were very large. He clearly enjoyed Vincent.

'You'll be pleased to know,' he announced, 'that a friend of yours is back in town.'

'Oh, good, I rather thought that would be the case.' Vincent rubbed his hands together. His tartan-lined carcoat shuffled. 'He's a walking disaster, of course, but principally because he's so woefully honest. I must say, I do like him. He makes me laugh.'

'Honest?' Markham spluttered into his gin and tonic. 'Now, Lovelady, I don't want to slander anyone or anything, and I know I'm not meant to know about it, but we do hear things, you know, and from what I can gather, his last little enterprise . . .'

'Well, yes, yes.' Vincent grinned. 'Not honest in the strictest sense, I'll grant, but really that was a singularly ingenious act of desperation. People are doing it every day and getting away with it. You'd be astonished, the number of people who want a new carpet so simply leave the taps on when they go out. It's the modern form of shopping.'

'God.' The corner of Markham's lips jerked back into his cheek. 'No wonder my bloody premiums are so big.'

'Yes, but no. Our friend is fundamentally honest. No side to him. No bullshit, if you'll pardon the expression. It's refreshing.'

'Hm.' Markham looked disapproving. 'You know, the difference between us is, you regard the whole damn business as a game. You're amoral. For you, Glaister's just a good player. For me, he's a villain just like any other.'

'Oh, no,' Vincent tutted. 'Villains are as disparate as saints. Their actions are my only professional concerns, but their motives are all that interest me when it comes to judging them.'

'Which is why he slipped the net. Glaister, I mean.'

'I saw no point in informing you insensitive clods, if that's what you mean. I had protected my underwriters. That's the sum total of my duty, you know.'

'Like I say. You're amoral. What about your duty as a citizen, then?'

'Oh, pooey,' said Vincent Lovelady.

Philip sat in the office. Myshkin snored at his heel. The light in Jim's room had been gulped up by darkness. Occasionally, outside, a horse snorted or danced on straw.

He riffled through form-books. He related his findings with the entries in Freddy's own records. Occasionally, he stood and strode from the the room to peer over a stable-door, appraising an animal before returning, puffing steam, to run his pen down the yellow pages of the Racing Calendar. Occasionally, he breathed, 'Yes!' and scribbled fast.

He was undoing all that his family had laboured to create.

*

First came the grumble, then the jingle and the panting as the mass of dull colour split into recognizable entities; men crouched, plumed with the steam of their own breath, horses striking out, shadows becoming light, light shifting to shadow as the ribs tautened and the damp skin shuddered and the hooves puddered their crazed tattoo.

And then they were gone, once more swallowed into a unit as they ran down into Swynsmere Bottom and swung round to the left to climb the down.

'Now,' said Philip softly, and the rain spattered his binoculars and pattered on his suede gloves.

It hurt to see. It hurt, because it should cause so much pleasure, because the thrill at seeing that beautiful animal moving like a bullet from its four-year-old rival as they climbed from Swynsmere Bottom must be constrained. Here, once again, was the dream, the thing for which many trainers pined in vain through long lifetimes. This was the big pools win, the crock of gold, the miracle which would make most grown men once more into jubilant, carefree children.

But Philip knew the mocking antic hidden inside this crock of gold. Having the dream yet checking the leaping heart hurt more than never having the dream, as monastic life on Mount Athos must be better than being wound up, tight and trembling, by women who then hung you out to dry. Fulfilment was just a whisker away.

At Philip's shoulder, the bowed cello voice said, 'So, my dear. Just how good would you say he really was?'

Philip half turned his head, then turned it back again fast as the wind bounced, flinging a handful of cold rain in his face.

'Goddamn it, Gerry,' he growled, and again he raised the binoculars to his eyes. 'You don't need to ask. You're a collector. You've got the feel. You can look through a thousand fakes and suddenly you see – damn, suddenly you just feel, no need to see – the real thing. Your hand starts trembling. Your mouth goes dry. Your arse twitches. Go on. You tell me how good he is.'

'Very, very good,' Gerry nodded. 'Mind you, I don't

133

share your trust in my judgement. I've backed enough pigs in my time.'

'That's different,' Philip responded. 'I couldn't tell one moderate violin from another, but because I've got the feel – know how to judge a horse, a hound, whatever – I once picked up a fiddle in a Prague antique shop and it told me, "I'm in another league. I'm class". Brought it back, sold it for twelve grand. Anything touched by the gods, you know? And that leering black bastard has been touched by some god with a nasty sense of humour. Loki, at a guess.'

'Maybe it'll turn out all right.' Gerry soothed. 'Maybe the Glaisters'll end up with a great stallion. A jinx is not necessarily for ever. What'll he be worth if he takes the Dewhurst?'

'And nothing else?' Philip shrugged. 'Say ten grand a shot. Forty mares a season, that's four hundred grand a year . . .'

'Tax free, if he's in Ireland . . .'

'Sure. And if he gets good sorts, or trains on to win something decent next year . . . God. Castles in Spain. This family doesn't do things like that. They have all the ability in the world, but they don't like winning-posts.'

'This one's already won.'

'Oh, sure, sure. Think he'll do something predictable, like just being useless? Bollocks. He'll look like he's going to win the Derby, then die at Tattenham Corner. It's in the blood. Still.' He turned away. He handed his binoculars to the lad who held Ludo's rein. He jumped up into the saddle. He gathered up the reins and looked down at Gerry's smooth pink face and those big, wet, beautiful violet eyes beneath the tweed cap. 'It's not my problem, is it?' he said. 'I'll be out of here a month from now.'

Ludo lowered his head. Philip rocked easily forward, said, 'Easy, lad,' and shortened the reins. 'Listen, we've got a lot to talk about. Can't invite you back to the house. Probably find it booby-trapped. Whyn't you go down to the Frank-lands? Tell them to rustle up some eggs and bacon – what? Half an hour?' He glanced at his watch. He wiped water from his cheeks and lips. 'Yup. Half an hour. Do you?'

Gerry nodded. 'See you there.'

He smiled affectionately as he turned towards the BMW and climbed gratefully into the warmth. He wiped the windscreen with his gloved hand and watched for a minute as, sitting his hack as though it were an extension of himself, Philip gave orders to the lads who rode about him.

Gerry shook his head. The black horse, he thought, wasn't the only one with all the ability in the world but an inability to bring home the prizes.

It felt good to be back here, beneath a marble washstand sky with the familiar fleshy swoop of the downs all about him and the warmth of Ludo's body between his thighs. It felt natural to be in charge here, to see rosy, glistening faces beneath skullcaps which nodded at his orders, to hear horses snorting and puffing as they wheeled and set off to do his bidding.

It was his land. His, not in terms of ownership so much as in that he knew its every inch better than anyone alive, his, in that, thereby, he belonged to it. He might hate it. He might never have thought to return here, but, he now realized, the place had often returned to him as he lay in the now distant darkness of the south.

He did not like the idea that this was his destiny, but it seemed natural to him to be on a horse, natural to be in England, natural to be appraising horses' actions, their condition and their wind.

He had been warmly greeted by the old lads up here, much as by the locals in the bar last night. Here, as there, there had been broad smiles, warm handshakes, even occasional tears. Here, too, there had been a couple of people who had expressed hope that 'now things would start running straight again,' or that, 'things would get back to normal.'

As one who regarded his own record at Swynsmere with no great pride, he had been mildly surprised to find his reign regarded with nostalgia. 'When you and your dad were around,' an old man had told him in the pub last night, 'you knew where you were. You heard there was a good thing, you knew you was all right for a touch. Maybe each way, but we still got something back.'

The old gaffer's companion had chipped in then. ''Strue. Listen, mate, I've not got a word against your brother, poor bugger, nice guy, all that, but Gawd, I mean, I've lost a packet this past year or so. We all have . . .' He had stared morosely into his almost empty pint pot. He didn't argue when Philip had offered them both a fill-up.

When Philip had returned with the straight glasses of the good local brew, he had encouraged them to talk. 'So what was the story, you reckon? What was different?'

'Well,' the younger man had said, 'it's not as if there weren't no winners, we had a few, just not like the old days.'

'Go on,' Philip had prompted.

'Well, just, when there was a hot thing – sort of thing you rely on to buy your Christmas presents, that sort of thing – I don't know. Well, you remember, Alan, we had two left at the start, didn't we? Two, well, their boxes broke down on the way to the races . . .'

Alan was shaking his head. 'Then there were three, four withdrawn at the last moment. Jesus! I mean, you suddenly couldn't rely on a bloody thing. I mean, what's the point of having a decent yard in your village if you don't get the odd bonus or so . . . ?'

All this was odd, much as the circumstances of Freddy's accident were odd, but now Philip could not help wondering whether his years in exile had altered his sense of perspective, whether he was not regarding as extraordinary events which, to others who lived here, were perfectly normal.

He rode back to the escarpment at the head of the string and, leaning back and whistling softly, allowed Ludo to bear him back to the village and into the yard. He jumped down, Western-style, on Ludo's near side.

'OK, Jim,' he called to Dobbs, the head man. 'I'll be back before you get the Deep Run and that washy rat boxed up. I'll set off for Fontwell round eleven. You want me, I'll be down at the Franklands with Mr Kilbride. Everything OK?'

'Sure.' Jim Dobbs nodded. 'Don't you worry. I've managed up to now.'

Philip pulled off his cap and his gloves. Water trickled from his hat down his collar. He sidestepped into the maroon Mini which had been in the yard since his time. All about him, lads and girls were already down to the business – tying up their mounts, mucking out, grooming, wisping.

Philip waved. The car jumped. The seat hit his back hard.

He drove down, past the back of the house and out on to the narrow road. The Mini seemed possessed of a mischievous daemon, but then, Philip had not driven for two years. The car seemed to bound when he touched the accelerator, stop like it hit a tree when he touched the brake.

Thus leaping and bowing, it made its way up through the deep, dappled freestone lane, out once more above the folds of the downs and down the hill into Swynsmere village.

Gerry Kilbride looked more like Gerry now. He had had a chance to sweep back his damp hair, which already showed signs of springing back into bouffant life. His rosy cheeks had dried in the warmth of the gas flames. Without his protective clothing, he was revealed in his more usual, incongruous feathers – a blazer with gold buttons, a pink button-down Oxford with monogrammed breast and monogrammed links, a Georgian Society tie and a tumescent silk handkerchief. His shoes were slippers made of conkers, with twin toggles flapping from each.

'Dearest Philip,' he extended a regal, chubby hand, 'how altogether wonderful to see you, and away from all that weather. You do look well, I must say. All sort of well-seasoned and rough-chiselled – and blond, my goodness! Very becoming in the beachboy sort of way. I've ordered breakfast. You, in keeping with your appearance, will eat quantities of kidneys and bacon. I have elected an enormous ham omelette. The tea is disgusting, but she tells me that the coffee, which is coming shortly, is delectable.

137

Now. Sit down and tell me all. How was your encounter with the emotional Alison?'

'Grim,' Philip sat. 'And very emotional. She was painting a green carpet red when I arrived.'

'Oh, dear, oh, dear. How – how unsubtle.'

'Yes,' Philip drawled. 'No, but I suppose . . . OK, so she's all sorts of crazed bitch, but she's been a fair wife to Freddy, I imagine, and I can see she must feel a bit hard done by. The estate *must* make provision for her.'

'Of course, my dear. Of course. It's quite clear now that the whole thing is untenable. The assets will now be realized and we'll all sit down and work out what she deserves.'

Philip winced. 'What I don't get is, why is she so anxious to keep the poor old boy alive? I talked to the doctor. He said there's no chance, and normally they'd just let nature take its course. Apparently they can't because Alison knows her stuff and has laid down the law.'

'I know. I've talked to her. She won't hear reason.' Gerry frowned. He shot his cuffs, and Philip saw again the puce birthmark which covered the outside of his left hand and forearm. 'Mind you, it never was her long suit. Reason. Still, we'll work on her. No doubt, in time . . .'

'And I'm not happy about this nonsense about Freddy's accident, Gerry. He hears some noise, goes out in the middle of the night – inexplicably without his inhaler – meets, we assume, one or more intruders, then she arrives on the scene, somehow sensing what's going on . . . It doesn't make sense. There are too many one-offs to make it simple coincidence.'

Gerry nodded. 'I know, I know, but what is one to do? I had a chat with old Hugh – you know, chief constable in these parts – and he said, you know, I mean, it plainly was an asthma attack, and you can't blame anyone for that, can you? And little Alison plainly did – and is still doing – everything she can to save his life. So what can one do? Nothing inherently disreputable about her conduct, even if a trifle extraordinary. Nothing criminal about the nature of his accident, even if you and I know he would never go out without his puffer thing. All right, if they can find the intruders, but they'll probably just prove to be tinkers out to steal tack or something. Just because they happen to run into an acute asthmatic, it doesn't make them murderers. Ah, good.' He looked up at the young and pretty waitress with a broad smile which drew a great diamond inside his face whilst making its overall shape that of a heart.

The smooth flow of fanciful nonsense continued as the slender girl with frizzy brown hair simpered and scolded and laid out plates, knives and forks, spices and sauces.

As he ate, Philip wondered, not for the first time, at the unlikely friendship between his grumpy, taciturn father and this voluble, almost camp lawyer. Gerry was something of an absurdity, but he was kind, genuine and sincere. Although his snobbery was evident, it was never unkind and his devoutness was unfeigned. After a successful career at the London bar, he had taken up a life of endless calls on the endless aged and impoverished princesses who are scattered about Europe. He shuddered from modern – particularly American – sensibility. Indeed, much as a sceptic might shudder from a ghost, he even questioned the existence of such a thing.

He behaved like a sponger, yet he was a hugely generous host and patron. He was in the habit of excusing his extravagance with the philanthropic claim that it hurt him to see his friends slumming. If, therefore, he would tell Philip in the old days, a young man would forgive an old man's grotesque self-indulgence, he really would be happier if he would have the foie gras and the Yquem or stay in his beautifully furnished flat in Hyeres sooner than undergo the hellish discomfort of the Intercontinental.

After years of such munificence, Philip had come to believe him. The idea that any fellow human (he admitted only limited numbers to this category) should suffer the mediocrity of, say, a Holiday Inn really would have caused Gerry to have sleepless nights.

His sexuality was a mystery. He certainly loved elegant women. He certainly loved attractive and vigorous young

139

men. If he possessed so commonplace a thing as a sex-life, Philip had concluded, it must have been in some extraordinarily recherché and quite beautifully decorated house which catered specifically for the requirements of his kind.

'What you said,' Philip reproved, 'when first I walked in here, was "tell me everything . . ."'

'Figure of speech, my dear,' Gerry waved. 'Thank God you didn't take me literally. Last thing I want to know is just what you did and with what and to whom in the lower fleshpots of the South of France.'

'No, but I do want, you disgusting, camp old queen, to know about what's been going on over here. First, how are the finances at Swynsmere?'

'Astonishingly, just creeping into the black.' Gerry swallowed omelette and impatiently washed it down with coffee. 'Lord knows how Freddy did it, but he *is* an accountant and was never as interested in matters Lucullan as you or I.'

'Or Dionysian.'

'Oh, no. Not Freddy. When I say into the black, of course, I mean only that the year's figures showed a profit. If an asset stripper or whatever they're called actually took a look at the overall position – the property's worth half as much, the horses a third as much – he'd feel as though he were stripping one of those Russian dolls. *Au fond*, there's precious little there.'

'So what do you reckon we're worth – overall?'

'Not my field, of course,' Gerry pushed away his plate and mopped his lips. 'The house is now unmortgaged, which is nice, and, of course, your papa sold off a two-thirds share of the gallops, so, unless a trainer buys Swynsmere, there's precious little chance of selling the remaining third. So you'd get, what? Four hundred, four hundred and fifty, for the house and yard? And that's a maximum. Well, that's your lot. And then, of course, there are the horses.'

'The horse,' Philip corrected. 'From what I can gather from the office files and records, I might get thirty for the two four-year-olds in training. Old Blazing Moon may have a couple more handicaps in him, but he can't go on much longer. They'll go to the October Sales. There are the two brood-mares. The old lame Nijinsky has been barren the last two years. She'll have to be destroyed. The other – well, what do you get for the winner of a selling-plate at Windsor who's so far got two jumpers and the winner – of a selling-plate at Windsor? No. It's Plutonium or it's nothing. Millions or penury. It comes down to that.'

'And if he does win,' Gerry pulled out an enamelled box of cachoux. He offered them to Philip. Philip shook his head. 'If he does win next week, what then?'

'I don't know.' Philip reached for his own Gauloises. 'Given that he's our sole asset, it would be a hell of a risk to run him next year without selling a share or two. On the other hand, I'd like to think that Sam had a healthy share in a valuable stallion. That sort of continuous income is not to be sniffed at. No. I'd say sell off half, preferably to someone who's got a stud in Ireland, this winter, keep him well insured, see what he can do then syndicate him as a four-year-old. I'd not breed from that line, but the market likes that sharp sort. And if we put him with, say, Liam Moran – Liam's good enough if he proves to be a Guineas chance and he's canny enough to invent injuries if he does what his sire did.'

'I believe Freddy did receive offers for Plutonium.' Gerry peered at his watch. 'I don't know from whom, mind you. You may find some record in the files.'

'I'll look.' Philip nodded. 'You going somewhere?'

'Oh, nothing important, my dear,' Gerry smiled sadly. 'Just a little memorial service at St Martin-in-the-Fields. You know how it is.'

'Sure,' said Philip, who didn't. 'So, how's Jenny Laing?'

'A trifle shell-shocked, I'd say.' Gerry raised a hand to the waitress. He mimed writing. He grinned his best avuncular grin. 'She's had a sheltered life.'

'And . . .' Philip paused. The very name still hurt to speak. 'How's Sam been getting on? I've talked to him, of course. He sounds . . . well, boisterous.'

'I think that's the word. I saw a rather nice piece of Meissen flying past my nose the other day and I had to retire to the loo to tell myself, "the word is 'boisterous', the word is 'boisterous'". No, he's an amiable enough child, though I'd sooner see him through the bars of a cage.'

'And Linda?'

'Bonny. Ring her. Find out for yourself. She's happy. That chubby blond fellow seems just the thing. A little dull, perhaps, but after you . . . He certainly seems to have a great deal of money.'

'Oh, he's got money, all right.' Philip inhaled with that tell-tale puncture hiss. 'Every goddamned speculator with a striped shirt and a baby face made money back in the bloody eighties. I'd not have him clean my fucking loos, but the City rewards idiocy and ineptitude.'

'Oh, he's not bad.' Gerry shook his head. 'Thank you, my dear,' he smiled up at the waitress. He pulled out his pen and spoke as he studied the bill. 'No. He may not be our sort, exactly, but one does understand the appeal of the big soft yellow labrador, doesn't one? There are a lot worse around.'

'Some consolation,' Philip sneered.

'Some,' Gerry agreed. 'Ring her.'

He signed his cheque with a flourish. 'Now. Call me if you need anything.' He stood and pocketed his pen. 'I don't think you'll need money, and you can send the bills to me, but if there's any problem, you'll let me know. I might ask young Jenny to come down if I'm too busy.'

Philip too stood; Gerry was holding out an open hand. Philip took it, then caught Gerry's wet eye, drew him close and hugged him.

They walked slowly to the pub's door. 'Just one other thing,' Philip said quietly. 'Do you know anything about the Herons?'

'Heron? Heron?' Gerry mused. He pushed open the half-glass door. 'Ah, you mean the spiv. Hotels, things like that. Bookmakers. Married poor Ivo Donovan's daughter, didn't he?'

'That's right. You still see Donovan?'

'Oh, of course, of course, from time to time. He collects English Delft. We meet at sales. Looking very old these days, since Pru died, poor thing. And I don't think he's

142

best pleased about his son-in-law. Why? Can I help?'

'Possibly,' Philip nodded. The rain had stopped. The air had an ether edge to it. Philip and Gerry walked to the BMW. Their feet crunched in unison on the gravel. 'Does Donovan still have power? Contacts, you know?'

'Oh, I'd say so, yes. Serious banker in his time.'

'Hmm,' Philip mused. 'Don't mention me to him, OK? I just may need his address, and I just may need to be anonymous. Tell you what. Can you give me a list of his closest associates and friends, particularly those with some clout?'

Gerry raised an eyebrow. 'Sure,' he said simply. 'Oh, dear. And I thought you'd been living quietly. Do you ever go anywhere without picking up a drama?'

'No,' said Philip, a little bewildered as he considered the question. 'No. I'm afraid not.'

Back in the office, Philip wrote:

Dear Mr Heron,
Thank you for the cheque via Mr Duggan. I would remind you, however, that my agreed fee was £2,000, of which you have thus far paid a bare quarter. If you really wish the nature of our deal to remain confidential, I earnestly advise you to pay the sum in full.
Yours sincerely,
Philip Glaister

There were ghosts aplenty at the races that afternoon. Car park attendants who waved and stared, trainers who vaguely nodded, even barmaids who said things like 'Ooh, hello.' None of them could hurt Philip, any more than, presumably, the diaphanous wraiths of legend, so whence came this cold, gulping stomach, this agitation of the limbs, this imprecise but powerful paranoid sense that these creatures *knew* things about him which he would sooner not have known?

Philip set his face against the curious stares and smiles.

He glowered. He glowered in the weighing-room as he deposited the jockeys' kit. He glowered as he strolled back out into the soft, halogen-in-mist glow of the afternoon. Occasionally he was greeted. He nodded and marched on, and often those who greeted him only then realized whom they had hailed.

He glowered at the two racing correspondents who approached him as he neared the racecourse stables before the first. To one, he said, 'Morning!' as though he had never been away, and swept on. To the other, he said, 'Hello. Back. Great Pity. Poor Freddy. Horses Running. No Problem. No Comment.'

The runner in the first was a washy bay, a six-year-old who was making the transition from moderate flat stayer to potentially competent hurdler. Philip saw him saddled, ran a last check on his legs and strode out to the paddock.

Again he was obscurely convinced that the burble of the surrounding crowd was largely concerned with him, his return and the reasons for his going. The owner, a Sussex man who, if asked, would have called himself a farmer (in fact, he owned a mere eighteen acres of hazel plantation and derived his money from Lloyd's and his wife) spoke of his animal, as most owners did, as though it were Philip's only concern in life. 'Nice to see you've been taking care of him – well, not you, your brother, of course. God, poor Freddy. Never known a family like it for luck. No. So.' He sniffed deeply. His gut shoved hard at the yellow alpaca of his waistcoat. 'Bit surprised not to receive progress reports, you know. Difficult times and all that, of course, but I pay you Glaisters good money – must be the better part of eighty grand over the years, and I appreciate a service, occasional telephone call, all that. Not much to ask, you'd think.'

'As soon as you pay the outstanding eight-and-a-half grand,' Philip said smoothly, 'I'll give you a call telling you that you can remove your horse within twelve hours. You can't get prompter service than that. Now, he looks fit, but I haven't had much time to gauge the opposition since I got back. By the look of them, I'd say he might be worth a small each-way bet. If it comes to a turn of foot, he'll be

144

there or thereabouts. If he gets caught up in an affray, forget it. He's too weedy just now. Ah ...' He turned towards the double line of jockeys who, like children let out from school, entered the paddock in crocodile, then split and veered, each to his separate owner and trainer. Philip recognized the colours. He did not, at first, recognize the jockey.

'Well,' the owner was burbling at his side, 'I didn't mean anything...'

'I never thought you did, Mr Freeman,' Philip smiled at the approaching form. 'I'd be grateful if you'd let me have the cheque within two weeks. I wouldn't like to have to seize your horse in lieu.'

'. . . never been spoken to . . .' The plush, pompous voice was that of a man torn between protest and pleading. It shuddered. 'In your father's day ... good whipping ... Always were bloody rude ...'

'I suppose – yes, of course, I mean, security, the future, all that. I mean, that's all beneath the mighty, noble Mr Stephen Shand isn't it? Thinking – just thinking for a moment, "Might this be a good idea?" That's all boring and middle-class, isn't it? Steve Shand is a cavalier. He doesn't fucking need to think. Just blunders in, ruled by his cock and some bloody arrogant idea that he's immortal . . .'

The words, the familiar crescendo of staccato screeches which would end in incoherent shrieking or in incoherent sobbing, still echoed in Steve Shand's head, two hours later, as he sauntered into the paddock. He had heard it all before, protested at its injustice many times. Not only women had accused him of arrogance and lack of foresight, though there had been many, many women. 'Why should you think you're different from anyone else?' they shrilled, usually because he declined to yield to this pusillanimous age's expectation of constancy.

When women complained, truth to tell, he did preen just a little, feeling himself the exemplar of a great tradition, misunderstood, cursed in its time, yet fondly recalled by each subsequent generation. When the accusation was made by owners and trainers regarding riding, however, it was serious. He also sincerely believed it to be unjust.

If he made light of falls, that was because such was his nature. It did not mean that he avoided them any less than his more apparently assiduous brethren. If he was inclined to make jokes rather than excuses to owners after a poor result, it was because he could see precious little point in insincere humility. He just wasn't that sort of guy. As to partying – God, try telling the Corinthians of the past – Dave Dick, Fulke Walwyn, Bryan Marshall – try telling them that they should not have drunk and fornicated for fear that it might damage their performances. So some jockeys had sleepless nights worrying about their wives' pregnancies or their children's exam results. Steve merely spent sleepless nights in other pursuits.

He *was* a good rider. That conviction was central to his whole life, his whole concept of himself.

Whilst his mother had lived, Steve had been an amateur. It was all very well to say that she had indulged him, but it was her canon that young gentlemen should divert themselves, so far as possible without hurting others. Steve was the son of her first, shortlived marriage to a spendthrift racing-driver who had, eventually, shot himself.

So poor Jack Quentin, the American collector of fine art and small girls whom next she had married, found he had to pay for steeplechasers to keep Steve happily and harmlessly engaged. Steve had had no objection. He had been brought up in the Vendée but educated in England. His English was perfect, though he had early on discovered that wholly to lose his accent in either language was not such a step forward as many language teachers maintained. He retained the French 'r' and the buzzing 'th' in English, and spread his vowels in the English style in French.

Three years earlier, Steve's mother, Mrs Jack Quentin, had died. Death had come rudely upon her, like a vulgar creditor or a policeman, affording her no time to prepare herself or make provision for her son. There she was in Les

Alpilles with her Belgian lover in his Di Thomaso when a careering lorry had forced them off the road.

At first Quentin had not seemed grief-stricken. His visits to select academies for young gentlewomen in the Marais had continued unabated. Sotheby's and Christie's were pocketing his cheques mere weeks after the accident. When it came to Steve, however, Quentin was inconsolable. The horses reminded him too much of his beloved wife. They must all go, and he would retreat to his château on the Loire.

Quentin had no desire to inconvenience his stepson, of course, to whom he acknowledged an inviolable obligation, so if Steve fancied working for one of Quentin's midwest newspapers or (starting at the bottom, of course, but with every prospect of rapid promotion) for the greetings card firms on which the American's fortune was based, Quentin, for one, would be overjoyed. Blood, he said significantly, was thicker than water.

Steve's first reaction had been to seduce Quentin's tiresome daughter Christina. The revenge of a runaway marriage would have been the sweetest imaginable. It had proved impossible, however, not because Christina would not have been willing, but because she had ankles like hocks of ham and believed, for example, that all men were equal, that all life was sacred and that everyone deserved respect, even in bed.

No. On reflection, it was not her *believing* in these things which offended him. She could believe in Easter bunnies and unicorns, for all he cared. It was her habit – and, it seemed, an incurable one – of talking about these beliefs at every opportunity which would unquestionably have blighted their married life. It was to his credit, Steve thought that such high principles on his part had prevented him from exacting that revenge even for the few years necessary to win a large divorce settlement.

Instead, he had turned pro.

Well, it beat work, didn't it?

But no. He struck his thigh with his whip. It was thoughts like that – jokes merely – which, coupled with

147

his reputation and his background, gave rise to the general idea that he was not, in the truest sense, a professional but merely a playboy, not to be trusted with valuable animals and unprepared to fight his corner in a rough house.

He spotted Philip Glaister standing with the owner, a grumpy old sod who looked as though he drank too much. He veered towards them, deliberately flattening the natural spring in his step and adopting a manner which, in so far as he was able to recollect such a thing, might suggest deference.

Steve had plans for his future, but, just for now, he needed work.

'Hello,' Philip said to the man with the slow, one-sided smile who stopped before him, his yellow cap set jauntily back on his crown. 'You won't remember me. Philip Glaister.'

Steve Shand crossed his arms. His whip tapped at his hip. He was perhaps five-eight, with heavy dark eyebrows, a blue chin and deep dimples. His eyes had a twinkle. Irish, you'd have said, had it not been for his swarthy colouring. French, then. Bedroom eyes, constantly flickering, constantly appraising. Fancied his chance. Probably with reason.

''Course I remember you.' Steve's voice was smooth as a purr. It could soothe, hypnotize or annoy the hell out of you. 'I rode – if you could call it riding – a beast of yours at Cheltenham five years ago. Those days, I was bouncing around like a sandhopper in the Sahara. Thought I should ride like these little flat monkeys, you know? Came off at the second last, and serve me right.'

It was a charming speech; it appealed to evident shared prejudice – no one who worked under both rules liked the flat – it was modest, and yet, like all self-criticism, it hinted at equality. It separated Philip and him from their younger selves, and from others younger. It thus flattered both of them. It was, in the subtlest sense, 'manly'. It spoke of fellowship, initiation, peerage.

Steve Shand was a clever man. Philip knew that, but he

148

knew too that such charm could never entirely be feigned. He could not help but like him.

'This one OK over fences?' he asked.

'Yeah. I 'ave schooled him a bit. He's improving all the time. If anything, he is a bit cautious, which is nice for me, but not so good for Mr Free-man, hey? No. Mr Glaister was working on schooling him upsides. He gets all confused when he's racing.'

'So you'll keep him out of trouble?'

'Best I can. He's too small anyhow. Another couple of years . . .' He shrugged. 'Well, we can dream.'

'If we couldn't, we'd have given up years ago.'

'So, you'll be coming from behind, eh?' Freeman could no longer stand being excluded.

'That, I am afraid, I cannot say. We'll see how it goes.'

'Ah, right. Right. Yes.' Freeman subsided like a parked Volvo.

The horses were led into the centre of the ring. Philip bent to flick Steve up into the saddle. 'At least you've got a fine day for it,' he murmured.

'Yes.' Steve placed his feet in the irons. 'That's OK. Only problem is, the ground hits you that much harder.'

'So don't let it hit you,' Philip advised simply.

Steve Shand grinned and saluted with his whip. He turned his mount away.

It was the injustice of it all which vexed Steve. Look at him. He rode well. He was good-looking. He spoke two languages perfectly, three competently. He knew about manners, drink, drugs, night clubs and clothes. Yet he must bow and scrape to the likes of Quentin – the likes, even, of Freeman. 'Meritocracy', they called it, yet it was anything but. What merit had that huffing, puffing yokel to justify his ownership of this animal? What merit had he that he could employ the likes of Steve?

But what did the future hold for him now? A few more years of slogging around British racecourses with little chance of enduring glory, inevitable retirement and what?

Marriage to an aged Jewess? A gigolo's existence like that of some of the nastier of Argentine polo players? Work for Quentin? No. He had not been bred to simper at Eurotrash nor to connive at the production of saccharine greetings cards. He had been reared to give – and to expect – better. That wonderful woman Duncan had understood. He had met her down at his stepfather's Loire château, just up-stream of Heron's. Of late, she and Heron had invited him several times to partake of their peculiar hospitality. They knew that he was out of the ordinary. Their ways were the ways of his forebears, unbound by petit bourgeois rules of propriety. Steve ardently wished that the world could be populated entirely by women like Angela Duncan and her friends, who would pass each morning through a cleansing, sacred fire and emerge ladies, like his mother.

He pulled the horse up at the starting gate. He narrowed his eyes down the fluffy green flock of the track. At his left, the starter was testing girths before mounting his rostrum for the off. At his right, Paddy Sheehan and Paul Tracey walked their animals in tight little circles, just settling them. The big boys, like Nick Storr, were not here today. They had bigger fish to fry at Newbury. They did not have to go pot-hunting around the tiddly provincial tracks. Steve had started his professional career too late. That was the trouble. None the less, he consoled himself, as so often before, that in the past year or so he had probably earned more than the champions.

The trouble was, it was never enough. The extra revenue had proved a boon. It had enabled him to be rude to Quentin. It had enabled him to buy a decent car. It had given him the chance to travel and to take his women to Tramp. It had increased the turnover, but done nothing to reduce the overdraft.

Steve was not a cruel man, but he saw no harm in his ambitions nor in his actions. In every story of his child-hood, the changeling regained his throne. That was nat-ural justice. In every story, too, it was ingenuity and a readiness to make the most of opportunity which character-ized the hero. Steve had not planned what had happened.

He had taken advantage of it. That was all. Worse things were done by grotesque little 'businessmen' every day of the week. And at last, it seemed, justice might be done. He might, after all, be a property owner, and able to educate his children as he had been educated, to carry on a torch too bright and too sacred for most dull modern eyes.

The chance was there, perhaps the last that would be offered to him. He must grab it and run for the flag.

They were moving forward now, sitting to the trot. Steve's cheeks jogged. The little horse had his ears pricked. Its black mane flapped, barely separated by the light breeze. It was a quiet start, this one. No one was in a hurry. There were no protestations to the starter, no conversation between the riders. The starter's hand arose and fell, and suddenly Steve, in common with the riders at his either side, rolled forward, his weight now on the irons. His legs were rock steady. There was no pressure on the bit save that which Steve slowly, deliberately exerted with his hands. He would give the field a minute to settle before deciding what he must do. Meanwhile, as the others veered towards the inside, he kept his mount at the centre of the course. He wanted room to move.

He pulled the whip through to his left hand in order to discourage the horse from joining the pack. There was talking and growling now from the men at his left as each looked for a snug and secure position on or near the rails. In green and gold and white, Paddy Sheehan, hugging the rails, held the lead whilst, a neck back on his outside, his compatriot, Aidan Kehoe, sat crouched low like an American quarter-horse jockey on an iron grey. Behind them, in double file, the remaining six in the field bowled along happily or strained against their straining riders' grip. They were going no sort of a pace. Steve clicked on, let out a reef.

He had never tried front-running with this animal before, so had no idea as to whether, as often happens, it objected to getting its nose cold. On the contrary, he was pleased to discover, the horse extended his stride and his head bobbed all the more once they were clear of the competition. He liked this game of Being Boss.

He liked it a bit too much. At the first, two or three lengths up on their nearest pursuer, he charged inattentively up to the plain birch fence. Steve had to check him, get him to put in a quick one before launching himself up and over. He jumped cleanly enough, but, unbalanced, pecked on landing. Steve felt his support suddenly drop away from him on his right-hand side. Suddenly the stained grass was altogether too close.

Steve sat steady. He did not allow the sudden pressure of gravity between his shoulder-blades to shove him forward. The horse pushed himself up on the near fore, looked about him for someone to blame for his indignity, then, hearing the others landing behind him with grunting and puffing and tinkling, bounded forward as though goosed.

'That's better, lad. Settle down,' Steve purred as he sat forward once more. 'You've got it all to do . . .'

Passing the stands first time round, Steve risked a glance over his left shoulder. The nearest contender was eight, nine lengths back. Those who had it in them to break from the pack would do so in the back straight, then it would be in the lap of the gods. If this little beast had the stamina, he frankly doubted that any of his rivals had the turn of foot to make up the lost ground. If he were going backwards, however . . . Well, there was a chance of an additional victory to add to the season's tally, and at least he had been seen and repeatedly mentioned by the course commentator. It was all to the good.

There was no justification for what happened then. The horse was going sweetly. He wasn't under pressure. There was all the time in the world to get him right. He had flown the open ditch going up the hill. He had turned into the back straight full of running. Steve was enjoying himself – dreaming a bit, he would admit later. The horse did not break his stride. He put himself absolutely right for the first plain fence out in the country. He took off with joyous enthusiasm.

152

He took off too fast. He took off too low.

Goddamn it all, Steve thought as the birch thudded and spat gobbets on to the turf ahead and the sky suddenly vanished and he was wrenched from the saddle, flung flailing forward. Goddamn it, it was his business to get the beast back, to stop him flying his fences on the forehand like a bloody hurdler. It might do for Arkle, but not for a pipsqueak novice like this one. How had he done it? How allowed the joy of the speed and the solitude and the confidence to overthrow his judgement?

He was cursing in French as his knees hit the animal's head. He was cursing in English as he hit the dry turf, shoulder first, and the wind was punched out of him and he rolled. The horse had ploughed through behind him with a huge grunt and a clatter. It stood. He did not bother. Its reins swung above his head. Its legs, like the turf and the trees, seemed to spin around him. He felt suddenly very sick.

And when the others had passed in what seemed a big parade of bass drums and glockenspiels, Steve sat up on the turf and twice lashed the ground between his legs with his whip.

This was no activity for a grown man.

Philip sat in the office. His eyes were slits. His teeth were gritted. His fingers straightened and curled. The object of his glare, an old-fashioned cream telephone, sat smug and secure on its broad base, unmoved.

Philip picked up the tumbler on his desk, hit his tonsils hard with a single slug of whisky. He gasped. He chewed the aftertaste. He pushed the hair back off his brow. He sighed.

The clock on the wall said ten past seven. The yard outside was still and dark. Twice already this evening, he had picked up the telephone and dialled. Twice already he had slammed down the receiver before the telephone could ring twice.

It was childish, he knew. So far, the ghosts which he

153

had encountered since his return had been, for the most part, harmless, even kind. His firm conviction that they would spurn him – his conviction, he acknowledged now, not without embarrassment, that they had been thinking about him as much as he about them over the past two years – had not been justified. The world was a nicer place than he had given it credit for.

Why, then, did he doubt the benevolence of this – these – dearest ghosts?

Whisky and reason did their work. He must take himself by surprise. Pick up the receiver, dial without thinking. Do it. Now.

He reached forward. Freddy's waxed cotton coat hissed against the desktop.

'Philip?'

He jumped. He looked up. His jaw retained its grim set. He replaced the receiver. He said, 'Oh. Hello.'

Alison Glaister was peering round the door. Her face was made up, her hair pulled tidily back. Her eyes were bright between their dark lashes. Her pink lips said, 'Sorry. Can I come in?'

'Of course, of course.' Philip jumped to his feet. 'Sorry. I was miles away. Come on in.'

She slipped round the door and closed it by backing against it. She kept her hands clasped before her crotch, her feet together, in first position. She was a figurine, a lamp-base, in her open-necked cream shirt and black waistcoat, her tight, bright blue jeans. She said, 'Look, I'm sorry, OK? It was – I was stupid. It's not your fault, all of this, and you're doing your best and it all just got on top of me and I'm sorry.'

'Don't worry about it.' Philip gestured towards a chair. She nodded.

'No, but I was stupid,' she said carefully. 'You and I – well – ' She caught his eye. 'We've had our ups and downs, but basically, well, we've always had some sort of – well it's like, you know, a rapport but we hate each other's guts, sort of thing. We get on but we just sort of send off sparks whenever we get together, like – I don't know – positive and negative jump-leads or something.'

154

Philip nodded. 'Sure,' he said. He did not resume his seat but perched on the corner of the desk and swung a leg. 'Honestly, I understood. I understand. You've had a bloody rough ride, and I've talked to Gerry, and whatever money we raise from the sale of this place – well, it's not going to be much anyhow, but whatever it is, you'll get first bite of the cherry. I don't need anything much, and Sam – well, if it's all invested wisely, he'll not be a pauper. Damn it, do a Glaister good to be born without his chops full of cutlery. And if Plutonium does his bit – well, we're talking serious money.'

'I know. Freddy said – apparently he got a huge offer, but he said no. It was all or nothing, he said. The family's fortunes or . . .' She had looked away, to the Petcorps Equisport spreadsheet on the walls. 'So, everything depends on that one horse. God.'

'Fairly horrific,' Philip admitted, 'given the jinx on that family. A lot of prayers are needed.'

'I'm praying.'

'Did . . . Did Freddy say who made this huge offer?'

'No. I don't think he knew. Just a bloodstock agent at the races.' She looked back at him. 'So, he definitely goes in the Dewhurst?'

'Barring accidents, yes. Why? It's what Freddy wanted, isn't it?'

'Yes, of course, just wondered.' She stood and trailed her limp fingers along the windowsill. 'You'll keep me posted, won't you?'

'Of course. It's more your concern than mine. Listen . . .' he said. He slid from the desk.

At the same moment, she said, 'Philip?'

'Go on,' he said.

'No. You.'

'No, go on. Sorry.'

'It doesn't matter. It's just . . .'

'Yep?'

'No, you say whatever you were going to say.'

'No, come on. Spit it out, Ali.'

'No, I was just thinking. Oh, it's silly. It's just – suppose, you know, someone wanted to train here. Find someone, you know, just starting up. I mean, would it be possible not to sell? I don't know, I mean, I could live in the cottage or something, maybe stay on in the house . . .' She looked down at her feet. With her fourth finger – a naked finger, Philip noted - she pushed a loop of hair back behind her ear. It was a pretty gesture, a little girl's gesture. She leaned back against the filing cabinet. The crow's feet creases at her crotch deepened. Philip looked at his feet, then quickly up again.

'I'm not with you,' he said. 'I mean, the way things are, there are going to be precious few people thinking of setting up on this sort of scale, and those there are will want to buy. Anyhow – sorry, but – you don't like horses, you don't like racing, I'd have thought you'd be glad to be shot of the place, get some money in the bank.'

'Oh, yes. No, it was just a thought. Just looking at alternatives. I mean, just if someone came along. I mean – what sort of percentage do you reckon I'll get when the place is sold?'

'I don't know.' Philip slid from the desk and strolled to the window which she had vacated. He said to the frosted pane, 'Fifty, I should think.'

'Yes, well, that's why I was thinking . . . I mean, house prices are low. If I could raise the money for the other half . . . Oh, I don't know. Forget it.'

Philip saw her white face move into the darkness of the window before him. 'Now,' her voice was very high and small, 'what did you want to ask me?'

'Freddy.' Philip was grim. 'Why are you so keen to keep air pumping through the poor sod? You know there's no point. He's dead. Isn't it time we let him go?'

'*No!*' It made the window-pane woof. He heard a crackle as she swallowed behind him. 'No,' she said softly. 'Not yet. Just a week or two more. Don't you believe in miracles, Philip?'

'In general, of course not. Name your miracle and I'll tell you whether I believe in it. Black being white, the dead walking, Freddy having a decent life, no.'

156

'Well, maybe not.' She was conciliatory. 'But I think I have the right to my own irrational beliefs and hopes just for a week or two, don't you?'

'I wouldn't want it. Not if I were Freddy.'

'He's not feeling anything. The doctor said.'

'No. OK. Two weeks, then?' Philip's shoulders were high and tense. The silence into which he spoke was thick and porous. 'Two weeks, then they can let nature take its course.'

'Yes. OK.'

'Right.' Philip rubbed his hands. 'Must get on.'

'Yes, sorry.' She stood still as he strode past her without looking at her. 'And – sorry, Philip, I'm not being nasty now, but if you'd just bear with me, leave me to my own devices in the house . . . I'm just adjusting, you know. I'd rather be on my own.'

'Sure, sure!' Philip was cheery. 'No. Don't worry. I'm having the time of our life up at Ma Bradley's. Don't you worry about me.'

When Alison had shuffled out into the darkness, Philip resumed his gloomy vigil over the telephone, daring himself to pick up the receiver and dial.

When it rang, he leaped in his chair. For a moment he told himself that it must be she, so intently had he been thinking of her. When he snatched up the receiver, however, it was to hear a man's voice. 'Philip Glaister,' it stated, not asked.

'Yes.'

'Plutonium does not run, right?'

'What?' Philip winced. 'Is this a joke?'

'Was it a joke, what happened to your brother?' The voice was very flat. 'Plutonium is withdrawn. He doesn't go. Understood?'

More even than what was said, it was the intrusion of this voice into the stillness and the privacy of the office which caused a flare of anger to streak across Philip's brain. 'Fuck off, shithead,' he said calmly enough, but he slammed the receiver down so hard that it rattled from its cradle.

It took him five minutes to calm himself. This time, he

157

did not delay. He needed to hear her. He snatched up the receiver and dialled.

The telephone in that big, Georgian-style redbrick mansion rang just three times before a man said, 'Yes? Hello?' The voice was cheery and youthful.

'Nugent. Philip Glaister.'

'Philip!' Nugent was, probably genuinely, delighted. 'Good! God, I was sorry to hear about Freddy. You must come over.'

That was David Nugent, Philip thought – all verve and enthusiasm, gabbling and giggling. Philip had trained for him and had found him amusing. After Linda's desertion, he had tried hard to dislike him, but still found it difficult. Nugent was blond and chubby. He glowed with condition and prosperity. Philip had characterized him to his friends as 'New Gent', which was almost, but not quite fair. Nugent's father had been a vicar, as Philip recalled, but young David had devoted himself wholly to Mammon and had made a fortune in the commodities market back in Thatcher's reich.

'Is Linda about, then?' Philip was brusque.

'No. Sorry. She'll be so disappointed. She was expecting your call. No, Sam's in bed, of course, and Lin just ran down the road for a drink with an old girl she met in Horsham the other day. You know how she picks up waifs and strays. *Refugium peccatorum*, I call her. No, but she's got to be back soon, we've people coming in. Pity you've missed her.' He giggled like a rusty motor. 'Whoops. No. Hold on, Philip. I hear a door. That could be her. Hold hard.'

The receiver clicked. Philip reached for his cigarettes as, on the telephone, he heard footfalls chiming in the big room. There was a kiss in there, then Nugent's footfalls sounded like panting.

There was clattering, breathing. 'Philip? Hold on. No, I'll be along in a second. Yes, yes, I know. Philip?'

'Hello?' Philip said, and he felt as though his heart had just sunk into a warm bath. 'Linda?'

'Oh, God, I am so glad to hear you. How *are* you? I gave

up on writing to you, and never heard *anything*. You must have been back. Mark says he saw you in January. I can't believe you didn't call.'

'No, well.' Philip found himself smiling. 'You know. Lots to do. Didn't want to rock the boat.'

'Oh, Philip!' she sighed. 'Don't talk gibberish. Rocking the boat never worried you. You were just running away. You should have called. Sam misses you. We all miss you. No, listen. You're back at Swynsmere, right?'

'Yes.'

'God, poor you. Freddy really is a goner from what I hear?'

''Fraid so.'

'Poor little Freddy. It all seems so monstrously unfair. I mean, there are we sinners, smoking, drinking, generally misbehaving, and it's the Freddies of the world that get the chop. He was sweet, really. Infuriating, but sweet.'

'Yes.'

'Right. Listen. You're coming over. Tomorrow? Sam's going to be so excited . . .'

'Listen, love, I'd love to, but not tomorrow. There's a ton of work to do.'

'The next day, then?' She sounded positively hurt. 'Please, Philip.'

And suddenly he knew that Nugent had left the room. Her voice was naked on that last plea. 'Linda . . .' he said softly.

'Yes?'

And there was a long silence.

'No, the day after tomorrow. Fine.'

'Good. Come,' again a pause, 'before lunch.'

'Sure. You're . . . OK?'

'Fine, fine! I've got to rush, we've got some chums in for supper. But everything's OK with you?'

'Everything's fine. I've missed you.'

'Mark said you were looking tanned and fit – I don't know.'

'Tanned, sure. God, I have dreamed of you, worried about you . . .'

'Well, you shouldn't go so far away, then, should you?'

159

'I couldn't stay so close and . . .'

'Well, it's no damned good. You shouldn't have gone. Sam misses you.'

'He must have grown.'

'He has. He's huge.'

'Are you . . . ?'

'I'm fine, fine. Don't . . .'

'Don't what?'

'OK, so, sort of round twelve or something. OK?'

'You know that I love you, you silly bitch?' Philip suddenly barked.

'Of course, idiot. We love you.' Her voice quavered, but she raised its pitch and gabbled on. 'Sam's fishing. He'll tell you. He caught . . . a six pound . . . grilse in Scotland . . . in the summer. You should . . . I'll show you the photographs. No. Listen. I hate the bloody telephone. I really . . . David's been so good, Philip.'

'I should bloody well hope so,' Philip croaked.

'Must go,' she breathed.

'Right.'

'See you.'

'Kid.'

He knew that the pet-name was a cruel valediction. She was his sister. He knew all her insecurities, all the pretensions with which she hid them. She would cry as she turned away. Come to think of it, he wasn't doing too well himself.

Philip's limbs were wool as he opened the back door of Mrs Bradley's house and tiptoed into the back hall. He kicked a plastic bucket, rocked sideways against a hanging coat and hushed himself.

He pushed open the inner, frosted-glass door and his toes sank deep into plush carpet. His coat made it sound as though he was skiing as he walked. In the sitting-room ahead of him, a female was belting out a torch-song. Applause made the television sound defective.

Philip slipped sideways into his room. He was not afraid of disturbing Mr Bradley, who, he suspected, would judge nuclear holocaust as good or bad television, and would be disturbed by nothing so much as a deficiency of beer. He was, however, afraid of disturbing Mrs Bradley, principally because she would insist on making him cocoa, filling a hot-water bottle for him and, probably, on engaging him in metaphysical speculation. He had discovered this unexpected interest last night. 'Do you believe in God, Mr Glaister, then?' she had whispered as, in powder-blue housecoat and pink fluffy slippers, she cut ham sandwiches for him.

'Yes, unless you mean, do I believe that God exists?'

'Well, yes.'

'No.'

'Oh.'

Philip approved Mrs Bradley's enquiries, but did not, at the moment, want to be a sounding board for her opinions. She had an unfortunate habit of coming very, very close to you as she spoke, occupying the body's Members' Enclosure. And she smelled of artificial violets.

But this evening he had failed in his bid to enter unheard. Even as he returned from opening the window and slumped down on to the bed to pull off his boots, there was a shy, shuffling knock at the door.

'Come!' he called, resolved to be gruff. He continued to tug at the left boot.

The door brushed open.

What walked in was not the short, scraggy twitching form of Mrs Bradley, but a figure of something akin, in a teenage magazine sort of way, to loveliness. It was a slender young man with fine features and blond hair puffed back and sprayed into stillness. A gold half-sovereign medallion hung between the plunging neckline of his frothy white shirt. His trousers were tight and black.

He smiled nervously. He said, 'Hi, there.' He tilted slightly, and had to support himself on the doorframe. He blinked.

'Gawd,' Philip stared. 'Who are you, then?'

'Sorry, mate. Tony.' The apparition held out a large hand. 'Son of the house, you know.'

161

'Yes.' Philip quickly shook the hand. He pushed at the right boot which flew off into the corner. 'Can I help you?'

'Nah, nah.' Tony smoothed his fossilized hair. His eyes were moist. He'd had a few. 'Just thought as I'd come and say, you know, wotcher, all that.'

Philip lowered his stockinged feet to the carpet. He relented. 'Good of you,' he said. 'Look, I'm going to bed pretty soon, but – would you like a quick drink?'

'God, yeah.' Tony perceptibly brightened.

'Have to be a toothmug.' Philip pushed himself to his feet. He padded to the windowsill and, reaching behind the curtain, pulled out a bottle of Famous Grouse. He span the lid, pulled down the toothmug and tipped up the bottle, which coughed. 'So. What do you do, then?'

'Ah, bit of everything. But had some bad luck, I have. Ta.' He sat crosslegged on the end of the bed. 'Well, bit of a villain, me. Just it always seems to go wrong. You know, good ideas, everything sorted, then something happens, you know, like there's a jinx. I've got a gift. Jeez. When I was fifteen, I thought I'd mug this guy. Jumped out, said, "Giss your money," he's only an army self-defence instructor, isn't he? Did a smash and grab, Christmas, got some booze from the window display. Invite, you know, a couple of mates, a couple of girls, fuck me if they're not display bottles all full of coloured water. Great party. Girls laugh themselves sick, don't they?'

Philip was staring wide-eyed at this rueful bungler. A smile twitched his lips. He said, 'Why don't you try something straight? You might be better suited to it?'

'I done things straight!' Tony yelped. 'It's just I want to pull off just one really nice little scam. You know, these other guys, flash buggers, lots of dosh, they've all done one, you know? Me, it just never works.' He whirled his toothmug of whisky around his head in apparent frustration.

Philip was spluttering faintly at this glorious confection who had appeared from nowhere – only begotten son of a metaphysician landlady and a compost heap – to relate this jeremiad. The confection looked splendidly morose.

'So last year,' Tony stated glumly, 'I think, this is it. Do

162

a creep, right? On my own. Tasty gaff out Lewes way, and I'm knocking off this bit of cuff works out there. I know it'll be empty, right? So it all goes like clockwork. I get in, clear up all this stuff – nice stuff, silver, snuff-boxes, cash – come down, there's the village bobby at the door. No problem. He's old and slow. I leap over the garden wall, all agile, like, land in a slurry heap. Now I'm stinking and I've got a sprained ankle, haven't I? Really heroic stuff. I hobble to the motor in the end, climb in, and fuck me, there's this patrol car behind me. Breakneck chase. Sure. Thirty yards of it because my ankle's hurting like hell and the car's no bloody good anyhow – straight into the bleeding village duck-pond. Eighteen months, I got for that. Jesus.' He drank and winced. 'I mean, villains ain't so darned bright, are they? There's top villains can't add two and two, so what's with me?'

Tony, Philip had decided, was a boon, a source of joy, a natural comic and a charmer. He could be useful, notwithstanding his avowed incompetence. 'So, what do you do now?' Philip struggled to keep his voice steady before Tony's doleful gaze.

'Plucking,' Tony said dolorously.

'Plucking?'

'And singeing. Yeah. Turkeys. You know, out Ripe. Batsfords Buttered Turkey Roast. I pluck 'em.'

'Tedious work.' Philip was sympathetic.

'Tedious! Gawd! But I've got a record, haven't I? Hardly going to give us a job in a bank, are they?'

'True.'

'No, I was just wondering if you had any suggestions, that's all.'

'As to what you might do?'

''Sright.'

'Well, Tony,' Philip took the toothmug from the turkey-plucker and threw it into the basin, 'I'll tell you what. Come up to the yard tomorrow, and I can show you round and we can have a talk because, funnily enough, I might, I just might, have something for you to do.'

*

Plump little boys become war heroes. Games stars become gross property-developers. Sweet, playful little girls become exploitative bed-hopping bitches. And you look at the papers and wonder at the conjuring trick which has been done, for, to those who have not watched the process, it is magical as the instant transformation of bouquet to rabbit or whatever. It has happened in a moment.

So Philip wondered, and resisted the growing conviction that sweet little Freddy had been a crook. As he read through the files that rainy day, he frowned, he told himself that the conclusion was absurd, he accepted that the absurd was possible and at last he knew that the impossible metamorphoses had indeed occurred without benefit of mirrors.

Freddy had been on the fiddle.

The awareness suddenly made Freddy seem more real than he had been since Philip had last seen him – alive and kicking, that is – all that time ago, nervously and apologetically helping to carry the suitcases to the taxi. And, being real, not merely a remembered amalgam of defined traits, Freddy somehow inspired Philip's understanding and affection more than ever before. Philip had been there, had undergone the same financial pressures. He too had sat at this desk and stared out into the yard and wondered how he could possibly keep the business going, the house warm, the lads paid.

It was perhaps harder to allow this business to go into liquidation than most others. It was, after all, a business devoted to nurture, a business founded upon endless hope. It was at home, too, and the welfare of yard and house were inseparable. The lads and girls were friends. They needed their jobs, of course, but, more than that, they too were devoted to their charges. Even the gruffest and most cynical amongst them would work through the night without thought of overtime if a horse was ill, and for them, as for Philip and Freddy, job and home were synonymous.

So Freddy too had sat in this chair casting his accountant's eye over the books, seeing them very differ-

164

ently from Philip, but unable to alter the bottom line or its implications, and he, like Philip, had been unwilling to go down without a fight.

The precise nature of his fighting was unclear. Five very hot favourites had been beaten during the past two years. So much was plain enough. A study of the form-book showed that they had come too late, been hampered or, in one case, cantered up sound and left the stalls lame. Another banker at the tail-end of last season had also contrived to get left at the start.

That there was money to be made by arranging for favourites to be beaten was obvious. Bookmakers like favourites to be beaten, and not even the most ardent of apologists for bookmakers would claim that there are not some ready to offer trainers and jockeys considerable sums to ensure this desirable result. As with geese and golden eggs, however, a trainer must balance short-term profit with long-term revenue. If too many good things get stuffed, rumours spread like a virus and the owners move elsewhere.

Freddy – to judge by the conversation at the pub – had been to the well too often.

The complainants at the pub, however, had also mentioned late withdrawals, and here Philip had to profess himself confused. Only bookmakers profit from beaten favourites, but bookmakers would derive no obvious benefit from the four fancied animals which, Philip discovered, had failed to reach the racecourse or to leave the racecourse stables. The market would simply have been adjusted, and no bet was valid on an animal which did not come under orders.

Philip picked up the telephone and called Jim Dobbs down to the office. Dobbs confirmed that, yes, on two occasions the horsebox had broken down on the way to the sports. Another hot favourite had been found to have knocked a knee just before leaving the Fontwell racecourse stables for the paddock. 'Run of bloody rotten luck,' he called it.

There was another anomaly here. On the first occasion

when the box had supposedly broken down, the race had been at Bath. For as long as Philip could remember, the Glaisters had stayed with Gemma and Jeremy Forsyth on the night before Bath or Wincanton races. It was a tradition. The Forsyths had a beautiful yard, and the practice had proved, in the past, to bring good fortune. On this day, with no apparent reason, Freddy in his car and the horse in its box had travelled down on the morning of the race. Had they not done so, of course, it would have been easy to arrange alternative transport for the horse to the racecourse.

When Jim Dobbs had gone, Philip rang Jeremy Forsyth. No, Jeremy told him after the usual exchange of greetings and sympathy, he had no idea why Freddy had broken with tradition on that day. They had been expecting him as usual. They had seen him at the races, questioned him, but he had merely been evasive. Busy, he had said, too busy. Things, you know?

It began to look, in other words, as though Freddy had wanted the horse to fail to arrive at the races, despite the inevitable penalty which he had had to pay for later withdrawal.

As the afternoon began to thicken, Philip pulled on a coat and drove down to Maynard's Motors. Joe Maynard sold motors, bent and straight. He also sold dope and dirty pictures to the stable-boys. As Philip walked into the Portakabin office, a young man with bakelite hair and a ring in his left ear stood. He muttered, 'Right. Sorry. Oh, hello.' He squeezed past Philip in the doorway.

The door rattled shut, the pinned-up invoices and the browning pictures of girls with wineskin tits flapped on the walls.

Joe Maynard was greyer and fatter than Philip remembered him. His face was like a seaside-postcard representation of several naked and adjacent bums. You could see every pore in the skin. He smiled to see Philip, and it was only then that a red haemorrhoid of a mouth appeared amidst the sagging spheres of flesh. His lips and his tongue crackled. He leaned back in his big chair. 'Well, well.' He spoke in a chortling cockney which made it sound more like 'Wow, wow'. 'Just look what we've got 'ere.'

'Hello, Joe.' Philip looked at the chair intended for customers. It looked unfit to accommodate a dung-beetle. It looked, too, as though a lot of dung-beetles had made use of it. He remained standing. 'Tell me. On or about September 11th and October 26th last year, you had the box in here, right?'

'If you say so,' Joe shrugged. The rest of him settled in layers, like silk unfurling. 'So?'

'Check it out. I want to know what the problem was.'

'Probably the engine went wrong.' A thin rasping laugh wriggled from him. 'That's usually the thing.'

Philip leaned forward, his fists clenched on the desk. 'Check it.'

Joe leaned back a little. That little berry of a lower lip shook. 'OK, OK. Gawd. September eleven. All this ordering about. Yes, sir, no, sir. Let's see.' He pulled a dark blue book towards him and flicked its grimy pages with a thumb like a saveloy. 'We been in the sunshine, 'ave we?'

'I have no idea where you have been,' Philip spoke on a monotone. 'Come on.'

'Shir-*tee*. 'Ere we are. September nine. Glaister.'

'No. After.'

'Oh, yeah. All right, all right. Hold it one. Yeah. September twelve. That's right. Broke down way out in the wilds.'

'What was the problem?'

'Water in the fuel system. 'Appens with diesel. Petrol engine now, burns your water up, dunnit? Diesel, you gets – you know, there's water about in, like, the pumps, things like that. There's a water filter, see, a trap, but it'll only 'old a cupful. You get water in the system itself, the 'ole thing seizes up, like. 'Ave to drain the whole shooting match, don't you?'

'That's it? That's all it takes? A cupful of water in the fuel tank?'

'That'll do it, yeah.'

'And the October date? The twenty-sixth?'

'Bloody Nora,' Joe grumbled. He snapped the book shut.

167

'Come on. I don't need to look it up, do I? Same thing, weren't it? Water in the fuel system. Gawd, I don't know. What's with you? You need a new one? Put a rag in. That'll work. Or I can give you a dodgy turbo-charger. They won't fix that by the roadside, though.'

'You told Freddy this?'

''Course I bloody did. Didn't know 'is arse'ole from breakfast time about engines, did 'e? So I tells 'im, that's the way to do it. Glass o' water, your diesel's fucked, I says.'

Philip winced. He still could not work out why anyone should go to the trouble and expense entailed in boxing up horses and taking them halfway to the races only to fake engine failure and return home. 'Right,' Philip pointed, suddenly fierce, 'do you know what this was in aid of?'

Joe Maynard gave another of his interesting shrugs. With some effort, he linked his hands behind his neck. He pushed his chair back with his knee. His smirk made his upper lip vanish, his lower bulge. 'Maybe.' He raised one black eyebrow. 'Maybe . . .'

He grunted. Suddenly he was doubled over the desk, his mouth open. It showed a lot of pink behind strands of spittle. The edge of the desk drove into his belly. His chubby hands flapped and flailed.

His head jerked back, whiplash. His chair's feet shrieked on stone. The chair toppled.

As he went down, as the chair's back smacked against the wall and split, he saw above shuddering flesh Philip's gritted teeth, Philip's dun hair flopping over glaring eyes. His crown hit the wall. The spheres sang in his skull.

The chair back scraped down the wall. A calendar thumped on the bridge of his nose and spread over his face, then he was down, his legs kicking like those of a baby at changing time. The desk's edge dug deep into his groin, and Philip was on top of him, grasping a clump of greasy hair, twisting hard. 'I said, *what was it in aid of*, you filthy, fat, fudge-packing crook?' Philip pestled out the words.

'I don't know,' Joe squealed and kicked. 'I don't know! Honest I don't!'

'Know that nice little red Porsche out there?' Philip jerked his head. 'I am going out there now, and I'm going to pulp it. Windscreen, lights, bonnet, roof . . . And if . . .' he added another twist to the greasy strands in his fist, 'if you haven't told me by the time I'm done, I'll start on *you*. Toes, shins, kneecaps and so, disgustingly, on. *Tell* me.'

'No. Really, I don't know. Really. No.' Joe's breath was hot and humid as the blast of a basement kitchen on Philip's face. It smelled of fish. 'Please, Philip. We don't know. Really. Please . . .'

'Mister fucking Glaister to you.' Philip jerked the big head further back. For once, Joe Maynard had just one chin, above a neck like a Lucien Freud stomach. '*Tell* me.'

'I don't *know*!'

Philip felt the words revving and skidding beneath his chest. Maynard's eyes were erratically shifting molluscs, but water gathered in the deep pink basins which were their shells. 'Honest, please, Mister Glaister. I just thought – shit – I mean – twice 'e dun get the 'orses to the races. I think maybe – maybe 'e's got some scam going. That's all, I swear. 'E didn't tell me nothing. Honest. It's an 'abit, Mister Glaister. Knowing more 'an the next guy, you know? 'Swat everyone wants, 'innit? A bit of the inside. But all 'e gives me – all 'e gives me is a pony, just to shut up.'

Philip looked down on the blubbery, blubbing creature who gasped for breath beneath him. He believed him, regretfully, if only because he knew that, at the prospect of personal violence, let alone a damaged Porsche, Joe Maynard would prostitute his infant daughter.

'Next time you dare to look me in the eye or speak my name,' Philip hissed, 'I shall render you.'

He dropped the head. He picked himself up. He kicked the toppled desk out of his way. He was wiping his hands on his trousers as he walked to the door.

'Er . . .'

Philip turned. Maynard had raised his head sheepishly above the desk. His jowls were very pale now, his hair tousled. 'Er, look, like, sorry, Mister . . .'

169

'That's better,' Philip bared his teeth. 'What is it?'

'Well, like, render me what?'

Philip's laugh was like a door slamming. A moment later, the door slammed too.

'Hold it, mate, would you?' Tony touched Philip's shoulder before the bar's doors stopped puffing. There was a grim set to his jaw. He was off to battle.

'Sure.' Philip did not care. He was glad just to be here in the warmth of the fire and the soft glow from the fairy-lights which studded the bar. After the swooping, speckled wind outside which sounded like an asthmatic in an echo-chamber, after the scents of Maynard's sweat and breath, he was even glad of the tinkling piped music and the funereal burble of conversation from the locals. A few of them worked for Swynsmere. Philip nodded. They nodded back. He was just a local again.

He walked to the bar, ordered Guinness and, finding a *Daily Mail* there, read it with one eye. With the other, he watched Tony, who was moving in on a dumpy little girl with a white face and a heavy veil of dark brown hair. It was an impressive performance. Tony parked himself beside her. He sniffed a bit. He ran those slender fingers through his beautiful coiffure. Then he sniffed a bit more. He frowned. He raised one foot then the other, studying the soles. He leaned over to the girl, an expression of disgust on his face. 'Is that you?' he asked.

'Sorry?' She was not good at aloof, but she did her best.

'That pong. Gor. Bloody disgusting. Let's 'ave a look at your shoes.'

Already faintly smiling, the girl raised her right foot across her left leg. Tony was down there, all elegance, giving the foot and the attached leg a once over. 'Nope.' He shook his head. 'Must be the other one.'

She raised the left foot, this time by kicking it backward. Tony grasped the shoe, sniffed, nuzzling in there. 'Nope. Lovely,' he announced with surprise. 'Oh, well. Must be someone else.'

'I don't smell anything.' She giggled uncertainly.

170

'Nah.' He straightened, gave her that blazing smile. 'Nor do I,' he admitted. 'Just thought I'd like to talk to you.'

Yes, he was in. She was smiling, flattered.

'Like a drink?' Tony pointed at her empty glass. He did not give her time to answer. 'Yeah, 'course you do. 'Ere, George! This girl 'asn't an ounce of flesh on 'er and you're just letting 'er waste away. Forget the fat old farts, this is a case of life and death.'

George lumbered over and busied himself with optics. Tony leaned in close to the girl. ''Ear you keep parrots, then, that right?'

Again the girl giggled. 'Nah. What you talking about, then?' Her voice was as high-pitched as a rivulet.

'Well, I'm amazed. I am ay-mazed. My mate, I says, she's a nice looking girl. 'E says, "She's 'ad a cockatoo", so naturally I thought . . . oh, well.'

Philip winced, but, God, she was laughing, hitting out at Tony in mock reproof, a little girl with her trusted playmate. Philip could not help wondering how Tony's technique would work in the salons of Mayfair. Probably brilliantly, if you happened to be Tony.

He gave him a chance to finish his drink, render his ultimate triumph inevitable, then he cleared his throat and leaned towards the two lovebirds. 'Mr Bradley?' he said. 'I am sorry. If I could just drag you away. The messages for you have been piling up all day. We've got some serious decisions to discuss.'

Tony rose to it like Georgie Best to a floater. 'Gawd. Don't they never leave us alone? All right, Phil, be with you in a sec. Just get us another drink in, there's a good chap.'

Philip allowed himself a small smile. Like a good chap, he bought more drinks.

'Bit of all right, that, eh?' Tony slid in beside him on the banquette a few minutes later.

'Absolutely,' Philip agreed tactfully. 'You manage to set something up?'

'Yeah. Disco Thursday. Might walk 'er 'ome tonight, if you don't bang on too long.' He caught the eye of the girl

171

at the bar. He waggled his fingers at her. 'So, what's it all about, then?'

'Ever hear about the poacher gamekeeper?'

'Sure.'

'Well, that's you. You made a lousy villain, let's see how you do as a cop.'

'You mean, legal, like?' Tony looked crestfallen.

'A cop, I said.' Philip raised an eyebrow. 'Since when did cops use legal means to catch villains?'

'Gor,' said Tony, and the grin returned. 'Lovely grub.'

In the darkest corner of the pub, over by the pool-tables, Vincent Lovelady watched with interest as Philip Glaister, with much cautious glancing over his shoulders, explained something to a flashy boy whose chest and fingers fired gold tracer whenever he moved. Strange associations automatically made Lovelady suspicious. They did not come much stranger than this.

Philip Glaister was a snob, he told himself. He at once corrected himself. No. Not, at least, a social snob. In his earlier investigations, Vincent had discovered that the stable-lads invariably spoke of Philip as odd, but a good mate, no side to him, always ready to muck in. The Swynsmere visitors' book, too, which Vincent had had cause to study in depth, had contained the names of has-been pop stars, lowly actors, a couple of nurses of inauspicious origins, an old nanny and an author whose fame did not extend beyond ferreting circles, in amongst the race-horse owners and the golden lads and lasses.

The class least represented in Swynsmere's guest list had, in fact, been the snobs – the respectable, the refined. Bank robbers might dine there, but bank managers might well be sent round to the back door. Bearded, barefoot men and girls in Oxfam gear might stroll amongst the designer dresses, but dark, three-piece suits and narrow ties were rarities. No, Philip's brand of snobbery would once have been seen as a political allegiance. He was a cavalier. He detested roundheads.

172

As a grotesque for a cavalier's collection, his present companion was not, perhaps, that extraordinary after all. The flares, the gold, the outrageous shirt and bootlace tie were effeminate, and it was difficult to imagine just what this boy and brusque Philip might find to discuss with such seriousness. Viewed merely as an acquisition, however, this graceful exemplar of bad taste as a fine art was not, perhaps, inapposite. Philip would take pleasure in introducing the lad to the likes of that solicitor of his, Snaith.

One thing, however, struck Vincent Lovelady as certain. Unless Philip had changed sex or sexual predilection during his exile, he and his companion were up to no good.

Vincent Lovelady had pursued his interest in Freddy Glaister's accident because he had That Feeling and because, in retirement, he could think of nothing better to do. On the face of it, there was no problem. The doctors were agreed that an acute asthma attack had caused Freddy's moribund condition. 'Acute asthma' would doubtless be written, in some form or another, on the inevitable death certificate. Vincent's business was insuring racehorses, and no claim had been made relating to a racehorse. The life insurance policy was with a sister company and was no concern of his.

But he was an insurance man, he knew the set up, and he had That Feeling.

Even that would not have been sufficient to send him snuffling around at Swynsmere again. Many stories in the newspapers gave him That Feeling, yet he ignored them. They were someone else's concern. Two factors combined to bring Vincent Lovelady to the Dog and Duck this evening. One was that Barbara had enrolled in a First Aid course which took her from the house for two evenings every week. The other was that – well, to be honest, he had *enjoyed* Philip Glaister.

It is a commonplace, of course, that the hunter must, to some extent, become his prey. He must see with its eyes, hear with its ears, think as it thinks. Vincent had imagined the thoughts and feelings of many hundreds of men and women, which was why, unlike his friends in the police, he was in no hurry to condemn. In Philip's case, sympathy had taken him longer than for any other subject besides that of a psychopathic stud-groom who had actually enjoyed eviscerating mares. Vincent had found Philip rude, assertive, self-indulgent, depressive and arrogant. It had been very difficult to see as such a man must see, to think as he thought, but Vincent Lovelady had made the effort, and he had enjoyed it.

Philip was funny and sceptical but essentially an enthusiast. He liked human beings. Had he not done so, his comedy would have been simply cruel. He despised human stupidity but did not consider himself free of that original sin. He parodied himself as ruthlessly as others. The only crimes which he did not allow were priggishness and complacency. His jokes were a hand shoved up a uniform skirt.

Vincent had found himself giggling suddenly as he drove home from Swynsmere. His attempts to repeat Philip's jokes or to replicate his mimicry had fallen rather flat with Barbara, who had been on a Psychology for Beginners course at the time.

But Vincent had liked brooding and reading in pubs. He had liked cloak-trailing – oh, a modest cloak, to be sure, and strictly within the bounds of taste and propriety – and, above all, he had liked preparing and delivering Glaisterisms (as he dubbed them) about his wife's friends and his colleagues. That he had delivered them only to the mirror or to his patient old beagle had in no wise diluted his pleasure. On the contrary, it made of Glaisterizing a guilt-free, solitary vice. Just as, for some, pornography was liberating in that it created the illusion of a demimonde free of sexual constraints or responsibility, so emulating Philip had given Vincent the illusion of liberty from niceness. It was heady, dangerous stuff, but it was fun, and Vincent flattered himself that he had a natural talent for this sort of thing. He did not – could not – like Philip, but, in some curious, fantastic way, he did envy him.

The effects of reminiscence, coupled with those of two

glasses of barley wine, were to console Vincent. He knew that he must either approach Philip now or go home and not come back. There had been moments in the past half hour when he had felt giving up to be the only sane, the only sensible thing to do, but contemplation of Philip and his nature made Vincent bold and careless of sanity and sense. He downed the last of his barley wine. He stood.

Philip saw him immediately. Vincent felt rather than saw the suddenly narrowed eyes, the suddenly tight set of the mouth, the sudden steely glint of the eyes. He felt like a Frenchman at some telepathic Agincourt. The arrows blotted out the sun. He very deliberately, however, did not look to the source of these emanations. With a voice only slightly higher-pitched than usual, he asked the landlord for another drink. With a gloved hand which was almost steady, he counted out the cash. Then he turned, very casually, fixed a smile of recognition on his face and, looking at a point about a foot above Philip's eyes, approached his prey.

'Ah, Mr Glaister,' he bleated, 'I thought it was you. It is good to see you.'

'I would that it were good to see you, Lovelady. Go away.'

'Lovelady!' mimicked Tony. 'Gor, is his name really Lovelady?'

'It is,' Philip sorrowfully shook his head, 'but you have the inflection wrong. The name is not a boast nor a statement of intent, but a hopeless imprecation, worn like a message on a beggar's back – "Love, lady?" His family have worn it ineffectually for generations, but what lady, pray, can bring herself to love this pimple on Beelzebub's buttock? Impossible! Bugger off, Love-lady.'

'May I join you?' Vincent was smiling very happily now.

'Tell me, Tony, if someone says to you "go away", "fuck off", "efface yourself", "evanesce", do you not consider that he has no desire for your company? At the lower end of the evolutionary scale, however – beasts such as weevils and other burrowing parasites – such linguistic sophistication is obviously unknown. Hence Rentokil. Listen very

175

carefully, Lovelady. No, you may not join us. You may – indeed, you must – leave, bugger off, begone.'

'It *is* nice to see you,' Vincent was coy. 'Just like the old days. I was saying to Barbara the other day . . .'

'Go away, Lovelady,' said Philip. 'Watch my lips. Push off.'

'No, really, I was saying when I saw about your brother's accident – I was sorry about that – I wonder how Mr Philip Glaister is.'

'Well, now you know.'

'And I knew you wouldn't hold it against me – that little contretemps. I told Barbara that.'

Philip stared bewildered at the little man in the hat. He felt that he was losing his grip. First Jenny Laing, now Vincent Lovelady, had blithely stood their ground when he had given of his best to be rid of them.

And as he watched Lovelady standing there with a smile on his face and the flush of alcohol in his cheeks, as he saw the ridiculous moustache, the ghastly titfer, the car-coat, the shiny trousers, an idea planted itself in his head and rapidly grew.

He kicked a vacant chair. 'All right,' he snapped, amazed at himself. 'Sit down, I want to speak to you. You know about villainy. You may be able to help.'

Vincent coloured still further as he tucked the coat neatly beneath him. He rapidly sat.

Unlikely associations made Vincent's nose twitch. Had he been sitting in the shadows watching this triumvirate of which he was now a part, a cokehead rabbit could not have out-twitched him.

'It's all arse about face, as I was explaining to Tony,' Philip said. 'I've been through Freddy's betting account. When he stopped those horses or prevented them running, he never once had a bet. On the other hand, he had several big winning bets in similar contests in which he wasn't engaged but which followed the same pattern – favourites scratched or suffering accidents – but that in itself is not remarkable. Backing the second favourite is a pretty successful general policy. So, let's suppose that Freddy was dancing to the tune of our mystery telephone caller. Another problem. The voice says "Scratch Plutonium", but Freddy hadn't scratched Plutonium. On the contrary, I think it seems clear that he was *protecting* Plutonium. That's why he had Ludo in Plutonium's box and vice versa.'

'That certainly seems a reasonable contention.' Vincent Lovelady wiped his moustache on the back of his hand. 'Yes.'

'Reasonable contention be fucked,' announced Philip. 'Oh God, why must you wear that ridiculous hat and talk such unutterable drivel? A little air to the skull might sort out the brain problem. It is obvious that was what he was doing. So we assume he had conceded to earlier demands to fix races and refused to concede to this one.'

'We may also assume,' said Lovelady, 'that whoever came to Swynsmere that night still has an interest in seeing Plutonium injured or in some way prevented from running.'

Philip nodded, then the full import of the words sank in. 'Jesus, you're right. Wouldn't lend me that hat, would you? Brain's in neutral. Tony, you know the way. Get down to the yard and patrol. I'll be up in an hour or so, see you comfortable, discuss tactics, OK?'

'But what about . . . ?' Tony winked towards his girlfriend up at the bar.

'I'm offering you money, man,' Philip barked. 'Go. Take your floozie with you if you think she fancies snogging in the straw and the rain. Just get down there. You see anyone who can't explain himself, fracture a limb or two, OK?'

'But my shoes!' Tony wailed.

'They're not shoes,' Philip was dismissive, 'they're plastic pumps. Go, man, will you? I'll buy you more shoes. I'll buy you new Carmen rollers. Just get down to the bloody yard!'

'All right, all right,' Tony pouted. 'Gawd, bloody night-watchman, nannying a load of nags, I dunno.' He waved

to his girlfriend. He mouthed, 'See you Thursday, right?'
He flung her a smile to keep her warm until then, and,
grumbling, loped to the door.

'Right, then.' Philip drew his chair closer to the table.
'You are an experienced truffle hunter, Lovelady. Sink
your muzzle into this little mess and see if you can come
up with anything.'

'If I can help in any way,' Vincent nodded, 'I will,
of course. If you could appraise me of the pertinent
details . . . ?'

Philip stared at him. 'Where do they teach you to talk
like that? "Appraise me of the pertinent details"? I'd like to
examine your phrenology one day, once they've removed
the more offensive things – hat, hair, skin, all that. There
must be an unsightly bump there where such awful official-
ese crap festers and proliferates. If you want me to fill you
in on the facts, tell you what's happened, bring you up to
date, explain the problem, why not say so? Right. Listen.
Something's badly wrong . . .'

It was half past eight when Vincent and Philip left the pub
and drove down to the yard. It was just after nine when
Vincent rang Barbara from the office to explain that he
would be late. It was half past ten when at last he left, his
arms full of papers.

'It will cost you,' he called back into the light, 'but I'll
keep it down as much as I can, and quite a few of the
things I can borrow.'

'Good.' Philip appeared in the doorway behind him.
'Maybe you have uses after all. I'll see you tomorrow
morning, and let's hope you can make more sense of this
rigmarole than I've been able to. Tony!' he called. 'Are you
still awake out there?'

Tony emerged from the shadows, tiptoeing uncertainly
over the cobbles. 'Yeah,' he said. 'Gawd, it's getting bloody
freezing out here, and about as much fun as watching
paint warp. Can I go home?'

'Nope. Not yet. We'll go back in a minute. Tomorrow,

178

Mr Lovelady is going to bring us some security equipment. Tonight we're just going to have to improvise. All right, Lovelady. You bugger off back to the good Barbara and polish up the grey matter. Drive carefully.'

'Thank you, Mr Glaister.' Vincent trotted back to his dark blue Lada Riva. 'I'm sure we'll come up with something.'

He sidestepped into the car. Tony and Philip watched as it coughed and shook and, with a sigh, moved off.

'Right,' Philip said. 'First thing, we move Plutonium – let's see, shift him over to that box where the brown colt is . . .'

'Not me,' Tony gulped. 'I can't be doing with those things.'

'What?'

'Horses. Bloody things fart and kick and they're bigger'n me. Don't like 'em, me. Bloody mad, they are, and the people as likes 'em, you ask me.'

Philip glowered at his ill-chosen lieutenant. He swung round and stalked over to the tackroom. Tony sheepishly followed. 'Well, I mean, I never said as I liked bleeding horses, did I?' he whined. 'I'm not your agricultural type, me.'

'I had noticed.' Philip switched on the light and reached down a leather headcollar. 'No. OK. I'll sort out the horses. You just cast an eye about here and see what you can find in the way of booby-traps, alarms, anything that'll give an intruder a surprise.'

Philip moved the Deep Run colt to an empty box. He led Plutonium, who tried to bite his hand off, to the newly vacated box, then installed the Deep Run colt into Plutonium's. As he did so, he reflected that Freddy had done just this on the night of his death and for the same reasons. Freddy had been on the fiddle, but had wanted the family's most valuable asset to run, threats notwithstanding. Was it possible, then, that there were two entirely separate groups of people stopping horses or preventing them from running – Freddy's group, as it were, and another, far more resolute and violent?

Philip knew that all this was futile. If some professional

villain with enough money invested truly wanted to nobble Plutonium, he would do so, here, in transit or at the racecourse. He could only try to deter whoever it might be in the short term.

Philip was surprised to find that he was seriously angry. In part, of course, this was merely his nature. When people threatened him or gave him orders, he reacted against them, just as certain horses stop so soon as the jockey produces the whip. But other influences were working on him. Freddy, that irritating, nagging, well-meaning little gadfly, had become very much more real and his plight much sadder since Philip had returned here to Swynsmere, seen what Freddy had seen, worried as Freddy had worried. Philip was convinced that Freddy had died because of another person. If it was not murder, it was none the less clear that whoever had been in the yard that night had not bothered to go to poor Freddy's aid as he had wheezed and droned and drowned. Philip wanted – he mocked himself for it, but the urge was there – he wanted revenge. He could beat up his brother if he felt like it, but no other bugger did, not whilst Philip lived.

He found too that he cared very much about Plutonium. Oh, he hated the bloody leery animal; he shuddered from the very sight of him, but he was none the less a Glaister creation. Years of hard work and worry and nurture had gone to create this brilliant pig, and, just as Philip would fight for an inheritance with infinitely greater passion than for an acquisition, so he felt now that, in defending Plutonium, he acted on behalf of his father, of Freddy, of Sam and of the countless lads and girls who had laboured and prayed for Erebus and for Swynsmere.

He felt quite delightfully primitive, in short, as now he and Tony went about their work. They stretched binder twine tripwires across the yard and attached them to aluminium buckets and dustbin lids on doors and window-sills. It was childish, perhaps, but at least it would serve to give any intruder a bit of a shock, and might – just might – awake Jim Dobbs.

Philip had entered the Deep Run colt's box for one last

180

glance around when suddenly he frowned and pointed upward. 'What the fuck's that?' he asked.

Tony, carefully keeping Philip between him and the horse, stepped into the corner of the box and gazed upward.

'Well, it's a light, isn't it?' he supplied helpfully.

'I know it's a light,' Philip spoke from the corner of his mouth, 'but what are those two wires doing?'

'Well, you need wires, with an electric light.'

'Tony,' Philip was gracious, 'I can't think how I ever lived without you. Don't be gormless, or more than necessary, anyway. I was aware that flexes were commonly used to conduct electricity to light sockets. If you will look more carefully, however, you will note that there are two sets of flexes there. One runs to the light. The other looks as though it serves the light, but in fact, if you look closely, you'll see that it goes up into the ceiling. It shouldn't be there.'

'You sure?'

'I ran this yard for six years, Tony. It shouldn't be there.'

'Cripes,' Tony whistled. 'Could be a bomb or something.'

'No,' Philip shook his head slowly. 'Bombs aren't usually on the mains. Get us a chair or something, will you?'

Tony crunched gratefully out into the darkness. He returned a minute later with a saddle-stand from the tack-room. He handed it to Philip at arm's length. He retreated again into the corner.

Philip tied the colt's head to the ring in the wall. He soothed and pushed the animal around until he stood directly beneath the light socket. He used the saddle-stand as a mounting block. He clambered on to the colt's broad back.

'Easy,' he told the horse as he stood. Beneath him, the animal shifted from foot to foot. 'Woah, now. Stay still, there's a lad . . .' He reached up and grasped the extra pair of flexes. His hand followed them up to the whitewashed ceiling. He tapped. 'Panel here,' he mused softly. He pushed, and a small square of thin plywood gave easily to his touch. He reached in. 'Red light,' he murmured.

'What?' Tony stood with his hands before his chest as though to halt a charging horse or the blast of a bomb. His voice was high-pitched.

'Well, well.' Philip's eyebrows were raised. He had pulled a little white box from the cavity. 'We are overheard, it seems . . .'

'What?'

'Ever seen one of these?' Philip held the box up for Tony's inspection.

'Yeah,' Tony nodded. 'That's a baby alarm, right? Shit, you mean someone's bugging us with a bleedin' baby alarm?'

'Sort of, yes, but I don't think that's the intention. What you said about nannying nags seems to have been taken still more literally by certain people.' Philip replaced the contraption and pulled the panel of wood back into position. 'Well, well.' He dusted off his hands. He jumped down into the straw. 'At least we know why Freddy came up here that night.' He smiled sadly. 'Clever old Floozo. Bet he did exactly what we've done tonight. That's why Jim Dobbs thought the sound was familiar. Bloody well should have been. A bucket hitting cobbles must be amongst the most familiar sounds in his life. It's something Alex and I used to do when we were playing here as children. Jesus.' He shook the memories from his head.

'You mean you're just leaving it there?' Tony was staring.

'Course I bloody am. Come on. We've done all we can.' Philip untied the horse's head. He picked up the saddle-stand and went out into the yard.

Tony slipped through at his side. Philip shut the lower door. Then he called back into the box. 'Night, Alison,' and he switched off the light.

The post van was leaving as Philip led his small string back into the yard the following morning. In the office, he rifled through the pile of envelopes and impatiently opened one. The letter was neatly typed:

Dear Philip,
Mr Heron and I are more than a little surprised at your effrontery. We acknowledge no 'deal' entailing a fee as to yourself. Mr Heron asked Mr Duggan to pay you the sum of £500 as a generous token of gratitude for your solicitousness during our sojourn at L'Hermitage. No other transaction took place, so your pathetic threats of disclosure seem hardly compelling.
Please restrain these fevered illusions and do not disturb Mr Heron further.
Yours sincerely,
Angela Duncan

Philip nodded slowly. He pulled out his pen. On a sheet of Swynsmere paper, he tried again:

Dear Angela,
Please don't try it on. My friends in France are perfectly capable of identifying the participants from photographs if you compel me to ask them to do so. I am sure that the tabloids would be delighted to know of the services which I rendered Mr Heron.
Please just pay up and we can forget the whole thing.
Philip

The dashboard of a Lada was an unsatisfactory desk. Philip had form-books at his feet, Freddy's betting accounts in his lap, various notebooks scattered on the dashboard. He was frankly confused.

Beside him, in car-coat and driving gloves, Vincent Lovelady seemed composed. 'You will notice some anomalies,' he said.

'I will, will I?'

'You will. First, as you have observed, there is no record of Mr Frederick's having bets on the races which we have reason to consider suspicious. On the other hand, he did

183

have some very successful bets on other races in which favourites were beaten.'

'I got that far.'

'Yes, but obviously we have to see if those races have anything in common. I'd like you to have a look at them. Perhaps you will recognize something that I would not.'

'What sort of something?'

'I don't know. Maybe a trainer of a beaten favourite in one race is the brother-in-law of the trainer of another in another. If we are assuming, and I think that we must assume, that these favourites were beaten by design and that Mr Frederick was privy to that design . . .'

'Now, that's much more like English,' Philip beamed.

'Thank you. Well, then, are there connections between them? Can we see the trace of a conspiracy?'

'OK. I get your drift. OK. Let's start with the Stratford race.' Philip reached down for a form-book. 'Here we are. March this year. The Lady Polly Waller Memorial Handicap Chase. Three and a quarter miles. Going good. Odds on favourite was Corinium. Well, he would be, of course. Bloody good animal, always was. Trained by Ferdy Black in Lambourn, ridden by Paul Tracey. Second favourite, Lilli Burlero, trained by Louis Lauderdale in Yorkshire, ridden by Steve – Steve Shand, that is. Freddy goes thirty-three grand to seven-and-a-half Sir Orfeo, I mean, that's going deep, for Christ's sakes. Something like a third of his total income. So maybe he's got a hot tip.'

'Maybe.' Vincent licked his moustache.

'Sir Orfeo is trained by Maria Thornton up in Yorkshire, ridden by Nick Storr; Corinium jumped the last in the lead, ran on one paced, easily headed in the straight. Lilli Burlero falls at the first.'

'Right. Could be a straight run race, could be fixed. Let's move on to the next one. Thirsk, wasn't it?'

'That's right. Flat race, so hardly any of the participants are the same. Seven-furlong sprint, won by Bay of Biscay, seven to two second favourite – oh, yes. He was trained by Louis Lauderdale, in fact, but then that doesn't make any sense, does it? If Lauderdale's hooking a horse in one race,

184

how come he's winning the next? Jockeys are all different. The favourite, Rosicrucian, dwelt badly, made headway but could make no impression on Bay of Biscay. Stewards' enquiry, actually. What did Freddy have on that one? Two grand. Two grand at seven to two. "Lovely grub", as our young friend Tony would say.'

'And then there was Warwick. What was that again?'

'That was the one big loss, wasn't it? Yeah, well, the participants there – hold on. Yup. Again, yes, some of the same jockeys, but there would be. You've only got a pool of twenty or so to draw on. Winner was Clarendon, trained by Rambo Dowty, ridden by Paddy Sheehan. Only problem is, bloody animal's a steaming hot favourite, isn't it? Freddy went for our animal, again ridden by Steve. Bloody thing ran a blinder too, but was caught in the last furlong and didn't have the pace to make up ground . . .'

'Mmm. No. I couldn't find a significant resemblance between any of the races,' Vincent said sadly.

'And what's it got to do with whoever came to the yard? OK, so he or she wanted to get at Plutonium. Do we assume that was linked to all these good things and to Freddy's stopping our animals? If so, what in God's name is the connection?'

'I don't know.' Vincent shook his head. 'And then there's the business of the inhaler, the strange behaviour of Mrs Glaister . . .'

'That's not so strange,' Philip objected. 'Not if she was listening on the baby alarm.'

'Well, no,' Vincent popped a boiled sweet in his mouth, 'but is hers a normal reaction? Woman on her own, middle of the night, hears a fracas, surely she calls the police first, doesn't she, not just run up, unarmed?'

'Good point.' Philip let the form-books thud down on to the floor. He reached for his cigarettes. 'No, but there are plenty of explanations for that. It was Freddy who was alerted by the alarm, right? So Alison may not have been in the same room. She comes in five minutes after Freddy leaves, just hears all the wheezing, worries about her poor

185

husband and legs it. She needn't have known that anyone else was there. No, I'd love it to be her, but it doesn't tally. Look how she fought to save him.'

'Hm.' Vincent unwrapped a sweet with a lot of crackling. 'All very dramatic, that.'

'Maybe, but if I were involved in someone's murder, I'd not be insisting on keeping that someone alive. There's always the danger – small, I'll grant you – that the victim will point a finger at you and gasp "murderer" before the last. No. Ali's all sorts of crazed, hysterical bitch, but she's sincere about Freddy. She wants him alive, *ergo* she didn't kill him.'

'No,' the boiled sweet clicked on Vincent's teeth, 'but I'd very much like to talk to her about her betting. Suppose she'd been laying against your losers, in cash, probably, so there'd be no evidence of any jiggery-pokery? That would account for the absence of tallying bets in the account-books. One anomaly out of the way at least.'

'True. One of many, but it's a step in the right direction. OK. Let's talk to her. We probably won't get anywhere but we'll give it a try. Right, it's just up here to the left.'

'Oh, I look forward to seeing the late Mrs Glaister again.' Vincent's right index finger arose and hooked to stroke his moustache. 'Indeed I do. Always had a soft spot for the late Mrs Glaister, I did.'

'For God's sake stop referring to her as "the late", would you? She's divorced and remarried, not dead.' Philip unwound the window to toss out a cigarette. 'Anyhow, it's never the soft spots that do the damage.' His fingers scrabbled slowly at the corduroy on his thigh. 'Listen, Lovelady. I could do with your help on another little matter.'

'Say the word.' Vincent was munificent. 'Just say the word. If I can, and if it's legal . . .'

'I need a photographer, or rather someone who can doctor photographs. Do you know anyone like that?'

'Mmmyees.' Vincent's hat bobbed. 'Yes, there was a case once. Dead horse. All sorts of fake photographs produced as evidence of natural death. We had a man then. He

186

showed me how it was done. The photographs were good. They'd have fooled me. He saw through them right off. Astonishing.'

'Would you arrange an introduction?'

'Oh, yes, yes. Of course. If he's still around, no problem. He's in East London somewhere. I'll look him up.'

'And another thing.' Philip gulped as the car turned on to the long, straight drive of deep washed gravel.

'Yes?'

'Do you know any pornographers?'

'Not personally,' said Vincent solemnly. 'No. I can't say as I do . . .'

Linda jumped down the steps two at a time. She said, 'Hello, sweet Mister Lovelady. What are you doing here? Come in and have a drink.' She ran round the car and flung her arms about Philip. 'Philip, darling. Oh, I am so glad to see you. God, you look roué and rough and lovely.'

She kissed him noisily on both cheeks, then quickly, lightly on the mouth. She stood back but kept his hands in hers. She blinked.

Philip blinked back. He had forgotten the scent of her, the sight of her, the feel; forgotten, that is, in that they were familiar as the scent of the nursery, yet had become, like the scent of the nursery, a dream, so transfigured as to render the reality shocking.

Look. Try to appraise her as a stranger might, not gilt by the light of past summers. What? She was a pale blonde – or, at least, a heavily highlighted mouse. Her hair was thinnish and straight and fell straight to her shoulders. She had pale eyes, a wriggling mouth, pink by nature, pinker by artifice, and a little, much kissed snub nose. Her face was startanned, spattered with little light freckles which she hated. Her breasts were full. She had a tendency to spread into cloudy Rubensian softness. One day her body would be welcoming rather than challenging, but her legs would never be less than perfect nor her smile less fresh than first frost.

187

Philip said huskily, 'Shame about the boat-race, kid.'

'Yeah,' she said, 'I know.'

'Damn your eyes. Damn the whole lovely lot of you.'

'Come on,' she urged softly, though her eyebrows arose as though she were questioning. She squeezed his hands. 'No. Everything's fine.' Her head swivelled from side to side like the pages of a skimmed book. 'Ah! Oh! Here we are!' She grinned up at the white portico. 'Sam! Come and say hello to Daddy!'

Sam was still Sam, still evidently his boy, for all that he was twice the size at which Philip had seen him last. He stood beside Nugent on the stoop. His face became broad. His eyes became nail-parings. His nose developed insect-legs. His teeth gleamed. He ran down to his mother. He grasped her black-stockinged thigh. He hid his blond head behind the thigh. He beamed out from between her legs. He hid again.

Philip's mouth was spread in a broad involuntary grin. His eyes were full. He held out a hand to his son. 'Come here, runt,' he said. 'By the right, quick march!'

Sam stepped out from behind his mother and goose-stepped to his father. Linda covered her mouth with her hand. Philip had taught Sam to march thus because he was blond and blue-eyed and because it affronted the neighbours.

Philip knelt. He scooped the boy up to him with a little cry – almost a squeak – and pressed the limber, wriggling body hard to him.

'Hello, Daddy, you know Bilbo? Well, you know he died, and now I've got a new dog, he's called Thistle and he's weed on the drawing-room carpet so he's shut in the back hall.'

'In the doghouse, is he?'

'Yes,' Sam laughed and felt Philip's cheek. 'You're all rough and brown, Daddy.'

'I fear so.'

'Did you know I caught a six pound grilse?'

'I think you told me four hundred and thirty-two times on the telephone.'

'He fought for twenty minutes. David landed him for

188

me. And I lost an even bigger one, didn't I, David?' He wriggled around to face Nugent.

'You did indeed.' The blond man walked slowly down the steps. His cheeks glowed. His chubby hands intertwined. 'No, he's turning into quite a fisherman, Philip. Good to see you. How are you?' He held out a hand.

Philip took it and quickly released it. 'Right,' he said briskly. 'Lovelady. What are your plans? You staying for a drink or heading on?'

Vincent had not stepped from the car. 'Oh, I think I'll head on,' he said meekly. 'Very kind of you, Mrs Nugent, and very nice to see you again, and you, Mr Nugent. Right. No, Barbara will be waiting, and you've given me a lot to do, Mr Philip. I'll call you tonight.'

'You do that. Thanks for the ride.'

Philip set Sam down and, with his hand on the boy's shoulder, turned towards the house. 'So,' he said loudly, 'I suppose there's quite a lot of news to be gleaned.'

'Well,' David Nugent was chummy, 'Lin here gave very clear orders. Large jug of Bloody Mary, she said, then sod off out of our way.'

'I did not.' Linda flapped at him.

'Well, that was the gist, and quite right too. No, I'll be back for lunch, but I've got a hell of a lot to do anyhow. Shopping, lawn-mowing. I don't know.'

'So, how's the destruction of the countryside going?' Philip was convivial. 'Destroyed any nice cottages recently? Buggered up any beauty spots? Purged any terraces or slums lately?'

'Oh, no, no. Not lately.' Nugent grinned and patted his wavy golden hair. He looked very like the sort of chubby schoolboy that people kicked just for practice. 'No. I'm afraid we're all rather in the doldrums just now. Recession, you know. Few small deals here and there. Nothing much, I'm afraid.'

'Good. My wrists ache from opening champagne bottles every time another bloody estate agent and property developer cashes in his Filofax. Still. Even jackals must live, I suppose, not that I'm quite sure why. Doesn't look as though you're down to your last Porsche, anyhow.' He looked around him at the high white hall with its cupola the size of the house. There were flowers on the console table, flowers on the mantel. The furniture was French, a lot of it carved and gilt and all of it too perfect. Every chair looked as though it had been newly unpacked, fresh from the factory. The floor-tiles were black and white.

'David's been having a really hard time actually.' Linda led the way into the drawing-room. 'The whole property market's dead. Still, we get by.'

'So I see.'

Again, this room, with its pale beige carpet, its embroidered Japanese screens, its vast *pietro duro* coffee table, was pristine. The paintings and bronzes were good but ordinary. They lacked the homogeneity afforded by a personality. They had been ordered – 'find me two quality horse bronzes, two nice racing scenes, two good flower-paintings . . .' rather than bought for love or inherited. The leather bound books sat smug as virgins on the shelves. There were coffee-table books too, and magazines laid studiously out on the *pietro duro*.

'Right,' Nugent clapped. 'I'll leave you be. I'll be back – what? One do you, Lin?'

'Fine.' Linda sat on the greyish sofa. She took Nugent's hand and smiled reassuringly up at him.

Nugent said, 'Really good to see you, Philip. Super.' He wheeled, and his footfalls were fast on the hall tiles.

'Philip, you really must try to be nice to David,' Linda scolded. 'He's been so good to Sam and me.'

'Hm.' Philip strode to the jug on the sofa-table. He poured out two large Bloody Marys. He handed one chuckling glass to Linda. He slumped down on the sofa and stretched his legs. 'I do try,' he said, 'and I am grateful to him. Doesn't alter the fact that he's a property developer and I've never talked to property developers and he's living with my wife when I'm not. Still, I'm civil, aren't I?'

'No.'

'Oh, well. I do my best, but all this – it's just so – so *nice*. It sets my teeth on edge. Why can't there be just one dead flower, one scratch on the table top? It's not decent. It's unnatural. It's suburbia writ large. Sam, go and get your dog and we'll see if we can't get him to chew the chair legs.'

'No, Philip,' Linda remonstrated. 'Don't start, please.'

'Oh, all right, all right. Is Sam's dog allowed in here?'

'Of course he is.'

'Well, can I meet him?'

'Can I get him?' Sam pawed at his mother. 'Please?'

'Of course you can, darling.' Linda gave him a squeeze. 'Just keep an eye on him. He is very young.'

Sam gone, Linda was serious. 'No, Philip. It won't do. Really. You may not like everything spick and span. All right. I don't feel entirely at ease with it either, but it's David's house and David likes things well looked after. That includes your son, so don't try and make Sam question him. He spends hours working with him, playing with him, teaching him to fish. You're a loving father – I've never disputed that – but you're not a good one, not like David is. And as for property developers – well, every house was built once by a property developer. I know you're thinking of the modern, spivvy variety who couldn't give a damn about the environment or the people they displace, but David's not like that. Really.'

'OK, OK. David's a bloody saint. No.' Philip drank and looked down at the chunks of ice in his glass. 'No, Nugent's all right. Just don't expect me to fling myself upon his breast and embrace him. You're happy. Sam looks great. Nugent's got – all this – without doing a stroke of bloody work. I suppose – I don't know – I suppose I'm bloody jealous. I don't know why I can't be a sweet little, spick and span, devoted, uxorious, sweet-violet crapping husband like Nugent. I can't is all, I never thought you wanted that.'

'Neither did I, Philip,' Linda sighed. 'Oh, and God, we had fun, you and I, but it's such a relief after those years, just to be spoiled and secure, you know? Maybe I'm a coward, but seven years with you is enough to make anyone a coward. Call me a mercenary if you like. Maybe I

191

am. I don't think so, but I never did claim that I could live with constant insecurity, nor with – well – poverty. I'm spoiled, OK, but I want the best for me and for Sam. Do you understand?'

'Oh, I understand.' Philip walked across to the drinks table. 'I was an adventure, a juvenile thrill. Now it's time to be responsible and comfortable and pampered.'

'Well, yes!' The corner of Linda's lips was tucked hard back into her cheek. 'I admit it. It's the old thing, you know? You love someone but can't live with them. And come on, Philip. Let's face it. I've heard the rumours. You've been having a hell of a lot of fun down there in the sunshine. You're better alone like that. You don't want me nagging you. It's like me. I'm a petite bourgeois at heart, but I loved you and thought I'd like to live in a lady's house – no heating, threadbare carpets, lots of fun. But it's not me. Not really. And you – you're a loner. Sure, you get lonely. Sure, you'd like to live with a wife and family in theory, but when it comes down to it, it just tears you apart. So ultimately David has nothing that you want. Don't resent him.'

'Oh, yes, he has,' Philip grumbled. Linda held out her glass to be topped up. 'He has the ability to make you happy.'

'But that's like wishing you were someone else!' Linda protested. 'It's pointless. You couldn't be like David any more than he could be like you. It's me that's at fault. I should never have thought I could be comfy on a bloody roller-coaster. Be nice, Philip, please . . .'

Sam's footfalls chinked out in the hall and chimed in the cupola. A small border terrier scampered into the room. It saw Philip and at once curled into a crescent so tight that its wagging rudder hit its nose.

'Come here, border.' Philip laid down his glass. He bent and picked the puppy up by the scruff of its neck. Hanging at arm's length from his fist, it whimpered and licked as though it might, with a great effort, reach Philip's face. 'Now,' Philip grinned, 'you little Geordie tyke. You've landed on your feet, haven't you? One seriously upwardly mobile little rat, aren't you? If I know these buggers, one year's time, he'll be roaming into the next county in pursuit of bitches and cats. I look forward to some happy hours ratting with you, feller.' The embarrassed puppy returned his grin. Urine spurted from its little cock. Philip hugged it to him. 'Ah, an ally,' he said, 'a spy in the house. Don't you dare clean that up, Linda.' He pointed at the tiny trail on the carpet. 'That's one little relic of me, one little imperfection. You can look at that and smile – or shudder. This, my beloved Sam, is a fine dog.' He handed the dog to his son. He suddenly shuddered. 'God,' he said, 'it's hell, coming home.'

'So, Philip, our horse. Seem well?' Nugent flapped open his napkin. He smoothed it on his thighs.

'Oh, fine, fine. Going well, far as I can see. What arrangements have you made for him, by the way? He'll have to be moving on soon.'

'Oh, he'll be going to Neil Munrow. You know, I've known him for years, poor sod, and his strike rate's good. Just never seems to get the owners.'

'When exactly d'ye want to take him?' Philip addressed the soup. He recognized it as an old friend – iced fennel soup – one of Linda's standbys.

'Whenever suits,' Nugent shrugged. 'I mean, if the money helps . . .'

'Nope. Thanks but. Sooner we clear the decks the better.'

'OK. Fine. I'll have him transferred next week. What about Plutonium, then? The Dewhurst.'

'He goes. He looks brilliant. If he wasn't Acheron stock, I'd say put your shirt on him. There's only Dulverton to beat, and I don't think his form stands up. His speed figures certainly don't compare.'

'You're lucky, Sam,' David slurped. 'Hell of a stallion if all goes well.'

Sam looked unconcerned by his share in a potential world-beater. 'Daddy?' he said.

'Hm?'

'Are you back for long?'

'Not very, old boy, no.'

'When I come to see you in the summer . . .'

'Yup?'

'Can I waterski this year?'

'Of course.'

'Is it expensive?'

'What? Skiing? No. Christian will take you out. Why?'

'Ah.' Linda reached over to ruffle Sam's blond hair. 'He's something of a financial whizzkid, aren't you, darling? David's been teaching him to draw up a cashflow. Every expense has to be accounted for, planned in advance. You're a shareholder now, aren't you, Sam?'

'Yes, I've got three hundred Allied Lyons and a thousand pounds worth of Hanson.' Sam was grave.

'Have you now?' Philip laid down his spoon. 'Damned sight more than I've got. God, I wish some sod had taught me to draw up a cashflow at your age. We weren't supposed to talk about money, so we were brought up in complete ignorance as to its workings. All very well when you've got millions, like the Royals don't carry cash. Fine for them, but . . . I was over thirty when I learned to do a cashflow.'

'I didn't think you'd approve, Philip.' Linda pushed back her chair and stood.

'Oh, but I do.' On the other side of the table, Linda picked up Sam's plate. She was just a dark shape against the big window. Outside, the sunlight was bright as tooth-ache. 'No, of course I do.' Philip placed his crumpled napkin on the table. He too pushed back his chair. The carpet said 'Sh!'

'No, Philip, sit,' said Linda from the sideboard.

'Please, Philip . . .' David was at his left shoulder, a bottle in his right hand.

Philip conceded. He rested his elbow on the back of his chair. 'No,' he spoke into the shadows by the sideboard, 'we all have to be bloody tradesmen today. Might as well start young. I don't like it, but I do approve.'

Sam was up now, waiting whilst his mother carved what

194

looked like leg of lamb. Philip felt very solitary, stuck there alone at the long mahogany table. Out there below the terraces, Nugent's llamas grazed. Occasionally there was a dragonfly glimmer as a car sped by on the road below.

'So, come on, Philip,' Linda called across. 'Come and help yourself.'

'Absolutely.' David had completed his circuit with the wine bottle. He was munificence itself. 'Tuck in.'

'It's a treat having David here,' Linda said as all four now stood uncomfortably at the sideboard. Philip helped himself to two small slices of pink meat. He scooped up gravy and turned back towards the table. 'Still eating like a bird,' Linda laughed. 'I don't know how you stay alive.'

Philip sat. Sam was at his side, carefully holding a bowl of carrots and roast potatoes. Philip helped himself to two of each. He kissed Sam just because he was there. 'No,' he said. 'How come? You been away, then?'

'Oh, business,' Nugent sat in the carver. 'Thanks, Sam.'

'I thought business meant sitting at home saying "block up this pensioner's drains" or "bulldoze this church before they can slap a protection order on it"?'

Nugent giggled. 'No, no. Got to get out there, see the sites, you know? "See the sites". Well, you know what I mean. If I'm going to find a worthwhile project, I have to be out in the field.'

'Oh, you've left a field, have you?'

'Philip . . .' Linda's tone was monitory.

'I've got a map,' announced Sam as he returned the vegetable bowl to the sideboard.

'Right, how many spuds for you?' Linda cooed. 'Twenty-six?'

'Lots, please. Yes. No, Daddy, I've got a map like in the films of the war, you know? You're on it. You're a little blue flag, but you don't move much.'

'That's me.'

'But, David, he's all over!' Sam grinned back at his stepfather. 'Manchester, Liverpool, Taunton, here, there and everywhere. Where was it last week?'

'Middlesbrough.'

'Ah, these exotic, evocative names,' Philip sighed.

'Well, we can't all sit on our arses in the sun doing nothing,' Linda reproved.

'There's a lot to be said for doing nothing,' Philip objected. 'At least I do no harm.'

Linda returned to her place at the foot of the table. 'That,' she said, 'is a very unlikely tale.'

'No, he's doing well,' Linda said, and the breeze picked up her light blonde hair and whipped it into a veil of floss about her face. She plucked at it. 'He's a nice boy, I think, and bright.'

'Yup.' Philip looked down at the paving-stones at his feet. They were walking very slowly in step about the walled garden. The flint walls were ten foot high and very much older than the house. 'You've done well, kid. And Nugent. I grant you. May be a berk, but he's amiable at least. God, I hope Sam doesn't grow up as nice as he.'

'No chance,' Linda smiled and her eyes shifted slyly sideways. 'He's your son.'

'Poor sod.'

They strolled down the steps to the twin urns. Below the ha-ha, in the field, Sam approached his New Forest pony. His right hand offered nuts. His left held a webbing head-collar behind his back.

The pony was not fooled. It took the nuts, then swung stiffly away on its hind legs. It lowered its head, bucked high and set off at an unconvincing terror-stricken canter. It slowed to a trot in the far corner and came to a halt at the creosoted post-and-rails fence, where it conversed with surprised looking llamas.

Sam set off in pursuit.

'This one,' Philip said, 'will run and run.'

'I know. Don't you remember doing this? I do. God, it was frustrating. Ponies are such sods.'

Over at their left, a white car was turning into the drive. 'Is that David?' Philip asked.

'No. No, that must be your taxi.'

'Bugger,' Philip sighed softly.

196

'Come on. We'll see you at Newbury.'

'I know. Linda . . .'

She turned to him. She took his hand. 'Stop being so gloomy, love,' she urged. 'Please? Everything's fine. In the long run, you know, it's for the best, for you, for me, for Sam. And we're always here when you want us . . .'

Philip nodded. He blinked. He said, 'Oh, fuck it all, woman,' and he drew her to him, pressed her to him. She bent at the waist. His lips found hers. He was shaking all over as he kissed her. She did not resist him. He did not find teeth in the way of his tongue. Her hands lay lightly on his shoulders. He continued to hold her to him as he gazed down into her damp eyes. 'God almighty, kid. I love you.'

'I know, my love,' she said. Her voice quavered. 'But that's not very relevant, is it? We've got to live. That's all that matters in the end.'

'Live? Like a grazing cow?'

'There are worse lives.' She was still and certain. She was unassailable.

'Shit,' said Philip. He released his grip and he turned away. 'Say goodbye to Sam,' he said, and he was fumbling for his cigarettes even as he strode towards the drive.

Lights came on as the car bumped into the yard. Jim Dobbs appeared almost instantly at the door to his flat. Tony peered out through the office window. Lovelady's men had been at work.

Philip jumped out. He waved to Jim. 'It's all right, Jim. It's me.' He counted change for the driver. The telephone was ringing in the office behind him.

'Oh, take the lot,' he snapped and forced a handful of coins into the driver's hand.

He swung round and pushed open the office door. 'Evening, Tony,' he said.

'Gor, you should see what those guys have done . . .' Tony started.

Philip snatched up the telephone. 'Hello?'

197

'You come in, there's buzzing in here . . .'

'Ah, Philip . . .'

'. . . buzzing in Jim's flat, lights . . .'

It was the voice. Philip hissed and winced. He pointed at the mouthpiece of the receiver.

Tony mouthed 'Oh.'

'What do you want, then?' Philip demanded.

'Have you decided to obey instructions, then?'

Philip wanted to study the voice. 'What instructions are those?'

'Don't be obtuse.' It was an educated voice. The vowels were open, not flat as in adopted standard English. The slight cockney accent was borrowed. It was a full voice, a fat voice. 'Plutonium. I told you he doesn't run.'

'I can see absolutely no reason why I should heed you.'

'Your brother's little accident, perhaps?'

'It was an accident.'

'No, it wasn't.'

'Prove it.'

'I don't need to prove it. Look what happened to Clarendon, then. That should satisfy you. Life could get nasty, Philip. Do as you're told.'

'Oh, go stuff yourself,' Philip barked. 'My horse runs.'

'Look what happened to Clarendon, Philip,' the voice taunted. 'Goodbye.'

The telephone clicked and purred. Philip frowned at the receiver. 'Has the telephone rung before?' he asked Tony.

'Yeah. Mrs Glaister rung, and a guy called Gerry.'

'But no strange voices? No one who put the receiver down when you answered.'

'Nope. What's 'e want now, then?'

'Same thing.' Philip replaced the receiver. He strode over to the bookshelves and pulled out a form-book. He ran a finger down the index. 'Christmas Rose, Citizen's Charter, Clarendon . . . Right. Warwick. Oh, shit, yes. That was the race Freddy dropped three grand on.'

'Whassis, then?' Tony was at his shoulder.

'The man says "look what happened to Clarendon." Well, what did happen? He won a race that Freddy didn't think he'd win. He laid against him. Trainer, Rambo Dowty. I think he still talks to me.' He moved over to the desk and sat hard. He picked up the receiver again. He flicked through the address book and dialled.

'So, what surprises have friend Lovelady's men cooked up?'

'Oh, it's all just, you know, for show. Lights, things buzzing and beeping. Doesn't do much good really. What we need's closed circuit TV, ultra-violet, all that.'

'Yeah, but they don't give those away with cornflakes, do they? I wonder . . . Oh, hello, sorry. Philip Glaister. Is that Mrs Dowty? Hello. Yes. No, thank you. Yup, he's fucked, I'm afraid. Yes, listen, is Rambo there? Thanks.' He covered the receiver with his hand. 'I was wondering if we could move him, but there's not much bloody point, is there? They'll get him or they won't. Oh, hi. Rambo? Philip. Fine, fine. Listen, this may sound a funny question, but you know your nag Clarendon . . . ? No, of course I bloody didn't. I was in France. They don't talk much about slow horses from Wiltshire in the bars down there. Why? What happened? Fricassée. Yes, I know what *fricassée* means. Yup, thanks. I can feel the sunlight on my shoulders just to hear you say it. What happened, man?' Philip listened in silence for a while. He frowned fiercely. 'God. How did that happen? Tinkers? Rubbish, man, tinkers nick horses, they don't – You're sure? No. No, I agree. It's a silly question, really. And she's a good girl? No, well. Shit. Oh, and what about the drivers? Glory. Thanks, Rambo. See you at the sports.'

Philip laid down the receiver with a snort and a sigh. 'Our friend,' he said, 'is not a pleasant man. He plays, as our transatlantic friends say, dirty pool, or is it hard pool? Or dirty ball? Whatever. Two nights after his victory at Warwick, Clarendon somehow escaped from his box. The girl who did him has twelve years' experience. Girls like that bolt doors when they're sleepwalking. So the horse got out, ran all the way up to the A303 where he met a Rover. The horse, with a lot of broken bones, remained alive for a while. The people in the Rover – a doctor and a hitchhiker – were luckier. They saw Equus appearing out of the darkness and that was the last they saw. The lights went out, for good.'

'Jesus,' Tony whistled. 'That *is* dirty pool.'

'Yup. I didn't think they'd go as far as killing horses.' Philip reached into the top drawer of his desk. He pulled out a half bottle of Bells. He span the bottle's cap.

''Ere, can I 'ave some of that, then?'

'Nope. You can have some money. In due course, I will give you a small hip-flask. I forgot to tell you. You're the highest-tech security fixture we've got. You come on at night and stay on till first lot.'

'You *whaaat?*' Tony shot up. He shoved his fingertips into the pockets of his white jeans. 'You got it wrong, mate. No, no.' He wagged a long finger as he walked. 'No, no. You got the wrong man here. No way. I got a life to lead. Gawd, stuck down here with nothing but nags and a mangy old mutt for company, I'd go mad.'

'Mad's fine. I'm not prejudiced. Anyhow, who said you had to be alone? You can bring your doxies down here. That day-bed will serve for whatever you do with women nowadays. It certainly served for what we used to do with them when I was eighteen. I don't assume it's changed that much. With all this *son et lumière* that Lovelady has laid on, I'm perfectly happy to have two people on guard rather than one. If it's a case of *coitus interruptus*, which, for your information, does not mean you've chucked the horseshoes overboard, I trust that you will none the less leap to your feet. If that doesn't frighten an interloper, nothing will. Oh, and you get two hundred a week and that hip-flask, but I'm warning you, Madame de Pompadour, I'll be coming in here at all hours, and if you aren't up and challenging me, with or without an engorged organ, I will kick the shit out of you and you'll be back playing Keystone Cops. Fair?'

'Two hundred?' Tony had sunk back into the Utility armchair. He took a deep breath. He ran his fingers back through his quiff. 'Yeah. OK. Yeah. That's fair.'

*

200

Angela Duncan read Philip's letter. Just as Philip had done, she pursed her lips and nodded slowly. She stood, sidestepped the desk and strolled over to the big bow-window overlooking the gardens of Eaton Place. Many of the trees were yellow now. Autumn was coming in.

With the Heron ménage and the Heron money, of course, autumn was not a grave portent. You could run from winter the year round. As summer followed summer, however, time refused to stand still. You could not take an aeroplane from your birthdays. They followed you, like Inter-Continentals.

Angela had done well for herself. She had been twenty-four when first she took the job with Richard. She had seduced him at the interview and, on discovering his penchant for pornography, had eagerly encouraged him to fulfil his fantasies in reality. She had made herself indispensable by her organizing ability and her confidentiality. Richard had had to trust someone. She had made herself wholly trustworthy. When Richard had tired of Serena and resolved to marry Charlie Vane's fiancée, Angela had set up Eledi's seduction, Angela had set up the cameras which incriminated poor dear Serena, Angela had conducted the negotiations which saw Serena off with nothing but her clothes, her jewellery and £60,000.

She was in no doubt as to the burden which she had taken on with such trust. Were she to betray Richard's confidence, his days of high-profile dealing might be done, but he had associates unpleasant and powerful enough to have her dealt with permanently. Each owned and depended upon the other. Angela, however, had ambitions. She was thirty-two now. Her age was beginning to show. No amount of make-up and exercise would prevent the drooping of the flesh, the wrinkling of her skin. She had no illusions. She was no beauty. Her attraction lay in her body, her overt sexuality (ironic, she had to acknowledge, in that she had never known orgasm), her readiness to smile upon and to indulge any desire. The time would come, however, when she must be superannuated, pensioned off. She must act before that day.

When Richard wanted something and was denied it, his

201

reaction was that of a spoiled child. He was vengeful and irascible. He had harboured resentment of Philip Glaister for a long time, but his desire for the Vespertine gene had far exceeded that rancour. Through Eledi, he owned Persephone, granddaughter of Vespertine, who had been covered four times by brilliant stallions but in whose progeny the gene had consistently remained recessive. Persephone had thrown two chestnuts, a bay and a brown, but never a black, never a champion. Richard had made offers to Freddy Glaister which would have saved Swynsmere twice over. Freddy had refused to sell the last remaining male bearer of the gene. The horse, he had said, was not his to sell. 'Woo Philip, then,' Richard had ordered. So they had come to L'Hermitage, and, meeting Philip and recognizing his kind, Angela had cooked up her own little plan.

That morning in France, she flattered herself, she had read Philip Glaister unerringly. She had known that his was an old-school morality. She had known that he would respond to a plaint from Eledi. She had known that he must return to England. Beyond that, it could not really be dignified by the name of a plan. She had brought them together. She had trained the video-camera with its mouse-ear microphone on them as they talked in the cloisters. She knew about the Fraser's rendezvous and would ensure that Eledi did not miss her appointment. She had left the photographs where she had known that Eledi would find them. She had a fairly shrewd idea as to what Philip would now seek to do with them. It would cause a deal of damage, but the damage would be laid at Eledi's and at Philip's doors, not at hers, and only she could limit that damage. If she proceeded now, she must be alert to contain the damage and emerge the heroine.

She hesitated, but autumn persuaded her. She must lay in stocks against winter. Eledi must go. She would give Philip what he wanted.

She returned to the desk. A shudder shook her shoulders as she typed, 'Dear Philip . . .'

*

Horses had been leaving Swynsmere steadily for their new stables and, with just five horses in the yard now, Philip was not overstretched. He oversaw first lot – the only lot – then rang Vincent Lovelady who, on hearing of last night's call, said, 'Ah, now. That is interesting. I have, by the way, the address you wanted. Have you, perchance, a pen?'

Philip wedged the receiver between his cheek and his shoulder. 'Go for it,' he ordered, and he wrote fast.

He had no idea as to whether he could trust Jim Dobbs, but he had little choice. He found him outside Allsfair's box, sweeping wisps of straw from the cobbles.

'Jim, a word,' he said briskly.

Jim raised his curly red head. 'Mmm?'

'We reckon we've got a nobbler. Someone doesn't want Plutonium to run. That's why we've got all the new gadgets.'

'I reckoned as it was something like that.' Jim clasped his hands on his broomstick and leaned his chin on them. 'So, what's the procedure?'

'I want the horse's feed to be kept separate. You can use the old gardener's shed over there. There's a disused chest-freezer which'll do for oats and bran. You can drive over to Mrs Greaves's every day for hay. Water – I haven't thought of an alternative source, but I suggest the tap. I don't like taking him off rainwater, but that butt is too vulnerable.' He nodded towards the large, iron-bound butt by the office-door. 'Take out all box light-bulbs after evening stables. These security light things will fill the yard, but it'll be difficult to tell one horse from another just looking into a box. Oh, and superglue the bolts every evening. Don't ladle the stuff on. We'll have to use solvent every morning to get it off. Just enough to hold someone up if they try a quick in-and-out. You'll find the glue in the office, and I'll get some more today. What else? Oh, yes, our friend the flower, you know? Guy with the lacquered beehive, he's going to be here all night and every night. Make sure he is, will you? He likes the girls, and I've given him permission to bring the odd one down here, so clear

203

your throat or something as you get close. I reckon that's all we can do.'

'Mrs Glaister's always up here too. You'd better warn 'er. Don't want 'er coming on strange men on the job, do you?'

'No,' Philip smiled. 'Poor Tony might be impotent for some time if that happened. I'll call her and tell her. She's always up here? I haven't seen her.'

'No. Nights. She's always strolling around. I mean, I seen her twenty times by chance, so, I mean, she must've been up here a hundred times when I didn't clock her, mustn't she?'

'When did she start this nocturnal meandering?' Philip raised an eyebrow.

'Oh, just recently. Never came up here in the past. Didn't want anything to do with us lowly lads.'

'Before or after Mr Freddy's accident?'

'Oh, before. Only sort of the week before, something like that.' Jim shrugged. 'Maybe she reckoned something was wrong and all.'

'Maybe.' Philip's lips drew back in a humourless grin. 'Well, it seems that everyone's alert. Has anyone else been hanging around?'

'Nope,' Jim answered quickly. His small eyes slid past Philip, seeking something to fix upon.

'Jim. No one?'

Jim's jaw jutted. His head arose. 'Nope. I said. No one I noticed. Just people as works 'ere.'

What or whom was Jim being so defensive about? Philip wondered as he strode back to the office, and what did Alison know? Were her wanderings in the yard mere late-night obsequies in memory of her husband?

Philip still found it difficult to believe in her grief. It was palpable in the facts, yet it was not borne out by her manner or by what he knew of her.

He looked at her now and he saw anger – and sex. Was that just his mind, harking back to that delicious, mad, disgusting hen-night when Alison had been transformed, when she had grabbed and gobbled and groaned, scrabbled all over him, ground her pubis into his face, ridden him in a frenzy with staring, unseeing eyes, shuddered, drooled and dribbled snot and saliva? Was memory blinding him, or was Alison's body speaking sooth?

Philip nodded slowly. If it were not for this disturbing and distracting memory, he would swear that Alison was getting it.

He could never understand how complacent husbands could not see the signs. He had once dropped the beautiful wife of a baronet at Paddington station after an afternoon's hot hot-sheeting. She had looked flushed, wide-eyed and beautiful, glowing with her own inner light. By evil chances her husband had been on the same train. 'There I was,' she said, 'with you still trickling down my legs, my hair all over the shop, tights torn, and he said I looked nice and then discussed the Chancellor of the Exchequer. I just could not believe it!'

Philip could not believe it either. You knew. You always knew. And if Alison was getting it, it was more than idle to speculate from whom.

'. . . if you'd just bear with me,' she had said, 'leave me to my own devices in the house . . . I'd rather be on my own . . .'

Was he to believe that she was alone? She had wondered whether someone – a trainer – could buy out the remaining fifty per cent of the house and the yard.

A little spying, perhaps, was called for.

There was no reason why Alison should not have a fling. Knowing her fierce appetites and Freddy's mild nature, it was in itself unsurprising and, to Philip's eyes, innocuous. If, however, she was still at it while Freddy, at her insistence, lay still and all but dead in hospital, what price her hysterical grief?

Philip's sense of propriety was not exacting. Within the limits of courtesy, it admitted of most human activities, but bonking the lover whilst the husband lay dying offended even him. An orgy at the wake was not only acceptable, it was positively therapeutic, but you buried the dead man before slipping into his shoes.

This line of thought recalled today's tasks. Philip had

business in London. He had done Odysseus. It was time to revert to Orpheus.

He was climbing into the Mini to set off for London when a large silver Mercedes hummed into the yard. Jim peered curiously from the box which he was mucking out. Philip frowned. He slammed the car door and stood stock still, arms folded, as the car came to a halt. A tall, fair man with a little round blond head struggled with his seatbelt, then with papers on the passenger seat. He emerged from the car looking flustered. He was a big man all round. Philip guessed that he had been a sportsman but was now running to fat. His body looked uncomfortable in the creased dark blue mohair suit. His hair was very short. 'Er, hi,' he said. He extended a large hand when he was still five yards from Philip.

'Can I help you?' Philip barked.

'Phil Glaister, right?'

'Philip Glaister. Yes.'

'Good to see you, good to see you. Ernest, Ernest Cormick.'

The hand was within shaking range now, so Philip, after a moment's scrutiny, unfolded his arms to shake it. 'Yes? And how can I help you?'

Cormick grasped the waistband of his trousers and worked it up over his paunch. He breathed deep. 'Nice place you got here.'

'Do you want to buy it? It's for sale.'

'Hey, no! No, no. No, but I did wonder if I could put just a little business your way.'

'We're not buying.'

'No, no, Philip. No, you got me wrong. I'm talking horses. I hear tell you've got a pretty prime bit of horseflesh, and, seeing as I was thinking of moving into the racing game, I just wondered if you'd consider selling to me. This is Plutonium we're talking about. Top dollar, if you're willing.'

'What exactly do you mean by top dollar? If he wins the Dewhurst, and there's no reason to suppose that he won't, he'll be worth the better part of a million – guineas, that is. Any offer would have to reflect that.'

206

Cormick swallowed. 'Hey, absolutely. I'm not – you know, I want to do this properly.'

'His dam got the twelve. He's got to be a serious Classic prospect.'

'Right.'

'Wrong, actually. His dam never got more than the mile.'

'Oh, sure, sure. You had me all – '

'So, how much do you propose to pay for, say, a half share in my horse, Mr Cormick? I'm not selling more than that.'

'Half? Well, I don't know. Say two fifty grand?'

Philip shook his head sharply. 'Who are you working for, Cormick?'

'Me? Hey, I'm not working for anyone. Like I said, I've got a few bucks and I've always liked the idea of owning a racing horse or two, and . . .'

Philip resorted to his best-practised *bon mot*. 'Bollocks,' he said. 'You don't know which end bites or kicks, man. You walk in here and make a crazy offer without so much as asking to look at the animal and without professional advice. Last night, some bugger rings up threatening me with trouble if I don't withdraw the horse from the Dewhurst. Today, you roll up with an offer so tempting that I know it's got to be a wrong 'un. You're under orders, and I don't like you, so the answer's no, Cormick. Sod off.'

'I'll up my offer, if that's what you want. I know things aren't too good at the moment . . .'

'No,' Philip snapped. 'The horse is mine. Someone's been putting a hell of a lot of pressure on me. Tell your paymaster, Cormick. Plutonium runs in the Dewhurst and he's not for sale. After the race, he can approach me in person if he dares, but I'll do business with the organ-grinder, not the monkey. Good day.' He strode over to the Mercedes and held open the driver's door until Cormick, with much grumbling, had climbed in and started the engine. The Mini followed the bigger car out of the yard like a cygnet behind its mother.

PART III

'I'LL HAVE THE sweetbread thing and the sole, please,'
Angela smiled up at the waiter. Her hair became a dark
glissade on to her right shoulder. 'Eledi?'

'Um, the *salade tiède*, please,' she laid down the menu,
'then the rabbit.'

'*Salade tiède* and rabbit,' Angela told the waiter, as
though Eledi's voice were inaudible to any save her. 'A
large bottle of sparkling mineral water – what? San Pel-
legrino if you've got it, and a bottle of the Château de
Tracy.'

'Certainly.' The waiter bowed and smoothly flapped the
two menus shut.

'Oh, look,' said Angela brightly, 'there's that Burchill
woman.'

Eledi nodded wearily.

'Isn't that what's his name – the composer?'

'Yes.' Eledi shifted uncomfortably. 'Steve.' She nodded
over at the curly-haired man, who waved.

Eledi had insisted. It was her birthday, and Angela had
supported her. Richard had raised his habitual objections,
but without conviction. He liked to torment and deny, but
he was not man enough to take on both of them, and
doubtless he had whores to visit, horses to buy or sell,
sleek bodies to be used or disposed of. Eledi had got her
way. Angela would accompany her to lunch at Fraser's,
then the latest Louis Malle at the Gate.

Eledi's imprisonment entailed no locks or bars. She could

211

have picked up the telephone and rung Philip at any time, but all her calls passed through a central switchboard, and, she knew from past experience, were heard. She could have left the house on foot, run down Eaton Place, plunged into the babble and the frou-frou of dress shops on Sloane Street, but her every move would be watched. 'You are a well-known woman,' Richard had explained. 'The paparazzi would love to catch you unawares, and there are kidnappers who would love to get hold of my wife. We cannot afford to walk around unsupervised. And why do you want to? Gerard is always there with the car, ready to take you wherever you will. For your protection, I have had to order that, if you insist on running about like an urchin, he stays with you. I'm not spying. You can do what you like, see whom you like . . .'

And so, strictly speaking, she could, under Gerard's eyes, under Angela's eyes and so under Richard's.

Richard was not rich. In the old days, he had been able to borrow enormously from the banks because of the income generated by his hotels, amusement arcades and clubs. He had boosted the value of his bloodstock by bidding vast sums for blood-lines in which he already owned large shares. The sums meant nothing. Often he had made a private deal with a yearling's owner before ever it entered the sale-ring. He could thus bid as high as he liked, knowing that it would cost him no more than the auctioneer's commission to reassure the banks and his partners.

Richard had many partners.

He owned ten per cent of this horse, twenty per cent of that. In effect, he was a bloodstock broker. He used his high-profile, high-rolling expenditure to lure other men's millions into co-ownership. There were Arab millionaires who were not sheiks, but wanted to emulate their princes. There was Kurt Glenn, the film star, who had merely wanted a Derby winner as a macho feather in his cap, there were plenty of Americans seeking to lose taxable money in something which might, in time, yield tax-free income and meanwhile bought status.

Some had been lucky. Others had suffered terrible losses. Richard, however, was always the official 'owner'. The press and the public saw him gallantly, philosophically smiling when his potential champion proved a pup or when his uninsured stallion died. A few days later, there he was at the sales again, conspicuously spending giddy sums on more blood. It was a good act. The sporting press and the racing public were unaware and did not care that Richard had lost only his small percentage and was now buying with someone else's millions.

There was a mystique to racing.

Richard was known to have had enormous success. He had won all the classics, several of them twice or more. No matter that hundreds of his horses never saw the racecourse, it was those successes which inspired investment from punters less familiar with horses and racing.

It had proved a hard juggling act to maintain as recession hit. Bloodstock prices had plummeted. Many of the hotels had had to be sold. The gaming clubs saw a tenth of the turnover that they had enjoyed back in the eighties when the disgraced Chris Wildman had been in charge.

Richard said that the banks could not foreclose. He was probably right. He had dug his trap too deep for them to climb out, and a complete disposal of Heron assets would prove fantastically expensive and tortuously difficult. Orders would have to be obtained and enforced in twenty or more jurisdictions.

More than any other asset in the world, perhaps, the difference between the value of a failed Heron foal and a successful one was to be gauged in figures more familiar to the astronomer than to the bank clerk. Every foal born, therefore, gave the bankers that nice, warm feeling resulting from the prospect of a crock of gold at the end of the rainbow. Better to sit tight, perhaps, and hope for a Derby winner, than to sell the gold with the dross.

The banks might sustain their investment, but they were certainly not going to increase capital outlay. The big players were thin on the ground. Richard's new partners were very different. They were mostly Americans, Latin or otherwise. So far from seeking publicity and status from their investments, they seemed to skulk. They skulked, to be sure, conspicuously, behind smoked glass in stretch limousines or in great mansions behind high walls and electronic gates. They were noticeable, not in themselves, but by merit of their towering bodyguards, who bulged in all sorts of places where bulges should not be.

Eledi knew little of such people or of their business. Richard did not talk to her about these things. She guessed, however, that they needed Richard only because their money came from questionable sources and had to find a way into the market. The sort of potential return which bloodstock offered was higher by far than they could attain, say, in the gaming houses.

It was these men, increasingly, whom Richard had been introducing into their parties. She could imagine his smug little smile. 'My wife likes to party. Tell you what, you just sign the documents and we'll organize a little celebration.'

She shuddered now as she sipped her Negroni and looked across the crowded restaurant. There were familiar faces in here. Some of them she recognized. Others were just parts of the kaleidoscope of gabbling, gawping faces which had constituted her life over the past ten years.

One thing only terrified Richard, and that was divorce. His first marriage had cost him millions. Another expensive divorce would set alarm bells jangling in every bank that had ever heard of Richard Heron.

Serena, Richard's second wife, had quietly stepped into shadow. Richard had sheaves of photographs of Serena with other women, other men. That was how he organized things now. He had had a pornographic dossier on Eledi before they had even made their vows at Chelsea Registry Office. The photographs and films were not those in which Richard featured. Those were destroyed. He kept only those pictures, those letters which incriminated his wives. Eledi had no doubt as to the nature of the evidence which Angela or Richard's friends and partners would give. If she walked out on Richard, she would be subject to the mockery of the world, the shame of her family and friends and

214

the reproofs of any court. The money did not concern her, save in that, vengefully, she would very much like to drag Richard down. One day, no doubt, Richard would find a new trophy and would inform Eledi that she could leave. Until that day, she was his possession.

She had slipped the envelope into the back of her cream silk body. It had rustled as she moved. Almost immediately on her arrival in the restaurant, she had gone to the loo, and slipped the sheaf of papers behind the little white plastic pedal-bin in the first cubicle on her left. She slumped down on the seat for a few minutes to consider just what she was doing, just what she was risking.

She still did not know why Philip wanted these pictures. For ten days now, she had wondered whether she should trust him – whether she could trust anyone – with them. In the end, she had concluded that this was her only chance and that, whatever Philip might do, whatever tribute he might exact, it could be no worse than the price which Richard Heron demanded she pay for her sins.

She was aware of the danger, not just of Philip's betraying her trust but of the photographs falling into any other hands. Hatred, however, had motivated her. Hatred had made her reckless. She did not know, had not dared to envisage what she would do with freedom and power if ever she attained it. Such freedom would be at best relative, for she carried many of her gaolers within her mind – her sick, bad body. What she wanted, more than anything else, was the power to alarm Richard, to make him beg or sue or woo or cajole. She wanted to surprise him. She wanted to laugh, just once, in his face.

Still more gratifying was that, should this venture come to anything, Angela too would suffer. Eledi had known love for Angela – desperate, solitary, first love as the awareness of her own nature and her consequent dependence and isolation had breached the dam of frigid respectability and had burst over her. Love was not converted to hatred. Her hatred for Richard was cold. Her betrayed love for Angela was as lustful and as passionate as back then when it was manifest in tenderness. She wanted to look into Angela's eyes, to soothe her, to kiss her as the poison seeped and spread through her veins. She wanted to love her to death.

Richard should have known that Angela would have her own little collection of moments of her triumphs. Angela was a predator and a performer. Eledi had been the sort of actress who found personal freedom in performing and unthreatening love from an audience, be it an audience of children or an audience of geriatrics. Angela was a show-off, not an actor. She lived for her triumphs, her rave reviews.

Eledi had found Angela's own stock of photographs in a file secreted beneath the lower drawer of her filing cabinet. She had removed an assortment, those which corresponded most nearly to Philip's description.

She had little faith in Philip's plan, whatever it might be. This, however, was an adventure. It might, at the least, bring things to a head. That was all that she wanted after the years of ambivalence – a surrender to the decisive force of the winds, a shove in one direction or the other.

She would be almost as happy – or unhappy – committed for once and for all to her life of haute couture and base sex, as she would be free. Freedom was more attractive only in that it presupposed the abasing of her tormentors. She wanted, more than anything, to shake off the illusion of a choice.

She looked down now at the mache and the rocket in her plate, the broken soft-boiled egg, dribbling already congealing yolk into the folds of crimson. Food mocked her. She laid down her fork. 'I don't know why,' she sighed, 'I don't seem to be hungry.'

'Darling, after all that fuss,' Angela smiled. She inserted a sweetbread with precision.

'I know. It wasn't the food. It's just – just getting out, seeing the world.'

'You ought to eat more,' Angela chewed. She slurped her wine. 'You're lovely, but you don't want – there's a point where it starts coming off your face.'

'I know,' Eledi pushed her plate away. 'Don't worry. I'm sure my successor will be all tone.'

216

'Come on.' Angela grinned a coach's grin. 'Don't get down. Successor. Idiot.'

'How long – it must be eight years now, isn't it? You, working for Richard?'

'Yup, and never a cross word. No. We've had problems, but, you know. Overall, it works. I wish I could like horses, that's all.'

'Have you – oh, I know you'll not tell me the truth anyhow:' Eledi tipped her glass up. She gasped. She reached for the bottle in the ice-bucket. 'Have you been – what's the phrase? Faithful won't do. Celibate certainly won't, but have you ever had an illicit passion, privately, in that time?'

'Aha,' Angela was arch. She gave Eledi the corner of her eye. 'Wouldn't everyone like to know? I've been tempted, but no, nothing to report.'

'Well, there you are. Don't you resent the various Mrs Herons? I mean, you're the kindred spirit, you're the faithful, long-standing friend . . .'

'God, no. I'd not be Mrs Heron if you paid me. Sorry, but. No, I like things as they are, thanks. All the privileges and none of the pains. I mean, terms of power, I've got the lot. I know everything that happens. I can hire or fire. I can write cheques.'

'What about – I don't know, affection?'

'Oh, affection, affectation. Shit, darling, I've got you, I've got my work, I've got playthings, I've got my teddy-bear. You give me affection, don't you?'

Her eyes were suddenly a maelstrom. Eledi clung to the outer edges for a moment, but found herself sucked into the darkness.

She said, 'Of course I do.'

'Well, there you are.' Angela tipped up her bowl to scoop the glutinous lemon and ginger sauce. 'You can have affection and the illusion of everything else you want or everything you want and the illusion of affection. I chose. I think I chose right. Slows you down, reliance on any one thing – sex, drugs, affection. You've got to take a little of everything. It's like – we're omnivores, right? So I

217

get hooked on one sort of food – Double Gloucester, say. Shit. I can't travel, I can't go to this restaurant, can't go to that . . . No. There are lots and lots of lovely things to eat. Best thing's to learn to love them all. Like you,' she said.

'Like me in theory,' Eledi admitted. 'Not in practice. I sleep with you . . .'

'Sh . . .' Angela pouted, frowned, glanced over her shoulders.

'I want to keep you, to go for walks with you, to . . .'

'Sure, sure.' Angela leaned forward. She laid a long hand on Eledi's. 'I feel that too.'

'No you don't.' Eledi spoke sharply. She withdrew her hand. 'You close your eyes, sure, and whoever it is, you can pretend. You're a spore on the wind. I don't know. Most people are the same as me. They want to stop somewhere, concentrate on setting down roots, learning, growing. It's not like food – well, it is in some ways, but there's more. Christ.' She shuddered and shrivelled. 'There bloody has to be.'

'Not in nice, twentieth-century bourgeois society, darling.' Angela leaned back. She stretched and crossed her legs. Her arms unfurled above her head like a lyre-bird's tail. 'Once, sure. You could have a nice, respectable love life and a nice, respectable, promiscuous sex-life. As long as you kept them separate, all was well. Not now. You're a whore or a nun today, darling. You are of the world or out of it. And if you want babies and gardens and so on, forget the naughty bits. You're lucky. We're lucky. Good God,' she uncrossed her legs and sat upright, 'what's *he* doing here?'

Eledi's head swivelled. She said 'Who?' and the colour arose in her cheeks as she saw Philip up there by the bar, scanning the tables through narrowed eyes. He wore faded jeans, a crisp striped shirt and a leather bomber-jacket. That familiar bang of ochre hair hung down over his left eye. He combed it back with his fingers. His left hand held a slim pigskin briefcase. He looked thin, nervous but fitter than ever here, amidst the pasty London crowd.

The Mâitre d' was at his side now, scanning a clipboard,

218

shaking his head. Philip scowled. His eyes fixed upon Eledi and Angela. He nodded. He stepped down the steps and strode towards them. Behind her, Angela drawled, 'That funny little chap, Glaister. Oh, dear.'

'Morning, Eledi,' Philip said cheerily. 'Morning, Miss Duncan. Don't forget you still owe me some money.'

'No, I don't,' Angela smiled up at him, 'I have written to you about that. Are you following me?' She was coy.

'Don't be ridiculous. I'm here in England on business. Never expected to see you again. Still, as you're here . . .'

'Let's not go over that in public, Philip.'

'OK.' Philip nodded. 'Well, I'll look forward to your cheque. So, enjoy your stay at L'Hermitage?'

'Very much.' Angela's voice was deep.

'Look, as you're here, do you think I could have a quick, private word?'

'I've got to go to the loo anyhow.' Eledi knew she spoke too fast. God, and I'm meant to be an actress.

'I can't think what Mr Glaister thinks we have to discuss.' Angela's voice had acquired an edge. 'Sit down, Eledi. Honestly.'

'No, listen, I really do need to go. Nice to see you, Mr Glaister.' Eledi smiled quickly – a morse flash only. She weaved between the tables.

Philip took her chair.

'Philip,' Angela unsheathed a long, long cigarette, 'your manners leave much to be desired, you know.'

'I'm sorry. I just had to talk to you.' Philip spoke urgently. 'I haven't been able to get you out of my head, damn you. God, when I think what I missed out on that night. There are few enough of us kindred spirits. I'm sorry, I was in a bloody awful mood.'

'What a touching little speech.' She leaned forward, pouting about the cigarette. Philip reached into his jerkin pocket. He pulled out a 'Cricket'. He flicked it once. Angela's eyelashes meshed against the smoke. 'So,' she threw herself back in her chair, flung back her long dark hair, 'you'd like to play now. I must admit I'm flattered, and you do have a certain reputation. The only problem is,

I don't usually engage in extra-mural games.' She set her head on one side. She appraised Philip. 'We'll have to think about this, won't we?'

There were two bottoms in that gasping loo, a deuce of hearts before the enamel of the basins. Their owners leaned forward as though to bathe in the mirrors. Eledi averted her eyes and pushed with her shoulder at the first cubicle door. It did not give.

She muttered something sibilant. She shrugged up an imaginary shoulder-bag. She flicked back her hair. She sauntered slowly over to the basin between the bottoms.

She placed her bag behind the basin. She snapped it open. She pulled out mascara, lipstick and comb. She played at imaginary repairs.

'God,' said the woman at her right. She was mid-forties, fifties, even, but had kept her hair long and had kept it russet. Her strained face was russet too. 'I don't know. London's brutal, isn't it? So dry! Time for a visit to Champneys, I reckon.'

'Time for a visit to the embalmer,' thought Eledi, who found her mood less than charitable. If only these women would leave. None the less, she said, 'It is horrible, isn't it?'

The woman at her left, a businesslike thirty-year-old with her mouse hair pulled back in a ponytail, snapped her bag shut and turned away.

Eledi bared her teeth at the mirror. Behind her, a loo coughed and gasped. The door of the first cubicle swung inward. A young girl emerged, and clicked quickly across to the basins and washed her hands like a professional mourner on a busy day. She moved to the hand-drier and grieved some more.

Eledi had been out here too long. She could not wait whilst someone else came in and locked herself into that cubicle. She had to get those photographs back. The whole thing had been crazy from the start. More than anything else, the commonplace, squalid tedium of the ladies' loo with its garish hygiene, its mocking functionalism, its idle chat, its assumed gender solidarity, made her sins seem the more grotesque. Those photographs could not stand up to such light.

Eledi plucked up her bag and walked to that loo. Eledi closed the door, then bent down to retrieve the package from behind the pedal-bin.

And something withered and whimpered in her belly.

They used to stand barefoot on blotting-paper at her school. The blood would all go to your feet, they said, so you'd faint.

She felt as though she were standing on a whole stack of blotters. Her skin prickled as the blood sank from her face and neck.

The photographs were not there.

Eledi felt sick. She extended a hand to the wall to support herself, and pulled the bin right out to check. Nothing.

Angela's tongue described the contours of her upper lip. 'I'll tell you what, Philip, dear. You come up with something exciting, something out of the ordinary, something new, you let me know. We're here for two weeks, then Florida, then back to the Loire.' She reached into her black Chanel bag. She flicked out a card. 'This is my private line. If I'm not there, someone'll tell you where I am. Consider yourself challenged. There is precious little new under the sun. You find it, we'll team up, OK?'

Philip cleared his throat which was suddenly full of mucus. Again his mind was filled with distaste for this woman but his body was receiving entirely contrary signals. 'OK,' he said. He nodded. He stood whilst yet he could do so with propriety. 'Thank you. I'll not let you down.'

'I do hope not.' She smiled brightly.

'I'll call you.' Philip tucked the card into his pocket. He caught her steady, unmoving soft eye. His breath caught somewhere about his breastbone. 'I'll call you,' he croaked. He picked up his briefcase and swung quickly away. He stumbled on the step up to the bar area.

221

Angela watched him with a triumphant little smile. The abasement of Philip Glaister struck her as no small triumph.

When Eledi returned, she looked at the empty chair, then at Angela's smirking face, then up at the door. 'Where is he?' she piped, then gulped. 'Where's he gone?'

Angela shrugged. 'Just gone. Why? You specially want to talk to him?'

'No. No.' Eledi sat as though uncertain that the chair was really there. 'Well, what did he . . . ? You know. What did he want?'

Angela was arch. 'I seem to have caught his fancy,' she laughed. 'Sweet, but not, I fear, my type.'

Eledi said, 'Oh,' then, 'Well, well . . .'

'Hmm?'

'Oh, nothing.'

For so long, everything had been contained, both within her and within Richard's well-ordered, high-security life. Now, she had lit the fuse.

Maybe there would just be a fizzle. If, however, the explosion came, someone would be very badly hurt.

Something wriggled in her gut.

She was already convinced that she had made a very grave mistake. What did she know about Philip Glaister, for God's sake? He was no longer the amusing undergraduate of fifteen years ago, any more than she was the eager young aspirant of those days. He could even now be rushing off to Fleet Street in search of the highest bidder.

'Oh, Jesus Christ.'

She had wanted fresh air in her life. Now, too late, she remembered.

Fresh air was cold.

In a doorway on Kensington Church Street, Philip stole a glimpse of the contents of the envelope. He had seen Eledi and Angela through the restaurant's smoked plate-glass windows. He had borrowed the cover of a large party of Americans to slip into the lavatory unnoticed before approaching their table. He flicked through the photographs without wholly removing them. He nodded slowly. He said, 'Good.'

He pulled out the single sheet of plain azure writing paper. Eledi had written, in capitals, FOR GOD'S SAKE, BE CAREFUL. I'M TERRIFIED. PLEASE GUARD THESE WITH YOUR LIFE. AND DON'T LOOK AT THEM. BURN THEM, ANYTHING. *PLEASE.*

It was an eloquent plea, unsigned. Philip folded it and tore it, folded it and tore it into scraps. He forced the scraps into a bin on a lamp-post. He stepped from the pavement and hailed a taxi. He read out the address which Lovelady had given him.

As the cab whined and shuddered towards the East End, Philip perused the pictures more thoroughly.

They were standard dirty pictures of humans behaving as humans will when they are sick and tired of being responsible administrators and wish to think as little, to be as undifferentiated as the beasts of the field.

Philip was no stranger to the passions which could occasion such abasement, but the still, uncritical camera made the indignity of it all appear incomprehensible.

No doubt, before things reached this stage, there had been music, drink, drugs, caresses, stimuli, giggles, dares. The camera recorded none of these – just the bare facts of coupling, the apotheosis which should have been left in darkness.

It was never fair. An overheard conversation between lovers was always embarrassing. Passion – even licit passion – always had about it a touch of the absurd, even, under brilliant light, of the disgusting. It was like a murder. The facts, the sight of a corpse, would turn the stomach. You knew that the passions which had brought this about were your passions too, that you too could know the high, heady intoxication of anger, but the accusing detritus of that anger was merely squalid and sad.

These pictures, of humans engaged in the most vital and life asserting of activities, recalled to Philip's mind nothing so much as those of mass graves at Belsen. The bodies seemed frail and soulless, the faces blank. The pictures spoke, paradoxically but eloquently, of mortality.

Eledi was in five of the eight pictures. Philip still found it hard to relate what he knew of her with what he saw here. It wasn't just the disparity between Eledi well-dressed and well-spoken and Eledi naked and disporting. She had always had, she still had, a childlike openness and clarity in her manner and her gaze which he found irreconcilable with her eager and indiscriminate contortions. It was not that her activities in these pictures were adult. On the contrary, they were as childish as blind man's buff (as if to underline the point, in one of the pictures, Angela lay sprawled and blindfold) but they were corrupt as Eledi was not, corrupt in that the participants had forsworn all illusions, all hope. He did not see Eledi thus.

He recognized the playroom at L'Hermitage as the location of one of the pictures. He recognized, of course, all of the girls. He thought, too, that he recognized one of the men, who presented him with a three-quarter back view. His pubis was hard against Anick's arse. Angela, barely recognizable as Angela, lay on her back, her face beneath their genitals. Another man, a bronzed, curly-headed beach-boy, all muscle and glossy skin, attended to her other end. Philip racked his brains, running through his acquaintances in the South of France, wondering who amongst them, if stripped, would fit this burly form closest to the camera. He failed.

He recognized, however, two other men in the other photographs. One was a well-known owner, the other a high-profile Italian banker, also an owner, who had received a lot of unwelcome publicity at the time of the Calvi affair.

In one regard, Philip was disappointed and at least mildly alarmed. Angela was in all the pictures, but in none of them was her face sufficiently clear to enable positive identification. A great deal more of her was on view, but he doubted that her tits or her arse were sufficiently distinctive to save him from a libel rap were he to publish them above her name. This might, of course, be merely because she liked, at such events, to keep her mouth as far as possible full. He remembered, however, Eledi's astonishment at the sudden licence granted her back in the cloisters of L'Hermitage. He could not help wondering whether Angela might not know a deal more of Eledi's actions than she was admitting.

Was there some way in which she might have overheard that conversation in the cloister? Of course there was. Future generations, no doubt, would grow up furtive as voles. They would know as a matter of course that microphones and hidden cameras were all about them. That knowledge would occasion a new, hypocritical puritanism or a new, glorious openness which would see cabinet ministers openly avowing that they visited prostitutes on Mondays, Wednesdays and Fridays because pretence was no longer sustainable. Philip, however, belonged to a generation which believed that a secret was anything whispered or explicitly confided. Of course Angela could have been listening. Of course she might be aware of Philip's machinations, but he could not see how she could turn them to her ends or those of her master.

Windmill Studios proved to be a tall red-brick Thameside warehouse whose blind arcades had now been given startled glass eyes. Philip ran up a grey stairwell to the third floor. He checked Lovelady's scrawl once more, rapped on a black-pointed door.

There were footfalls and calls of 'Hold it' and 'Coming' before a slight man with a silver fringe appeared in the doorway. His eyes were hyperthyroid – lemur eyes – round, bulging and heavily hooded. 'Yes?' he said, though it came out as 'Yis?'

'Guy Bonallack?'

''Sright. What can I do for you?'

'Vincent Lovelady sent me. He thought you might be able to help with a little problem. My name's Philip, Philip Glaister.'

'Oh, Vince,' the little man pulled the door open. 'Gawd, he's a funny bugger, isn't he? Come on in. 'Fraid you'll have to wait a bit. I'm working. Giss ten minutes, will you?'

Philip followed him into a huge, light space with arched windows staring aghast out over the river. Up at his left, there was an octagonal stage or plinth, circled by screaming white lights.

A woman stood there, one leg cocked, one hand on her hip. Her hair was blonde and bubbly as spume. Her breasts were better described as jugs – large and full to bursting. She wore only black eyelashes and plain white knickers. A Swiss-cheese plant stood in an ornate neo-classical jardinière beside her. The jardinière stand reached higher than her tits. The plant towered above her.

Beneath her, with his back to Philip, a young man with a long pony-tail knelt holding up a large sheet of white, reflective paper. A camera stood on a tripod beside him. Another camera, a polaroid, was on the floor. 'Help yourself to a coffee, Phil.' Bonallack snatched up yet another camera by its strap. He skipped up on to the stage.

'Right, then, Marcie, doll, let's 'ave the "ooh, it's just gone up me" look, right? Deep breath, then. Ooh, it's lovely. Nice and hard and warm. Come on. Lick those lips. That's a girl. Six million people are going to want to lick those titties. Gawd, just think of it. Six million people lining up for a quick lick. Tell us when you want to breathe. Let's try a couple . . . That's it. Stick 'em out. This way. Eyes wide. You've never *seen* one so big. Nice. Right, Frank, let's try it round there. Get some light on the underside. Hold it. No, tell you what, girl, you kneel down and hug that thing to you. Sideways on. That's it, but look at me. Little smile? Frank, you do a Polaroid for us?'

Philip leaned on the white Formica bar and watched, amused, as the girl pouted, smiled and fluttered her eyelashes. She was a mere piece of furniture before the dancing Bonallack.

Bonallack was lithe, light and sprightly. In his black shirt, tight jeans and white trainers, he sprang this way and that, crouching, kneeling, never once easing up on the mildly obscene patter. He was a creature of the sixties. The fringe and the refined cockney spoke of that era. The banter was sub-Bailey.

It took a further fifteen minutes for him to finish his work, during which time Marcie was doused with water and Philip was co-opted to hold another reflector. At the last, Bonallack wrapped his camera-straps and said, 'Right, Frank. Pack up, will you? Marcie, doll, thanks. Dry off. I'll let you have a set of contacts tomorrow. Think we got some nice shots there. Right.' He turned to Philip. It was like seeing a television change channels. 'Phil. Come through with me. We'll talk.'

He took Philip's upper arm. He led him into a little office separated from the studio only by a glass partition. There was no desk in here, just shelves cluttered with rolls of film, magazines and books, two deep armchairs and a window seat. 'Right.' Bonallack pressed a button on the wall. Fiddles stitched Bach into the stillness. 'So. What's Vince up to, then? Take a pew.' He sat on the window seat and so became merely a silhouette.

Philip sank into one of the armchairs. 'Vincent tells me you know a lot about making the camera lie.'

'Yeah, well. A sideline, isn't it? Tabloids use mocked up photographs, you get a libel suit. I can usually prove that it's a fake. Vince's business, you get some clever clogs thinks he can rig photographic evidence, you know, for a claim. See, what it is, every photograph's different. Different lighting, different definition, different contours. I've mugged up a programme, does a breakdown of the light and shade, right? Identifies the light source and its intensity, OK, so shadows should fall here, here, x depth here, y depth there, that sort of thing. You got another suspect claim, then?'

'No.' Philip reached for the envelope inside his jerkin. 'Can you do the faking?'

'Yeah, sure.' Bonallack shrugged. 'Hey, this legal?'

'Oh, yes. Or rather, it's not illegal. You know Lovelady.'

'OK, OK. I'll check with him later if that's OK with you. Hey, mind if I smoke?'

'Of course not.'

'You?'

'Not for me. Anaesthetic. I like fascist drugs.'

'Yeah, I can see that. Nah. Take it easy, I say. There's enough bleeding stimulus, isn't there?' He jumped down

227

from the seat. He opened a little cupboard and pulled out a long, bulky joint. He broke two matches before one flared. He drew deep on the joint and sat in the armchair opposite Philip. He leaned forward. 'Give,' he said.

'Confidential?'

'Man, I've had pictures of cabinet ministers and choir-boys. The cabinet ministers are still cabinet ministers. It's my business. Give.'

Philip studied the little man's face. He nodded. He handed over the envelope.

Bonallack drew out the photographs and leaped to his feet. He walked back and forth with a slight jiggle, bouncing on the soles of his feet. The joint hung from his lips. He blinked against the smoke.

'Standard dirty pictures,' he said. 'Wide-angle distortion on all of them, except this one which shows telephoto condensation. One in five hundred, I'd say. Two of them – these two – are exposed, taken with a hand-held. The rest I'd guess are spy pics, probably set to shoot every thirty seconds, fixed focus. Not good, but good enough for black-mail, I suppose. You'd need an image intensifier to get a positive on these two in the background, but their hus-bands or wives would know them.' He swung round and fell back into the armchair. 'Gawd, I mean, why do they do it? Don't they get hangovers, feel sick after? They must, but they come back for more.'

'Did hangovers ever deter you from having another jar?' Philip demanded.

'Nope, but – I mean, some of these girls are lookers. Could have anything. Look at the locations. They're not exactly hard up, are they? I mean, sure, I can dig the thing itself, get out of it, sure. I use this . . .' He waved the joint. 'Some women lose their tempers, some people drink, sure. I can dig that, but this . . . It's kind of irrevocable, isn't it? You done it, you can't wipe it out, say "sorry", start again.'

'That's why you do it again and again,' Philip nodded. 'It's a trap. It's like murder, whatever. You do it once, sure there's a hangover, but soon you need to escape again, and now nothing less will do the trick. Next time, eviscerate, bathe in the blood. Each time, you cut out all the tamer pleasures.'

'Shit.' Bonallack was up again. The sun had come out. The river winked behind him. 'Oh, well. What do you want done, then?'

Philip pulled himself to his feet. He stood at the photographer's shoulder. 'I want you to take this woman's face off the pictures, then put it back in such a way that you could detect it as a fake.'

'You *what?*'

'It's got to look good, good enough to convince at first sight, but, when it's sent to an expert, he's able to say with certainty, "That's a fake."'

'I get you.' Bonallack grinned. 'Yeah. Challenge, that. Superimpose so it looks like the real thing, only anyone who checks it out . . .'

'That's it. It's a delicate balancing act. A newspaper gets it, sends it to an expert . . .'

'Most likely me.'

'Fine. All the better. But whoever, he'll say, "You can't publish. That's a fake." Same time, I want it convincing enough for them to be interested.'

'Bit of creative brushwork'll do it,' Bonallack mused. 'And if it comes to me, I can say with certainty "that's rigged", can't I? Yeah. You're all right. Giss a couple of days.'

'And you'll look after them?'

'Man, man,' Bonallack slapped Philip's shoulder. 'Get it into your head. I'm straight. I'm secure. You think a little guy like Vince is going to employ a dopehead glamour photographer if he hasn't checked me out? Anyone looking for the pics?'

'No.'

'Well, then, know where I'll keep them?'

'Tell me.'

'On the open shelves, in a file full of this shit. That way, anyone burgles the place, he thinks this is just another shot from a blue movie, right? and you can't blackmail blue movie performers, can you? I got a safe. It's a great safe. Cost me a bleeding fortune. Know what I keep in there?'

'Go on.'

'Dope, condoms, a grand in fuck-you money. It'll keep a pro burglar busy for a couple of hours getting to that lot. Don't worry, Phil.' He waved through the glass screen to Marcie, who, now fully dressed in a tight sweater and a busy, boxy little skirt, teetered across the studio. He flicked open a desk diary from the bookshelves. 'Come and see us, what? Midday Thursday?'

'You're on,' said Philip.

'Sorry, were you waiting for someone?' The large woman in a floral print spoke in jolly tones. She chortled as though sucking pebbles.

Philip watched Jenny Laing up there by the front door, crouching to shake hands with a little boy in a uniform blue coat and a blue and red quartered cap. The little boy turned away and ran to his mummy, who for some reason wore a husky. Jenny turned her attention to a pair of blonde little girls.

'Sorry. I say. Are you waiting for someone?' the woman demanded.

'No. No.' Philip growled, then he realized what the woman was thinking. 'No, just Jenny.'

'Oh. Oh, jolly good. She'll be free in a mo.'

At that moment, Jenny looked up. Her hair was pulled back in a pony-tail. She saw him. She frowned, then her eyes snapped wide open. She smiled slowly, wryly, then grinned and waved. Philip instantly regretted having come here. What was he going to say? What could he propose? 'I just wanted to see you?' Come on. 'Wondered if you'd like to come for a walk, have dinner?' She'd probably respond much as he had to her unannounced arrival in France.

He shifted from foot to foot. He was angry with himself.

It had been an impulse only - a sudden whim. He had

230

not thought to have to stand about on the street being gawped at by mothers, teachers and children.

Oh, he had thought of Jenny since his return - thought of her with some admiration and amusement. Had he run into her at a party, he would have chatted with her, chaffed her, but to seek her out like this, to subject himself to such public indignity was proof positive of premature senility.

She was walking towards him now. She held a little girl's hand. It was strange to see her in the muted ochres and greys of Ladbroke Grove. In his memory, she was all tanned flesh and flashing hair, bright hues against porcelain blue. She looked smaller here. Her hair seemed darker, but her eyes were still bright watery grey flecked with gold – wishing-well eyes. Her lips still told silently of amusement at just about everything.

He still liked the cut of her jib.

'Philip,' she said simply. 'What are you doing here?'

'Oh, I was just passing.' Philip was airy. 'Thought, good God, that's where Laing works, you know? Thought I'd come and shove buns through the railings. Well, seen you in harness now. Be on my way.'

'Don't be silly,' she chided. 'I'll be with you in a minute. We've just got to find someone to take Melanie here home. Come on.'

She turned back towards the school. Philip found himself following her, up the steps and through the front door into a hall decorated with children's paintings and lined with low coat-pegs.

'Hello,' said a pretty young thing who was stacking chairs. 'No one come for Melanie?'

'No,' Jenny's voice rang. Her heels clattered on the boards. 'We'll give mummy a call, shall we, Melanie? Probably got the school-runs all mixed up. Come along, Philip.'

They made their way through a classroom where a woman with an iron-grey bun said, 'Jenny, Melanie,' and stared at Philip, down another corridor past a clanking kitchen and so into a sitting-room of some sort.

231

Philip stopped in the doorway. Two women sat on the sofa. One sprawled in an armchair with coffee before her, a cigarette in her hand. A redhead with a disturbing resemblance to the Duchess of York stood with her thumbs in her waistband and her egg-timer legs set wide before the fire.

Talk stopped.

'Come on in, Philip,' Jenny called over her shoulder, 'and shut the door. You're letting all the heat out. Girls, this is Philip. Now, Melanie,' she led the little girl round the desk. 'Let's see. Fisher . . . Fisher . . .'

She picked up the telephone receiver and tapped out a number. Her eyes smiled wickedly at Philip. She covered her lips with the mouthpiece. She hummed something as she waited. It was the only sound, a tuneless 'tum, tum, tum . . .'

Philip stood stock still, wondering why a man should feel such a total prat when surrounded by women. His cordial hatred for Jenny Laing was reawakened. 'Right, Philip,' said the Duchess of York lookalike, so loudly that he started, 'take a pew. Have a coffee. Take the weight off your pins.'

'Yes.' One of the women on the sofa shifted along on her well upholstered bum. She patted the sofa beside her. 'Come on. Sit down. Are you a new parent or what?'

'No.' Philip perched like a dysentery sufferer on the very edge of the sofa. 'No, I'm Jenny's probation officer.' Behind him, Jenny started to speak into the telephone.

'*What?*' the Fergie clone guffawed.

'Sorry. Have I said the wrong thing?' He tipped his head back to look at Jenny. 'Didn't she tell you? Oh, I believe the headmistress knows, and is prepared to give her a chance to reform.'

'Philip!' Jenny squealed. She slammed down the telephone. 'Philip is an acquaintance from the South of France,' she explained. Philip was gratified to see colour in her cheeks. 'He has a wicked imagination and lies like a trooper. No, listen. Melanie. Mummy's already left. She's on her way. Your granny said she left ten minutes ago . . .'

232

There was a knock on the staff-room door. Smiling female faces turned towards the girl who entered. She was older than Melanie - ten, perhaps, or eleven. 'Sorry, Miss Laing,' she chirruped, 'Mrs Fisher's here for Melanie.'

'There we are, Melanie.' Jenny pushed the little girl forward. 'Mummy's here!' She steered her to the door. 'Come on, Philip. I'm going to take him away before he can do any real damage.'

'Ah,' the Fergie clone complained, 'we were hoping to learn something!'

'Hard luck,' Jenny called back from the open door. 'See you tomorrow!'

Philip shuffled nervously behind her. He said, 'Thanks for your hospitality, ladies.' He pulled the door to behind him, then turned back and stuck his head through the jamb to deliver his parting shot. He was rewarded with chortles as he shut the door.

'What did you say to them?' Jenny demanded. She stopped to pull a coat down from off a peg.

'I mentioned I was also the headmistress's probation officer, too,' he informed her. 'It seemed only right in the circumstances.'

'God, I'll get carpeted if that gets back to the old bag,' she laughed. 'You are a sod.'

'Well, who was enjoying my discomfort, standing there feeling like a sucking-pig at a bar mitzvah?'

'OK, OK.' They rattled back through the hall. 'You did look a little nervous. Shades of your rapacious friend on the beach.'

'You like to see me uncomfortable, don't you?'

'Well, why not?' She shrugged. 'Hello, Mrs Fisher. Off you go, Melanie.' She wrapped her scarlet coat around her and strolled down the steps. 'You're so bloody confident all the time.'

'You believe that?' Philip raised an eyebrow.

'No. Not really. You give the impression, though.'

'Oh, sure, the impression. Would you sooner I wandered about whimpering and whining "please don't hurt me". All these self-analysing, self-pitying jerks only serve to lower the race's morale. I don't like whingers about me, so I'll not whinge myself.'

'Fair enough,' she said as they emerged on Holland Park Avenue, 'but you don't have to deter everyone you meet. It takes a brave man to battle through to you.'

'Or woman.'

'Or woman.'

'Yeah, well. I like people with guts and a sense of humour.'

'Don't you get lonely in there, Mr Philip Glaister?'

'Sometimes.' He shrugged. 'Better than being plagued by traitors and hypocrites.'

'Tell me about Theresa Villiers.'

'Theresa?' Philip skipped to keep up with her. 'What about her?'

'Tell me about her and you.'

'God, that's going back. What's to tell? We went out for a while. It didn't work out. We split up.'

'You split up?'

'Well, I left. God, that was ten, eleven years ago.'

'I know. She was really cut up about it.'

'Yes. She told me. We were laughing about it the other day.'

'The other day?'

'Six months back, something like that. I was at a dinner with her and Jack, her husband. You know that they have a place down at Antibes?'

'She hated you back then.' Jenny's eyes watered in the cold wind.

'Well, of course she bloody did. I walked out on her. Her vanity was affronted.'

'And that's all?'

'Of course it's all. What is this? A bloody interrogation? Sure. Relationship's not working, you can let it limp on, lot of pain and destructiveness all round, or you abort mission. End of story. A lot of immediate agony and affront, but we all recover. That way, most of my exes are still good friends, Theresa included. It's two souls slowly killing one another that does the harm. Shit, woman, what's all this about?'

234

'Nothing. No. You're right. I was stupid. No, Theresa's my step-sister. My mum married her father.'

'Your mother married Simon Villiers?' Philip stopped and stared. 'You mean, you're Diana's daughter?'

'Yup. She ran off with him when I was ten. I used to see you when you came to pick up Theresa. You were super-man first, then public enemy number one.'

'So that's the Gerry connection.' Philip smiled. 'Well, bugger me, so you were . . . God, yes. I remember. You had a brace, didn't you? Skinny little thing with hair down to her bum.'

'That was me.'

'Dear God. Well, you've improved. I'll give you that.'

'You are gracious, sir.'

'I am rather. So, all this time you've seen me as the evil seducer, is that right?'

'Something like that.'

'I never understood that. Theresa was as keen as I. I'm not a rapist. Why do I get the blame? The wicked Sir Jasper and poor little girl who knows no better. I don't remember Theresa like that. Where are we going?'

'What? Oh, I don't know.' She stopped at the entrance to Notting Hill underground. 'Where do you want to go? What's the time?'

He glanced at his watch. 'Just after four. Well, I don't know. Don't care. Just thought I'd drop in on you. Haven't you got anything to do?'

'I have plenty to do, thanks.'

'Well, I don't know . . . What are you doing this evening, then? As I'm here.'

'No plans. Do some ironing, prepare a project for next week . . .'

'Where's the boyfriend?'

'Who said anything about a boyfriend?'

'Don't be stupid.'

'I am not being stupid, Philip.'

'You're saying no one's . . . You're saying - well, what about whoever you went to Italy with? Where's he?'

'I went in a party. Yes, as a couple in a party, but . . .

235

Anyhow, that's none of your business. I am free this evening. What were you going to suggest?'

'Well, what is there to suggest in this God-forsaken town? Dinner, I suppose. Tea, dinner. We could walk across the park, have tea at the Ritz or something. Then if you want to come back and change or something, there's a restaurant I've read about, fish place. Probably no good, but. Give it a try. Or you can do the ironing.'

'You don't care?'

'No. Well, yes. I'd like you to come. Boring, eating on one's own.'

'What do you send on Valentine's Day, Philip? Red roses, or just the thorns?'

'Sorry. I'm just . . .' He pouted. 'I don't know. OK. I'd really like you to come out with me, OK?'

'I'd love to come.' She shook her head sadly. She caught his eye then and gazed at him very solemnly. Then the corners of her lips curled downward. Her eyes curled and wrinkled. 'Well, one thing that can be said for you,' she said, 'you say something, I reckon you mean it.'

'You can count on it.'

Goddamn it, thought Philip. He gunned the Mini's engine and leaned forward to urge it on. That woman got to him. She was infuriatingly cool and reserved, yet affectionate and funny. It must be the teaching that did it – the familiarity with tantrums and trauma. She amused him.

They had been ejected from the Ritz because Philip had not been wearing a tie, and anyhow the Palm Court was full. They had given Fortnums a miss because they had agreed to boycott the Fountain restaurant until the old decor was restored. They had had tea in the end at the Piccadilly Hotel, where they had caused a number of raised eyebrows by talking too loud.

One thing he had discovered about the Laing here: she had an uncontrollable giggle which started as a quiet fiddle exercise but rapidly became a honking, whooping, gasping sound which had her doubled up and begging for mercy.

It had been Philip's description and imitation of Lovelady which had first occasioned this performance, his account of the cardigans and the shiny-seated Terylene trousers, the knitted ties and the hat. 'The Queen,' he had told her, 'was at the National Stud when she saw an artificial vulva. She asked what it was, and was told, and she said, very regally, "What will they think of next?" Well, that's Lovelady's titfer for you. It's a What-Will-They-Think-Of-Next hat. Colts bend down to sniff it.'

He had moved on to the lovely Tony and then to Alison, outlining the problems at Swynsmere with a series of caricatures. Jenny had coughed and spluttered and whooped, retching up her laughs, until at the end, Philip had said simply, 'So, what am I to do? You told me it would all be so simple. Just come back. Dispose of the animals. Oversee Plutonium's triumph. Thanks a ton.'

She had sobered up at that, sat straight and wiped her eyes. 'I didn't know, I didn't know anything.'

'I know. Still, what would you do?'

'There's nothing you can do, is there?' Her hands thudded down on her denim skirt. 'Well, I mean, there is. If you really think there's a risk that they'll harm Plutonium, you could just withdraw him from the Dewhurst and run him next year. Or sell him to your crazy American bidder.'

'Neither works, alas,' Philip sighed. 'Everyone wants good two-year-old performances in their blood-lines. Bloody silly if you ask me, racing the poor buggers before their bones are set, but that's the way of it. And this family – to date, at least – has never trained on. Plutonium could be a busted flush by next season. He wins the Dewhurst, he'll come out top of the Free Handicap, favourite for next year's Guineas. Horse like that, overwinters badly, you invent the odd accident, the odd virus to explain why he's not running, he's still made the grade, he's still a desirable stallion. Even if he gets no good stock – and this brilliant bloody precocious gene seems to be dominant, so he should – that gives us three years, say eight grand a covering, minimum, that's three hundred and twenty grand clear and we can still flog him on to Chile or something.'

'Aren't there any other races this season?'

'Not that he's entered for, no. It's October, damn it. Flat-racing's a summer sport.'

'Well, then, you'll just have to run him and hope for the best. He's insured, isn't he?'

'Yes.' Philip had shuddered at the mention of insurance. 'He's insured. If he wins, his insurance value will go up proportionately. If they get to him now – what? Seventy, eighty grand?'

They had paid their bill and headed back for Jenny's flat. They had strolled up Bond Street for a look in the shop windows. 'Time was, I used to haunt this place,' Jenny had told him; 'never get time to come here now . . .' They had cut across to Grafton Street, down Hay Hill to Berkeley Square, and so into Curzon Street.

Philip had been filling the silence. 'That,' he had said, 'is my barber's. I have my hair cut there or nowhere, so I can get pretty shaggy if I don't get back for a while. Once, I had a Frenchman cut my hair, but Mr Alex, he's a Cypriot, always shaves me, does the facial, the works, he plucks at my hair with a sneer and says, "Oh, yes, yes. Anyone can have it off. It is how you have it off that matters."'

He had turned his attention to the other side of the road. 'The Market, God. I came here to get laid when I was fifteen. Paid my fiver or whatever and there was this big, thick bush, slobbering at me like a Newfoundland and just as bloody smelly. I ran faster than I've ever run in my life, and she was whining in Welsh. "Ah, come back, love, there's nothing to be frightened of." Nothing to be frightened of? Christ, you'd need a machete and a Davy lamp. There'd be skeletons in there of overambitious jockeys, people like that. Put me off for a whole year, and even then – it was a tiny Chinese – I insisted on a lifeline and harness. Crockford's,' he had pointed, 'God, I've seen a few million lost in there. You know the story. How Crockford died on the morning of Derby Day?'

When Jenny shook her head, he had continued, 'Oh,

that's one of the oldest chestnuts in racing, God knows if it's true. Crockford, the founder of this club, had a huge bet on something in the Derby, and in those days, huge bets were huge. Anyhow, unfortunately, on the day of the race, he dies. Trouble is, there's a rule of racing which says – '

And then he had stopped talking, stopped walking, just stared at the pavement in front of him.

'Yes?' Jenny frowned back at him. 'Philip, are you OK?'

'I . . .' he had goggled and gulped. 'Yes. I've just been so fucking thick! I can't believe it. The bitch!'

'What are you talking about, Philip?' Jenny had come closer, had touched his hand.

'Alison! Listen. Crockford died on the morning of the race. There's a rule of racing that says that if either party to a bet dies, the bet shall be void, for God's sake! So they propped poor old Crockford up in that bow window. They even took him for a ride through the park in his carriage, all to give the impression that he was still alive! That's what Alison's doing, isn't it? That's why she insists on keeping poor old Freddy in a state of consciousness slightly lower than the average carrot. If he dies, all bets are off!'

'But what bets?'

'Plutonium! It has to be.' Philip was walking again, fast, his fist slapping into his left palm. 'She asked for two weeks. Freddy must have a whole load staked on Plutonium!'

Then he stopped and swivelled to face Jenny, who was scampering to catch him up. 'Or could it have been against him? No. No, he couldn't have laid against him. Either he or Alison could have nobbled the animal at any time. No, they want him to run. They want him to win.' They turned into swooshing, shuddering traffic on Park Lane. 'Anyhow, can you see Freddy hooking that horse? Who could pay him enough to make him throw that much away? No. Freddy was defending his investment that night.'

'Which means . . .' Jenny had spoken, but a lorry had trundled by and pulled her words away.

'What?'

239

'Which means,' she had shouted in his face, 'that some-one is out to get your horse and that that someone is either a murderer or is perfectly happy to watch a man die!'

'You are consoling.' Philip too had been shouting, but the traffic stopped at the lights. He had lowered his voice. 'But you are right.'

They had dined early, because Philip was itching to get back to Swynsmere. They had eaten turbot with blackened skin. They had drunk Prosecco Malvolti. He had walked her back to her house off Campden Hill Road. They had walked in silence. At the door, as if in some formal dance, he had turned to her, she to him. He had said, 'Well. That was fun. I'll – I'll call you.'

'It has been fun. You'll go easy, won't you, Philip?'

'Ha.' He had flicked ash from his cigarette with his thumb. 'Easy . . .'

'Not your style, easy?'

'Doesn't seem so.'

'Well, kick 'em hard then lie back and enjoy the effect.'

'Hm.' He had nodded and drawn on the cigarette. He had flung it away. It had bounced on the street, spraying sparks. He had turned his head to watch it.

'You're not alone, you know,' she said in a small voice. 'You've got a lot of friends.'

'A lot of enemies.'

'No. A lot of people who don't like hearing the truth about themselves, but not enemies, no, I don't think so.' She had paused. She had clasped her hands over her shoulder-bag. 'So where's your car?'

'Just down there somewhere.' He had pointed vaguely, irritably. 'Bugger it.'

'Don't worry.' She had tried to laugh. 'You'd better be on your way.'

'Yup. Yes. Right.' He did not succeed in shaking himself from his reverie.

'I'd ask you in, but I know you want to be on your way, sort out the dread Alison.'

'Yup. That's right.'

She reached into her bag for the keys then. At their jangle, he at last looked up. His sinews stiffened. 'Good. OK, then,' he said. He backed away from her. 'Fine.' He turned on his heel and, with a little flap of the left hand, lowered his head and strode off down the steep pavement.

She had climbed two steps towards her front door before she turned to watch him go. He had felt her gaze on his spine. He had very much wanted to turn back, to say, 'Jenny, look, I don't know if it's pity or amusement or what. I like you. I'd like to be with you for a while.'

He did not make speeches like that any more.

Miss Manners would not, have approved of Philip's technique. The car swept up a wake of gravel which must have spattered the windows. He stepped out and he slammed the door.

The car rocked. He strode to the front door. He raised the knocker and rapped twice, hard. He waited for ten seconds, rapped four more times and pulled the bell. He stood back. He flapped his arms about his chest. He stamped. He snorted. Twice more he returned to rap and ring before at last the carriage-lamp above the porch came on and Philip adopted a posture of studied casualness.

'Who is it?' called Alison's voice as bolts were shot.

Philip did not answer. A chain rattled. Philip saw a straggling dark tendril of hair first, then a hand round the door – a bad female habit, this. Pull the door sharply, smash her fingers, shove hard and you'd have an invalid grovelling on the mat. Philip had done it once in Belfast.

The triangle of light on the tiled hearth grew more obtuse. Philip stepped forward. He was through before she could move. 'Alison,' he said.

'Philip!' she called, high and loud. 'What do you want?'

'I'm not deaf.' Philip turned to face her from the centre of the hall. He had slapped his leather gloves in his left palm before he realized that it was a cliché. 'I want to talk to you.'

241

Alison was busy locking up again. She wore an embroidered cream satin dressing-gown over, so far as Philip could see, little else. 'There is a telephone.' She pushed back the stray strand of hair which at once fell back again. 'I asked you to leave me alone.'

'I know. Why?'

'I wanted to be alone. I told you.' She bustled back in. 'With Freddy and . . . I just wanted my own home to myself.' She stood between Philip and the foot of the stairs. She untied the strap of her dressing-gown and tied it still tighter around her. She still wore make-up. It was unsmudged.

'Alone?' Philip raised an eyebrow. He looked up towards her room. 'You're sure?'

'Not that it's any of your business,' Alison bit her lower lip, 'but yes.' She stood to one side. 'Please. Turn the place over.'

'No. No.'

'What was it, then? I don't actually very much like these Gestapo techniques. You said this was my home.'

'So it is.' Philip smiled sweetly. 'So it is. I just thought you'd like to know. I've decided to withdraw Plutonium from the Dewhurst.'

He watched her very carefully. He watched the initial recoil, the gasp, the involuntary jerk of the hands towards her mouth. One hand caught the other, dragged it down, twisted it into submission in front of her belly. She swallowed twice, three times. She looked down at her hands. 'All right,' she said. 'Let's . . . let's talk about it. All right.'

'Nothing to talk about,' Philip shrugged. 'I've decided.'

'I think this concerns all of us.' She spoke sharply, then with more delicate modulation as she walked towards the kitchen. 'No. Come on. Talk to me at least. Come on. I'll get you a drink.'

Philip followed her across the hall, up three steps, through a swing door and into the back hall. The kitchen was to his right. It was in darkness. Alison was a wraith in there, over by the Aga. The hot-plate hissed. Philip switched on the light.

The kitchen had barely changed since Philip's departure – had hardly changed, he should say, since Linda's departure. Linda had painted the walls this sandy gold. Linda had stencilled the ivy festoons below the ceiling. Linda had overseen the laying of the York stone flags and had brushed the pitch pine table to this undulant honey hue. Nothing had changed, not the copper saucepans nor the cork noticeboard nor the marble worktops. Alison, like a ghetto-dweller, had been a lodger here because she had been too idle or too frightened to be anything else.

'Tea?' Alison asked. She stood with her fingertips on the table. Behind her the kettle rattled and fumed. 'Or something stronger?'

'Something stronger, please. I've just driven back from London.'

'Scotch, I suppose.'

'Yes. Thank you.'

She padded over to the work-surface by the window. She picked her way through half-empty bottles of wine until she found the Bell's. She pulled it out. She reached into a cupboard above for two glasses. She placed bottle and glasses on the table. She waved towards them. Philip span the lid and tipped the bottle twice.

'So.' Alison perched on the table. 'Why this sudden decision?'

'You know why.' Philip pulled out a chair. He sprawled like a man in an engraving of a hunt-breakfast.

'No,' she said patiently, 'I don't. I don't know why. As I understand it, he's unlikely to train on and this is the last race in which he can establish himself as stallion material. It's essential that he runs.'

'Yes, but there are other pressures, aren't there?'

'What? Sorry. What are you talking about?' It was unconvincing and she knew it. Her shoulders sank. She looked down at the drink in her hands. 'OK. OK,' she looked up at the central light, 'so you've had calls.'

'Yes.'

'So? You're just going to give up because of a few silly threats? Give up all that money, everything?'

243

'He could have run elsewhere.' Philip shrugged. 'No need to stick with the Dewhurst. He could have run at Longchamps, couldn't he?'

'Yes, but . . .'

'But he couldn't because you had an ante-post bet on him, hadn't you? How much was it, Ali?'

'You have no evidence of that,' she yapped. She clamped her legs tight in defiance.

'I have evidence; circumstantial, it's true. You know the thing I really despise about your gender at its worst? It's the endless blood denial, the endless insistence that what you did last night never happened or, if it did, that someone else did it to you. You're a greedy, raunchy, dishonest little bitch. Nothing wrong with that, but face up to it, will you? Turn off the open-my-legs-and-a-light-comes-on bit. You don't want Freddy kept alive because of your deep, enduring love for him, yea, even beyond the gates of death. Oh, it looks good, I'll grant you, but it's crap. So acknowledge it. You want Freddy alive because you want your bet kept alive.'

'He'd want it too.' She was sullen.

'I have no doubt of it. He must have laid the bet. How much?'

'It's the second leg of a double. Eighty-four to fourteen.'

'Hundred?'

'Thousand.'

Philip whistled. 'Nice. But you weren't to know that your race-fixing friends were going to lay against Plutonium, were you? That's why you had that baby-alarm rigged out there. That's why Freddy was up there, wasn't it? He was trying to protect Plutonium against his former friends, wasn't he?'

'Friends,' she tutted and rolled her eyes heavenward.

'Wasn't he?'

'Yes.'

'So. Tell me. How did it start?'

'Oh, it's all so easy for you, isn't it?' She slid from the table. She walked to the stove where she removed the singing kettle and slammed down the cover. 'So easy,' she

244

whinnied. She picked up the whisky bottle. Shakily, she poured an inch into her glass. She now leaned back on the table and gazed down at Philip. Her eyes were frosted glass. 'You swan in, work out what's been going on, and you don't see half of it. You don't see a hundredth part of it. Day after day, bills coming in, creditors knocking at the door. God! Some of the debts were yours. Doesn't matter. It's a Glaister debt. It's ours. And then – ' she gulped and gagged, 'and then suddenly Freddy's got some cash. Oh, he tried to hide it, but suddenly he had money. We were thinking about a holiday this spring. Seychelles was the idea. He gave me presents, that sort of thing. He was jumpy, but happy. The rows stopped. We went out to dinner, all that . . . He didn't tell me. I worked it out. God, he was so bloody transparent . . .'

'You challenged him?'

'Of course I didn't. I didn't need to. I reckoned I could make a killing on my own account. It was easy. When he wasn't going to win, he was all jumpy. He'd sit at that desk and scribble the name of the bloody horse over and over. Sometimes the name of the racecourse. Some bloody conspirator. God. So what would you do, you've got a sure-fire indicator what's going to win, what's not? I laid against the horse. Not a lot of money, but enough, and it was always easy to see who was going to win. I tied them up in doubles sometimes, with the yard's good things . . .' She shrugged. Again she gulped whisky. 'I didn't know who was giving the orders. I assumed some big bookie or other. I didn't want them sussing out what I was doing. That's what happened with Plutonium. I had two grand on a sharp two-year-old we had at Goodwood, Forsan, doubled it up with Plutonium. Forsan came in at sevens so I've got fourteen grand riding on Plutonium, ante-post at sixes. You realize what that money would mean?'

'You bloody bet I do.' Philip too topped up his glass.

'Then – I couldn't believe it – Freddy started scribbling "Plutonium" and "Dewhurst" on the blotter. Jesus. I had it out with him. He didn't know much. It was incredible. Someone had been ringing. He didn't know who. He, like me, thought it had to be someone fairly heavy duty. This someone just said, "Don't run so-and-so" or "So-and-so doesn't win". They threatened him. They also rewarded him. Carrot and stick. The rewards were bets on other fixed races – never more than two thousand a time, and it had to be spread. He had your old aunt Celia doing it, his barber, I don't know. Anyhow, I said, you know, please. I mean, this is serious. Eighty-four grand. This is a once in a lifetime chance. We've got to make a stand. So much depends on it.'

'So he set out to protect the horse.' Philip did not look at her. He too was glowering at his glass which he held at arm's length on the table.

'Yes.'

'For you. For your bet.'

'Yes. Why not? We knew they might hurt the horse. We didn't think . . . Come on, Philip. No one was to know he'd have an asthma attack.'

'Where was his inhaler?'

'What? I don't know. I don't know, Philip. You believe me, don't you? I couldn't understand either. I searched his pockets while we were waiting for the ambulance. I . . . Jim will tell you. I had him searched. It wasn't there. Maybe just a once in a lifetime mistake. I don't know.'

'Hmmm.' Philip mused. He stood and carried his glass over to the sink. Two dinner-plates stood in the draining-rack. Philip remembered that china. Linda and he had had it on their wedding-list at the GTC. He ran a finger round the blue and gold rim.

'Still, the horse does not go,' Philip announced.

'*What?*'

'He doesn't go. Freddy was right. It's too much of a risk. Even as he stands, he has a value. I'll not have him hurt for your greed.'

'*My greed?*' She did not know which word to stress, so she stressed them both.

'Yes, Alison.' He raised his eyes wearily to the steamed-up windows. 'How come the bet was in Freddy's name? You used one of his accounts. How come? Because if anyone was going to get hit by these big baddies, whoever they may be, you wanted it to be Freddy, not you. And who was up there protecting the horse that night? Freddy, not you. But it was you that laid the bet, wasn't it? You that stood to profit.'

'Shit!' she shrieked. At Philip's right, a glass smashed and tinkled in the corner. A hand tugged roughly at his sleeve. He turned to find her glaring up at him, her trembling face just inches from his chest. 'Just you listen for a minute, Mister fucking sanctimonious Philip Glaister!' Her fists were by her hips again. Her eyes were hard and grey as ice. 'My greed! Have you ever thought why I had to do all this? Have you? No money to entertain? Having to switch off the lights and check the supermarket receipts? The nagging, the rows? We didn't have any of this in West Byfleet, oh no. Everything was good then, but you blew it, you with your gay blond extravagance. You don't think I've seen the holiday snaps, the jolly bloody parties, all swigging champagne and fucking Linda in her designer rigs? Jesus! And there were we, picking up the tab. Thanks a lot, Philip. My greed. And now you won't risk your – your – precious horse? Oh, and who gets the cash if it proves to be a stallion? Not me. Oh, no. You and your precious son is who. I've worked for the yard and the land and the house and I ask you to take one small risk and, oh, no. It's my greed. Just think a bit, Philip. Isn't it time you paid some dues? Well?'

He opened his mouth to speak.

She said, 'Isn't it?'

He said, 'Alison . . .'

'Well?'

'Listen!'

'Isn't it?' she shrieked. She stamped. Like a prosecutor pointing, she shoved away the tears. Mascara-painted Mikado eyes. Her shuddering lips curved downward. She said, 'Oh, God.' She covered her face with her hands and turned away.

Philip watched her back. She looked very slight and frail. Her shoulders bobbed, upper-case to lower. Her right hand was wrapped tight over her belly. Her left still covered her face.

He said, 'Alison, look, I understand. I admit . . .'

'Please, get out. Go,' she sobbed.

'No. Listen. I know I was wrong. I didn't know at the time. I was young and stupid . . .'

'Please. Please, Philip. We can talk about it tomorrow. Not now. Just leave me alone.'

'No,' he said firmly. He laid the glass down on the draining-board. He stepped forward. His two steps seemed very loud in the stillness of the house. He raised a hand to her bouncing right shoulder. 'No. I'm not going to leave. We'll sort this out. I'm fucked if I'll leave this unsettled.'

She swung round with a little squeak. Her forehead hit Philip's chest hard. Her arms were around him, her head nuzzling in.

Philip said, 'God.'

'Oh, I'm sorry, Philip.' She looked up at him, caught his despairing frown and again lowered her head and clasped him tight. 'I'm sorry. I'm sorry. What is it about us?' An uncertain giggle shook her. 'I don't know. It's one thing or the other, isn't it? Oh, I'm sorry. It's just, all that time . . .'

'I know,' Philip soothed. 'I know.'

'It's just so stupid,' she squeaked. 'So stupid. Oh, God. We should be friends. We're in the same boat. God, I mean, we could be close, having fun. I don't know.' She raised her head again, pulled his down. She kissed him, softly at first, on the corners of his mouth, his chin. He closed his eyes. He neither yielded nor resisted.

'Come on,' she breathed against his mouth. Her hand was rubbing his cock now, massaging, moulding. God-damn everything, he was hard too, with those wet lips sliding over his cheek, her tongue hot as it flicked at his ear, her pubis rasping against his thigh.

She pushed him back on to the table. 'Come on,' she said again, 'I owe you this.'

Somehow she had unbuttoned him, somehow extricated that treacherous organ. She smiled with clenched teeth. 'Oh, yes,' she murmured. 'Nice.'

248

He looked down on her as she descended, on the splayed hair, the bulging cheek, the little bobbing breasts, the legs, one kneeling, the other raised. God, but his sexuality was perverse.

She was looking up at him now. Her smudged eyes sneered. Her lips opened in a snarl.

Philip surprised himself. No sudden upsurge of honourable motives inspired him. It was his recreant body which, for once, recoiled from the thoughts which assailed him. The picture of Freddy laid still and empty in the hospital, the memory of this woman's passion, her vampire's passion, whether in anger or in lust, and of its aftermath, the awareness that her motive for her actions was money – all this constituted a cocktail far from erotically intoxicating.

He said, 'No.'

'Come on. Philip . . .'

'No.' He pushed her away. 'No, Alison. Sorry. Is this how you got Freddy to risk his life? God, you're my big man. You'll not let me down. I'll look after you. Was that it?' He tucked his now limp cock back into his trousers. 'No, Alison. You're a lovely wee thing, and I'm sure someone'll be grateful, but not me. Sorry.'

It was hateful and horrible. Every shuffle, every breath, every whisper of fabric as she wrapped the dressing-gown around her and he tucked in his shirt seemed amplified a thousand times over.

Philip gulped down the remaining whisky. He said, 'Sorry.' He made for the door. She stood shaking and glaring after him. Her mouth was shiny and twisted.

'Plutonium is scratched,' Philip snapped back at her as he unlocked the door. Then he hurried to be away from the smell of Scotch and sex and out in the cold air of the night.

Sleet streaked like arrows across a grey sky washed with dirty yellow. Sleet pattered on the horses' flesh, briefly spangled their rugs and whipped at Philip's cheeks until they burned. Linda's cheeks were livid, Nugent's even

249

more so. They looked like a couple, these two, with their chubby smiling faces, their pale blonde hair. Between them, Sam, every inch a Glaister, winced and narrowed his eyes against the flicking of the sleet, but he held his head high and he grinned, enjoying his moment of glory in the centre of the paddock. He wore a tweed cap and a little tweed suit. His nose glistened.

Philip hunched Freddy's Barbour close about him. It only reached down to mid-thigh. 'Well,' he said, 'I suppose I should say I'll be sorry to see him go. Load of bollocks. Nice enough nag, but I'd be happy never to set eyes on another horse outside Westerns. I've seen Munrow, told him what I know. He'll box him up after the last and take him down to Marlborough. God. I wish it were two weeks hence and the whole business wound up.'

'Plutonium's the last, then?'

'Praise God.' Philip licked sleet from his upper lip. 'Yup. Couple of jumpers still to go. And one old handicapper. Then the Dewhurst. When that's done, I can sleep.'

'No accidents to date, then?' Nugent was watching his horse.

'No.' Philip frowned. 'Why should there be?'

'Just you said that family trips over its own feet. I thought you were expecting accidents.'

'Oh. Of course. Oh, no. It's too soon yet. He'll get our hopes up first. It'll be the night before the race or in running. They like a good joke, these animals. Nothing predictable like a long illness.'

'Ali bearing up OK? David, we must give her a call, have her over.'

'Seems OK,' Philip shrugged. 'I haven't seen much of her.'

'Hello, there,' said that mellifluous voice behind him. Sam was beaming. Philip turned. Steve Shand stood, hands on hips. 'Hello, Mr Glaister. Mr Nugent, Mrs Nugent. Hello, young 'un. How're you doing?'

Sam writhed with delight. His mouth wriggled. His eyes became wrinkles. He shouted, 'Fine!'

Philip had seen a poster of Steve on Sam's bedroom wall, up there beside the cherished cashflow projection and the absurd campaign-map of Nugent's movements. Steve was a real live hero. Oh, there were two photographs of Philip up there too – Philip on Ludo taking the Taxis, mere seconds before they crumpled, Philip on the Swynsmere gallops looking glum, but those were pictures of another, alien age. Steve was real because he was now.

'Good, good!' Steve's lopsided smile was infectious. 'Filthy conditions, eh? You going to be a jockey, then?'

Sam was tongue-tied. He nodded. Linda and Nugent smiled down at him, indulgent.

'Right.' Philip wiped his lips on his wet sleeve. 'I've got things to do. Steve knows the animal better than I. You chat to one another. See you in the stands.'

He strode towards the centre of the ring, where a big youngish man with short brown hair and a large belly stood shouting down at his jockey as though from the top of a cliff. 'No bloody cop saying "he put down, sir". It's not up to him, is it? Might as well put the weight on him, forget about you bloody monkeys. It's your fuckin' job to stop him puttin' down, isn't it? Get him right, man. So he's on the forehand. Get him back on his hocks. Obvious enough, isn't it? God. Sorry, Mrs Carver. Sure you wouldn't like to put on the colours, ride the animal yourself? Damn sight better chance than you have with this little berk. God, I don't know . . .'

Mrs Carver, a rubicund, dyed red-head, wobbled and clucked. The jockey was smiling and nodding. He'd heard it all before.

The horses emerged from the strobe-light sleet. Rambo Dowty's animal, a huge lop-eared bay, was dancing like a high-mettled two-year-old. 'Oh. Hello, Glaister Philip.' Rambo flicked the rug back off the animal's back. 'Hold on. Right. Up you go.' He pulled down the irons with a snap. 'Try to do something other than just sit there, would you, there's a good fellow? Glaister here'll tell you. There's more to it than that. And remember, there's not much of a market for Persons of Restricted Growth in the circuses these days, so it's do the job properly or spend the rest of your life bein' chucked at walls by drunken Australians. Take your pick.'

251

'Sir.' The jockey's bum slapped into the saddle. He gathered up the reins in his left hand, saluted with his right. He winked down at Philip and Mrs Carver. He turned his mount away.

'God, I don't know,' Rambo sighed and watched them go. 'D'ye know Philip Glaister, Davina? Philip, Davina Carver. Want something, Phil?'

'Just a quick word.'

'Well, I want to get out of this.' Davina Carver shivered. 'Will I see you in the box?'

'Yes, yes. Be there in two shakes.' Rambo waved. 'You go on. I'll just have a chat with this feller. Get two large hot whiskys together, one for the blast and one to last. So, Philip, what was it?'

Mrs Carver had waddled on. Philip dropped in beside Rambo and they walked slowly towards the stands. 'Clarendon,' Philip said simply.

'Christ, man, I told you, didn't I?' The big man turned his head and snapped angrily. 'Not my fault the bloody creature got shredded. Having a party that night. I can only think some silly bugger got pissed and went messing about in the yard. God almighty, I've had enough of this. Bloody Old Bill went on long enough. It was an accident, and there's an end of it.'

He lowered his voice as they joined the turbulent stream of people that bubbled away from the paddock. He lowered his voice, but it was still sufficiently strident to cause heads to turn.

'It could happen to any of us, man. You know that. Your animal out there can kick a racegoer. You're not liable, are you? They're big, dangerous buggers, ain't they? You mess with them, you're in trouble. That's the long and short of it.'

'Yes, Rambo,' Philip looked down at his feet as he walked, 'I'm not disputing that.'

'What, then? Come on. What is it?'

'Did anyone threaten you before Clarendon's race at Warwick?'

Rambo's head jerked sideways. There was a moment's

tell-tale silence. When he spoke, it was much quieter. 'Threaten? Come on. Nobody's going to threaten me. Must be bloody mad.'

'No one asked you to hook the horse?'

'Fucking crazy,' Rambo mumbled. 'Hook the bloody thing? Come on. What are you talking about?'

'Or to have an accident on the way to the course?'

'What difference would that make? Accident on the way to the course? So? Readjust the market. No one's advantage. You're barking.'

His lower lip almost totally eclipsed his upper now as he swung to his right and into the new stand, which more closely resembled a second-class airport than a viewing area for a popular sport. He made no effort to hold the door open for Philip, just barged through and made his way fast towards the stairs.

'Clarendon wasn't meant to win,' Philip persisted, 'and you know it. He did win. That's why he was released.'

'Bollocks,' Rambo rapped down the stairs at him. 'You've lost your marbles, man. It was an accident. I told you. Now sod off, will you? Leave us be.'

Philip stopped climbing. 'And you've been obeying orders ever since, haven't you, Rambo?' he called up gently. 'They've got you where they want you, haven't they?'

Rambo stopped at the bend in the stairs. His right arm shot out, pointing down the well. 'You say that again, matey,' he said between stiff lips, 'I'll have you for slander.' He looked down at his shaking finger. Strands from his quiff fell down over his brow. He hooked the finger, hid it behind his back. 'Ah, God,' he moaned, 'I can't help you, Philip. Sod it. Leave it.'

For a moment his eyes caught Philip's. They begged. Then he turned away and ran up the stairs, two at a time.

The letter arrived early the next morning. Philip cut it open. He made an irreligious but none the less heartfelt sign of the cross before pulling out the single thick sheet of Wedgwood blue paper. He unfolded it. His lips curled in a smile as he read.

Dear Philip,
I had thought better of you than this. For two thousand?
The papers are hardly going to be interested in – or believe in
– your grubby services, nor in the word of your little friends
against Mr Heron's and mine.
*   If this is your surprise, it's pretty pathetic. You've had your*
five hundred for services rendered. Think yourself bloody
lucky. We've eaten bigger blackmailers than you for breakfast.
*   Piss off, basically.*

*   Angela Duncan.*

'Yee,' said Philip softly, 'ha.' He folded the letter carefully, slipped it into his breast pocket and patted it twice, just to make sure.

'There are birds,' announced Bill Gregory, 'and there are horses. Both are inordinately stupid, incredibly specialized – freaks – in that, so far from acquiring adaptability like the majority of successful species, they each have but one skill. Dogs swim, hunt, see, smell, hear, intuit. They have speed, wit, fur – there are even naked dogs. The poodle or the spaniel may perish, but the species, being diverse, should be safe. The horse can do just two things – follow, and run like the clappers. Herbivore, eternal victim of predators, he survives by running fast until, one day, he runs slower than the rest of the pack and, because he follows, saves his fitter fellows by dying. These birds . . .' he indicated the hooded peregrines which roosted on their blocks, 'are much the same. They know hunger. It is their driving force, their motivation for everything they do. They have no loyalty, no love save dependence based on hunger. They are specialist killers. They fly higher and they swoop faster and steeper than any creature living. That's all they know. The solitary life of the assassin.'

'But you like them.' Philip followed Gregory out into the cold lemon light which squirted from the low black clouds.

254

'Yes, and I don't like horses. Not one jot.'

'You make your living through them. I was always told that you were the best in the business.'

'Yes, yes.' Bill Gregory led Philip through the parterre and up the steps towards the Lutyens mansion. 'But that's like saying that I used to make my living on the Stock Exchange, so I ought to like rubber or coffee or mining. No. I can work out what they're going to do, but don't ask me to like the bloody animals.'

'This garden Jekyll?'

'Yes, yes.' Bill Gregory pushed himself up the steps, his hands crossed on his cavalry-twill covered left thigh. His right leg remained stiff. He emitted a long, low, clogged grunt with every step. He stopped now, apparently to survey the terraces below, the fishpond and the orchard surrounding the stables where the falcons rested. He and Philip's father had been friends for many years.

He puffed and swallowed every other word. 'This is what horses have bought me, if you will: the gardens, the house, my own falconer ... But it's not horses; it's facts, figures, endless hard work at my desk. I gave up the Stock Exchange because I found that handicappers ran truer to form than shares. There are far fewer imponderables to deal with.'

'Dad always told me that you never punt at the races?'

'I never punt at all. I'm not a gambler. A gambler has no place in this business. I very rarely go racing, because I am susceptible as anyone to the appearance of a horse or its resemblance to my cousin Katie or a coincidence of names and numbers. That's not my business. That's the market I'm laying against. My business is on paper.'

'You've done well out of it.'

'Yes,' he sighed with no undue pride. 'Yes, I've done well. Nowadays, retirement, I've got investors. I lose, I lose nothing. I win. I keep half. I have maybe eight, ten bets a year.'

'And the bookies take your bets?'

'The bookies, so called.' Gregory's jaw ground sideways. His straining gut sank. 'Bookies haven't dared take a bet

255

this twenty years. Certainly not from me. No, I have to use endless subterfuges to get a bet on. That's the exhausting bit these days. I used to enjoy it . . .' He turned slowly and, trailing his right hand round the little fountain with its pitcher-carrying boy at the centre, continued his lumbering progress along the broken flags towards the high double bays of leaded diamonds, the steep-pitched gables and the towering chimney-stacks of the house.

'So, sorry, I know you can't give away trade secrets, but can you tell me something of your – well, how you do it?' Philip walked sideways alongside him.

'There are no secrets to give away.' Gregory raised eyebrows like curls of spindrift. 'It's very simple. Most handicappers run at more or less precisely the same speed over a given distance under a given weight. That is why they are handicappers. A few are ungenuine, but you ignore them, however brilliant. The official handicapper handicaps on finishing position in relation to other horses. I keep a handicap based very precisely on speed figures. An animal may finish sixth and five lengths off the pace in the hottest little handicap of the year. I don't care about where he finished. If his adjusted speed figures say that he's better than a five-lengths winner of a funeral cortège, I'll back him. That simple. Of course, I need to keep my ear to the ground, watch videos, that sort of thing, make sure they weren't hampered, make sure they were off, but basically that's the sum of it.'

They had reached the pergola now, with its crazy festooning of bare wisteria branches. Night was closing in. Already the sky above the house seemed tarnished.

'You stick to handicaps, then?' Philip asked.

'And classics, yes. Classics are easy. Two thirds of the runners in the Derby, say, shouldn't be there at all. The breeding tells you. You get seven-furlong sprinters in the Guineas, milers in the Derby. Then there are the French and Irish contingents, whose form must be tested against the home-grown entry, and God, it can take some complicated lines to do that. Then there are the talking horses, the flash numbers that flatter in their two-year-old season, the royal horse which is backed down by an loyal public, the American raider, the brilliant speed-merchant who has never mixed it. Discard the lot and you're left with precious little else. Your animal, Plutonium. Case in point. He'll win the Dewhurst. No doubt about that. He'll be quoted for the Derby. Not a hope. It's like putting a greyhound in a marathon. Forget it. I doubt he'd make the Guineas unless it's a particularly poor year. I don't trust that family anyhow.'

'Nor I.'

'And then, you see, if you're alert, if you know your way about, you get to know about every yearling that can possibly win the Derby, say.' They stepped on to the gravel at the side of the house. Security lights flooded the drive and touched the dead leaves of the rhododendron and azalea bushes at the two men's left. Bill Gregory stepped into the long porch. 'I can usually get, say, a hundred to one. There's so much that can go wrong between the yearling and the three-year-old stages. That's where I need friends; ring me up, say, so-and-so's not going well, so-and-so's injured himself. I sell the bet back to the bookies. Couple of weeks before the race, I've got perhaps the top four or five contenders at a hundred to one. By now they're on the open market at seven to two, fives, a hundred to eight and so on. I lay 'em off.'

'What?'

'I turn bookmaker. Sell back say a hundred quids' worth. I can't lose.'

'Neat.'

'Yup, but work.'

'Sounds it. Not for me.'

'No.' Gregory pushed open the heavy oak door. 'Special temperament, it takes. You know something? There's a way to make money without the work.'

'There is?'

'Yup. Proven over the years.'

Philip stepped into a large panelled hall. An adzed oak staircase jerked at right angles up to a balustraded gallery. Up there were two huge oils of Arabs with falcons and salukis. A giant stone fireplace gaped beneath a panoply of spears.

'Yes, yes.' Gregory puffed. He turned left into his high, dark study. 'It's proven, all right, but how many people have the temperament, the complete lack of avarice or imagination to do it?

'Sit down, sit down.' Gregory waved his huge right hand, and sat himself heavily at his desk. His left hand lay idly on his computer keyboard. 'Right. Try it in theory, just looking at the newspaper results for a few weeks. What you do, you set yourself a target – a modest target, say fifty pounds a day. Right? You pick the smallest meeting in the country and you never bet on a Saturday, right?'

'Right.' Philip found his feet kicking vainly as he sank into the deep blue armchair. He righted himself.

'So, you back the favourite in the first to make you your fifty pounds. He obliges, you stop. He loses, you back the favourite in the second to win fifty pounds plus your losses in the first. He wins, you stop. Same again next race. If you've lost three times in a row, you stop, start again tomorrow. You count the number of times in a year that no favourite has come in in the first two races at a small meeting. Minimal. It's discipline that punters lack. Only discipline.' He reached into a cedarwood box for a stubby Havana. 'You'll stay for dinner?'

'Thank you,' Philip said, 'I will.'

'Good.' Gregory made three popping noises. The flame from his lighter flared. 'Good. It'll be early. Pot luck.'

'Fine by me.'

'Good.' He looked up sharply as the door at Philip's right slid inwards. 'Ah, Jeremy. Good. Drink, Philip?'

'Whisky, please.'

'And the usual for me.'

'Yes, sir.' The butler, an unwarrantably slender butler with auburn hair bubbling over his collar, nodded and turned towards Philip. 'Good evening, sir.'

'Evening, Jeremy.'

'Please tell Mrs Cook to lay an extra place for dinner.'

'Of course, sir.'

258

'And leave us alone till then. All calls through to Clara, please.'

'Fine.'

The door swished back and clicked shut.

'You have a cook called Cook?' Philip queried.

'Yes, yes. And Jeremy is called Stewart. Pure coincidence. My secretary, on the other hand, is called Troia, which means prostitute in Italian. This is entirely inapposite, I assure you.'

'Pity.'

'Now, I assume you want to know just what your brother's been up to?'

Philip's head shot up. His eyes snapped open. He frowned. 'You know he was up to something?'

'Oh, yes, yes. Of course. Quite apparent. I wasn't sure what, of course, but various things were very clear.'

'How many other people will have known?'

'Just from the signs, you mean? Oh, probably just the professional punters and a couple of bookies. Students of form may have noticed oddities, but they haven't got the suspicious nature or the sixth sense that we have. Probably just six or seven people in the land.' Gregory swung round with remarkable agility. He flicked on his computer, which hummed and beeped. 'Let me see, now,' he murmured. 'It's not just him, by the way. No ...' He tapped a few keys. The legend on the screen was replaced by a climbing haze of letters and figures. Gregory turned back to Philip. 'No, it's perfectly simple,' he said. 'What we seem to have here is an attempt at short · odds, sure-fire race-fixing. You've got a race – here, this one at Sandown. Look at my handicap. At the overnight declaration stage, we've got Sabrina Fair, trainer R. Dowty, twelve points ahead of the two other animals with any chance, see? The six others are just makeweights. You can ignore them. Look at the timeform ratings ...' He pressed another key. The numbers by each horse's name were replaced by other numbers. 'See? Same story. It's a three-horse race. So, Dowty's horse is injured in the racecourse stables. His presence in the race has intimidated any other would-be contenders. We have a two-horse race. One of those two isn't off, you've got as close to a racing certainty as you can get. The odds will reflect that, but that makes no difference. I'd lay a thousand pounds to win me one if I were that sure.'

'So who rides the two remaining contenders?'

'Your man, Steve Shand, and Arnold Murray.'

Philip was leaning over Gregory's shoulder now, eagerly scanning the screen. He reached into his inside breast pocket. 'Try these,' he said.

'What are they?'

'Either races in which we had mysteriously beaten favourites or non-starters or races where Freddy had big winning bets.'

In the light from the screen, the folds in Gregory's face seemed crevasses. His eyes were filmed. He looked down at the list. 'That one,' he stabbed with a fat finger, 'I recognize. That one, that one, that one . . .' That long, wounded wild boar grunt trundled up from his belly. 'Well, Mr Glaister. We have some work to do before dinner . . .'

'Confidential,' said Vincent Lovelady, 'is relative. I mean, supposing I've been having an affair. That is confidential information. I do not want it plastered all over the newspapers and I certainly do not want Barbara to know, but that doesn't mean that I can't tell my best friend at the Mechanical Music club, does it? He doesn't know Barbara and he's not going to tell the newspapers, even if they were interested. Similarly, he can then use his knowledge in a discreet illustrative story. "I know this chap in the insurance business who's got the same sort of problem," he'll say to his chum, and that's all right by me. Do you see what I'm driving at?'

Toby Bolus saw what Vincent was driving at. So much was clear from the alarmed, ping-pong spectator shifting of his eyes. He was a broad-framed, thin but genial looking man in his mid fifties. His thin brown-grey hair jerked upward in a little ducktail above his collar. A maroon silk handkerchief ballooned from his crimson and brown checked jacket.

260

On Kellow Hoyle's death from Aids six years ago, his leisure empire had been broken up. The bookmaking side of the business had been snapped up by Josephs, to whom Toby Bolus, an erstwhile Guards officer and rails' man, was odds layer and figure-cruncher in chief. All the Joseph's betting-shops had taken on the Hoyle's name and with it the youthful, trustworthy identity which Hoyle had so brilliantly fostered. Where Hoyle's had been a poor relation to the big five bookmaking houses, it now had more outlets than any other turf accountants in the kingdom. Toby Bolus was at its heart.

Five years back, Hoyle's accounts had shown large, inexplicable losses. Vincent Lovelady had investigated. No one at head-office, on the instructions of the underwriters, had been exempt from his intrusive enquiries. At length, he had identified the guilty party as a junior employee, victim of blackmail, who had been writing losing account bets at ten per cent their actual worth and had channelled the shortfall, through the computer system, into his own well-managed betting account.

The bright young man had been asked to leave.

In the meantime, Vincent had discovered that Toby Bolus kept a young and promising actress in a cottage near Fen Ditton.

'So you're saying,' Bolus was gruff, his cheeks puce, 'that you will not abuse any information that I may give you?'

'Surely you can rely upon my confidentiality, Major Bolus.' Vincent smiled up at him. 'I seek information only to guide my investigations. The source of that information will never be divulged. Nor, of course, will any other, incidental information which I may accrue in the course of any of my investigations . . .'

The pitch of his words did not return to the tonic. He allowed them to hang on a casual fourth, admitting all sorts of developments and variations should the need arise. A modulation to the dominant was not out of the question.

Bolus wanted the tune at an end. 'I understand,' he

said, and he raised a hand as though to mop his brow, but instead merely pushed at his widow's peak with his fore-finger. 'Right, you had better come with me.'

He set his jaw and pushed back his chair with the violence characteristic of impotence in one accustomed to potency.

'What we have here is a curious scam but in many ways a very successful one.' Bill Gregory nodded to Jeremy, who poured claret from a silver and crystal ewer. The dining-room occupied one of the bays overlooking the terraces. It was decorated in a ponderous would-be Chinese style – swagging *famille rose* style flowers and dragons on a vellum field between blind relief-carved columns of ebonized wood. Luckily the lights – fringed Chinese lanterns – were low.

'No,' Gregory had to shift from one ham to the other in order to pick up his glass, 'let's just suppose. Let's suppose that someone – your brother, say, for the sake of argument – gains information that can be used to coerce jockeys or trainers. They're all members of a paedophile ring, say, and he has evidence. Alternatively, he threatens them with violence or, I suppose, though it seems unlikely, they're all in it together. So he picks certain races in the calendar such as we have seen – one, maybe two hot favourites and nothing much to touch them. In six of the fourteen races over sticks, your man Steve Shand was on one of the remaining animals. In every case, he lost. Otherwise, we have a wide selection of jockeys and a grand total of four trainers, your brother included, whose horses have run or travelled erratically and thus have been ruled out of conten-tion. On each occasion, if you knew for a fact that x was not going to win, you could say with certainty that y would. The animals who didn't reach the track or the ones scratched at the last moment served the purpose of keeping declara-tions down. By the time a horse is reported injured or whatever on the day of the race, it's too late for a trainer to say "Christ, mine could win this turning handsprings". He's already failed to declare his animal. Bad luck. The fix is on.'

He made that growling, gravelly noise again and set to his carpaccio with vigour. His eyebrows bobbed each time he swallowed. Philip, as usual, had eaten two mouthfuls then laid down his fork. He had brought his whisky in with him. He bit out a finger's width and laid the tumbler down.

'As for the people we reckon to be involved,' he gasped. 'As for . . . We've got Steve, nearing the end of his career, expensive tastes, and by all accounts broke . . .'

'Dowty, who obviously stood up to them, but got intimidated very effectively . . .'

'Freddy, who desperately needed the money . . .'

'And a rag-tag-and-bobtail selection of second-rate riders. On the flat, the equivalent of Shand would seem to be Jimmy Furlong.'

'Who's not bad, but he used to have a gambling problem when I was training, so presumably still has.'

'And it would seem, from your brother's experience, that the co-conspirators are rewarded by information about races in which they are not personally involved. In other words, they don't incriminate themselves by having a punt against their own animals, but they're informed of other sure-fire winners.'

'None of which gets us any nearer to understanding . . .' Philip stopped talking as Jeremy re-entered with a covered charger and placed it on the sideboard.

'Thank you, Jeremy.' Gregory raised his head as the resplendent butler removed the plate. 'We'll look after ourselves now. I'll ring when we want you.'

'Sir.' Jeremy reached for the claret.

Gregory flapped him away. 'I was pouring claret before you were born,' he huffed. 'I told you. We'll manage.'

Jeremy scuttled away. Gregory pointed at the sideboard. 'Help yourself, lad.'

Philip stepped up to the sideboard. Behind him, the ewer clucked. On the salver, he found six plain roast partridges wrapped in vine-leaves, sautéed potatoes and cabbage. 'Pot luck, indeed!' He helped himself to two of the birds with particular relish. 'This meal,' he announced, 'gives

263

me more pleasure than most. First, because I cherish the partridge above all other birds, and the French version, like the Frenchman, has little red legs, no taste and runs away squawking as soon as you shoot at it; second, because I have never had a meal paid for by bookies served by a butler paid for by bookies in a house paid for by bookies. Cervantes was wrong. Hunger is a fine sauce but vengeance is the best.'

'It still affords me satisfaction,' Gregory admitted. 'I feel a little like a latter-day Robin Hood – not that I give to the poor, but at least I rob those who rob the poor.'

No weightlifter with a deadweight made more noise than Gregory in lifting himself from his carver. He rocked to the sideboard. He stabbed three partridges, one by one, with the carving-fork and shook them on to his plate. 'No, you were saying ... ?' Philip could feel the rumble of Gregory's voice behind him.

'Just it brings us no closer to understanding who is responsible.'

'That's the trouble.' Gregory sat.

'It's just so strange that they'd ask him to do something which he so obviously couldn't afford to do.'

'Yeees.' Gregory clove a complete breast from one bird. He studied the pale pink flesh. 'Yes, except, of course, that there's an ante-post quotation on the Dewhurst. Probably the last of the year.' He popped the breast sideways into his mouth. He chewed.

'But the bets can't have been laid before Freddy was involved. He's been on the fiddle for eighteen months.'

'No.' Gregory gulped claret. He swallowed, breathed out heavily and started again. 'In theory, unlikely, I grant you. I can't work that one out. No, but what you've got here is a very clever scam, you think about it. Murder's an easy crime. I can't remember the exact figures, but I think it's something like ninety per cent of murders are domestic and ninety per cent of those which aren't are unsolved. That's because, you kill someone unconnected to you, you leave nothing behind to give you away. Trouble with theft, you take away the evidence, otherwise it's not worth doing. This scam is racing's version of that newest crime, consumer terrorism. You know, you ring up a major food company, whatever, say, "We've put arsenic in your baby-food." It's incredibly effective. The only thing that gives the criminal away is that he has to pick up the ransom money. Here you have consumer terrorism with no such problem. The criminal terrorizes trainers and jockeys and he picks up his ransom from the bookies and the Tote, anonymously and, to all appearances, legitimately. It's neat.' He anatomized another bird. 'It's very, very neat. It must be stopped.' He spoke with all the solemnity and sincerity of a statesman. 'I will give you every assistance that you need. I owe all this' he swivelled his head to encompass the room, 'to straight-run races. And I don't like bullies.'

'Nor I.' Philip raised his glass in a toast or a pledge. 'Don't worry,' he said, with more confidence than he felt, 'we'll screw the bastards.'

'It begins to make sense.' Vincent was enthusiastic later that night. He bounced on the velveteen banquette, leaned forward, rubbed his outstretched hands.

'Gor, yeah,' Tony put in. 'Wish I'd thought of that. You mean, you just ring up, put the frighteners on someone – "your 'orse don't run" or "your 'orse runs slow" – place the bets and clean up. Nice one.'

'Not so nice,' Philip reminded him. 'Remember, it only works if you're prepared to be nasty if someone calls your bluff.'

'Yeah, but . . . I mean, just hurt an 'orse. It's not like murder or something, is it? And you could be making a pile.'

Philip and Vincent turned to look at him where he sat in yellow, broad-collared canary yellow shirt, white jeans and cowboy boots which, it seemed, he had attempted to emboss with a hot needle. Neither man had to speak. They just looked.

'Yeah.' Tony looked down at his perfect nails in the

pulsing light of the gas flames. 'Yeah, well. I mean . . . I don't mean . . . I mean, it's nasty, sure, but I mean, cows, horses . . . I know you guys get all worked up, but . . . Oh, well.' He gave up before their glares. 'OK, OK. So I don't understand. I'm not saying as I'd do it. Just it seems a pretty perfect sort of scam is all.'

'So we need to have a word with the good Mr Shand,' Vincent told Philip.

'Yup. Which, at this moment, we cannot do because the said Mr Shand is in Ireland. Back tomorrow, I gather. Tony and I'll catch up with him.'

'It could be run by a jockey . . .' Vincent considered.

'It could, and that would explain a lot of things.'

'Like what?'

'Like the fact that Myshkin didn't bark that night. Like whoever is ringing seems to know the yard's routine inside out.'

'Hold on.' Vincent frowned. 'So we're now definitely associating the two things – the assault on Freddy, or rather, the abortive assault on Plutonium, and the race-fixing?'

'Yes, surely. Freddy turned renegade. That seems obvious.'

'Hmm.' Vincent was oracular. 'Well, I grant you, that seems reasonable. Except, if you're right, why did the intruder go to all that trouble and then not nobble the horse? Anyhow. Let me tell you what I've discovered. I have a friend . . .' he started. He looked up very suddenly as the landlord boomed, 'Time, ladies and gentlemen, please!'

'Have we time just to run through this?' Philip asked.

'Yes, yes.' Vincent subsided with much moustache-twitching. 'Not a great deal to tell, really, but. No. I have a friend in the bookmaking industry. This person was prevailed upon to give me information as to those account punters who appeared to have profited largely from this – as you call it – scam. I say, Tony, I don't want to be a killjoy or anything, but shouldn't you be down guarding our horse?'

Philip let the 'our horse' pass. 'Yes, you bloody should,' he snapped. 'Jim's on till closing-time. Get down there now.'

'Hey, I wanted to hear the rest of this,' Tony whined.

'Don't worry. I'll keep you abreast, as St Agatha might have said. Get going, and patrol like we arranged, at twenty minutes, thirty, thirty, twenty, ten.'

'I was waiting for Debbie.' Tony was glum. 'She said she'd be here. She was working late, stocktaking at Safeways . . .'

'If she comes in, we'll send her down. Please, Tony . . . ?' Philip's patience was heavily exaggerated.

Once again with a *moue* and a heavy shrug, Tony unravelled his long frame and slouched to the door.

'So, what have you got?' Philip looked down upon the deep cleft in Vincent's hat.

'Well, we have several account punters in various parts of the country who won on two or three of our selected races after investing more than usual. Two examples – and, mark you, we're only talking about one bookmaker – a Mr Charles Jerome of Battersea and a Mrs Frances Combe of Broadway, Worcestershire. Both of these opened accounts within the last two years, bet seldom, small and habitually lost, save on seven separate occasions, each linking to one of our races, when they laid sums of between two hundred and seven hundred pounds and, on every occasion, won. In Mrs Combe's case, there was one exception. A five hundred pound losing bet.'

'Clarendon.'

'Absolutely.' Vincent's expression was smug as he raised the glass of barley wine to his lips.

'Well done, sleuth!' Philip slapped his shoulder.

Vincent leaned forward as though retching. 'Oh, dear, oh dear,' he said. He flicked at his trousers, dabbed at his moustache. For all his discomposure, he could not conceal his pleasure. 'So, will you go and see them tomorrow?'

'Not a bit of it. They're yours. Take Tony if you want some muscle. He's up and about by lunchtime. Besides,' Philip downed his whisky and stood, 'tomorrow I have other fish to fry. Tomorrow I swap hats.'

'Oh, yes?'

'Yes. Tomorrow,' Philip pronounced, 'I cease to play Odysseus. Tomorrow, I am Orpheus again.'

Alison's methods the previous night may have been unsuccessful. Her accusations and her evident desperation, however, had had their effect. As Philip drove down to the yard these combined with his own bloody-mindedness to harden his resolve. If it were possible, Plutonium would run. The lights were burning in the hall and the library. He thought for a moment that he might knock on the door to tell her so. Then, he thought, perhaps not.

He noted with approval the lights about the yard. The headlights picked out Tony's long, lean frame, turned his silk shirt and his shock of hair white as he swung round, staring.

Philip jumped from the car. 'All quiet, then, Tony?' he rapped.

''Lo, mate. Yeah. Nothing. Seen Jim.'

Philip noticed that Tony was performing a strange jiggling sort of dance between him and the office door. He saw the dim flush of light from the window. Hell, Tony must have muffled the standard-lamp with a blanket or something.

'OK, OK, Tony.' Philip smiled. 'I'll knock, right? And I'll only be in there a second. Or you want to go in and warn her?'

'Yup. I mean – sorry, but you said . . .'

'It's all right, Tony! God, a bit of young lust is like a breath of fresh air. No. No problem. You just go on in, tell her I'll avert my eyes.'

Tony nodded, gave him a quick nervous grin and dived for the door. Philip heard the footfalls, Tony's voice, a girl's. He knocked gently.

'Yeah, OK.' Tony called.

He was kneeling, sheepishly proud and protective, at the head of the makeshift bed – the mattress from a Z bed laid on the floor by the desk, two blankets, a New Zealand rug atop the whole. The girl's white knickers and her black and white bra lay on the floor beside full coffee mugs which no longer steamed.

The girl from the pub looked coyly up above the rug. Her shoulders seemed very white. A smile played on her glossy pink lips. She tried a little 'Hello'.

'Hi,' Philip grinned. 'Sorry about this. I'll be out in a second. Stay warm. Tony, you should bring a heater in here.' He made in the half-light for the desk. He kicked fabric, looked down. A skirt. He sidestepped and sat at the desk. What he wanted was his mail. What he wanted still more was the half-bottle of Scotch in the second drawer.

He said, 'Cover your eyes. Just a moment.'

He reached for the light switch. There was a slight fizzing, a pop.

The room on the periphery sank back into darkness, but bright light slammed at Philip. Fire spat into his face and neck.

He was blinded, so he did not know that it was the bookcase that smashed against his crown. He was deafened, so he did not know if it was the girl or himself who was screaming or simply the searing pain within his skull.

He wanted to be unconscious, but the pain went on and on.

Jim Dobbs, fuddled by sleep, dazzled by the white lights, hard-tit cold in his pyjamas there, did not know what he was seeing, only that it did not belong out here in the night. A dream had escaped.

There had been the screaming, the fierce roar.

Now he saw a naked girl shouting, 'Get him up! Get him up!'

There was Tony: all in pale blue, straining to reach up into the water-butt, his shirt-sleeves dark and drenched, his face dripping diamonds.

There was – there were – the legs of an upside-down man kicking in the butt.

Jim said, 'What – ?'

'Give us a hand, for Christ's sake,' Tony spluttered.

Jim said, 'Um.'

'Go on!' the naked girl shrilled. 'Give him a hand!'

She turned to face him. The swirls of her pubic hair reminded him of a horse's tail, splayed in running.

Her hands were pushing him, pulling him towards the butt. He mumbled, 'All right. Right. Yes.'

He climbed on to the brick stack on which the butt stood. There was a lot of sploshing and surging of water. Water splashed his face and soaked his chest. The legs vanished.

A head appeared, a head from nightmare or mythology, a head so horrible that Jim leaped backwards and toppled back on to the cobbles. He stared up wide-eyed.

The head had weed for hair, weed which dribbled down over eyes and chin. The head was spattered with blood which welled, it seemed, from greasy, unbroken skin. It opened its mouth. It said, 'Grrahh!' It spat.

Jim sussed it. He was awake. 'Mr Glaister?'

'Who d'you think it is?' Tony snarled. 'Come on. Let's get in. Debbie, you'd better get some clothes on. Come on, Phil, let's get you out. Jesus! Come on. Get you out of those clothes.'

Philip nodded. 'Thank Christ.' He spat and kept spitting as he clambered out, heaving himself out on Tony's shoulders. 'God, I stink!'

'Somewhat,' Tony agreed. He grunted as Philip's weight slumped on his shoulder. 'Come on, Jim. Give a hand.'

Jim Dobbs checked his pyjama flies, then, with a shudder, took up his position at Philip's left shoulder. The two men half carried Philip back into the office. The girl had pulled on a sweater and a skirt. She had switched on the central light. She turned. She said, 'God, what a mess.'

'We've got all the First Aid stuff, antiseptics, so on,' Jim volunteered. He let Philip gently down into the one armchair.

'Get them,' the girl instructed. 'Tony, you going to ring the police?'

Tony looked to Philip. Philip shook his shaggy head. 'Not yet. We can sort this out, I hope.'

Jim Dobbs tottered out, studying his hands, plucking at his pyjamas. The girl carried the horse rug over to Philip. 'Let's get this over you, then get those clothes off.' She was brisk. 'You must be freezing.'

'I am,' Philip shuddered, 'except where I'm burning. Jesus. What was it?'

'Well, I smelt petrol, sure of it.'

'Must have cut open the light bulb,' Philip mumbled, 'put in petrol and some sort of nitrate. Probably topped it up with detergent so that the burning bits would stick. Switch on the light – bang.'

'God, we must get some of that glass out of you . . . How you weren't blinded . . .'

'I don't know.' Philip's teeth rattled. 'I think . . . There was something strange. I raised an arm, I think. Reflex.'

She unbuttoned his shirt beneath the rug. She eased him forward to strip it off. 'Thank God for that,' she breathed.

Jim was back. Debbie quickly and efficiently lined up iodine, cotton-wool bandages and plaster. She demanded water. Tony filled an ashtray from the tap in the corner. Debbie started dabbing. Philip started wincing and hissing.

'Right,' he said over her shoulder. 'Tony, you've been here since just after closing-time, right?'

'Yeah. Debs was already down 'ere waiting for us, weren't you, Debs?'

'Yup. Hold still,' she told Philip. 'Yup. Wires crossed. I was down here just after ten. Sat here twiddling my thumbs.'

'And obviously you didn't turn on the desk-lamp.'

'Nope.'

'And no one came here?'

'Nope.'

'So, this was done earlier. Jim. Who's been round the yard today?'

'Just the usual, Mr Glaister,' Jim said easily. 'No one's been in the office. No one's got a key. 'Cept me.'

'And you wouldn't give a key to anyone else, would you?'

'Nah. Course not!'

271

'You seem to be worried about your flies, Jim.'

'No. No. Just, you know, ladies . . .'

'Tony?'

'Yup?'

'Take off his trousers, would you?'

''Ere . . .' Jim protested, 'what the fuck – ' But the 'fuck' was forced from him as his back hit the floor. He flapped and clawed, but Tony was quick. He straightened, the striped flannel trousers flapping from his hand.

Jim Dobbs's face was bright red. His cheeks bulged. His hands clasped his genitals. He curled himself into a wood-louse crouch. 'What's this all about?' he whined, truculence mingled with pathos. 'You can't do this. I need my trousers . . . Is this a joke or what?'

'No,' Philip said calmly. He leaned back. Debbie held his right eye open wide. 'I like to have you at a disadvantage. Always helps the memory. Who's been here today, Jim?'

'I told you.'

'I know you told me, like you told me the other day that no one had been here when the telephone rang. But someone was here, wasn't he? And that someone has a key, hasn't he?'

'No, of course not.'

'Tony,' Philip said, matter-of-fact, 'kick him, will you? Break, say, three of the less significant ribs, initially.'

'No!' Jim barked. 'No. You touch me and I'll . . .'

'You'll what?' Tony's voice was flattened by a smile. 'Facts of life, mate. You are bollock naked on the ground. I got clothes on and I'm standing up.'

'Fucking yob,' Jim sneered.

'So, are you going to tell us?' Philip said, adding an 'Ow!' as Debbie extracted a shard from his cheek and staunched the bleeding. 'Are you going to tell us? What did he give you, Jim? Tips, was it? Or was it just hero worship? What did he tell you? Just an innocent prank, something like that? When did he get back?'

''S afternoon,' he mumbled.

'Stand him up, Tony,' Philip ordered. 'He doesn't speak too clearly.'

'Get your 'ands off me . . .' There was thumping and

scuffling. Jim snapped, 'Awright. I said, this afternoon. But 'e didn't do this. 'E wouldn't do this.'

'He did, Jim.'

'Any'ow, 'e works 'ere. Nothing wrong with 'im being around.'

'Hit him, Tony.'

There was a soft thud, then a hiss as of a burst ball, a metallic keening.

'Pack your bags, Dobbs,' Philip snapped. 'Security is paramount in your job. Don't look to me for a reference.'

'Your – your reference wouldn't be worth shit,' Jim croaked.

'Get him out of here, Tony. Please.'

'I'll talk to Mrs Glaister,' Jim gabbled as Tony propelled him from the room. 'I'll talk to the press. I'll tell . . .'

The door slammed. The room seemed to sigh.

'So you're saying . . .' Tony sauntered back. He looked down at Philip. 'Who are you saying done this?'

'I can't quite see why,' Philip's hand arose by reflex to grasp Debbie's, 'but he's the only one who knows the workings of this yard and who has the freedom to come and go, and he's been involved from the outset!'

'What's his name?'

'His name,' Philip said sadly, 'is Steve Shand.'

The face Philip saw in the mirror the following morning was an abstract expressionist mess. He looked as though he had been in a fight with a pack of cats. The glass had pocked and scraped his skin. He had bathed twice, but Penhaligons' best had not been sufficient to drive the stench of stagnant water from his nostrils.

He was down in the yard at half-past six. There were only two jumpers left in the yard, and they would go this afternoon. Of the two flat horses, only Plutonium needed exercising. The other would be let down now, put out.

Philip rapped on the door to Jim Dobbs's flat. Dobbs looked sullen when he came to the door. He instantly adopted a still more sullen pout on seeing Philip.

'You want?'

'See you. Look, you admit making a mistake? You know who pays you?'

'Sure.'

'And you know your duty's to your paymaster?'

'Maybe.'

'Try "yes" and you can stay on another month, have three months' pay in lieu of notice and a glowing reference.'

'Decided you need me, then, have you?'

'Nope. Decided you made an honest mistake. Steve's a charming man and you saw no harm in it. What? He said, "Don't tell the guv'nor . . ."?'

''E said 'e couldn't take some private 'phone calls at 'ome. Jealous woman, you know? 'Ad a girl rang 'im 'ere.'

'He conned you. Pay you in tips?'

'Yeah.' The sullen lower lip reappeared. 'Bloody good tips an' all.'

'Oh, yes. I make no doubt of it. I could tell you precisely which races you won on. How much were you allowed on?'

'Twenty.'

'Hm. So, how often was he round?'

'Well . . . Not sure as I owe you anything . . .'

'Come on, Jim. You blundered, you got caught out. Don't get all fucking self-righteous with me. You want to be out on your ear, you hold out on me. Tell me.'

'Well, not a lot. Just the odd evening, some nights.'

'Some nights?'

'Yeah, I'd catch 'im 'anging around, like. I mean, I thought . . . I mean, you know, we was looking out for someone trying to nobble Plutonium, weren't we, and 'e's 'ad enough opportunity, 'asn't 'e? So it weren't 'im. So I thought, you know, I mean, another pair of eyes . . . I still don't believe 'e'd do that – explosions, that sort of thing. It's not like 'im.'

'Whether it was him or not, have we an agreement? You don't mention a thing to him this morning, OK?'

'Yeah. OK. You didn't 'ave to do that with my trousers, you know.'

274

'That's past. Leave it.'

'So what am I meant to do if he comes back, eh?'

'Don't worry,' Philip said quickly. 'He won't be back.'

Dobbs caught the look in Philip's eye. He swallowed a jagged chunk of air. 'Like that, eh?'

Philip nodded. 'Like that.'

'Top of the morning to you, Philip.' Steve stepped from his silver XJS with a smile like a slash in a sack full of jewels. 'Jesus, you run into a window or something?'

'Sort of. The glass ran into me.'

'God. Car?'

'Don't worry. I'll recover.'

'Narrow miss there. Right eye.'

'It missed, though.'

'You want me to mount up here?'

'Why not, you've got the time? Yes. You've just got the Deep Run to school, right?'

'Yup.' Steve scratched his head. He gazed around the yard. 'I suppose this is the last time.'

'Yes. They'll all be gone by next week.'

'Shit. I don't know. I'll miss the old place.' Steve blinked. He was sincere. 'It's still the loveliest training establishment in the kingdom, for my money. A proper house, a gent's house. This yard. Classy, old fashioned. The gallops. It may not be trendy any more, but it's pukka.'

'Pukka doesn't cut the mustard any more, for better or for worse,' Philip said sourly. 'That's what my father thought. A gent's place, classy, all that, a lovely place to live, a wonderful way to live, a glamorous, old-style folly. It doesn't work that way. Not any more.'

'It should,' said Steve with certainty. 'God, property developers could move in here.'

'Count the property developers amongst your owners,' Philip sighed. 'It's a spiv's world. Married, monogamous, monotonous and mealy-mouthed frauds. They're the rulers today. We're fossils.' He too was sincere. He too smiled sadly about the yard. 'Money without land. Power without responsibility. The prerogative of the harlot. Ah, well.' He shook himself from his reverie. What was it about Shand that got him talking like that, opening up? 'Good. I'll not be coming up there today. Leave it to you.'

Steve nodded. He reached into his car for the skullcap and the whip.

Philip watched him, the ease of him, the confidence, the one-sided smile, the twinkling eyes.

What was this about? Was it loyalty to a younger brother for whom he cared little? Loyalty to Swynsmere, which he had long hated? He didn't know. He didn't know even how Shand fitted into all this, only that somehow, deviously, he did.

And whatever the reason, Philip narrowed his eyes, drew a bead on the smiling, stocky man, thought 'I'm going to do you, Shand,' and he felt angry, though still he could not say why.

London again, and Tony at his side, pointing at theatres, recognizing names from TV. Horns howled on Tottenham Court Road. The street was blocked solid by a demonstration. A leaflet was shoved under the windscreen-wiper. Unborn children. Right to life.

Philip gunned the engine, swerved left then right, ducking out through Soho in screeching jerks. Tony whooped, then resumed his old tune. 'Ah, come on. Show us, will you? I mean. I won't tell. Wouldn't recognize anyone anyhow.'

'Nope,' Philip snapped. 'Leave it be, Tony. You want smutty pictures, there's plenty available in the newsagents here. I told you. These are confidential.'

'Ooooow!' Tony whined in frustration. 'It's unfair. Where we going, anyhow?'

'We're going to see some nasty people, some very rich, very powerful specimens of vaguely human ordure. Don't give your name, and watch my back, all right?' Philip drew up outside a black glass tower block. He pushed open the car door.

''Ere, you just parking here?' Tony gaped.

276

'I just did. Come on.'

Together they strode into the softly lit reception area. There was a long terracotta bed full of New Zealand flax and sweaty, dark green plants against one window. Water splashed in the courtyard garden beyond. A buffed girl sat alone at a horse-shoe shaped reception desk.

'Mr Glaister to see Mr Calza,' Philip announced.

'Yes, sir.' The voice was smooth as the auburn hair, the shiny skin. The smile was white vinyl. 'Have you an appointment?'

'I rang this morning.'

'Yes, but we have no record that an appointment was made.'

'Take this in to Mr Calza.' Philip handed her an envelope. 'He'll see me.'

The woman looked stern. She pressed a button on the console before her. 'Olivia? Lynne here. Could you come and pick up a letter for Mr Calza at Reception? There are two gentlemen here who want to see Mr Calza.'

The receptionist gave Philip a defiant look. She said, 'Please take a seat. It may be a long wait.'

It was a five-minute wait. Philip smoked. Tony patrolled, frustrated, confined. A dark, trim girl in black emerged from the lift. She said, 'Mister . . . ?'

'Glaister,' said Philip.

She held out a hand. Philip handed her the envelope. 'Strictly private and confidential,' he said.

'May I ask what this is in connection with?'

'Tell him Herons.'

'Herons?'

'Herons.'

The girl shrugged and clicked back to the lift.

There was a lot more silence. 'Jesus,' Philip threw his cigarette into the plant-pot. 'This is the bit I don't like.'

'What's the deal?'

'Any minute now, we could hear police sirens or we could be escorted from the premises by a bevy of bruisers and lowered into the waters of the Thames with kerbstones for pendants. I don't think so, but . . .'

'Oh,' said Tony. 'Gawd. I don't even know what this is about . . .'

'You wish you were back plucking?'

'Nah.' Tony grinned.

The fountain splashed some more. Philip wished that it would stop. His bladder ached. He stood. He walked around the hall. He peered out through the smoked glass.

The girl reappeared as he sat again. He jumped up.

'Mr Glaister.' She was frosty. 'Mr Calza will see you.'

Philip nodded. He followed the girl to the lift. Tony was taking his instructions very literally. Philip could feel his breath, smell his after-shave at his shoulder.

They travelled to the nineteenth floor in silence. The dark girl stood back to allow the two men to pass. Philip said, 'No, after you.' The gallantry of suspicion.

Standoff.

Her grey eyes gazed straight into his. Her lips twitched. 'Very well,' she said. 'Thank you.'

She walked out, her tight black arse rustling as it shifted from side to side. She led them into another reception area, this one brightly lit. A deep beige carpet muffled their footfalls.

The girl nodded to the receptionist. She swung to her right and bustled down a broad corridor lined with doors. Two young men in suits walked towards them. Philip's fists clenched, but the girl nodded and walked on. The men passed.

The girl led them through a door at her right. An anteroom, a vacant desk. A further door.

'Mr Calza, Mr Glaister,' the girl announced.

'Thank you, Olivia. Leave us be, would you?'

The girl about-wheeled. The door dragged through the carpet, clicked quietly shut.

The man was a burly silhouette against the broad glass window. He said, 'Mr Glaister, sit down, please. And your – your friend.'

Philip said, 'No, thank you, Mr Calza.'

Calza moved round the big partner's desk. Philip had seen him at the races and in the papers. He was a big man

278

with big black eyebrows, a high forehead and a heavy belly. He was one of those businessmen never more precisely described. He owned businesses. He owned millions. He imported and exported. He inspired whispered speculation. His investment in bloodstock via Richard Heron had started only in the last three years.

'You have sent up a fake photograph,' Calza's voice was deep. He stood like a duellist, six feet from Philip. 'I would have sent you away, but I am curious as to just what you thought you could obtain by this clumsy device.'

'It is not a fake,' Philip said calmly. 'I'll submit it to any test you like. It's for real.'

'Let's pretend,' Calza purred. 'Let's just pretend. The picture's real, you say. All right. If it were, what would you want from me?'

'Not I, Mr Calza. My employer.'

'Your employer? You used to be a trainer, didn't you?'

'Yes.'

'Your employer. What, then, would your employer want?'

'Increased investment. There's a yearling coming up at Keeneland. Four hundred and fifty thousand dollars for a half-share.'

'Hmm.' Calza walked to the end of the desk. He leaned forward, considering. 'I don't understand. If you are referring to the person I think you are referring to, why has he not first approached me without this – this ugly threat?'

'I don't know,' Philip said mechanically. 'He doesn't discuss things like that with me.'

'And how do I know that you aren't engaged in a little personal free enterprise, Mr Glaister?'

'I get a wage, that's all. I don't stand to profit, do I?'

'No, no.' Calza shook his heavy head, incredulous. 'All right. Say, just say – again playing let's pretend – say I said "Go to hell," what then?'

'I leave that to your imagination, Mr Calza. I imagine that Mrs Calza would be interested. And the newspapers, your business associates, I don't know. I'm just guessing.'

'But that would also implicate Mrs Heron, wouldn't it?'

'That does not seem to concern my employer.'

'Ah, so that's the way the wind blows, is it? I see. Another nice, cheap divorce.' Calza straightened. He suddenly barked, 'I think your employer is making a very considerable mistake, Mr Glaister.'

'You do?'

'I do indeed,' he nodded, 'I do indeed. Come to that, you haven't exactly endeared yourself to me by this little visit.'

'I'm only the messenger, Mr Calza.'

'Yes, well, messengers have a way of getting associated with their messages, Mr Glaister. So. I am expected to increase my investment in Heron bloodstock by four hundred and fifty thousand, am I?'

'That's what I'm charged to tell you.'

'And I suppose this goes on and on, doesn't it?'

'Sorry?'

'I don't get the negatives, anything like that?'

'I have not been apprised as to my employer's plans in that regard.'

'You cannot make a bigger mistake than this . . .' Calza murmured, and, standing there, slowly shaking his head, he looked as dangerous as anyone Philip had ever seen. 'So, Mr Glaister, what's the yearling?'

'Doyley Carte out of Otterburn. Tuesday afternoon.'

'Very well, Mr Glaister. You may leave. And, Mr Glaister?'

'Yes?'

'Don't let me see you again. Don't let me hear of you again. Lie very, very low for the rest of your days.'

Philip gulped. 'Yes,' he croaked, and, by reflex, 'sir.'

An electrical discount shop, a bookmakers', a corner pub . . . Philip sidestepped a pushchair, danced with a Sikh. He stepped off the pavement into the road. A lorry grumbled by, mere inches away. A Pepsi can yelped beneath its wheels.

Back on to the pavement then, Tony dogging his heels. A newsagents, an office suppliers, The Star of Delhi, a bristling wino drooling in the doorway, clasping his Cyprus sherry close, a minicab joint . . .

A seaside rock awning then. Pictures in the window. Blonde girls and mustachioed men, naked but patched with white towels, sat on slats in a sauna, looking cool. Male and female heads smiled above the swirling of a jacuzzi. The neon scroll above the door read Las Palmas Unisex Health and Fitness.

Philip swerved in, pushed open the glass door. More pictures on the walls, a list of available services and a little Japanese girl on a high stool behind the counter. She wore white shorts. She clasped her knee. She smiled, 'Harro.'

'Hi. Right. What's on the menu?' Philip studied the tariff. A special set you back forty pounds: half an hour's shiatsu, half an hour's sunbed and unlimited use of the jacuzzis, the sauna and the gym. Philip could use the shiatsu. His shoulders felt like joints from the freezer.

Another time. There was business to be done.

'We'll just take the basic, please.' Philip reached into his back pocket. He laid three ten-pound notes on the counter. 'You busy?'

'Norra the moment, no.'

Outside a police siren sawed. The sound swallowed itself. The girl handed Philip and Tony rubber wrist bands with numbered keys. She drew two small towels from the pile beside her. 'Changing-room through there,' she nodded.

Philip pushed through a slatted door and into a narrow room lined with tin lockers.

'What? We strip?' Tony gaped.

'Nah. Dress up in eighteenth-century court dress before jumping in the jacuzzi – what do you think, dumbo?'

'No, come on, but, I mean – everything?'

Philip hung his tie in the locker. He unbuttoned his shirt. 'Of course everything, Tony. What's wrong with that? Tell you what. I see anything I haven't seen before, I'll scream, right?'

Philip pulled back the green and white shirt. He kicked off his shoes as he worked at his cufflinks. 'Come on, Tony. You can't look worse than the average Englishman. Come to that, nothing can look worse than the average English-man.'

'Yeah, no, but . . .' Tony started nervously to pluck at the buttons on his rainbow shirt.

'But me no buts.' Philip hung his shirt on a wire hanger.

'Yeah, but it said "Unisex" out there.'

'That's right.' Philip pushed down his trousers. He carefully lined up the creases. 'Come on. The towel will preserve your maidenly modesty. Anyhow, Debbie didn't look so shell-shocked the other night.'

Philip, in common with many men who appear sham-bolic when dressed, stripped well. His shoulders and stomach were well muscled, his chest deep, his legs strong. Tony, when deprived of his finery, was not so prepossessing. His ribs stared through his white skin. There was a cyclone of fair hair about each nipple. His chest was shallow, his limbs stringy. He clutched the towel very tight. 'Gawd,' he gulped, 'I feel a right berk.'

Philip led him out into a large blue room where two men and two women lay naked on loungers, sipping fruit juice and watching MTV. A cockatoo strutted in one cage, a mynah in another. There were potted palmy plants. Tony said 'Gawd' again as he clocked the tits, the casually exposed genitalia. He jumped when the mynah whistled.

They walked on to the bar, where two girls, one a pony-tailed blonde, one a luscious Hispanic, sat wearing nothing but thongs. Tony groaned, 'Oh, my gawd.'

The Hispanic girl said, 'Apple, orange or mineral water?'

'Water for me, love,' Philip said. 'Tony?'

But Tony stood transfixed by the bobbing breasts. His jaw had dropped.

'Tony,' Philip coaxed. 'Do you want a drink?'

'Er . . .' Tony licked his lips. 'Yeah, lager, please.'

'No, Tony. This is a health club. Fruit juice or water.'

'Oh, right. Yeah.' Tony wrenched his eyes up towards the ceiling. 'Orange, please.'

The dark girl pushed the drinks over to them. 'Steve Shand around, is he?' Philip asked casually.

282

The dark girl shrugged. The blonde said, 'Steve? Yep. He'll probably be in the gym. Or the steam-room.'

'Thanks.' The two men picked up their drinks and wandered on. At their right, two jacuzzis swirled and bubbled. There were chairs and tables about the plunge-pool at their left. 'Oh, Jeez.' Tony moaned as more nudity assailed his eyes. There were sauna cabins then and, at the left, the glass door of the steam-room. Philip downed his drink. He shed the towel. He pushed the door and sidestepped in. Tony lingered in the doorway, still clutching the towel to his groin. 'Shut the bloody thing, man!' Philip barked.

'Oh. Yeah. Sorry.' Tony pulled the door shut behind him.

He coughed.

Philip sat on a bench. The figures in here emerged from the wreaths of steam like images in a developing photograph. Beside him, a long-limbed woman in a G string sat with her eyes closed. Beyond, a balding man with rolls of suet dough where his waist should have been sat brooding on a clutch of heavy hanging testicles. Tony sat nervously on the other side of the room. He yelped and leaped up. 'Hey, sorry,' he said. He had sat upon a foot at the end of an extended chubby leg. 'Look, I mean, I'm really sorry. I mean, I didn't see ... I mean, it wasn't deliberate or anything . . .'

'It's OK.' The woman's voice was amused. 'Don't worry.' She removed the leg.

Tony sat again. 'Phew. Hot, isn't it?' he announced.

'That,' Philip informed him, 'is the general idea.'

'Gor, I dunno. Why do people do this?'

'I like it. Reminds me of old times.'

'Yeah?'

'Yup. Riding days. You have a bender, you spend the night in one of these places.'

'The whole night? Jesus.'

'Yup. Sweat off pounds. If you're still putting up overweight, have a bath in Epsom salts. That gets the heart going. Then piss-pills or diuretics. Makes you think twice about gorging yourself.'

283

'Lor, I bet. Shit, I can't hardly breathe.'

'Go on, then. Pop out. See if our man's in the gym. Don't let him see you.'

Tony gratefully arose and staggered to the door. He returned three minutes later. He wiped his nose on his arm. 'Yeah,' he sniffed. 'He's in there, pumping iron.'

'Alone?'

'Yeah.'

'Let's go.'

The gym was at the very back of the building. Tony pointed at the door. 'This is it,' he said.

'OK. Straight in,' Philip murmured, 'quick and quiet. Don't give him a chance to think. When we've subdued him, you come back here and keep other punters out, right?'

Tony nodded.

Philip pushed the door.

Steve Shand lay flat on his back on a black vinyl-covered bench. The balls of his feet rested on the floor on either side. He wore gold satin shorts and a grey T-shirt. He was pulling a chrome bar downward. The bar was connected by a pulley to the stack of weights at his head.

'Hello, Shand,' Philip was at his side before Steve could move. 'You haven't enough weight on there.'

Steve's mouth opened. He released the bar. His head arose. His eyes veered, alarmed, from Tony at his one side to Philip at his other. Philip laid a hand on his chest. He pushed him back down. 'Easy,' he said. 'Tony, let's have a bit more weight on there, shall we?'

'Sure.' Tony held a clump of Steve's hair in his right hand. He bent. He pulled out the peg and moved it four or five weights further down.

'Hey, what's going on?' Steve babbled, half grinned. 'I mean, what's the joke?'

'No joke, Shand,' Philip snapped. 'Just helping with your exercises. Spin him round, Tony.'

Together they swivelled Steve's body around so that his stomach was where his head had been. He wriggled and kicked, tried to roll from the bench but the four hands held him firm. 'Hey, come on. What the fuck are you up to?'

'Shut up, Shand,' Philip ordered quietly. 'And lie still, let's see if you can pull this, hmm?'

'No. No, look, what's going on? No, look, please . . .'

'I said shut up and pull. We'll talk afterwards.'

'No!' Steve whined, 'It's too heavy, for God's sake!'

'I told you. We'll help you. Pull.'

Steve strained against the bar. Philip nodded to Tony. He grasped the end of the bar and pushed it downward. Philip pulled Steve's legs through the gap which opened up between the raised weights and those remaining.

The weights with their black iron spike hung directly above his groin.

'Right. That's enough help, Tony,' Philip said calmly. 'Let him take the strain now. Mind the door.'

Tony nodded. He released the bar. It sagged. Steve released a long clogged grunt as the weight arose against his hands. 'Christ!' he wheezed. He screwed up his face. 'What are you doing?'

'We thought you might feel more like talking in that position,' Philip said. He strolled around the bench.

'I – I can't talk. If that thing comes down . . .'

'If it goes down, a spike with twelve kilograms on it will plunge straight through your intestines.'

'Christ almighty,' Steve's arms shook. Sweat wriggled down his shoulders. 'Quickly, then. What do you want?'

'Race-fixing, Shand. You're deep in. Tell me the story.'

'There – is – no – fucking – story. I got – telephone – calls, same as – Freddy. God. Please.'

'Who made the calls?'

'I don't know. I s-swear I don't know. It's a man, that's all. He just tells us – what to do. I got paid – in – tips. My – my girlfriends – backed the horses for me. Please, Philip, Mister Glaister, please help . . .'

'What about the night Freddy died?'

'I don't know anything!' His body shook violently. Tears dribbled from the corners of his eyes. His legs gave little convulsive kicks.

'So why have you been hanging about the yard?'

'S-same as you. Same as Alison. Protect – Plutonium.'

'So why'd you put that fucking bomb in my office?'

'I d-d-didn't! I didn't know about any bomb!'

'I don't think you've got enough weight on there, Shand.'

'No! No!' he yelped. 'Oh, God, please. I didn't do it! I don't know about any b-bomb. Please, oh, God, please!'

His shaking arms were giving now. The spike hung just above the satin of his shorts. He was sobbing, drooling. His neck was swollen and purple. 'Please. I didn't know. I didn't know. I didn't know . . .'

Philip looked down upon him with a cold, unmoved eye. 'All right,' he said at last. He grabbed the bar in both hands. He pushed downward.

Steve squirmed out from between the weights. He floundered like a banked fish. He toppled to the floor where he lay hugging himself, bent and sobbing. A pool of golden liquid spread from under the golden shorts. Philip released the bar. The weights clanked down.

'You believe him?' Tony asked from the door.

'I have to.' Philip walked over towards him. 'Look at him. The buck, the ladies' man.'

'But where does that leave us?' Tony protested. 'I mean, someone that knows the yard, someone that the dog doesn't bark at . . .'

'It leaves us,' Philip snarled, 'altogether too fucking close to home.'

'I have a memorial service to attend, Philip,' Ivo Donovan had told him on the telephone, 'then a board meeting. Believe it or not, I still retain a consultative role at one or two firms. I anticipate that I will not be free until half-past three, maybe four o'clock. You say that this is urgent?'

'Yes, sir.'

'You can give me no indication as to the precise nature of the matter?'

'Aside from the fact that it relates to Eledi, no, sir.'

'How very mysterious. Very well, Philip. I assume it must be important. Lord. I haven't seen you – you must have been damn near in short trousers. Listen, will this take long?'

'No, sir. Half an hour at most.'

'I shall be, then, at the Lowndes Hotel at four o'clock precisely. I would be grateful if you would be as punctual. I want to get off before the worst of the rush hour.'

Philip was more than punctual. He was in the foyer of the hotel at a quarter to four. He gave his name to the receptionist. He informed her that he would be awaiting Mr Donovan in the bar. He told Tony to keep quiet for the next half hour or so. His stomach gulped and whimpered. He wanted this interview over.

His fears were several. First, he did not relish being hated by a man whom he believed and remembered to be decent and honourable. Second, he did not look forward to the hurt that he was going to do. Finally, he had no desire to cause the old man to suffer a heart attack.

On the last count he was to some extent consoled by the sight of the man who strolled in at three minutes to four amidst the troika tinkle of tea. The figure was upright, slender and strong. The skin was tanned and glossy. The hair was almost as white as the shirt. The eyes which scanned the bar were sharp and clear. You'd put him down as a cricketer, perhaps, or a fencer.

Philip swallowed and stood. He stepped forward. 'Mr Donovan?'

'Philip. I'd have recognized you. You're your mother's son.' His hand was warm and dry. 'Sorry to be so curt on the telephone, but really, the least time I can spend in this hellhole . . .'

'I'm with you. I'm sorry about this. Can I get you a drink or something?'

'I don't think so, no, thank you. I would sooner know just what all this cloak and dagger stuff is all about.' He laid his briefcase on the chintz-covered bench. He sat beside it. Philip pulled out a gilt chair. He sat and gazed at Donovan across the table.

'I suppose I should have kept in touch,' he said, 'but, what with Eledi's marriage and so on, we seem to have been pretty much estranged. You probably heard that I made a cock-up of Swynsmere. I now live in the South of France.'

'I see.'

Philip took a deep breath. 'And Mr Heron was down there recently. He engaged me to do certain things for him on my return to England.'

'What sort of things?'

'I was to approach various people, including yourself, with certain incriminating photographs – of your daughter.'

'You were to do what?' Donovan winced.

'Mr Heron wishes to be rid of Eledi. He does not, however, want an expensive settlement. He wants me to show you these photographs and urge you to advise your daughter not to make trouble.'

'I am aware that Mr Heron is a shit, Mr Glaister,' Donovan said smoothly, 'but this implausible story needs some confirmation.'

'I have a letter here from Miss Duncan, Mr Heron's assistant.' Philip pulled Angela's letter from his pocket. He handed it over.

Donovan read. Philip saw his lips forming the words, 'Piss off.' Donovan laid down the letter very carefully. 'I see,' he said. 'And?'

'Well, as you see, they declined to pay me the full sum.'

'So now you turn to me in hope of revenue, is that right?' Donovan's voice was suddenly harsh. 'You have turned out, in short, to be not only a blackmailer, but a treacherous one at that?'

'I was merely trying to help you, sir,' Philip soothed. 'I assumed that you would rather have these photographs yourself than have them seen by Mr Heron's cronies or by the press.'

Donovan's eyes narrowed. His upper lip arose in a sneer. 'Dear God,' he breathed, 'I thank God that Tom is dead. He always said that you were a wrong 'un. I mocked him. Said you couldn't judge like that. But by God, Tom knew his men and his animals. If I had my way, *Mister* Glaister,

I would spit on you for the vermin that you are and walk out of here.'

'I think you'd better see the photographs first, sir.'

Donovan disdainfully held out a hand. Philip handed him a brown envelope. 'I wouldn't look at them here, sir,' he said huskily. 'They are – unpleasant.'

Donovan glared. He arose. He picked up his briefcase. His hip hit Philip's arm as he strode by.

Philip slumped and puffed out air. 'Jesus.' He closed his eyes. He clasped the bridge of his nose between finger and thumb. 'This is hard.'

'God, poor sod, seeing his daughter like that,' said Tony.

'Get a waiter. I need a large whisky.'

The waiter and the whisky had arrived before Donovan returned. He walked stiffly now. His eyes were red-rimmed and staring. His lips twitched and trembled before he could bring himself to speak. His voice was hoarse. 'They're fakes,' he said.

'Maybe,' Philip shrugged. 'I wouldn't know. Mr Heron just gave them to me . . .'

'That bastard, Heron. No maybes. They're fakes. Oh, the locations are right. Those are Heron's houses, and that bitch, Duncan. Oh, he'd do it right, but those photographs are fakes. I'll prove it.'

'I'm sure you will, sir.'

'And then I'll advise her to sue the little shit for every bloody penny.' His voice arose. Two good ladies with gardens on their heads turned.

'Easy,' said Philip. 'I'm glad to have been of some service.'

'And you expect payment, I suppose?'

'I'll leave that to you, sir.'

'Well, I suppose . . . I do not like you, Mr Glaister, nor what you represent, nor the sort of filthy work you are prepared to do. However, forewarned is forearmed, and the good Mr Heron is going to find a lot of his business deals going mysteriously wrong thanks to your treachery. I'll prove these photographs to be fakes, then . . . My Christ, the deviousness of the man. Anyhow.' He flicked open his briefcase. 'Fifteen hundred you were owed. Fifteen hundred you will get.'

'That's very good of you, sir.' Philip was humble.

Donovan pulled out a large cheque-book. He scribbled fast in a jagged, sloping hand. He placed the cap back on his fountain pen. He blew the cheque and threw it across at Philip as though the touch of it offended him.

'Are there more of these?' He pointed at the envelope.

'I don't know, sir.' Philip pocketed the cheque. 'These were the ones I was given.'

'Mr Richard Heron may think he invented dirty play,' Donovan said. He threw the envelope into the case. He flicked the clasps and stood. 'He will discover that there are fouls he never heard of. Goodbye, Mr Glaister.'

'But he'll prove they're fakes!' Tony protested as Donovan strode from the room.

'I hope so,' said Philip. 'Then he'll never believe any others to be real, will he? God,' he said sadly as he tore the cheque in two, then four, then eight, and piled the scraps in the ashtray, 'I've never seen a man age five years in as many minutes.'

'This guy Heron's not going to like you much, is he?'

'Ah, you get used to it.' Philip downed his drink, and wished that it were true.

Vincent Lovelady stood in his own sitting-room, Pooter paterfamilias. He had shed the coat and replaced it with a cardigan. He had at last removed the hat, exposing five or six thin black streaks across his cranium.

'The first of our account punters,' he consulted his clipboard, 'was one Mark Ellsworth. A nice young fellow. Very nervous, very unsure of himself, very lost. He used to work in the City. Came in at the end of the eighties boom. He seems to have wanted to be like the people in the films. Striped shirts, you know, red braces, power-lunches, big cars, all that sort of thing. He couldn't understand why it didn't happen. He took to playing at casinos. He lost more than he won. Silly boy. Sold furniture, big overdraft . . .

Then a form arrives in the post, nicely printed, offset litho, he thinks: "A Regular Income Can be Yours," that sort of thing. He'd already thrown it in the bin when the telephone rang. It was a man. He did not give a name, but he told poor little Mr Ellsworth that he had been specially selected. The caller knew all about his debts, everything. All he had to do was fill in the form giving details of his bankers, his credit cards, date of birth, all that, and send it to an address in Walthamstow. I checked it out. It was, predictably, an accommodation address. Then, the caller said, Mr Ellsworth merely had to place bets on account as instructed. He was even sent the cash – two hundred pounds – to cover the first bet. The animal won. He got to keep fifteen per cent. The remainder he put in a brown envelope and handed to a taxi driver waiting for him at Moorgate. And so it went on. He'd get a call – always the same voice – he'd place the bet, keep his fifteen per cent and send the bulk off in black cabs at pre-arranged times and pre-arranged places.'

'Neat,' Philip chewed at a finger. 'So, when did the bookies pull the plug on him?'

'What?'

'Well, modern bookies don't bet, for God's sake. You keep winning, they close your account pretty sharpish.'

'Oh. Ah. Yes. No, I'm afraid that was never to be Mr Ellsworth's problem. He's the sort who always thinks that he could do a little better himself, you know? He saw all these winning bets and he started to study systems, form and so on.'

'Oh, Christ,' Philip groaned.

'Precisely. The bookmakers were only too happy to have his account. He was soon losing more than he won. He shared the general view that the mystery caller was not a man to be trifled with, so he needed money to make good the deficit . . .'

'I don't want to hear this.' Philip clutched his brow.

'Yes, I'm afraid . . . Yes, by now, he'd lost his job in the City, taken a job in a gent's outfitters.'

'Hand in the till?' Philip sighed.

'Yes. He'd be in stir if it hadn't been for Gambler's Anonymous. He got a suspended sentence.'

'Dear God, but our friend has done some damage.' Philip brooded.

'The second victim . . .' Lovelady started, but just then the door swung open. Barbara Lovelady entered with the tea-tray. There was a deal of clinking and clattering then, as tea and milk and sugar were distributed and Tony charged his plate with scones and jam.

'There now, I'll leave you gentlemen,' Barbara simpered.

'No, no. You just stay here, dear. I'm just running through what little I've discovered. Barbara's intuitions have often helped me. No, now . . . Yes, our second victim is one Catherine or Cathy Trappes. She, too, it seemed to me, though she was anything but specific, had been in some sort of trouble. Much the same thing had happened. The form, with which, presumably, our man obtains the betting account, then the telephone calls. She is, frankly, a silly, spoiled sort of woman. She sells fashion sweaters to department stores and boutiques, which takes her around the country a good deal. She said that this betting business was marvellous. She used the word a lot. Everything was marvellous or ghastly. She never told her husband about it, she said. It had paid for a few little luxuries, a holiday in Minorca, that sort of thing. The bookies did stop accepting her bets, at which she was deeply chagrined. When the account was closed, however, because of the itinerant nature of her calling, she was encouraged to continue to place bets in cash, provided that it was always in a different town. She paid her eighty-five per cent to our informant by leaving envelopes of cash at the reception desk of various hotels in Leeds, Stockport, Cardiff and so on for collection by one Major Player.'

'Major Player?' Philip snorted. 'Some joke.'

'Yes, does it tell us anything?'

'A rather jovial sense of humour,' said Mrs Lovelady.

'And a certain arrogance, I'd say.'

'I think it limits the age group too,' Philip mused. 'I don't think "Major Player" is a phrase much used by people over the age of, say, forty-five. At the same time, if our man was to pass for a bona fide major at these reception desks, he'd have to be – what? Thirty-five, minimum, wouldn't he?'

'Good thinking.'

'Did you get a list of dates?' Philip asked. 'The dates when Mr Ellsworth paid his money in London and the dates when Mrs Trappes did her bit at the hotels?'

'Yes, indeed.' Vincent unclipped two sheets of paper. He handed them to Philip. 'Though I'm afraid that Mrs Trappes was woefully vague. Still, by reference to her diary, we did manage to get some idea as to her itinerary.'

'So,' Philip studied the lists. 'If we knew the man who was in these cities on these days and in London on these . . .'

'We'd have our man.'

Philip shook his head, incredulous. 'Dear God,' his voice thudded, 'we've been looking for a big, vicious organized criminal. The whole thing only *works* because of that presupposition. All these people have been jumping when commanded because they're afraid. And it's all illusion.' He hit the paper hard. 'It's all one great bloody illusion! Dear God in heaven! We've been looking for an ogre. We've found a bloody dwarf on stilts! Look at it, this special form of consumer terrorism. What does it take? A telephone, a certain amount of knowledge of form, Christ! I could have done it. The weak crumble, the compulsive gamblers do their bit, the Alisons and Steves of this world cash in on their own account, suddenly you've got a whole gang of co-conspirators, all motivated by greed and fear. And all it takes is a telephone!'

'And a certain amount of ruthlessness.' Lovelady was frowning down at Philip. 'Don't forget Clarendon, and the attack on you.'

'The attack on me wasn't an attack. It was a dramatic warning. As for Clarendon, OK, I don't like people who hurt horses, but ultimately, Tony's right. A horse is only a horse when all is said and done.'

'And Freddy?' put in Tony.

'Freddy collapsed because of asthma!' Philip protested.

'All right, I still don't understand why it happened, how it happened, but there's no question of murder. No. What we've got here is a little man with a bright idea. Reward your victims with sure-fire winners, bully them with threats, let them do the rest. He's not even a particularly bad man, just a greedy man with a bright idea. He breaks one rule! A chaos follows.'

'You're talking like you know this guy.' Tony licked jam from a thumb.

'Know him?' Philip sighed and shook his head. 'No. I thought I did, but no.'

Tomorrow it would all be done. Plutonium would be a champion or a busted flush. The last horse, save Ludo, would have left Swynsmere. Philip's task would be done. He would be free to return to the Villa Locarno, to his lessons and his wheeler-dealing, free to start dying again.

That was what he wanted, he thought, as he drove up through thick rain which smashed and wriggled on the windscreen and the wipers slurped it up. He had done the usual things: he had fought a war, adored women, married, got a son. He had socialized, but always uncomfortably. He had run a business, but always unhappily. He had developed the skills necessary to be a man, a mixer, an intriguer, but he had never felt at ease in that role.

He had been at ease only out in the country with a horse or crashing through a snipe bog with a dog, only on the moor with his prey for company or amidst the dark conspiratorial murmuring of the surf, bobbing out there on the long-board beneath the corkscrew cries of the wheeling gulls. He had been at ease, strangely, as a soldier, because there too a force greater than he had ordained his movements. And he knew ease when a woman whimpered and sighed and screamed and held him close. And left in the morning.

He might have the gifts of the socialite, but he did not see why his gifts should dictate the course of his life. He mistrusted human beings. Oh, he liked them, but he found their passions squalid and discourteous. He was happier on his own.

An old friend had once told him, improbably, 'You're the most moral man I know.' Philip's answer: 'Well, I would be. Your acquaintance ranges from the cathouse to the doghouse.'

'No,' said the friend, 'but everything for you is moral. You can be immoral, but I've never known you amoral. Every human action hurts or delights you.' To which Philip had answered, 'Bollocks, man. Presumably this is the preamble to touching me for a loan?'

But it was true. He did not live by conventions or rules, though he respected conventions and dearly loved ritual and courtesy. Human actions *did* hurt him, moving him to anger, pathos or amusement. He felt like a nun at a stag night. He was better on his own.

He would be sad to leave England, for England was, willy nilly, home. He would be sad to leave the hedgerows, the copses, the gentle violets, greys and greens, the gentle social distinctions.

But they had left him before ever he left them.

The man who loved England left her. Everyone now was out of place. Everyone was covetous. Everyone was alienated. No one had a home or a neighbour. The day when every Englishman's home was his fiefdom was gone. The day when friends were born friends and mutual aid was the principal motive, when communities served individuals and individuals communities, that too was gone. The day when every man or woman had pride because he had his function, be it village idiot, farrier or doctor, was gone.

England was a memory, replaced by a vast Monopoly board. He was better in a foreign land, better on his own.

'Da-dee!' Sam scrabbled down from his chair at the kitchen table. He flung himself at Philip. He wrapped himself about his knees.

'Woah, there.' Philip wiped rain from his eyes. He pulled

off his damp cap. He hunkered down to give his son a hug. 'Sorry. I'm sodden. It's pissing down out there.'

'I know. I was going to put Barcas over the new gymkhana fences, but even I couldn't go out in that.'

'Even you?' Philip drew him to him, felt the warm plush skin give against his cheek. He smiled. 'So, what are you up to, then?'

'Playing with my computer.'

'Your computer?'

'Yes, I told you! David gave me this really brilliant Apple Mac, and I've got a modem now, so I'm logged into CIX, so I can find out everything.'

'You've got a what?'

'A modem. Modulator demodulator.'

'Ah,' Philip nodded. 'And this modulator thing is the key to omniscience, you say?'

'What?'

'See? The future is a foreign country. They speak a different language there. What does this mod thing do for you?'

'Anything. It means I can link up with thousands of computers through the telephone. I asked it about rain. Did you know there was prepitation . . . ?'

'Precipitation.'

'Oh. Anyway, it rained on Ballysomething lake for three hundred and forty-nine days in 1954. Did you know that?'

'I didn't, but I knew something was missing from my life. Where are Mummy and Nu . . . and David?'

'Mummy's about.' Sam had returned to the gleaming machine on the table. 'I don't think she's dressed yet. David's in his office.'

'I'll find the sloven,' Philip announced. 'You find out what that thing has to say about life, will you? I could do with some pointers. Whoops. Hello, border.' Philip had to stop short in order to avoid the crescent terrier at his feet. He pushed through the baize door and jumped up the stairs two at a time to the big sunny hall.

'Linda!' he bellowed. The chandelier tinkled like a shimmying dowager. 'Linda?'

He was halfway up the main stairs when she emerged on the landing. She wore a dressing-gown of pale blue grey silk shot with pink. Her hair fell like a stream in a wind, then trickled in rivulets down her shoulders. She wore no make-up. She looked very young.

'Philip!' she cried, then, 'Philip? God, what's the matter? What have you done to your face?'

'I had an argument with a light bulb.' Philip stopped climbing. She was coming towards him, her eyebrows raised at the centre in genuine concern.

She raised her hand to his face. 'God, what happened? You're a mess.'

'Don't worry, I'll recover.' He caught the hand, held it tight and gazed up at Linda, wondering. Linda held his gaze for a bare few seconds before its weight proved too great. She looked down at their clasped hands. Nugent's rubies and diamonds glistered about her finger like a fresh wound.

He said, 'Linda. If anything happened to Nugent . . .'

'Nothing's going to happen.' She looked up sharply.

'You are happy with him, aren't you?'

'I'm . . . Yes, I've told you. Look at all he's done for Sam. He's . . .'

'He's a modern man. He's teaching Sam things like cashflows and computers. God save us. All right. If he lost all his money, then?'

'Oh, come on, Philip,' she snapped. 'It's different for women.'

'What is?'

'For you, money's a thing apart, OK. For us, position, power, money – they're all part of the person. I know you want to make me feel shitty, but . . . No. All right. If we went bust, I'd do my best to hold on.'

'You didn't with me.'

'That wasn't just the money. You know that.'

'So there'd never be . . .'

'No, Philip. How can you even think it? Come on. Please.' She pulled her hand away. 'I love you dearly, but I could no more live with you if . . . if you were dry and a billionaire and . . . If it all went wrong with David, I'd – I don't know – I'd take the veil or something.'

Understanding seeped into Philip's brain like water into peat, crackling as it permeated the cells. Not for the first time, he realized, he had been insane all this time, grieving, hoping, dreaming whilst all the while the world was moving on. The rift between Linda and him was an accepted fact, its permanence never questioned by anyone save himself. Even Sam had taken it on board. His future with Nugent looked rosy and assured. Only Philip had somehow, in the deceptive dementia of grief, maintained hope despite the bare, historic fact of Linda's marriage. Now, like the long denied fact of death, the penny dropped.

'Oh,' he said then. 'No, well, who wants a lazy fat old sloven anyhow? God, woman, it's ten o'clock.'

'We wealthy women.' She grinned quickly. 'They haven't milked the asses yet.'

'Oh, blame the vassals every time.' Philip glanced at his watch with no interest in the time. 'So, where's Nugent's den, then?'

'Down there.'

'Down where?'

'In the basement. Through the cinema.'

'Through the *cinema*? I always had the feeling that something was missing at Chatsworth. Oh, well. Right, I'll see you tomorrow at the sports.'

'Sure. Still going to win?'

'For once,' he was surprised, 'I think we just might.'

'Why's that?'

'Because there are enough people who want us to lose. The gods might get confused.'

'Why do you want David?'

'Oh, just a word. Horse stuff.'

'Oh. Be polite, won't you?'

'You know me,' said Philip.

She said, 'Yes.' Her eyes were sad as she watched him trot downstairs.

*

'Ah, Nugent,' Philip said to the blond head at the desk in the window.

The blond head half turned. A chubby hand slapped the desktop. 'Philip!' Nugent said with surprise. He pushed back his chair. He stood. 'How good . . .'

His head jerked downward. His bum jerked back. His eyes bulged. He vomited air. Philip stepped backwards. He hooked a tight, two-fingered fist into the bridge of Nugent's nose. He calmly swivelled, raised his left foot and dragged his steel-quartered heel down Nugent's shin.

The blond man stood doubled and still. He clutched his shin with one hand. With the other, he reached out, grasping as if for an invisible rail to support him. His face was bright red, his mouth open wide. No sound emerged.

He toppled forward. He sucked with a honk like a donkey. The exhalation burbled through blood. He clung to his shin and gave a wavering, plaintive little whimper, 'Oooh?' Then, as he obtained breath and the pain slammed into his brain, 'Ah, ah, ah, ah!' A series of staccato high-pitched cries which jerked up from his swelling and receding stomach. Blood splashed from his nose on to the Bokhara.

Philip sat on the desk. He watched.

'Oh, G-God!' Nugent gurgled at last. 'Oh, Christ, oh . . .' and again he bent double, forcing down the shock and the pain.

Philip reached for a jade-handled paper-knife. 'Do I kill you?' he mused. 'That is the pressing question now. You have stolen my wife, my son, my brother and my peace of mind. You have threatened me, you have bloody near blinded me and you have killed a damn good novice chaser. I reckon that little lot would be taken as justification for homicide, don't you? And you have done these things for what? For money, a commodity of which you have a great deal more than I. Yes, on reflection, I should kill you, don't you think?'

'I . . .' Nugent wiped his face on his sleeve. 'I . . . God Almighty!'

'Now he prays, the nice boy. Oh sure, I bet you read the

bloody Gospel at the village church, don't you? You're not like me. You're respectable, monogamous, clean-living, devout, a good husband and father – and you manipulate and hurt people for your personal profit, but that's business, isn't it? Christ, you polished Shanks of Barrhead sepulchres, lagged with waxed cotton. Yes, I shall kill you. I will kill you as an ecological duty.'

'No?' Nugent inhaled like an aged harmonium. 'Listen to me at least, Phil-ip . . .' The 'ip' emerged as a hiccup.

Philip bummed a cigarette on the desk. He flicked it up to his lips. He lit it. 'All right,' he said. 'Speak to me.'

'C-can I clean up a bit?' Nugent pleaded. He was on one knee now. Still his chest bobbed and his left hand fluttered at the pain.

'Nope, I haven't time and I don't trust you. Sit down there and do your begging. Now.'

'God, what have you done to me?' Nugent tried to arise but his leg would not sustain him. He dragged himself to the chair and with much wincing and thrashing of his hands at last contrived to sit. His check shirt was almost entirely red. Blood spattered his jeans. He covered his face with a hand. 'Oh, God,' he moaned again.

'Get on with it,' Philip ordered. 'Make the most of your remaining minutes.'

Nugent said something like, 'Bob boo doo go.'

'I can't hear you,' Philip snapped. 'Don't worry about the blood. There's going to be a whole lot more anyhow. Lower your hands.'

Nugent lowered his hands. He sniffed and blinked. Blood still trickled over his lips. He said, 'What do you know?'

'Everything, I reckon. How you fixed races, how you rang trainers and jockeys with threats, how you paid with tips on other fixed races, how you paid fifteen per cent to mugs to place bets, how you've laid against Plutonium, how you did this to me with that petrol-in-the-light-bulb trick . . .'

Nugent nodded, resigned. He said, 'I'm sorry. I was told it couldn't do too much harm, just be a bit scary. And I'm sort of a familiar figure round the yard, you know, and I knew the routine . . .'

'Of course you did. If you didn't know anything you could just casually ask Linda. Shit.'

'Look, it was just a sort of joke, Philip. You have to believe me.' Nugent wiped a hand across his face, smearing the blood into a ragged gash.

'I'll believe what I want to believe,' Philip growled. 'Get on with it, Nugent. When did you start this filthy joke?'

'It started ... Oh, God – when? Back in eighty-four, when I was starting up, I was – I was with Glendale, the petfood people. There was a guy there, put razor-blades and needles in cans, rang up, asked for money. He got forty grand out of us before we caught him, and we caught him because he was using the cash dispenser. I thought then, God, you know, if it weren't for the method of payment, that's damn near the perfect crime. Why not get the payment through bookmakers? No direct connection between the random punter and the – the . . .'

'Blackmailer is the word you seek.'

'OK. Right. Anyhow, it was just a thought. Everything went well. I made money, lots of money, bought race-horses, bought this house, all that. It was all so easy. Then – then Linda, and Sam. And then ... Oh, Christ, I was knee-deep in remortgages when the crash came, and . . .'

'You couldn't live without your fucking BMW.'

'It wasn't that,' Nugent blurted. 'It wasn't. I could have ... I know you think I'm just materialist but ... I don't know. I think I could have coped, but Linda, Sam ... Linda needs comforts. She kept saying, you know, how nice it was to have money and security after, after all the years of worry and . . .'

'And you thought she'd walk out if you went bust.'

'I – I didn't know. I thought she'd ... I thought she'd be unhappy, anyhow.'

'God, but I hate uxoriousness,' Philip snarled.

'And then,' Nugent gulped, 'then there was a classic horse, Legal Aid, you remember? He was inexplicably tailed off in the Guineas. I rang the trainer, said, "You saw what happened to Legal Aid. It could happen to all your animals. Solarus does not win." And then, then Jamie

Carroll was mugged up in Manchester – nothing to do with me, but I rang him, said, "You've got a choice, you can be very rich or you can have more of the same treatment." And it worked!' he suddenly squealed. 'I mean, it was that easy! It's not worth a trainer's while to insist on winning this race rather than another, and a lot of jockeys will choose a couple of easy races a year and lots of winning tips rather than potential trouble.'

His pleading eye caught Philip's. Philip merely snarled. Nugent raised his plump hands and let them fall on to his thighs. 'It was – I mean, the temptation . . . It all just – snowballed. I was making big money. I couldn't let it drop. I had this house to run, holidays, school fees . . . I'd have stopped when the recession stopped. It was just . . . Oh, Christ. It was like falling off a bloody log. Plutonium . . . God, it was silly. Vindictiveness, I suppose, laying Dolly Varden to beat him, but I didn't expect – come, on, yours is a tiny yard. I wasn't to know that you'd have a bloody superstar, was I? Anyhow Freddy was mine. He was one of the first . . . I knew the set-up so well. I could scare him by knowing what happened yesterday. So I laid doubles, a stack of them . . . There's over two hundred K riding on Dolly Varden. So . . .' he shrugged wearily. 'There you are. That's it. Just a silly wheeze that got out of hand.'

Philip stared. 'That's it?' he hissed. He stubbed out the cigarette on the Morocco desktop. 'That's it? Christ, man, I don't like your fucking bullying scam, but I'm not a moralist. That's the way you bastards do things. But that, Mister New Gent, is not fucking it. My brother is as good as dead. Not a word about this little matter? Perhaps it doesn't trouble you? Perhaps such things are trivial in your eyes. God,' he shifted the paper-knife in his palm. His hand closed about it. 'I'll be doing the world a service.'

He straightened. He took a pace towards Nugent. Nugent raised an arm across his face. 'No, Philip!' he yelped. 'No! Listen! I had nothing to do with it, with – with Freddy. I wasn't there. I was as shocked as anyone. Please. You must believe me. I said it was me, just like I told Jamie Carroll that it was me who mugged him. I had to get you

302

doing what I wanted, and I knew – I knew you wouldn't be as easy as Freddy. But I didn't touch him. Honestly. I swear.'

'The dog wouldn't bark at you. You know the yard. You wanted Plutonium out of the race.'

'Yes, but . . . Ask Linda! She wouldn't lie! Ask Linda.' He pointed at the desk with a shaking finger greasy with blood.

Philip frowned, then he understood. Nugent was pointing at the telephone. 'What do I press?' he demanded.

'Just the Intercom button, then six.'

Philip laid down the knife. 'Not a sound out of you, Nugent.' He hit the keys. He waited.

'Hello?' Linda's voice. The sound of water lapping.

'Linda. Philip.'

'Gosh, where are you?'

'Still with Nugent. Look, we were trying to remember. The twelfth of last month, where were you?'

'Oh, Lord. You know me. I don't know where I was yesterday. Why?'

'Oh, just an invoice I've got from the vet,' Philip improvised. 'He says he was at Swynsmere that evening and you and Nugent were there. Nugent reckons he was elsewhere. It was the night Freddy collapsed.'

Philip watched Nugent where he sat with his head in his hands. His frown deepened as he listened to the voice in his ear. '. . . All those vets are bloody crooks. No, I can tell you, we heard – Alison rang at half-past eight the next morning to tell us, and we were walking around with duvets in our skulls. David should remember. We had had a duty dinner – God, twelve people, National Art Collections Fund. Didn't stagger to bed till two, and then there was Ali at sparrow-fart gabbling about poor Freddy . . .'

'Thanks.' Philip said quietly. 'Enjoy your bath.' He laid down the receiver. 'So, you paid someone and he panicked . . .'

'No!' Nugent shook his head. His jowls juddered. 'I didn't. I've never nobbled anything. I wouldn't have the guts. God, I'd hardly know where to start.'

'Don't give me that,' Philip spat. 'What about Clarendon?'

'That was a coincidence, that's all. I was at Rambo's party that night. He was the first person to cross me, but I like Rambo. No. He'd stood up to me. Fair enough. Cost me fifteen grand, but. No, we were at the party. Linda was with me. She was with me full-time. Ring her again. She'll tell you. We joined in the chase after the horse. All the guests did. Someone else did it. Oh, God, it was useful, *but it wasn't me that did it.*'

Philip was exasperated. Everyone was guilty of greed and manipulation, yet everyone was protesting innocence with regard to Freddy and Clarendon. Reason told him that these were two coincidences too many.

Nugent had had abundant motive for both deeds, yet protested his innocence and, unless he had paid a lieutenant, had had the opportunity to do neither. Steve Shand had had opportunity enough, yet, certainly where Freddy was concerned, had every interest in keeping him alive. No one else, save Alison, whose motives were the same as Steve's, and Jim Dobbs, who would hardly have invented the story of the interloper and so aroused suspicion, had had the means to enter the yard unchallenged.

Which left Philip back where he started.

He said softly, then, more forcefully, 'You are wrong. You did it. You killed Freddy and you killed Clarendon. You broke a young compulsive gambler called Ellsworth as well. You corrupted countless people by your greedy little wheeze. You broke the rules. You put a pinprick in the dam, and, as a result, the whole rotten thing has collapsed and crumbled. You made your victims into fellow villains by breaking their spirits and stimulating their greed. You have destroyed lives, the lives of everyone who noticed your scam and the lives of everyone who did your bidding. You put temptation where there should be no temptation, and all for the sake of your petty fucking avarice, your drooling devotion to a floozie . . .'

'And your son,' Nugent croaked, 'and your son.'

There was silence, broken only by the bleating of some distant sheep.

Philip whispered curses as he strode from the room.

The Mini's brakes whined. The gravel had barely stopped its pattering when the door slammed. Philip hitched up his trousers. He was at the front door in two paces, head down.

The rain had stopped. The garden sizzled. The sky was bruised and bloated.

He tried the door. It was locked. He called, 'Alison?'

The name chimed in the walls and was puffed away by the breeze.

He turned away. He ran up the bank to the walled garden. He leapt over the beds to the gate in the wall.

The birds trickled in the fruit trees and the borders. The gate clinked. Myshkin tottered up. Ludo's head turned.

Otherwise, everything in the yard was still.

'Where are you, you bastard?' Philip muttered. He walked quickly down the gleaming cobbles. Absently he stroked Ludo's snip in passing. He stood tiptoe at Plutonium's box. The horse stood in the shadows there, head hung low, for all the world posing for the old engraving, *The High Mettled Racer Shortly Before His Demise.*

Vincent Lovelady sat, knees clasped close to his chest, in the corner.

'Damn it, Lovelady.' Philip unbolted the door. 'You're an honest man. A prat, but an honest man. All honour to you. It's a rare breed.' His feet crunched on the straw. He pushed the horse out of his way with a 'Get on, you bugger.' He sat beside Vincent. 'So, what's been going on here?'

'We're taking it in turns. The others are in the office.'

'The others?'

'Tony, Debbie, Mr Shand.'

'Shand?' Philip started. 'What's he doing down here?'

'I don't know. Just said he wanted to help. He seems very subdued, very sour.'

'Well, Plutonium won't be attacked here today.'

'No?'

'No. Half an hour from now, he'll be on his way. If your man decides to persist, it'll be at the racecourse tonight or tomorrow.'

'You know who it is?'

'Yes.' Philip nodded sadly. He sucked on a strand of straw. 'Yes. A modern man. The best mentor for my son.'

'Ah,' said Vincent. 'Oh, dear.'

'A wheeze, he said. 'A joke that worked.'

'I can see how it would. And – in what condition did you leave him?'

'Shaken, but he's got two hundred grand riding on the second favourite. If Plutonium wins, he goes down. I think he'll still try. He's fighting for his life.'

'I'm surprised at you, Mr Glaister.'

'At my restraint?' Philip sighed. 'So am I. But, God, Linda's happy. Sam knows about computers and cashflows . . . Oh, if I told Linda what he's been up to, she'd leave him. She's straight as a die, but what's the fucking point?'

'What about Mr Freddy?'

'He didn't do it. He swears he didn't get anyone else to do it . . .'

'Hmm.' Vincent looked up sharply as Plutonium stamped.

'It's all right,' Philip reassured him. 'He's a pig, but he's generally quite quiet at this time of day.'

'What do you know,' Vincent said softly, 'about Jack the Ripper?'

'What? Not a lot.' Philip shrugged. 'Chopped up strumpets in London. Lot of crappy theories, but he was never found. Surgeon, they think, or the Duke of Clarence or something.'

'That's the thing.'

'What?'

'All this stuff about his knowing about surgery. It all comes about because the coroner was a very silly man. He had discovered that an American medical publication was giving away a free human uterus with each copy sold, and because it was his discovery, he was convinced that this must be the Ripper's motive. The police told him that it wasn't so – the uterus was only removed in one of the killings and lots of other organs in the others – the police surgeon explicitly stated that the murderer showed no surgical skill or knowledge, but the coroner wasn't having it. In his summing-up, he said that the murderer was plainly familiar with surgery or post-mortems. You see? We've assumed from the outset that the attack on Mr Freddy was connected with the race-fixing. Let's run this race without the favourite. Let's assume that there was no connection. Oh, he was out in the yard because of the race-fixing, but he was attacked for some other motive. What motives are there?'

'Greed?'

'Yes. So who profits from Mr Freddy's death?'

'Well, Alison, from the life insurance, but she loses overall because of the rule about dead men's bets.'

'Ah, yes, and she knew about that rule and instantly tried to save his life. The original assailant, however, may merely have thought of the life insurance and getting Mr Freddy out of the way. He may not have known that obscure rule of racing. Give me another motive for murder.'

'Lust?' suggested Philip.

'Indeed. Put them together, and you have a classic squalid little killing, haven't you?'

'You mean Alison and someone . . . ?' Philip bit the straw. 'That someone attacks Freddy because – yes, with the life insurance, they could buy the Glaisters' share of the yard. She talked about that. She hears the attack on the intercom, realizes what it means, comes charging up to keep Freddy alive. Dear God . . .'

'You see, I have been aware for the past two days that Mrs Glaister has an intimate relationship. It is widely known in the village.'

'Which brings us back . . .' said Philip.

'Indeed it does.'

'The bugger.'

*

Philip walked very slowly past the empty boxes. He needed time to think.

It had been greed which had made him try on the insurance scam – greed much hedged about with love and nostalgia, of course, but greed for all that. How had that started? With a stray mention by some novelist friend of Linda's to the effect that insurance companies did not do their post-mortem homework. The scribbler could not be held to blame. That germ had lodged somewhere in Philip's brain and had proliferated. Oh, there had been other factors, of course. A germ needs the right conditions in which to breed, and Philip's brain at the time had been a foetid hothouse. He had lost his wife and son. He faced the loss of Swynsmere, the dismissal of his staff and, perhaps worse, his father's sneer still clear through the veil.

But somehow, it was expectation which was most to blame, he concluded as he stepped into the tackroom and methodically examined Plutonium's racing-bridle, leathers and girth. He had expected the standards of a gentleman, expected to pass on to his son a way of life which he had inherited – and he had less excuse, perhaps, than Nugent, in that he had at least been born to a culture and educated in its privileges, whilst Nugent had apparently magically acquired wealth – and Linda – and must be all the more terrified of their loss.

In both cases, however, it had been dependence upon wealth, status and a woman which had justified the crime to the criminals. After his life as a beach-bum, he could look back with frank amazement upon this dependence, but he could not deny that it had been there.

It was not that he had acquired a profound respect for the proprietorial rights of banks and insurance companies. Far from it. If a bank left its strongroom unlocked, he would still have no qualms about strolling in and helping himself. It was merely that he no longer very much cared whether he owned a mansion or not, and he reckoned, in truth, that there were charming women enough to go round. Above all, however, he had lived in a climate where quality of life was prized and greed seemed a laughable waste of energy. Here, greed was the norm. It seemed odd to him now.

It shocked him none the less to recognize that his motives had been the same as Nugent's – the same, even, as those of Freddy's attacker. The differences lay only in the nature of their crimes. The man whom now he must judge was guilty of bullying, perhaps of murder.

And his worst mistake had been to choose Philip's brother for his victim.

You didn't do things like that.

'Hello:' Steve leaned back in his chair and smiled over his shoulder. 'Mr Glaister!'

'Hi,' Philip nodded to Tony and Debbie. 'All well?'

'Fine, fine. Mr Lovelady's out in the box with the horse,' Tony was quick to explain.

'I know. I've seen him.' Philip noticed the blue nylon grip by the desk. 'All packed up? Good. You going along for the ride, Debbie?'

'Thought I might,' Debbie was coy, 'if I may?'

'No problem. After your good offices the night before last, you can ask for anything, up to half my kingdom. Where's Alison?'

'She's gone down to Wykeham to do the shopping and see Mr Freddy,' Steve drawled.

'Who?' Philip blinked.

'Mr Freddy. Your brother.'

'No, who's gone there?'

Steve frowned. 'Ali.'

'Ah, yes, of course.' Philip nodded. He wondered why he had been so dull as not to notice before that Shand referred to his employer by his title and to Alison by her Christian name.

Philip pulled out a chair. He reversed it and sat astride. Shand avoided his gaze, but faintly smiled. His crown rested in his clasped hands.

Not for the first time, Philip felt sorry for Alison and Freddy. It was no wonder that Freddy, struggling to make

309

a go of Swynsmere, had succumbed to Nugent's blandish-
ments. It was easier still to see how Alison, bored, frustrated and angry, had fallen for Shand. She was not a
racing woman. She would have known little of Shand's
renown as a cocksman. No doubt he had flattered her,
assured her that he loved her. No doubt he had painted
colourful, idealized pictures of their lives together when
Swynsmere was theirs.

Freddy, Philip knew, had bedded just two women before
he married – a tart and a drunken Sloane. Steve Shand
must have made Alison feel like a Stradivarius which for
years had been in the hands of a punk banjo-player. Now
she had found her virtuoso.

She had been easy meat.

And God, Shand had come close to attaining his ends.
Alison would own half of the house and the yard. She
hated racing but would, no doubt, for love, have ploughed
her insurance money and her winnings into buying the
other half. Steve Shand, for a few soft words, a few hours
of exertion and the expense of a few milligrams of semen,
would have been master of Swynsmere.

Yet again, Philip was tormented by the idea that it had
all, in part, been his fault. It was arrogant, perhaps, to
suppose that, had he and Alison's maid of honour not
taken Alison to the outer regions of sexual convention, she
might never have regarded Freddy's horizons as claustro-
phobically provincial. It was fair to suppose, however, that,
had Philip made a fist of running Swynsmere, Freddy and
Alison would have remained in West Byfleet, where the
worst consequences of her yearnings would have been a
slight tilt to the tumble-drier or a smile on the face of the
double-glazing salesman.

Philip despised Nugent, but he could not condemn him.
Nugent, after all, was little more than his wealth. He could
not believe himself loved without it. Fate had dropped in
his lap the chance to extend his life, to fulfil his needs and
to still his nightmares by little worse than a few telephone
calls. Philip too had tried a scam in order to prolong the
dream.

Philip despised Shand. Some atavistic, primal anger even made him hate him, but again, he found, he could not condemn. The smugness, the smoothness, the sexy smirk were all components of an illusory shell. As he had shown yesterday, the invertebrate within was a pathetic, ageing, cowardly creature. Shand needed money and position with which to maintain the illusion no less than an addict needed drugs. If he could attain them by sex, that made him no worse than many millions of women – no worse than Linda.

Only three questions now remained to be answered. The first was, had Alison known of Shand's intention to dispose of Freddy? The second was, how had Shand attained his end? The third, of course, was, what was Philip now to do?

The answer to the third question depended very much on the answers to the first and second.

The horsebox trundled into the yard. Philip spent the next fifteen minutes supervising Plutonium's loading. He passed the horse's papers to Jim who then joined Tony and Debbie in the cab and, with whoops and waves, they were on their way.

The yard was very quiet then.

Steve Shand stood slapping something invisible from his hands. Beside him, Vincent Lovelady, who had helped with the loading, panted slightly from his exertions. His hat was askew. Philip stood slightly apart from the two men, his dog at his side.

'Well,' he said, more loudly than he had intended. 'That's the lot. The last horse has left Swynsmere.'

'You've still got the old hack,' said Steve.

'Yes. I'll deal with that.' Philip's face was grim. Vincent looked rapidly from Philip to Shand. Philip caught his glance. 'Lovelady, would you do me a favour?'

'Certainly. Whatever I can.'

'Go and wait for me up at the pub. I have unpleasant business to attend to.'

'You are quite sure, Mr Philip?' Vincent asked. 'I wouldn't . . .'

'I'm sure,' Philip said sharply.

'You know that – you know that putting down your own animals is illegal?' Vincent almost pleaded. 'It's against EC regulations.'

'Fuck EC regulations.'

'Er, yes, but I wouldn't want you to get in trouble . . .'

'I'll be OK, mate.' Philip laid a hand on the little man's shoulder. 'Go on. Get on with you.'

Vincent looked close to tears, but he climbed into his car. He was shaking his head as he drove off.

'So.' Philip turned on his heel. He strode back into the office.

'Listen, Mr Glaister . . .' Steve followed. 'About yesterday. I mean, God, that was a nasty trick you played . . .' He laughed nervously.

Philip reached up to the cabinet on the wall; unlocked it.

'I mean, you're not going to hold it against me, are you? I mean, sure, I shouldn't have been betting, but, I mean, it was Mr Freddy who was at it first.'

'And you told no one else?' Philip pulled down the rifle and the box of slugs. He worked the action.

'No. Well, Alison . . . She guessed something. She asked me if anything was going on . . .'

'And you told her?'

'Of course. No reason to hide anything from her.'

'And thereafter you bet together?' Philip slid three rounds into the empty breech.

'Well, yes. Well, no. I mean, we backed the same horses, but she bet on the account Mr Freddy had for her.'

'Why not her own account?'

'She couldn't. You'll have to ask her that.'

'I will,' Philip squinted down the barrel, 'when she gets out of gaol.'

'What?' Philip heard the rustling and thumping as the man moved behind him. He did not turn. 'You mean you're going to stop us? You?'

'Why not me, Shand?' Philip was cool. 'Because I once tried a con with the insurance people? It doesn't disqualify me from making moral judgements. I've certainly got enough to get you and Alison warned off every racecourse

312

and training stable in the world. Won't do much good to your social asp – '

It was at that moment that Shand made his move.

It was a surprising move.

For a second, Philip panicked. The forearm round his throat was like a beam. That was to be expected. The shock lay in the cloudy cellophane which was clamped over his nose and his mouth. Philip's hands flapped uselessly. He was pulled back so that he could gain no purchase with his legs. His crown was against the cold, hard leather of Shand's leather jacket. The zip was a cold slash on his ear. He reached back. His right hand touched the crisp hair at Shand's sideburns. The hair shifted away. The hand at his right shoulder moved down to force down his arm. The hand on his face remained firm.

Philip slid from the table. Articles falling from the table slapped on the floor. Something rolled and rattled. Shand went down with him, kneeling now, his knee shoved hard in the small of Philip's back. His hand still bent Philip's nose, crushed his lips.

The rustle of the shirt became a roar. The creaking of the leather was loud as the rocking of a sailboat. Philip flailed and kicked. His hands grasped air and his feet found no leverage.

The swelling had started in his chest. Like a flood, it arose, now taking up half his lungs, now welling up towards his windpipe. 'Idiot,' flashed through his brain, 'you goddamned fool . . .' But there was more. There had to be more. Freddy had not suffocated . . .

It was too late to worry now. He had to get out. His breathing became shallower and shallower. His vision smeared. Burning scraps of something swirled and circled behind his eyelids. He arched his back, pushed his hips upward, knowing that it would be the last effort before asthma took its critical toll.

Shand grunted as he forced him down again.

'Oh, yes. Now who's the big man?' Shand ground it out through clenched teeth. 'Now who's the fucking big man? Nobody treats me like that, common little Glaister man. Filthy little English farmer. No one treats me like that . . .'

313

The arms were gone now. The plastic was gone from his face. It made no difference. Philip's head fell back on the floor. He was breathing in a cupful of air with every second. Oboes and air-brakes were playing discords throughout his body. Pain seized his bobbing diaphragm. Tears seeped from his eyes. His right hand shook as it made for his pocket. It missed, then, at the second attempt, slid in. The inhaler was in there, cool and smooth as his child's skin.

'Uh, uh,' Shand's voice, soothing, 'not that one, filthy little peasant.' His hand reached in over Philip's. It prised his fingers from the inhaler. 'Here we are, this one . . .'

Philip was gazing up as if from the bottom of the Thames, but he saw through the murk the familiar shape. Yes. Freddy's inhaler. OK.

He nodded, almost grateful. He saw the flap arise. The spike sank into the foil blister.

He turned his head to exhale, turned back, eager. The mouthpiece tapped on his teeth. He sucked.

Grains pattered at the back of his throat. He sucked them further in. He gulped.

He felt his body contracting, doubling into a tight ball like a hedgehog. He clutched at his stomach which had turned to ice. His breathing was now no more than hacking, honking, coughing. His heart thumped hard as a heavyweight at his chest wall.

He knew then that he was dying.

'Little more?' said the coaxing, gloating voice, distant now as a windblown blast from a radio on the beach when you're in the surging surf, and suddenly Philip was clear of his shuddering, twitching body. Suddenly he was free of pain.

Plutonium was before him. Good luck. Linda, smiling. Sam, cuddling close. Sorry. Sylvie, seen from between her legs. The sea, the cool, blessed sea. His father, scowling. The Taxis, looming. The sea, the cool, blessed sea . . .

He resented the manhandling. He wanted to be back there, floating. He resented the weight of his body, the musty smell of the office floor. He had enjoyed the lightness, the freedom, with the promiscuity of a bee drifting from bloom to bloom, to flit from this vivid image to that.

But breath was in his lungs again and blood crawling heavy in his veins. His eyelids flickered. His chest rose and sank. Dull smudged colours became separate and defined. There was dusty, oily wool beneath his fingers and – if he must return, let it be to this – a woman astride him, a woman's hair whispering about his chin and throat.

He blinked. He tried his voice. 'Alison . . . ?' It came out like sandpaper. 'Where's – Where's Sh – Shand?'

'Over there.' She sat back on Philip's thighs. She drew a hand over her brow. She was flushed. 'Phew!' She clambered to her feet. 'I had to hit him. I didn't have time to argue. God, that was close.'

'What happened?' he managed to gasp out.

'Same as Freddy. You were a goner, far as I could tell. I thought that Steve might have done him, but . . .' She shrugged. She rested her fists on the desk and stared into the middle distance. 'I just prayed that it wasn't so. God,' her eyes rolled upward, 'this leaves me without a husband or a lover. Shit, Philip, you do mess up my life, don't you?'

Philip pulled himself up on to his elbows. 'So, how did he do it?'

She slouched wearily to where the inhaler lay on the rug. 'At a guess . . .' she murmured. She opened the case. 'Yes. Very nasty. Very, very clever.'

'What is it?' Philip pulled himself to his feet. His legs shook, but held. He supported himself on the furniture as he walked over to her side.

'Look,' Alison pointed. 'Tiny holes in the next two blisters. He sticks a syringe in it, right? Taps out the drug, injects in something else. Powdered beta-blockers at a guess.'

'Why beta-blockers?'

'Because beta-blockers precipitate asthma attacks is why, and because the stock I have in my medicine cabinet has been going down. I thought I'd imagined it.'

'So you have an asthma attack and you inhale something that causes asthma . . .' Philip stared at the thing in horror.

'That's right.' She laid the inhaler down. 'The plastic spike destroys any evidence of tampering, the powdered beta-blocker's gone because you've inhaled it, and no one's going to look twice at an inhaler when someone plainly died of asthma. Anyway, you think about it, you could be miles away by the time the asthmatic inhales. It's bloody nearly perfect. Only trouble with Steve, he was impatient. He'd probably doctored Freddy's inhaler already, but when Freddy went running out to the yard, there they are, all alone at night, so Steve induces the attack, then administers the poison. I came downstairs, heard the wheezing and so on on the intercom. I just got there too late. It was a carbon copy. Get the heart started, pump in the cortico steroid. My luck. I lose Freddy, I save you.'

'Sorry,' Philip rolled down his sleeve, 'and thanks.'

Philip walked unsteadily over to where Steve lay on his face, groaning and slowly scrabbling at the carpet. The hair at his crown was dark and glistening. 'What did you hit him with?'

'That gun.' She pointed. 'It was on the floor behind you.'

'Christ,' Philip whistled. 'You were bloody lucky not to shoot yourself.'

'What?' Alison stared. She felt for the chair behind her. She very suddenly sat. 'You mean – that – thing – was – loaded?'

'One in, two up the spout, safety off.' Philip nodded.

She laughed. She set her head back and she laughed at the ceiling. Her head fell forward into her hands. Her laughter turned to jerking sobs and squeaks and deep, French horn inhalations. Philip returned to her. He crouched down and took her hand. 'Woah, there, Ali,' he crooned. 'Thank you. Really.'

She shook her head. She gripped his hand painfully tight. It took three minutes for her to discharge the pent bitterness and worry and disappointment of the past years.

She looked up at last. She blinked at the light, rubbed her eyes on her white sleeve. She said, 'God,' then, with a little laugh. 'Sorry. Idiot.' She sniffed. 'So.' She slapped her thighs. 'What now? God. Joke. On top of everything, kill

316

myself for you. Yup. Anyhow. What do we do? Call the police?'

'I don't think so.' Philip took a deep breath. He stood with a long grunt. 'No. Embarrassing all round, and unsatisfactory.'

Shand had pushed himself up on one hand. He shook his head. He blinked and moaned. 'Oh, God . . .'

Philip walked over to him. He grasped his collar and pulled. 'Come along, my beauty.'

Shand sagged. Philip heaved the man up and then slung his body over his shoulder. He made for the door.

'Where are you going?' Alison's voice was thin and light.

Philip pulled open the door. He said, 'You don't want to know.'

Philip dragged himself wearily up the steep, rickety wooden staircase. At his back, Shand drooled curses. Twice Philip had to stop and lower him on to his feet while he recovered breath before lifting him again.

'Leave me alone, peasant.' Shand raised his head and ineffectually struck at Philip's neck. He sagged again. 'Filthy little shit, deranged moron . . .'

'Yes, yes.' Philip kicked open the door. 'Here we are.'

Philip set him down on the granary walkway. Shand sneered. His eyes veered this way and that. 'Where?'

Philip grasped Shand's hair with one hand, his shirt front with the other. He took aim, then propelled the limp body backwards so that the back of his head thudded into the low oak beam. Shand buckled and moaned.

'That should satisfy forensic,' Philip said briskly. 'The execution chamber is where, Shand.'

Shand shook his head. 'Where? Wha . . . ? The fuck . . . ?'

'Come along.' Philip pushed him to the edge of the walkway. 'This is where we say goodbye.'

He shoved, but suddenly Shand was alive again. In the reflected orange light from the tons of grain below, he sidestepped free of Philip's grasp and swung round. He crouched in the fighter's stance. 'No, you don't,' he snarled. His eyes shifted from side to side, but too slowly. They were still glazed.

'Oh, yes, I do, your lordship.' Philip swivelled. He kicked at the back of Shand's knees.

Shand toppled forward without a sound. He hit the piled up grain with a beanbag thud. He lay flat for a moment, then groggily pulled himself to his feet. Philip watched as his right foot sank deep in the grain, precipitating a small avalanche from above.

Shand spat out grain. Unaware of the danger, he vaguely flicked at his shirt front. 'You come here . . .' he growled.

He took a step forward with his left leg but his right would not follow. He lurched forward into the grain. More corn pattered down on to his body, then a major fall slid like snow over his legs.

'God!' Shand tried to pull himself up but found himself floundering. 'God, this is . . . Get me out of here . . .'

He was struggling to free arms and legs, and all the time he was sinking deeper. 'God,' he called again. 'Please. It wasn't just me . . .'

'It never is,' Philip sighed. 'Who else, then?'

'She said . . .' he gulped. 'She said, "Get them to sell us the Vespertine . . . She said, just think, you have the woman, the commission, the yard . . .'

'But it didn't work if Freddy was still here, did it?' Philip mused softly. 'Who said, Shand?'

'Pl . . .' Shand spluttered and spat. 'Please!'

'No, Shand,' Philip called down. 'You don't want to spend the rest of your life in prison, do you? Amongst all those common little villains? Who was it? Who egged you on?'

'Please!' Only his tilted back head now showed above the ever rising grain. He spat and blinked. Instinct made him try to tread water.

Instinct was wrong.

He was digging his own grave.

'Please!' he bellowed. 'Please!' he whimpered. The final plea was just a muffled groan.

318

The grain surged twice, then it was still.

Philip turned away.

He stepped out into the stairwell. Alison stood on the landing. She gazed wide-eyed up at him.

Philip nodded. He trudged down towards her.

'I suppose it's fair,' she said in that little voice.

'It's fair,' said Philip, and he took her arm.

Philip led Ludo slowly out to the paddock. The horse was lethargic. His hooves scraped on the cobbles. His head hung low. Convinced of the old boy's telepathic powers, Philip sang and talked as he walked alongside him.

> 'Yes I ken John Peel
> And Ruby too,
> Ranter and Ringwood,
> Bellman and True,
> From a find to a check . . .'

His voice cracked on the top note. He cleared his throat. 'Ah, God, boy, but we have heard the chimes at midnight, have we not? I have shared so much with no man or woman. The fear, the fun, the freedom . . . I envy you. I really do. You've done no damage. You've never worried. Never even had any balls to torment you with longings for things you don't really need. Lucky sod. You've just eaten grass and chatted to Myshkin and once in a while put in a buck or heard a horn or seen others racing and you've perked up and gone for it. Christ, you must have a clear conscience . . . And if you dream – what? Back at Prestbury Park before the crowds or at good old Pardubice wondering just who put that fucking drop there, and with that eejit flapping around on your back, getting in the way? Ah, well. Here we are.'

He pushed open the gate. He released the clip on the headcollar. Ludo shook his head, then lowered it, raised his rump and kicked back twice. He set off at a jubilant canter about the field's perimeter. His hooves cleaved a dark trail through the gleaming grass.

Philip walked to the trough where he had left his rifle. The horse had reached the far corner. He gazed out over the valley. He span on his hind legs. Again he set off at a canter towards the gate.

Philip squatted. He shouldered the rifle. In theory, he should walk right up to the horse, draw an imaginary cross between ears and eyes and place the muzzle at that point. He could not do that. Ludo bowled up. He brought himself to an emergency stop. Water-drops spurted forward from his fore-hooves. He held his head high. He was looking for Philip.

'Here, boy,' said Philip softly from behind the trough.

The horse saw him. He pricked up his ears. His eyes met Philip's.

'Goodbye, old friend,' Philip said. He squeezed the trigger.

Swynsmere was empty. Ludo was dead. Myshkin was dead. Freddy would be dead by tomorrow evening. The daily bustle and clatter was an echo only. The long battle was lost.

Philip locked up the office. He had dug a grave for Myshkin. He had called the knackers to remove Ludo. It had been a day of bloodletting, a day of valediction.

He had nigh forgotten Shand.

He turned back at the archway. He was ambivalent about Swynsmere as he was ambivalent about England. He loved both perforce, yet hated them. He was glad to be rid of them, yet grieved at their loss. As with a nagging mother who dies, it was perhaps an idea of what they might have been, a memory of what they had been that he mourned.

The fabric of Swynsmere was good. The idea of training and racing was delightful. The buildings, the horses and the downs were beautiful beyond anything to be found in his new domicile, but only ugliness could keep them alive.

The horses must be run by accountants and bred for a quick buck; the buildings must be modernized, depersonalized; the downs must be ripped up into prairies of corn.

Sam, with Nugent for his mentor, might be fitter for such a world than his father.

He would go down now for a drink with Alison. Maybe, death being death, they would find temporary warmth and reassurance in a wild, forgetful tumble, but he would leave by midnight. When he returned to Mrs Bradley's he would yet have much to do. He must pack. He had letters to write.

He had done what he could. He wanted to be home.

'What's up with the woman, for Christ's sakes?' Richard Heron dibbed a feather carnation into the buttonhole of his grey suit.

'Oh, you know Eledi.' Angela flicked invisible specks from her tight black skirt. Her tightly waisted suit jacket was of pink tweed. Her broad-brimmed pink and black hat lay at her side on the brocade sofa. 'She's having a fit of the artistic temperaments. I'll go to see her before we go.'

'Damn it, I give the woman enough. Least I can ask is that she puts in an appearance on the big days. If I've got Calza and his like spreading bloody rumours, I'm going to need the best PR possible.'

'Don't worry about Calza,' Angela said irritably. 'I told you. I've dealt with him.'

'What got into the bloody wop anyhow?'

'Glaister. Eledi managed to get him some pictures. Glaister tried to blackmail him, used your name.'

'Little *shit*!' Heron thumped the table beside him, knocking over an ornament, which he ignored.

'Precisely. I think you should be worrying slightly more about Eledi, though. She's a threat to us all. I'll keep Calza sweet. But if she tries a trick like that again, your whole operation could collapse. *And* you can kiss goodbye to the Jockey Club. Mud sticks. You need investors. Bad.'

'You're right.' Heron nodded. 'You're always right, damn

it. I'll think about that. Jesus, I can't be outbid by the Arabs again on the Royal Mail colt at these sales. It looks bad. And your efforts with Shand . . . God, if we had the Vespertine gene . . .'

'Shand was a bloody fool to get rid of Freddy Glaister. He thought Philip would prove more pliable. He was wrong. I could have told him that. Freddy would have yielded to pressure in the end.'

'Yes, but that's Shand's type, isn't it? Prospect of a yard of his own, the Glaister woman and – how much did we offer him?'

'A hundred and twenty.'

'You wound him up too tight.'

'Easy to say after the event, Richard. It's not my fault. All I said was, "Get them to sell us the Vespertine gene and there's money in it for you." Yes, I knew he had been screwing the Glaister woman and I knew he had his eyes on that yard. I suppose he never reckoned they'd call Philip back. He and she could sell Plutonium, he'd get the cash and they'd be away. I do not hold myself responsible for whatever he did. God, I mean, if I say, "There's two million in that security van," is it my fault if someone robs it? Anyhow, for your information, I have two backers for the purchase of the Royal Mail. I've also calmed friend Calza, it was not easy. If you want to stay afloat, your best bet is to be very, very appreciative.'

Heron jiggled the knot of his tie. He turned from the Venetian mirror, beaming. 'You've got the money for the colt?'

'I have.'

'Who is it?'

'Ah. That I will tell you after the sales. You just bid with confidence up to two and a half million.'

A frown flickered across Heron's face, then the sleek smile returned. He stepped forward, both hands extended to take hers. 'Angela, you are a marvel. Bless you. What would I do without you?'

She ignored his hands. 'It doesn't bear thinking of, does it?' She stood and sidestepped around him. 'I've been thinking, though. If I'm raising the funds, I think it's about time that I was cut in on the profits, don't you? It won't do you any harm to have me as a nominee partner, will it?'

'In . . .? In the Royal Mail?'

She picked up her patent handbag from the sofa. 'In all the horses we buy from now on. It seems only fair, doesn't it? God knows, I've worked for it.'

'Oh, I'm not denying that, but Eledi . . .'

'Eledi won't object. We can't keep a viper in our bosoms.'

'I'll have to think,' Heron snapped. 'I don't want any more . . . I don't want her upper-class friends telling tales . . .'

'Leave it to me,' said Angela. Her fingers were on the porcelain door-handle. 'As ever, leave it to Auntie Angela.'

'He's a handful, all right,' Glenn Norwak told Philip. Beneath him, Plutonium did his peacocky firewalker dance. His neck was bent, his tail raised. 'Nice sort, though. Throws to the sire all right. I was watching the videos last night.'

Plutonium snorted and steamed. Philip nodded. 'He's the spitting image. Bad, brilliant genes seem to be dominant, damn it. Why can't we just have the brilliant and not the bad for once? Listen, I've got no instructions. Just remember he's temperamental and try to keep him going smoothly. If the pace is slow, take it up and stay up front. If they go a lick, lay him up. He can do either thing. He's fast away and faster still at the finish. Do your worst.'

'No sweat.' Jim Dobbs took the horse's head. The welted, wizened Australian dismounted. 'I reckon maybe we'll have to do it off the pace. There's a lot of straight sprinters in this field.'

'You'll save everyone a few heart attacks if you do.' Philip walked alongside Glenn. The jockey's head came no higher than his breastbone. 'Thank God, you guys have a stopwatch built into your brains.'

'Have to, don't we? It's the way we're trained, against the clock.'

323

In his earlier races, Plutonium had been ridden by Eric Hunt. Philip had replaced him with Glenn. Now in his forties, Glenn was one of the best, most experienced jockeys in the world. He was famous for his storming last-minute finishes. Just sometimes, he mistimed them by a split second. More often, he got his mounts up to win by a short head or a neck.

He was a jockey, but he was also a horseman. Philip had seen him win off the pace by coaxing, balance and perfect timing. He had seen him make a tired horse change legs two furlongs out. Eric Hunt would have thought changing legs to involve transplant surgery. Glenn handled a whip with the sleight of hand of a conjuror. He was strong.

Plutonium was a big, bad adolescent. He needed Glenn.

'What do you think of the going?' he asked.

'Ah, should stay good.' Glenn stopped to look out over the heath beneath its spangled sweat of dew. The sky was pale blue and clear but for ragged streaks of high cloud. 'Nah. Fine day, I'd reckon.'

'Good.' Philip smiled and waved at the gleaming BMW which bumped over the turf towards him. 'Right,' he touched the jockey's shoulder, 'I'll see you later.'

Norwak saluted with his whip.

Philip turned to Jim, Tony and Debbie who flanked the horse like a statesman's security guard. 'Jim, take him back and settle him down. One of you two come with me and get some breakfast. T'other stay with Jim.'

A car's doors thumped. Philip grinned at Gerry Kilbride, then at Jenny as each stepped from the car. 'Gerry, morning. Jenny, it's really good . . . I'm really glad to see you.'

She came round the car. She put her arms around his shoulders. She kissed his lips. 'I'm glad to see you,' she said, and her mouth curled into an embarrassed little smile. 'I had to be here . . .'

She stepped backward, trailing her fingers down his arms until they rested on his. Philip swallowed. He looked away. 'Ah, Debbie. Good. Gerry Kilbride, Jenny Laing, this is my saviour, Debbie Stone.'

'How do you do, my dear?'

'Mr Kilbride. Miss Laing,' Debbie simpered.

Gerry took her elbow. 'Do you look after the horse?'

'No, I look after the men who look after the horse.'

'Oh, very much more difficult.' Gerry rambled on to her his smooth, soft tones.

Philip said to Jenny, 'How's school?'

'Fine. What have you done to yourself?'

'Oh, the face. Light bulb exploded.'

'God. Any nearer to solving all this?'

'Yup. Got it sorted.'

'And after this?'

He shrugged. 'Back to the sun, I suppose.'

'You'll be rich. You don't need to.'

'Come on.' Philip broke from her gaze. 'I'm hungry. So, I imagine, is Debbie.'

'Where are you leading us?'

'Stable-lads' café.' Philip drew out a cigarette.

'Good. So. How's our horse?'

'My horse,' Philip corrected, 'is fine. All things being equal, which no things are, he'll win.'

'You look tired, my dear,' Gerry said softly.

'I am. Weary with toil, weary even unto death. No. People insist on doing things to you over here. It's like being a fire hydrant or a lamp-post. You stand still, doing nothing offensive, and everyone comes and pisses on you. Still, Swynsmere's all but wound up. No horses, no live-stock. You can put it on the market now. Give the proceeds to Alison.'

Gerry cocked his head. '*All* the proceeds?'

'Yes. She's deserved it. Oh, I know, I know,' he answered Jenny's querying glance, 'but it's time she had a break. I've written it all here,' Philip reached into his breast pocket. He pulled out two long envelopes. He replaced one. 'There are bills to be paid. There are special payments – Tony, Debbie here, Mrs Bradley. After that, she can have the rest. I've waived all claim.'

'You must be pretty confident about the horse.' Gerry took the proffered envelope. He pulled open his dark blue

325

coat. He thrust the envelope into the pocket of his tweed suit.

'No,' Philip grinned. 'It's just, I'm cheap. I've got my income. I don't need any more. I'd only drink it. Waste.'

'You are OK?' Gerry was watching him with those pale, prying eyes. 'You worry me. Things difficult at Swynsmere?'

'No, no, Cakewalk. I'm fine. I just want to get back where I belong.'

'Where's that, I'd like to know?' Gerry was gently jolly.

'So would I.' Philip held the door open on the smoke and the clatter. He cast a quick, worried glance at Jenny. 'So would I.'

'Oh, dear, oh, dear.' Angela strolled into Eledi's bedroom without knocking. She closed the door softly behind her. 'You have blundered, darling. You have most gravely blundered.'

Eledi sat up in the four-poster. She leaned back against a large, square pillow. Her lower eyelids sagged. Her eyes were veined and glazed. 'Go away,' she intoned in a voice from a vaulted tomb.

'No, no, Eledi.' Angela transferred her black kid gloves from her right hand to her left. 'You are going to have to listen this time. You've been a naughty, naughty girl, haven't you? So silly, to break trust like that. You had so much going for you – money, nice houses, nice friends, anything you wanted. Richard's been so generous to you.'

'Generous!' Eledi shrugged and smiled sourly. 'Sure. Like he's generous with his horses. Gives them oats and the very best hay, nice monogrammed blankets. All they have to do is look good and perform well. Generous, my arse. So, what am I supposed to have done?'

Angela sat decorously on the side of the bed with her stockinged legs curled beneath her. 'You're pretending that you don't know?'

'I'm not pretending anything.'

'You shouldn't have trusted Philip Glaister, you know. Very silly.'

326

Eledi's lips went white. She babbled, 'What? I don't know what you're talking about.'

'He asked you for pictures, didn't he? And you, like a treacherous, ungrateful girl, gave them to him. Pictures of you doing your favourite naughty things. And why did you think he wanted them? Hmmm? Philanthropy, was it? No, dear. Blackmail. He went round to dear Piero Calza and demanded money. He went to your father and demanded money . . .'

'No!' Eledi stared. Her lips twisted. Her eyes filled and stared. She shook her head and her hair flapped like a dog's ears. 'No. He wouldn't! He couldn't!'

'But he did, my sweet sacrificial lamb. Listen.'

She clicked open her handbag and stood. She pulled out a cassette. She moved over to the Ansafone on the pretty chest-of-drawers. She flicked it open, removed one cassette and inserted the other. She closed it and pressed *Rewind*. The tape whirred and clunked. She pressed *Play*.

There was a click. Angela's voice emerged. 'Hello?'

'Angela?' A man's deep voice.

'Yes?'

'Piero.'

'Piero, how nice to hear you! Are you here in London?'

'You know damn well I'm here in London. I've just had your filthy little emissary round.'

'What are you talking about?' Angela laughed.

'Glaister. With those pictures. And your absurd threats.'

'What? No. This has nothing to do with us.'

'So how come the pictures existed? How did Glaister get hold of them? Don't lie to me, Angela. I'll pay, but you and Heron will regret this.'

On the bed, Eledi clutched herself. She shook. Tears dribbled down her cheeks. Suddenly a sob burst from her like vomit. She sank back on to the pillows and curled up, croaking and drooling.

'. . . I'll come round at once and find out what this is all about . . .' Angela's voice was saying, 'I solemnly swear that we sent no threats and that Glaister has nothing to do

327

with us. I don't know anything about pictures. You must believe me. We don't want any payment of any sort . . .'

Angela reached out a long finger to stab at the *Stop* button. In the soft orange light from behind the curtains, her expression was invisible. The tape whirred forward. There was a click. From the bed, there came a deep, clogged groan like that of a mare in labour.

'Miss Duncan?' – Ivo Donovan's voice. There was chirruping from the bed.

'Yes?'

'I've just seen Philip Glaister. I paid him for some pictures. Fake pictures.'

'Nooo?' Eledi's fist hit the pillow again and again. 'Please.'

'Just so's you know, Miss Duncan. You and Heron are corrupt little fuckers and I'm going to finish you both. It doesn't matter how. I'm going to prove that these pictures are fakes and then I'm going to destroy you.'

'Mr Donovan . . .'

'That is all, Duncan.' The telephone clicked and purred.

Angela Duncan switched off the machine. The chinking and moaning from the bed continued.

'But he'll find that they're not fakes, won't he?' Angela crooned. 'So much for your trustworthy old friend. So, those indecorous pictures are out on the streets now. God knows how many more people Glaister will try to sell them to. The newspapers, of course. Richard will have to divorce you. The shame would be too great for him. You know how proud a man he is. It should make the Pulitzer case look very tame. And as for all your old friends, well, we've seen what they think of you. Of course, you may well get television parts with all this publicity, but that won't last long. Scandals never do. Within a year, producers will want people looking at the character, not ogling the actress who liked to gang-bang. Oh, dear. I don't like the prognosis at all.'

Eledi's fists were clenched. Her knees arose to her chest. She released a suppressed shriek of pure rage.

'Your poor father,' Angela droned on. 'He'll probably

take you in, but you'll always know that he's seen you like that. Poor Eledi. Poor, poor Eledi. I know what I'd do. There's a nice bottle of Smirnoff Blue Label here, and there's all that lovely soothing Diazepam in the medicine cabinet. You could have a lovely, calm, sleepy morning. Lots and lots of peace. There now. I'll leave you to think about your plans.' She strolled over to the bed. She bent and kissed Eledi's wet cheek. 'Bye bye, darling,' she said coolly. She wheeled, for a second off balance. She righted herself and her footfalls puffed as she walked to the door. There was bright light, then the door sighed and clicked shut, and the room sank back into amber darkness.

Hell, Philip thought as he watched his companions at breakfast, publicans and sinners have nothing on the crowd that I gather about me. Look at my friends – whores, world-weary divorcees, one old pansy, failed villains, Lovelady . . .

On the other hand, he consoled himself. Just look at my enemies: Heron, a manipulative bastard; Shand, a murderous little monomaniac; Angela Duncan, a corrupt nymphomaniac; David Nugent, a boyish bloody fool . . .

In the eyes of the world, these were respectable enough. In Philip's eyes, his ramshackle team of outcasts and wilful outsiders warranted a deal more respect. He even felt affection for Lovelady in this moment, perhaps because he was not here . . .

And Jenny?

Philip watched her, the way she leaned forward to hear Debbie, joining her in mild mockery, no doubt of him, the way she turned her head to involve Gerry, then looked up through the smoke. Her flashing eyes caught his.

And there was a moment of stillness. The eyes had a question to ask. Incredibly, she had resolved to invite him further into her confidence and her life. He must accept now and accept the consequences, or, pleading a previous engagement, miss the party – and the hangover.

She was strong. She was graceful. She had what he

would like to have – a poise and elegance which sprang from self-esteem. That did not mean, he knew, that she was immune from hurt.

He wanted very much to know her. There was a little easeful death promised in those eyes. He ached for it, but he feared himself. Something weak and mewling inside him would seek to dominate her for fear. Something strong in her would yield to it for love.

He had had enough of doing damage.

Yet surely, the child within him protested, this was no time for altruism. How many straightening flushes would he be dealt in this game?

It was his duty to play the cards. Maybe his jinx was no more than that – a bad run, a losing streak. Maybe the dark cards would prove a king and an ace . . . ?

No. He shook his head sadly. This time he avoided her gaze. The dark cards were dealt him early on. They were the same in every hand. He would sooner they remained dark. Win the small hands by bluff. Never go for broke and show.

He smiled. Him with a nursery-school teacher?

Garn.

He was gruff, tough, grumpy Philip Glaister.

The child within him wailed.

'Mr Philip?' That quavering bleat was unmistakable. Philip turned his head. The crowd on the steps above him parted like corn when a badger lumbers through. 'Excuse us. So sorry. Mr Philip . . . ?'

A green nylon arm emerged from between the two cover- coats immediately above, then a shoulder then Lovelady's shiny, crimson face and the hat with its speckled, wedge-shaped feather. He pulled his wife through after him. Barbara Lovelady was flustered. In a salt and pepper coat and a black fedora, she blinked through oblong glasses. She touched her cropped dark chestnut hair. She writhed a bit. She said, 'Ooh. Hello. I told Vincent we shouldn't disturb you, but he would have it.'

'Quite right.' Philip was jovial.

He rolled up his racecard and thrust it into his coat pocket. 'Gerry,' he touched the dark blue shoulder below. 'You remember Lovelady, don't you?'

'Lovelady . . .' Gerry's plush cheeks bulged. 'How could I forget? A model of discretion and acuity, as I recall.'

'And a great help in recent problems,' Philip conceded. 'Amazing, really, but there you are. Even dwarves start small.'

'And have we solved "recent problems"?' Lovelady asked. He was conspiratorial.

'Solved?' Philip sighed. 'There's no solution, is there? But something like justice has been done, I suppose.'

'In relation to Mr Freddy . . .' Lovelady murmured.

'Yes. You were right. If I'd read romantic novels, I'd have seen it straight off. Greed on one side, tenderness on the other.'

'And, as for the, um, horses business . . .'

'I have yet to carry out the sentence there. After this race.'

'Oh, dear.'

'Oh, it's all right.' Philip raised his binoculars. The contestants for the first race were down at the start. The jockeys' silks glittered. 'You can come with me if you like. Make sure I do it properly.'

'I think I'd better. You have a way of getting into trouble, Mr Philip.'

'You've noticed?' Gerry called up. His eyes were fixed upon the racecourse. 'You're being frightfully mysterious, you two.'

Jenny ducked beneath Gerry's binoculars and straightened at his side. 'I got seven to two against Spinning Jenny,' she announced. 'Is that good?'

'Jenny?' Philip said. Above them the course commentator said, 'And they're away . . .'

She turned. She was lovely. 'Yup?'

'You haven't met . . .'

'Mr Lovelady,' she grinned. 'I'd know you anywhere.'

The perfect family. They stood there on the third step up,

331

discussing the racecard. They smiled as they chatted. She had stepped from the shampoo ads, he from the four-wheel-drive pages in glossy magazines. They had even kept the gloss on their plump skin and plump hair. And the child, Philip's son, was one of them, in his striped shirt, his tweed suit and his Barbour.

As Philip and Lovelady drew closer, the bruises on Nugent's face became apparent. He looked up. He said, 'Oh,' then 'Philip! Mr Lovelady!'

'Hello, Daddy!' Sam called, but he did not run over for a hug. He was grown up today.

'God, what a pair,' Linda kissed Philip. 'My two champions. You looking like a spotty adolescent, and David – he had an argument with one of the llamas. He lost.'

'Ah,' Philip caught Nugent's eye. 'Bad luck.'

'Is he going to win, Daddy? Is he going to win?'

'I think so. It's out of my hands now.' Philip's eyes never left Nugent.

'I've put twelve pounds fifty on him. He'd better jolly well win.'

'A lot depends on it.' Philip nodded slowly. 'Nugent. A quick word.'

'Yes. Sorry. Absolutely.' Nugent burbled. 'Lin, darling. Sorry. Secrets. Presents, you know.'

'I don't like all this sudden chummy secrecy.' Linda was only half cheerful. 'It feels as though you're comparing notes.'

'No, no. Business.' Nugent explained. 'Silly. No. Look, I'll be a few minutes. See you down at the paddock. Or back here.'

'Philip, we'll see you later, won't we?'

'Sure, sure. Before the race. Watch it together. See you later.'

Philip walked at Nugent's right, Lovelady at his left. Nugent limped and winced with every stride.

'So?' Philip said softly.

Nugent glanced at Lovelady.

'Oh, don't worry. Mr Lovelady knows everything. Several people know enough to see you warned off or sent to gaol.'

'Oh, Christ,' Nugent wheezed.

'But if that happened – oh, it would please me well enough, but it would leave Sam and Linda on their own. What was your plan, Nugent? Today? Have you got sugar lumps about you? A syringe? What? Llama medicine?'

'Something like that. Shit, Philip, if Plutonium wins, I might as well be in gaol. I'm finished. Dulverton has got to win.'

'Don't plead to me, Nugent. I'd be delighted to see you and all your kind finished.' Philip ducked under the rails and on to the course. 'But I have a son who has been hurt once and I don't want him to suffer another loss. That is the one thing which prevents me from ruining you.'

'You mean . . .' Nugent was pathetic in his eagerness. 'You mean Plutonium . . . ?'

'I mean as far as I'm concerned, Plutonium runs to win. But I'm going to tell the people watching him to go off and enjoy themselves. All except Jim, of course, but Jim knows you. He wouldn't stop you. Of course, maybe you'll kill the animal. Doping is hardly a precise science.'

'You mean . . . ?' Nugent was affronted. 'I can't – I mean, with you knowing . . . I mean, you're just going to let me . . . ?'

'Yes.'

'Mr Philip?' Lovelady shook his head. 'I am a witness to this. I can't permit . . .'

'And then you'll report me, is that it?' Nugent panted a little. His cheeks were flushed.

'Why should I do that?' Philip sneered. 'I've told you. I could stop you right now if that were my intention. No. Off you go, with my blessing. Take your childish prank to its natural conclusion. But first, please cast an eye over this.' He pulled the second long envelope from his pocket.

All three men stopped walking. Lovelady watched Nugent closely. Philip was nonchalant.

Nugent ripped the envelope open with his thumb. 'What is this?' He blinked as he unfolded the single sheet of paper.

First his lower lip shook, then his hands, his jowls, his whole frame. He said, 'Bah . . . but . . . You can't . . . You shit . . . You shit! . . . This . . . You can't do this.'

'I've done it, New Gent,' Philip spat. 'I faxed my instructions to Weatherbys yesterday evening. Plutonium is now yours. Say thank you.'

'You – you *bastard!*' It came out of him as though under pressure.

'Not a very pleasant response, do you think, Lovelady? I give him a valuable present and he abuses me. My nanny always told me to say "thank you".'

'You – you've given him Plutonium?'

'Certainly.'

'But he's worth – well, if he wins today . . .'

'Oh, hundreds of thousands. And in eighteen months' time, Nugent, and, by proxy, my son, will have a valuable asset. If he doesn't win today, of course, Nugent will save his bacon for the moment, but the likelihood is that Plutonium will be nigh worthless.'

'But the prize money today . . .'

'No, no. I get that. Plutonium becomes Nugent's at four o'clock this afternoon. Neat, don't you think?'

Lovelady's moustache worked this way and that. He nodded. His eyes wrinkled. He held out his hand. 'Mr Philip,' he said, 'you're a gentleman.'

'Oh, scarcely that,' said Philip, but he took the hand and shook it warmly. 'Right then,' Philip was rueful. 'I'm away.'

'You'll not stay for the race?' Lovelady asked.

'No, no. Bloody farewells. Don't like them. They turn round, they'll say "Oh, is he gone?" Turn round again, "Oh, hello. Have you been away?" No. Anyhow, if Plutonium does his bit, I'll regret my decision. If not, I'll be spitting fire. I'll keep my equanimity, thank you. Don't worry. There's money set aside for you, for Tony, largesse for all and sundry.'

Philip walked fast past the stands and towards the car park. Lovelady had to skip to keep up. He said, 'It's not the money. You're going to be missed, you know.'

'No. The world is full of little mutually dependent units that do their thing smoothly enough. I'm not very good at being a constituent.' He stopped very suddenly. He said, 'Wait.'

Up at his left, three stories up, he had caught sight of a candy pink figure on the balcony of one of the boxes. He suddenly realized that his time-marking speech to that woman in the restaurant had not, after all, been so far from the truth. Angela Duncan had haunted his sweetest nocturnal dreams, even his nastiest diurnal nightmares. She was holding out her glass. A burly man with close-cropped blond hair was tipping up a bottle. Angela looked very assured, very respectable.

Philip had recognized the orange label on the champagne bottle before he recognized the man who held it. He had seen him twice before – once, when he had driven into the Swynsmere yard with his absurd offer for Pluto-nium, and once, in a black and white photograph, his coarse, skin-gauntleted hands clasping Anick's buttocks to his groin. Ernest Cormick, he had called himself.

And he was Heron's man.

Angela's glass was full. She turned to scan the race-course. She saw Philip standing there, stock still amidst the moving people like a stepping-stone in a stream. She raised her black-gloved right hand. She waggled her fingers down at him. She called something over her shoulder. Heron was quickly there. She leaned back. She said some-thing. She pointed down. Then, in full view of the racing public, she pouted and kissed Heron's throat.

She turned back to Philip with a triumphant little smile. Her eyebrows were raised. She raised her glass. She threw back her head and laughed.

'Oh, God,' Philip murmured. 'Heron wanted the Vesper-tine gene.'

'What?' Lovelady bleated.

'That's all it takes, isn't it? That bitch beds Shand, seeds the idea, offers him money, the yard . . . It's like Nugent. Throw a pebble and start an avalanche. Greed does the rest. Christ! That's why they were there that night. In France. They already knew! They knew about Freddy before I did . . .'

'What?'

'And then that conniving bitch . . . Oh, God. You saw the way she kissed him? Oh, God, Eledi . . .'

Philip started striding towards the car park again. His fingers shook as though to shed water. 'Now, Mr Philip, this doesn't mean you're going to set off on another quest, does it?' Lovelady called after him.

'No, no. Don't you worry, Lovelady. I'm going home. A lesson I've learned. Revenge takes itself. One day, Charlie Vane, Eledi, Micky, all of us . . . One day it'll come, and it'll be all the sweeter cold. It'll come, though. I promise you that. Jesus!' he roared. 'I need to get out of this cesspool. Now.'

'Forgive me, but – what about that Miss Laing? You ask me, that's a fine young lady, and she – well, she likes you.'

'And I like her. And you can tell her, anytime she fancies an irresponsible holiday – remember; relay those words exactly, an irresponsible holiday – I'll be a damned sight more hospitable than last time. Tell her she's on the very short and ever shrinking list of much beloved friends. God,' Philip was talking to himself now, 'I wish I could set up house with the Laing, but that's like Bertrand Russell on his deathbed, reportedly saying, "I wish I could have a priest." It's not the nature of the beast.'

'Many a man would envy you.' They had reached the car now. Philip jingled keys. Lovelady leaned on the roof. He rested his chin on his hands.

'Many a man is a bloody fool.' Philip opened the driver's door. 'I know my limitations. That's all I've ever learned. Cut your cloth, and, to mix metaphors and platitudes, cultivate your own garden. *Basta cosi.*'

He sidestepped into the car. He jiggled the gearstick. Lovelady walked round the back. He rested a hand on the open door. He looked down at his feet. He kicked the turf with his toe. 'Mr Philip?' He was hesitant.

'Yup?'

'So you're just driving off? That's it?'

'That's it.' Philip's fingers drummed on the steering-wheel.

'Oh. Well . . .'

'Oh, Goddamn it, Lovelady,' Philip barked. He climbed from the car. His hands clapped on Lovelady's shoulders.

'Yes, you silly bastard. You creep on to that list too. Come on. Be seeing you, mate.'

Lovelady blinked up at him. His lips worked. He opened his mouth but no sound emerged.

Philip was back in the car. The door slammed. The engine wheezed and growled. Philip said, 'Call me sometime, OK?'

He waved once and the car was moving.

Lovelady stood very still as he watched the maroon Mini jerking across the mud-streaked turf to the gates. His vision was misted.

'A wrong 'un,' he croaked at last. He licked his lips. 'Ah, well . . .'

He took a deep breath. He turned back towards the stands with a proud little smile. 'But not a bad man, Philip Glaister,' he murmured. He felt that he was now an acknowledged member of a small but very exclusive club.

He hurried now to be back with his fellows.

Eledi lay in the brown and orange light for many hours after Angela had left. Outside, the traffic sporadically swooshed by.

The tears dried and for a while she lay still, but soon the facts of solitude and of treachery again singed and withered the edges of her perception, and grief punched at her diaphragm, forcing out a sob, and she had to curl up again, clutching her belly, until the fit of blindness and of convulsive jerkings was done.

She had trusted to the past as most trust to the future. If she had idealized it, so be it. There had been decency there, and order, and if once it had been, so it could be again.

That thought, she realized, and that tenuous logic, had been at the heart of her life, as much as the cognate beliefs of a lost Eden and a possible Paradise motivate the Christian, even in the fat of his sins. Without this faith, she could never have arisen in the morning, never have summoned a smile.

Until now, however, she had been separated from Eden. It had existed in the videos and in her dreams, for ever preserved in its perfect, timeless because immutable form. Now Eden revealed itself to be polluted. Everything was as corrupt as she. The garden to which she had hoped to return had been ploughed up, paved and turned into a shopping arcade. Philip, who had inhabited that Eden, was as bad as Richard – worse, for he had not the excuse that he had never known it.

If angels were become devils, all hope of redemption was gone.

For a while, then, she considered the option offered to her by Angela.

There was dignity in a quiet death which no amount of calumny could diminish. Death – the peaceful and picturesque variety – transfigures. It can make virgins of whores and heroes of villains. Presumably, in death, she would be spared violation of her modesty and her pride, whilst in life, both would be pilloried and scorned. She did not belong – save there, below the waist – to the world in which she found herself. That the devil could be in her was a datum of her faith. That devils might surround her was a nightmare. The only prayer, then, was suicide.

It would be a courteous act, too, in that she would spare her father further agony and that such friends as remained could reconstruct her in the guise of an angel.

Twice, then, she moved towards the bottle, twice poured herself half a tumbler of vodka and downed it in one. Once, she went to the bathroom and threw two Diazepam down her throat. Then she looked at the little brown bottle in her hand.

She sneered.

Rebellion had played little part in her life. It had consisted in occasional mockery, occasional snaps and snarls and wriggles before concession. In essence, she realized, her readiness to be a good girl in childhood had been no different from her willingness to embrace corruption in adulthood. She had read somewhere that the respectable middle class, those most affected and inspired by peer pressure, were those most likely to become addicted to heroin.

So she, wanting to please or appease a more powerful will, had yielded first to her father's, then to Richard's will.

She was not unique in her compulsive desires. They were nigh universal. One master, however, had taught her to check them, the other to give them rein. Suddenly, betrayed by both, she was alone. A horse whose rider has fallen can choose to stay by its prostrate rider, to run on with the field, or – and the prospect was terrifying – to run elsewhere, to please no one, to violate every rule of training.

She could die. That would be a statement, but a statement dictated to her by Richard and Angela.

If all else were destroyed, though, if her damnation were beyond doubt, why should she not make another sort of statement?

She could, for example, kill.

Philip strolled into Les Oliviers and sat at his usual table. He opened his book – the latest James Lee Burke. His usual 51 pastis was delivered. He nodded, faintly smiled. He tried to lose himself in the swamps and bayous of Louisiana, but for once the mellifluous voice of the cajun poet had no power to move him.

It had been thus for the month since his return. He had tried to return to the normal routine. He had taught his pupils. He had slept with Sylvie. He had come down here to drink with the mob and play a little chess. He had taken nocturnal trips with Felix and Charlot to pick up malodorous illegal immigrants from the North African coast.

Nothing had served to afford him tranquillity. Something was now missing in his formerly sufficient existence. There was unfinished business.

He just did not know quite what it was.

Again and again he had taken tally of his last hours in England. He had imperfectly avenged his little brother. He had, at least, given him freedom from the grasp of so-called life. He had obtained freedom, too, for Alison and, maybe, for Eledi. The papers recorded that she had enrolled at Clouds' House, a Scottish clinic for addicts. Heron could not expose or divorce her when she was making so well-publicized an attempt to sort herself out. It was a good move.

He had safeguarded Sam's horse, who had broken from the field as though electrified to take the Dewhurst by four clear lengths. He had taught Nugent a lesson. So far, so good. In Eledi, he had rediscovered an ancient love; in Jenny, he had found, perhaps, a new one. Neither of these did he count to his credit. He had made friends – Ali, Jenny, Tony, Debbie, above all, perhaps, the incredible Lovelady.

That at least he counted amongst the profits.

He had made serious enemies. That was bad news. Heron, Duncan, Calza and Donovan hated him. They might seek to hurt him.

Overall, after a week's thought, he reckoned that he could cope with that.

There was nothing, then, so far as he could see, which properly qualified as a haunting concern, yet some part of the equation obtruded and denied him peace of mind.

Vengeance, of course.

He wanted to see Heron and Duncan brought down, but he had analysed his feelings and had discovered that what he had said to Lovelady was true. He was in no hurry, and he had unwavering faith that their time would come. Everyone who had gravely sinned against him had, in time, found their own hell. It had not taken his volition – or, at least, it had taken no more than his volition. On this occasion, through Ivo Donovan and through Calza, he had even, perhaps, initiated Heron's relentless slither down the primrose path.

One day, he and Charlie Kilcannon and Eledi would get together and would toast their enemies' downfall. He knew that.

John Waghorn clattered on to the veranda and sank with a deep sigh into the chair opposite him. He hailed a waiter and demanded his usual scotch and soda. 'Well,' he cleared his throat like a motorcycle, 'reckon that's it for another year. Last of the buggers gone.'

'Yup.' Philip gazed out over the harbour. There were

merely black embers now where formerly gin palaces had blazed.

'Game?'

'Not tonight, thanks, General. Reckoned I'd turn in early.'

'OK, are you? No troubles? Always turn to me, you know, need a hand.'

'No. Thanks. No, all's well. Just a little bit tired. I'll be fine.'

'Just so's you know.'

'Yeah. Thanks.'

'Ah, well. Stick together, you know.' Waghorn pulled a *Daily Telegraph* from his pocket. He puffed and grumbled and occasionally guffawed as he worked his way through it. Philip grew restive. He ordered more drinks, but nothing served to still his nerves. His right knee bobbed. His fingers scrabbled at his thigh.

He wanted to be somewhere else, but he knew that, when he got there, he would want to be somewhere else. For a man who had preached and practised the doctrine of the easy life, he had an unseemly and, to him, distasteful urge to *do* something.

He stood at last. Darkness had fallen. He would at least have a chance of sleep. If it would not come unbidden, he would drink whisky and listen to music until it arrived.

'See you, General,' he said. He patted Waghorn's shoulder, waved to Theo and jumped down into the street.

He remembered how he had pursued Jenny Laing down this promenade. The memory made him smile. She had written to suggest that she might visit him over Christmas. That was a nice thought to take to bed with him. Sam would be out too.

Maybe that was the trouble, he thought as he trudged up through the darkness beyond the town. Maybe this restless dissatisfaction was not so much a symptom of malfunction as of recovery. Maybe, after all, the resolute detachment from the ways of the world which he had turned into a philosophy was no more, in fact, than a fearful avoidance of anything that might hurt him. Maybe – and the thought alarmed him – he actually wanted to get in there and mix it, to get involved, to take risks, to fight. He had gone home and had confronted the ghosts. He had survived. He had found himself more than fit to engage in tawdry human intercourse, and day-to-day politics.

Was his refuge here, after all, merely temporary? Must he, by his nature, return to all the tedious business of life and love, buying and selling?

He did not like to think it.

He turned in at the gate of the Villa Locarno. Above him, L'Hermitage was a ghostly grey block which seemed to float just below the silver-edged clouds. There might be a storm tonight, one of those Mediterranean storms in which a lightning flash lit the clouds with tremulous purple for minutes on end and the wind whipped the sea into peaks.

That would afford some relief.

He padded up the steps, two at a time. In the shadow of the doorway, he pulled out his keys. He picked through them.

Suddenly there was a rustle at his left shoulder, a rapid inhalation. Suddenly a dark figure masked the moonlight.

He crouched. He dropped the keys. He swung round, too late. He said, 'What . . . ?' even as he felt the skin above his kidneys yield and burst, even as the white-hot pain shot up his back to be replaced by no more than a dull throbbing, even as he heard his own blood splashing on the flagstones.

'Fuck you!' a female voice was shrilling somewhere. 'Fuck you! Fffah!' as the blow which he had started as soon as the figure had appeared now struck home, driving the navel nigh to the backbone. There was a grunt then as his elbow thudded into the collar-bone, snapping it cleanly. His assailant doubled up, slowly span and sank to the ground, wheezing and coughing.

'Christ . . .' Philip leaned against the door for support. The sky was suddenly blurred and wheeling fast. He had to blink as he felt for the right key. He pushed open the door. He staggered in.

342

He reached for the light switch. He missed it twice before at last it gave with a click and light flooded the room. Everything was veering.

He lurched into the doorframe. His breaths were short and shallow. He reached for his inhaler. He squirted two quick blasts. Only then did he turn. 'Oh, Christ,' he groaned deep. 'You silly little bitch.'

Eledi Heron retched. She clutched her stomach. She gasped and wheezed. Her whole face was screwed up tight. 'You – you bastard!' Her gulp jerked her whole frame. 'I trus ... I trus ... I trusted you!' Tears oozed from the corners of her eyes. Her hair had been scraped back and tied, but streaks of it were daubed across her face and tangled over her drooping lower lip. Her face was white as the moon's.

'No, you didn't.' His voice came out rasping and reson-ant. The hand that covered the wound was warm and sticky. Still he heard the tell-tale dripping on to the door-step. The wound had developed a pulse of its own. He had to make a conscious effort to force his eyes open. 'You trusted that bitch, Duncan, didn't you?'

'She – she played me the tapes,' Eledi gasped. Her eyes too seemed to veer as though she had just stepped from a fairground ride. 'You blackmailed my father. You black-mailed ...' But as the pain in her body sharpened, she buckled again, gagging.

'Listen to me.' Philip had to force the words out in a constipated grunt. 'I *fixed* the bloody photographs. Your father will have checked and found them to be fakes. I drew that bastard Heron's sting. Oh, God. You've done – a little – damage – here,' he said as he slowly slumped down the doorframe to the floor. His head lolled.

'No?' Eledi whimpered. 'Oh, please, no?'

'Yes.' Philip's eyelids sank for a second, then snapped open. 'Check with him. But not now. Now ring for an ambulance and get the hell out of here. Take – take the knife with you. Throw it in the sea ...'

She was crawling towards him as again his eyelids fell. He felt his breath on his cheek, her wet cheek against his. The

343

whisper of her hair, the rustle of her clothing were amplified in the still night. It was nice, here in the darkness, with her holding him, her whining and snuffling like a bereft dog in his ear. 'Oh, Philip. Oh, God, I am sorry. Oh, Christ . . .'

An executioner's pillow was pushing hard down upon the top of his brain. He took one last deep breath before, he knew, he must sink into the blessed darkness.

'Operatics,' he mumbled. 'Fucking actresses. Ambulance. C'm see me in hosptl . . . Got a lot of work to do, you 'n me . . .'

She was saying, 'Yes, Philip. Oh, God, yes . . .' And suddenly it was cold where her warmth had been. He was sinking sideways. In his mind, he was floating untrammelled as a sleeping swift above the soothing rushing of the sea. He could alight here or there as he chose . . .

An idyll.

And whether it would be interrupted or no was no longer of concern to him.